To Susan

I hope you enjoy the "ride."

Riders

A Novel

R. K. BROWN

Best regards,

R K Brown

Riders is a work of fiction. Names, characters, places and events are either products of the writer's imagination or are used fictitiously.

ISBN: 978-1-7325776-0-2 (Paperback Edition)
ISBN: 978-1-7325776-1-9 (eBook Edition)

Cover by Yocla Designs.

Also by R.K. Brown (published as Robert K. Brown)

The Neighborhood
Sonnets
A Stone of Hope
Blind Luck

*To Mary Lynn, with whom I'd gladly
live a thousand lifetimes.*

Prologue

NOVEMBER 9, 1918
PASEWALK MILITARY HOSPITAL
PROVINCE OF POMERANIA, GERMANY

THE NURSE MOVED slowly down the drab, poorly lit hall of the hospital, her senses accosted by the sights, sounds and smells of wounded men. She kept her head lowered, eyes focused on the floor, in an attempt to avoid visual contact with any superior who might give her an assignment other than the one which she desired. No, more than desired. The one to which she was irrevocably committed.

It was time to take the ambulatory patients outside for a little morning sunshine and fresh air. Although it was a typically brisk November day, the men would not mind the cold. They seemed to respond well to these brief opportunities to feel sunlight on their faces and to fill their lungs with air that did not carry the stench of blood, urine and rotting flesh.

There was an established pattern for the movement of the men. The four nurses assigned to that ward started at the back of the large, windowless room, sequentially evacuating the cots on the right-hand side, then those on the left. Her objective was a soldier in the last group of four—the third cot inside the door on the left, number thirty-eight. On the previous morning, she had misjudged her timing only slightly, arriving back in the ward to find another nurse approaching bed number thirty-eight just seconds before she got there. She had almost asked the nurse to move to the next soldier, but Herr Doctor Forster had chosen that moment to stand at the foot of the bed as he updated the patient's medical chart. Not wanting to risk creating a suspicious or possibly contentious scene, she had reluctantly postponed her plan. But it needed to be today. There were rumors of an armistice, and things could change quickly after that.

She'd been very careful this morning. She knew that two of the nurses were still outside and the third, a heavyset, middle-aged *Grossmutter*—grandmother—was waddling slowly down the hall ahead of her. The old woman was a compassionate, hard-working caregiver, but was infuriatingly slow in everything she did. It was difficult to follow behind and not overtake her without appearing to be purposely sluggish and lazy—she, herself, being a youthful, energetic thirty years old—so she concentrated on moving as slowly as she could without drawing unwanted attention to herself. This could very well be her last chance.

She glanced behind her to make sure neither of the other two nurses were close, and then knelt on one knee as if retying a shoe-lace. She didn't look up at the sauntering old woman ahead of her, instead mentally calculating her prodding progress down the hall. When she felt she had allowed a sufficient gap between them, she stood, smoothed the front of her smock, and continued toward her soldier.

She reached the entrance to the ward a mere two steps behind the old woman and quickly proceeded to bed thirty-eight. She exhaled a sigh of relief as she found herself looking down at the gaunt, pale young man. "Guten Morgen, Gefrieter." *Good morning, Corporal.*

His steely blue eyes darted in her direction, but did not appear to be focused on her. He had been blinded in a British mustard gas attack in Belgium the previous month. But she was convinced the blindness was temporary. In fact, Dr. Forster—Professor Edmund Forster, chief of the Berlin University Nerve Clinic and a consulting psychiatrist at Pasewalk Military Hospital—had rigorously examined the soldier and had been unable to determine an actual medical reason for the blindness. He'd gone so far as to conclude that the young man was "a psychopath with hysterical symptoms." The good doctor might live to regret that diagnosis.

She gently touched the soldier's arm. "Would you like some fresh air?"

He moved his head in a subtle, almost imperceptible nod, as if acknowledging her would compromise his brooding despondency. Like many of the soldiers here, his face was thin and his complexion pasty. With dark brown hair and a thick, drooping moustache, both in need of trimming, he looked more like an artist than a soldier. A dreamer. Not a romantic dreamer, but a pragmatic and determined one who would obliterate any obstacles, human or otherwise, that stood in the way of realizing his dreams. Dr. Forster might be right—the young man might very well be a psychopath—but was that necessarily a bad thing? Sometimes the world needed someone who was crazy enough to do the things that no sane person would attempt. History had been shaped by such psychopaths…and the future would be too.

She helped him to a standing position and, draping his hand across her arm, proceeded to guide him out to the hallway. She imagined that if he could see her, he'd be a bit livelier. She was a very attractive woman—tall, slender but nicely proportioned, with wavy auburn-red hair that reflected sunlight as if it were infused with microscopic diamonds. Her sparkling green eyes and fair complexion—smooth, creamy skin punctuated by a few light freckles on her nose and cheeks—gave her the look of a gentle, loving soul. But that would be wrong. The body was that of a thirty-year-old Aryan beauty named Marlene. But the soul was that of a one hundred and fifty-year-old Egyptian man named Anwar. And there was nothing gentle or loving about him.

It had been pure happenstance that Anwar had come to occupy this particular host three weeks earlier. For the previous forty-eight years he had ridden the body of a diamond merchant with shops in Berlin, Munich and Dusseldorf. It had been a very rewarding ride, providing both wealth and status. He had even learned quite a bit about gemology, and had developed a great appreciation for diamonds. The thing he liked most about them was that so much value could be concentrated in so little mass. As a result, he carried a small leather pouch on his person at all times. In the event he was ever unable to access his sizable bank account, the diamonds in the pouch would sustain him for a couple of years—longer if he cut back on his opulent lifestyle.

The pouch had, as always, been in his coat pocket as he dined at a small restaurant in Pasewalk on the evening of October 16th. He had visited a local jewelry store that he planned to buy—steal actually, because the owner was on the verge of bankruptcy and had been forced to accept half the price he had been asking—and Anwar, in the guise of wealthy jeweler Jürgen von Bartow, was celebrating his latest acquisition with a bottle of Riesling and a teeming plate of sauerbraten. The heart attack came on suddenly, and Anwar's century and a half of parasitic self-preservation would have ended right then and there had it not been for the intervention of a beautiful, auburn-haired nurse. Her medical skills were not sufficient to save the jeweler's life, but she reached him in enough time for Anwar to jump from von Bartow's body to hers before succumbing to oxygen deprivation resulting from a fibrillating heart. That was the only downside to being a rider—if a host dies before the rider can make a jump to another living body, the rider dies too. Even immortality has its limitations.

But that was not the case with Anwar on that fateful evening. Twenty minutes later, the lifeless body of Jürgen von Bartow was covered with a black cloth and carried from the dining room on a stretcher, and the young, beautiful and very much alive body of Frau Marlene Reichert, tightly gripping the pouch of diamonds, walked away amid admiring looks and accolades from the restaurant staff and clientele.

The woman's purse contained her identification papers, including her address and place of employment, as well as a key which Anwar had correctly surmised would open the door to her small but well-kept apartment. He was at first concerned that he knew absolutely nothing about nursing, but was relieved to discover on his first day of work that Marlene was rather low on the hospital's organizational chart and was therefore relegated to menial tasks that required little medical training. It would be a temporary ride anyway. Anwar had never occupied a female body before, and found the curse of menstruation to be particularly distasteful. But even more pressing was the fact that the rumored armistice would mean that the woman's husband, having spent the past two years on the eastern front, would likely be coming home soon. The passionate reuniting of a young married couple after two years of separation—with Anwar in the role of the sex-starved woman—was a scene he would avoid at any cost.

So he had immediately initiated the search for a more suitable host. And had found him—the frail, emaciated young man now being escorted out the doors of the hospital and into the bright sunshine of a glorious November morning. The soldier immediately squinted and shielded his eyes from the sun's glare, another indication that his eyes were still functional and the blindness was temporary.

Most of the seating in the garden area was taken, so Marlene and her patient continued along the gravel path to a small clearing on the other side of the hedges. There were a couple of benches alongside a narrow brook, so they slowly made their way to the closest one. No one else had come down this far. They were hidden from the others by the hedge, and the sound of the water bubbling over the rocks would muffle their conversation. It was perfect.

Still, Anwar felt there was little time to waste. Another nurse, or perhaps one of the patients, could decide to take a little walk and their solitude would end. Two or three minutes were all Anwar needed. And then anyone who came down there would simply find a confused, blind soldier and the lifeless shell of a beautiful young nurse. There would, of course, be an investigation, but a body with absolutely no markings or any evidence of a struggle would eventually be written off to death by natural causes. Unusual for a person this young, but not unheard of. Her co-workers would recall that she'd been acting strangely for the past three weeks—withdrawn, uncommunicative, melancholy. The stress of wartime takes its toll in often unpredictable ways.

Sitting side by side on the narrow wooden bench, the nurse rested her hand on the soldier's arm. "What is your name, Corporal?"

He turned his head slowly, his red-rimmed eyes staring blankly, but purposely, in an attempt to see the person beside him. It was a moment before he spoke in a soft but confident voice. "My name is Adolf."

Anwar knew he had made an excellent choice. This was going to be one hell of a ride.

Chapter 1

MIRIAM GAZED ACROSS the choppy surface of the lake, savoring the warmth of the late afternoon sun. Early May was generally a glorious time in northwestern New Jersey, with warm days and cool, oftentimes chilly, evenings. A prelude to summer and a welcome escape from the icy clutches of a long, drab winter. The quaint, Alpine architecture that dominated the community of Lake Mohawk, an affluent enclave within the township of Sparta, was beautiful when covered with a fresh coating of snow. But this winter had not provided much snow, just month after month of cold, gray dreariness. She was glad this had been their last winter here. Forty-six had been enough.

She turned to her husband seated beside her on the cushioned glider at the edge of their dock. "Days just don't get much more perfect than this, do they, *kochanka*?"

He took her hand and gave it a squeeze. "No, this one has been special."

She reached for the bottle of chardonnay on the end table. "Ready for a refill?"

"Sure," he said, lifting his glass to her. "Might as well finish the bottle out here. I'm in no big hurry to go inside."

She studied his face as she poured the wine. He looked tired, haggard even. She'd always known that this body that had loved her, protected her, pleased her…oh God, how he could please her… wouldn't last forever. Human bodies weren't built to. But she'd hoped they would have more time. Unfortunately, that wasn't to be. Last week, after several days of tests, Peter had gotten the diagnosis she'd feared most—pancreatic cancer. Stage 3c. Which meant that without aggressive treatment—and possibly even with it—his life expectancy was measured in weeks. Twelve at least, maybe more, but they couldn't afford to gamble on any more than that. Treatment wasn't an option they would pursue. It was time for them to move.

"How about a salad for dinner?" she asked, lifting his hand to her lips. "Caesar, maybe. I have some shrimp in the freezer that I could sauté and throw in if you like."

He turned to look at her. "How about blackened?"

"Blackened? You know how that smokes up the kitchen."

"Okay, okay. Sautéed will be fine." He looked out at the lake and smiled. "There's certainly no reason to cater to the whims of a dying man. No special treatment expected here."

She punched his shoulder. "You bastard. I should've known you'd play the *dying* card to get what you want."

He chuckled. "Just wanted to try it out to see if it works. Will it get me what I want *after* dinner too?"

She smiled and inched a little closer to him. The sun was down behind the trees now and the air was getting chillier by the minute. "We'll see. But you can't keep me up too late. I have another meeting at Rutgers in the morning. I've been looking through the applications and I think I may have found our girl. I interview her at nine-thirty."

"Is she pretty?"

"Judging from her picture, quite pretty."

"So you think I'll like her?"

She snuggled in closer and rested her head on his shoulder. "You'd better like her. In fact, you'd better love her."

MIRIAM ARRANGED her two pages of interview questions on the table in front of her. She was in a small conference room in the Finance Department of the Rutgers Business School in New Brunswick. She had identified four potential contenders on the Newark campus—three MBA candidates and one MS in Global Affairs—but the young lady she was meeting this morning seemed to be the most perfect fit. There were a lot of attributes that Miriam desired in a candidate, but three were absolutely essential—good health, good looks, and no close family connections. Finding all three in one person was always a challenge, but the *curriculum vitae* of this woman seemed, at least on paper, to put her clearly in the lead.

At precisely nine-thirty there was a soft knock on the door. Miriam looked up as an attractive, but not particularly memorable, face peered around the edge of the door. "Are you ready for me?" she asked, her voice quiet and somewhat tentative.

"Yes, of course," Miriam said, rising from her chair. "You're right on time."

The young woman stepped inside and eased the door shut behind her. She seemed to hesitate a moment before placing a folder on the table and extending her hand, as if intimidated by the immaculately dressed, seventy-ish woman with expensive-looking reading glasses hanging from a platinum chain around her neck. "I'm Julia Crutchfield," she said.

"Miriam Ebersole. It's a pleasure meeting you, Julia."

The two women shook hands and sat across from each other. Miriam assessed her candidate as Julia began to pull out the contents of her folder and organize them into three stacks in front of her. So far, Miriam was pleased with what she saw. Julia was fairly tall for a woman—about five foot nine—with long sandy hair. Her complexion was light and unblemished, without a trace of make-up. Her blue eyes, partially hidden by the tortoise shell frames of her glasses, were clear and bright, shining with intellectual curiosity. She had the taut, slender figure of a runner. Miriam knew from the *CV* in front of her that Julia had attended Rutgers on a track scholarship while earning her undergraduate degree in accounting. Overall, a bit mousy—perhaps even nerdy—but brimming with potential. Cut and style that hair, maybe lighten it a shade or two, replace the glasses with contact lens, add make-up and a stylish wardrobe, and this young lady would be striking, if not actually beautiful.

"So," said Miriam, appearing to study the *CV* again, although she had it practically memorized, "you are completing your MBA in the fall."

"Technically it's an MFNA—Masters of Financial Analysis—but yes. All I have to do is write my thesis and get it approved, and I'll be ready for Wall Street." She smiled, and then blushed, adding, "Well, that's my goal, at least. A job on Wall Street."

Miriam smiled and arched the brow over her right eye. "Get started making a lot of money so you can pay off those student loans, right?"

Julia looked down at the table, re-aligning the corners of the three stacks of documents in front of her, although they were already positioned perfectly. "Actually, I don't have any student loans. My parents and my brother were killed in a plane crash several years ago—remember that commuter plane that crashed in upstate New York during a snowstorm?—and they left me enough money to finance my education." She looked back up and smiled sadly. "But that money is almost gone, so I have to start thinking about earning a living now."

Miriam was already aware of that sad story, but acted as if she were hearing it for the first time. "I'm so sorry, Julia. I can't imagine how difficult that was for you." She took a deep breath and smiled. "But I'm sure your parents would be extremely pleased to see how you've used the money. A lot of young people would have blown it on less admirable pursuits."

"I suppose," Julia whispered.

"So," Miriam said, her voice more cheerful now. "What are your plans for your thesis?"

Julia seemed to brighten as soon as the talk returned to academics. "I've applied for a summer internship with BD—Becton

Dickinson—the medical products company headquartered in Franklin Lakes. If I get it, I'd like to do an analysis of foreign currency valuations on stock prices, both in recessionary and growth markets. I believe a statistical tool can be developed to predict long-term financial returns for international businesses. The tool would have to be customized for each company, of course, but the parameters would be universal."

"And would that be a paying internship?"

"No, unfortunately not. But if I can find a cheap apartment and maybe a weekend job, I think I can stretch out my remaining funds enough to make it through the summer."

Miriam leaned forward and folded her hands on the table. "Julia, the reason I'm here is to offer you an alternative summer internship. It would pay a small stipend per month for a maximum of four months, but would include room and board. And, from what you just told me, I think the subject matter would be right up your alley."

Noting the look of interest on the young woman's face, she continued. "My husband is independently wealthy, and has dabbled in day trading for almost twenty years now. I say dabbled, but in reality he has tripled the value of his investment portfolio during that time."

Julia looked at her intently, her eyes shining behind her glasses. "How did he do that?"

Miriam laughed. "Good question. That's where you would come in. Peter, that's my husband, knows what he does, but doesn't know how to define it as a process. What he wants is to find someone who can study his results and develop a statistical tool—a predictor, if you will—that global investors can use to generate returns higher than the Dow, the S&P index, and other traditional indicators." She paused and studied her candidate's face. "Sound interesting?"

"It sounds fascinating," Julia replied, her voice enthusiastic.

"Excellent," Miriam said. "I was hoping you'd feel that way. Like I said earlier, the more I've learned about you, the more I've become convinced that you'd be perfect for this job." She paused a moment, staring directly into Julia's eyes. "But, to be frank, Julia, there are factors other than academic that my husband and I are concerned with."

Suddenly, Julia looked worried. "Like what?"

"Well, as I mentioned, we would offer room and board. But having someone live with you for four months is a big adjustment. We're both in our seventies and, for lack of a better term, a little old-fashioned. On top of that, my husband is having some health issues. Having young men coming out each weekend would be a little disruptive."

Julia brightened. "Mrs. Ebersole, I can assure you that wouldn't be an issue. I don't have a boyfriend, or any really close friends here at school for that matter. So, it would just be me."

Miriam smiled warmly. "Then I think you would be perfect for this opportunity, Julia. Absolutely perfect."

Chapter 2

PETER REMOVED HIS glasses and rubbed his eyes. He was seated at his kitchen table, directly opposite a large bay window that provided a panoramic view of the lake. It was June 27th, and summer had settled in, bringing warm, sunny days that made living on the island in the middle of Lake Mohawk almost worth the exorbitant housing prices...and ridiculous real estate taxes. He knew he wouldn't have many more mornings like this. The house had gone on the market in mid-May, and had sold in three weeks. The buyers, two doctors from Minneapolis with two teenaged kids, wanted to move in and get settled before the start of the new school year, so the closing had been set for August 1st. Just four and a half more weeks, and so much to do. It would have been taxing on a healthy man in his thirties. For a man in his mid-seventies, fighting advanced pancreatic cancer, it was exhausting.

It had been a month since Julia Crutchfield first arrived, and Peter had taken a liking to her right away. Miriam's assessment had been spot-on. As he watched her load the dishwasher with their breakfast dishes, he tried to imagine what she would look like after the makeover. She was pretty to start with, in a plain, unembellished way, and he believed she could be quite stunning with a little help.

She was tidying up the counter-top by the sink when she turned to look at him. "Would you like some more coffee or do you want me to pour this out?"

"I'll take another cup," he said. "Maybe the caffeine will give me a little more energy."

She smiled as she took his cup, filled it, and set it back in front of him. "How many times are you going to read that?" she asked, nodding at the *New Jersey Herald* on the table.

"I don't know," he sighed. "This is just going to take some getting used to."

He picked the paper back up and focused again on the short article on the first page of the local news section, starting to read it for about the tenth time.

Lake Mohawk Arts Benefactor Laid to Rest

SPARTA, NJ - Miriam B. Ebersole was buried Thursday, June 26th, after being discovered dead by her husband, Peter K. Ebersole, on the morning of June 23rd. Mrs. Ebersole was found in bed, and appeared to have died in her sleep sometime during the early morning hours. Her autopsy, conducted by County Coroner Richard Schaefly, determined her death to be by natural causes.

A neighbor, who preferred to remain anonymous, was quoted as saying, "It's not surprising, really. Miriam has been under terrible stress for the past few weeks. Her husband was recently diagnosed with terminal cancer, and they've been working frantically, trying to sell their house and move back to Colorado, where they lived before moving to Lake Mohawk in 1970. I believe the pressure just got to be too much for her."

Mrs. Ebersole maintained a low profile, as many residents of the small but exclusive Manitou Island community have done through the years, but was known for her generous support of the arts. In 1975 she and her husband established the Ebersole Performing Arts Trust, which over the past forty years has provided over two million dollars in financial assistance to promising Sussex County students who wanted to pursue careers in music and dance. Several beneficiaries of this trust have gone on to have successful Broadway careers, including

Lisa Anne Carlisle, who won a Tony in 2009 for her lead role in a revival of *South Pacific*. Ms. Carlisle is currently on tour in Europe and could not be reached for comment.

Sparta High School principal Delores Finney said that Mrs. Ebersole's support of promising students was not restricted to the performing arts. "She was a champion of academic excellence," Ms. Finney told this reporter. "It wasn't widely known, as per Mrs. Ebersole's wishes, but several students have received financial support to attend college and study art, literature, even the sciences." At the time of her death, Mrs. Ebersole and her husband were providing a paid internship for Julia Crutchfield, a graduate student at Rutgers University Business School, who said she was "devastated by the sudden, tragic loss of this remarkable woman."

Mrs. Ebersole's sole surviving family member is her husband, Peter. "They never had children of their own," said Ms. Finney, "but they have played a vital role in the support of the children of Sussex County for over forty years. She will be missed."

Peter folded the paper and set it gently on the table beside his coffee cup. "It's a really nice article," he said.

"And the funeral was nice too," Julia said, walking around the table and gently lowering herself onto Peter's lap. She kissed his forehead and brushed a few stray hairs back behind his left ear. "For some reason, these endings are always sad. I suppose it's like moving out of a house that you've lived in for a long time. So many memories made. The end of an era."

"And the start of a new one," Peter said, kissing her neck. "And if we don't decide on a replacement for Peter Ebersole pretty soon, you may be starting that new era without me."

"Stay strong, *kochanka*," she said, pushing his head back and tilting his chin up so she could look into his eyes. "Because you know I would never go anywhere without you. Never in a thousand years."

Chapter 3

ROBERT MARTINEZ made one more adjustment to the already perfect Windsor knot of his Italian silk tie before walking into the bedroom to retrieve his Armani suit jacket from the wooden valet next to the dresser. It was good to be back in his favorite suite in his favorite hotel. The 1,350 square foot Master Suite—powder room off the entry foyer, spacious living room with a grand piano, dining room to comfortably seat six, fully equipped kitchen, and a sumptuous bedroom with a king-sized bed and a massive master bath—provided all the amenities he felt he deserved. The Rosewood Mansion on Turtle Creek catered to the most discriminating clientele, and few were more discriminating than the wealthy manufacturer and founder of the new American Values Party—the AVP— who had checked in late the previous evening for perhaps his tenth or twelfth visit to the exclusive Dallas hotel.

He strolled into the dining room, where a clearly nervous young man from room service was setting the table with a light lunch for six. The boy was apparently new and was obviously star-struck by the handsome, fifty-year-old man whose face had adorned nearly every newspaper, magazine and television news program in America for the past four months. "Just about done, sir," the young man said, using his hand to smooth out a nearly undetectable wrinkle on the white linen tablecloth. "The soft drinks, tea and water are set up on the bar, and the coffee service and dessert are on the buffet table."

"Thank you, Brian," Martinez said, making sure to use the name on the gold plated tag pinned to the young man's breast pocket. People loved to hear their own name, especially from the mouth of someone famous. "Are you new here at the Mansion?"

"Yes sir," the boy replied, a look of apprehension in his eyes. "Two months." He glanced down at the table, obviously concerned that something might not be meeting the expectations of his famous guest.

"I thought so," Martinez said, noting the kid's nervousness. "I've stayed here a few times before, and I don't remember seeing you. But you handled this set-up like you've been doing it for years. I'll make a point of telling the desk manager what a great job you did."

"Thank you, Mr. Martinez," the clearly relieved young man said. "It's been an honor to serve you, sir."

Martinez handed him a folded twenty dollar bill and opened the door, ushering the young man into the hallway before he could launch another effusive accolade. Within an hour, every member of the room service staff and anyone else who would listen would hear how the man that many people thought could become the next President of the United States had complimented the server and called him by name…and tipped him generously. Martinez smiled. He wanted every single vote his fledgling party could get in the next mid-term election, so he went to great lengths to make sure no one had anything negative to say about him. Or, if they did, that they were appropriately "persuaded" to keep it to themselves.

He walked to the center of the foyer and knocked on the adjoining door as he turned the deadbolt from his side. After a few seconds he heard the other lock turn and the door opened to reveal his company COO, senior campaign strategist, and American Values Party second-in-command. "About ready, Arthur?"

Arthur Stephenson nodded affirmatively before following Martinez into the dining room of the suite and studying the table. "Rather light fare, don't you think?"

Martinez grinned and shook his head. "I don't think our guests will have that much of an appetite after they hear what I've got to say." He glanced at his watch. "Have you heard from any of them yet?"

"Two," Stephenson said. "Mitchell and Blankenship landed about a half hour ago." Ben Mitchell and George Blankenship were declared AVP congressional candidates for Wisconsin and Pennsylvania, respectively. "The other two should be landing shortly." They were Glen Arbuckle of Virginia and Patrick Ellis of California, each working to get on the ballot in his home state.

"Perfect," Martinez said. "Do you think they know why they were invited to an impromptu lunch meeting?"

"I imagine Ben Mitchell has a pretty good idea," Stephenson said, stepping over to the buffet to pour a cup of coffee. "His comment last week that he'd represent the views of the people of Wisconsin on immigration policy, even if they conflicted with party views, got a lot of press play. He has to know that caught your attention. The other three have been a little less flagrant in their deviations from the script we gave them, but enough that they might figure they're due a little dressing down."

Martinez smiled. "What they're due is a major ass-reaming. I think we made it pretty clear at the outset that everyone has to stay on message...*my* message. We're offering the American people a different path than the Republicans and Democrats, and we have to be very consistent in explaining what that path looks like."

"We'll make sure they understand by the time they leave here this afternoon. It's our way or the highway."

Martinez poured a cup of coffee and added a splash of cream. "I'd prefer to tell them it's our way or the graveyard." He smiled. "Figuratively speaking, of course."

The two men settled into opposite armchairs in the living room with their coffee, and Stephenson's feet, on the coffee table between them. Few people were this casual in the presence of Robert Martinez—not even Maria, his wife of twelve years—but then, few people dared think of themselves as Martinez's equal. Arthur Stephenson did. The two men relished different roles, but both realized that neither would be where they were without the other.

Roberto Rivera Martinez had been born the only child of a legal Mexican immigrant—Martinez never missed a chance to emphasize the word *legal*—and a poor second generation Mexican-American girl from his neighborhood. His father died in Viet Nam when Roberto was four years old—another thing Martinez never failed to emphasize—and Roberto grew up poor, but proud. And smart. He attended Baylor on a full academic scholarship, graduating with honors in just three and a half years. Like many students, he took off six months to travel after graduation. But unlike his friends who wandered through Europe, Roberto hitch-hiked the backroads of Mexico and Central America. It was an experience that shaped his destiny.

He returned to San Antonio in late summer of 1989, took the vowel off the end of his first name, and landed a job as a salesman for a small, locally-owned toy manufacturer. He was nothing if not brash. After a year on the job, he paid his own expenses to drive to Bentonville, Arkansas, where he camped out in a seedy motel for five days, refusing to leave until he had a Walmart supply contract. The resulting volume demanded an immediate four-fold increase in manufacturing capacity and a significant reduction in cost, which was beyond the imagination and capabilities of the owner. So he brought Robert in from the field and put him in charge of the project. There were bumps along the way, and a few casualties, but Robert single-handedly transformed the company from a local niche manufacturer to a regional player in less than a year.

It was a small, family-owned business, and Robert found himself doing a little bit of everything. Within two years of his fateful excursion to Bentonville, he was essentially functioning as the COO. He managed to structure a compensation plan for himself that paid a nominal base salary but provided a significant incentive for growth. By 1996 he had saved enough money to buy the old man out. Eight years later, with new supply contracts to make cheap toys for two worldwide hamburger chains to put in their kids' meals, he took the company public. The initial stock offering raised nearly a half billion dollars.

Before long he was being courted by the Republican Party as a future gubernatorial candidate. The idea of holding political office appealed to his ego, but Robert refused these overtures for two reasons. First, if he was going to enter the political arena he didn't want to be bound by someone else's rules. And second, he had his sights set way beyond Austin.

He knew the American public was often wary of bachelors in leadership roles, so he found himself a suitable wife. He married Maria Sanchez, an attractive middle school teacher ten years his junior, a month before his thirty-ninth birthday. It was a bit of a surprise to the public when they announced their engagement. Martinez had never been linked with any one woman for any period of time, nor did he appear to live the life of a wealthy playboy. Some even whispered he might be gay. But that was not the case at all. Robert Martinez loved women. Lots of women. He just loved them one night at a time…for a price.

As Liberty Toys, Inc. continued to grow, Martinez found himself needing to again increase manufacturing capacity. Part of his solution was vertical integration. He started looking for a mold designing company to buy, and that's when he met Arthur Stephenson.

Stephenson Molding Technology was a small but successful designer and builder of plastic injection molds for everything from shaving blade cartridges to disposable medical devices. It had all the capabilities Martinez needed, and Stephenson, in his late fifties, was not averse to the concept of taking the money and retiring somewhere in Europe. But Martinez saw something in the older man that made him think they could accomplish great things together.

At the final negotiating session before inking the purchase, Martinez said, "You're too young to retire. Why don't you come to work for Liberty? I need a COO who can facilitate the integration of our two companies. You'd be perfect."

Stephenson had eyed him suspiciously. "Why would I want to do that? I can have a lot of fun in Europe spending the eighty million dollars you're giving me."

Martinez had smiled. "Seventy-eight point five, but let's not quibble over details. I believe you can have a lot more fun with what I have planned."

He'd been right.

THE SIX MEN took their seats around the table a few minutes past noon. Martinez and Stephenson took the positions at either end of the table, occupying armchairs with higher backs than the four side chairs. Despite the amicable chit-chat since the arrival of the four candidates, Martinez could tell that his guests appeared a bit apprehensive. His goal, over the next few minutes, was to turn that apprehension into unbridled fear.

"Gentlemen, I took the liberty of ordering chef salads for everyone," he said. "I hope that's okay."

He really didn't care if it was okay or not, but was pleased to see heads nodding and hear voices murmuring approval. He waited until everyone had removed the covers from their plates and had begun the process of selecting from three choices of salad dressing before continuing. "Arthur and I appreciate you flying in for this meeting on such short notice. We felt it was important to gather our four most promising candidates for a brief strategy session."

He noted the tentative smiles when he threw them that bone. The poor bastards were probably beginning to think that the party founder actually valued their input. He would put that false notion to bed very shortly.

"As you know, we have a rare political opportunity in front of us. The American electorate is feeling, to use the politically correct term, *disenfranchised*. I have another term for it—they are thoroughly and damned near universally *pissed off*. The last presidential election offered them the choice of two of the most unpopular candidates in recent memory. It didn't take a Harvard political scientist to realize that, no matter who won, half of the nation was going to be disgruntled. And despite all the campaign rhetoric about working together to address our country's many problems, we're seeing more polarization than ever. Every major issue from the disastrous budget deficit to the war on terror is in limbo. These stupid bastards in Washington just keep kicking the can down the road and blaming each other for the lack of progress. The American public is fed up with both parties, as they should be. They are looking for a viable alternative, and the American Values Party provides them with one."

Martinez looked around the table. The four candidates were nodding their heads and glancing his way every minute or so, but seemed more focused on their salads than on him. He looked across the table to Arthur, who gave him a nod. It was time to get their attention.

"I founded the AVP to give the American people a choice. Over time, we'll have to address a myriad of issues, but our strategy at this stage is to focus on three. One, we will gain control of our borders—particularly our southern border—and then we will deport every man, woman and child that is here illegally. Two, we will balance the budget with absolutely no tax increases, and we will do that by dramatically curtailing entitlement programs and eliminating the socialist giveaway programs that are bankrupting us. And third, we will withdraw from the United Nations and tell the world that our foreign policy will be built solely around the perpetuation of American interests. No foreign aid, no military support, no humanitarian support or anything else that doesn't directly contribute to the strength and well-being of the United States. These three issues are front and center in the minds of the American voter, and we will be consistent and unambiguous in telling the voters how we will address them. Any questions?"

He looked pointedly at Ben Mitchell, who held up one finger as he finished chewing a mouthful of salad, and then said, "Well, Robert, since this is a strategy session, I feel compelled to share my thoughts. I agree that these three issues are the most important ones we can focus on. They certainly are in Wisconsin. But our proposed solutions, although directionally consistent, will need to be tailored to reflect the personality, if you will, of our various state electorates. For instance, everybody wants something to be done about the immigration issue, but voters in Wisconsin may have a different perspective than voters in the border states. To be successful, our strategy has to appeal to a broad range of voters."

Martinez noticed the other heads nodding, but he ignored them and leaned across the table toward Mitchell, getting as close to the man's face as possible without rising from his chair. "You are correct, Ben, that this is a strategy meeting, but there is a nuance that you missed." Without warning he suddenly slammed his right fist onto the table so hard that salad dressing from the serving bowls splashed across the linen tablecloth like blood spatter from a sniper's head shot.

"The purpose of this meeting is not to *debate* our strategy," he shouted, spittle flying from his mouth, "it is to clarify our strategy. *My* strategy. And if you are going to run for Congress using my money, my organization, and my name, you're going to run on my strategy. Not some mish-mash of ideas that is similar to my strategy. *My strategy!* Are we clear on that?"

He had their undivided attention now, as evidenced by their wide eyes and gaping mouths. Each candidate still held his fork, but no one was using it. They weren't moving at all, as if fearing the slightest twinge would send Martinez into another fit of screaming fury. But instead of screaming, Martinez spoke in a low, icy voice. "Arthur has put together a strategy statement on each of our three critical issues, along with a list of talking points. And I expect those talking points to be followed to the letter."

He turned his head to fix his gaze on Glen Arbuckle. "So, Glen, you will not see anything there about grandfathering current Medicare beneficiaries with respect to fixing entitlement programs. Everybody has to play by the new rules. And Patrick, I don't give a rat's ass if California farmers depend on Mexican migrant workers to harvest their grapes and avocados. If those workers are here il-legally, they're going home. No exceptions."

He shifted his attention to the youngest man at the table, an insurance salesman and former Army Ranger from Arlington, Vir-ginia, and spoke in a soft, almost fatherly, voice. "Glen, I'm going to cut you a little slack, because you're young and new to the harsh realities of politics. I know that your district is home to many of the career politicians, both Republican and Democrat, who make up the current Washington elite. I've noticed you being a bit deferential to your neighbors on foreign policy differences. But let me ask you something. Do you know the difference between those politicians and the Taliban leaders you caught in the crosshairs of your sniper rifle in the Pamir Mountains?"

The young man started to speak but Martinez cut him off with the wave of a hand, which he then used to slam the table, again shaking plates and splattering more salad dressing across the now ruined tablecloth. "Nothing!" he yelled. "They are just as much your enemy as those ragheads in Kunduz. They may not carry assault rifles or have explosives strapped to their chests, but they have no more love for you than the Taliban fighters you killed, and they are just as eager to cut off your head, or your balls, or whatever else it takes to remove you as a threat to their hold on power. You don't give credence to their views, and you don't offer to reach across the aisle and negotiate once you're elected. It's kill or be killed; you got that?"

Arbuckle nodded, but said nothing. Martinez lowered his voice and said, "I recruited you to run on the AVP ticket specifically because you were a soldier. Start acting like one."

Now regaining the cool demeanor that defined his public persona, Martinez leaned back in his chair and looked at each of the four men in succession. "Questions?"

Ben Mitchell shook his head and the other three simply stared back, looking shell-shocked. "Good," Martinez said. "Arthur, see that each one of these gentleman gets a copy of the talking points you put together. I look forward to hearing them reiterated on the campaign trail." He again locked eyes with each candidate in succession. "Word...for...fucking...word."

He then rose from the table and strode out of the room.

THIRTY MINUTES LATER Martinez and Stephenson sat in the living room, ties loosened and shoeless feet resting on the coffee table. Martinez chuckled. "I think the meeting went well, don't you?"

Stephenson smiled. "For us. I'm not sure our candidates had a lot of fun."

Martinez rose from his chair and walked toward the bar separating the living room from the kitchen. "I'm not interested in their fun. I'm interested in their obedience. If we're going to turn the American political structure on its ass, we'll have to operate with synchronized precision. There won't be any room for ad-libbing. Everyone has to be in lock step."

"*Sieg Heil,*" Stephenson laughed.

"Whatever it takes," Martinez said. "How about a drink? I could damned sure use one."

Stephenson glanced at his watch. It was two o'clock. "A little early for me typically, but this isn't a typical day, so why not?" He smiled. "I don't suppose you had them stock the bar with Laphroaig by any chance?"

Martinez laughed as he walked behind the bar in the kitchen. "It wasn't by chance at all. I ordered it specifically for you. Eighteen years old."

"Couldn't spring for the twenty-five year old stuff, huh? You cheap bastard."

Martinez poured them both a healthy drink and handed one to Stephenson. "You're in for a treat for dinner tonight. The Mansion Restaurant is one of my favorites."

"Looking forward to it," Stephenson said.

"I made the reservation a little early. Six-thirty. I want to get a good night's sleep and be ready for an early wake-up call."

Stephenson took a sip of his drink and grinned slyly. "No entertainment tonight?"

Martinez smiled. "Well, I have a friend who might drop by for a quick visit. I've had Maria with me damned near everywhere I've gone for the past six months. A little change of pace will do me good."

"Just be careful. You don't want to become known as the new Bill Clinton."

"I'm not worried about that," Martinez said. "Clinton's indiscretions only came to light because he didn't have a way to shut up his critics. I, on the other hand, have you."

They clinked glasses and then settled back in their chairs to savor their drinks. They were two men of equal talents, but different personal desires. One craved recognition, the other having decided many years earlier that true power usually resides behind the scenes, away from the public eye. They were both cunning, ruthless, and totally lacking in empathy. And brilliantly adept in making the world believe otherwise.

Theirs was the perfect partnership. A match made in hell.

Chapter 4

KRISTEN CONNELLY CHECKED her perfectly coiffed blond hair and meticulously applied make-up in a compact mirror before nodding to Mitch, her camera man. She was ready to go, positioned in front of the discreet Rosewood corporate symbol right outside the hotel entrance. Over the past few weeks the American Values party had started to gain traction and was now garnering a significant amount of media attention. Which put her and the up-start *Political News Network*—PNN—in a perfect spot. The report she was about to record was slated to be aired at eight-thirty that evening on *The Political Pulse, with Ron Archer.* The nightly 30 minute program, hosted by PNN's evening news anchor, had a respectable rating, particularly among viewers who considered themselves to be conservatives. These viewers loved Martinez and, because of Kristen's generally favorable coverage of him, loved her as well.

She watched as Mitch raised one hand over his head, fingers extended, and counted down from five, starting with his thumb. When he got down to his forefinger, he pointed it at her and she began.

"This is Kristen Connelly with an exclusive update on the American Values Party. I am standing outside the historic Rosewood Mansion at Turtle Creek in Dallas, where earlier today an unannounced meeting was held between AVP founder Robert Martinez, chief advisor Arthur Stephenson, and four of the party's most highly touted congressional candidates. Ben Mitchell from Wisconsin,

George Blankenship from Pennsylvania, Patrick Ellis of California, and Glen Arbuckle of Virginia are all reportedly close to qualifying to be on their respective state ballots in the next mid-term election. All four are polling close to their incumbent opposition, and could be indicative of the new party's appeal in all parts of the country.

"I was told a few minutes ago by a source within the AVP organization that Martinez called the meeting—referred to as a *strategy review session*—to pick the brains of his four rising stars so that other party candidates for the House, Senate, and three gubernatorial seats can benefit from their early success. According to my source, Martinez listened attentively to each candidate's views on what is working well and what is not working well, and solicited their help in refining the language used to articulate the AVP positions on immigration, balancing the federal budget, and revamping foreign policy. I was told that Martinez was very pleased with the outcome of the meeting, and most appreciative of the four candidates' willingness to disrupt their schedules so they could come to Dallas and share their ideas with him.

"In just the past six months, the American Values Party has tapped into the deep dissatisfaction a significant portion of the electorate has with the status quo. According to recent polls, the president's popularity is lower than that of any first-term president in recent history at this stage. Congress isn't faring any better in the minds of the voters, and the calls for cleaning house and imposing term limits has been loud and frequent.

"The AVP does have its detractors, most notably the Hispanic population's disdain for the party's proposed immigration policies. *Brigada de Proteccion Hispana*—The Hispanic Protection Brigade—the grassroots organization formed specifically to protest those policies, has become increasingly vocal and is said to be growing by hundreds of members every day. That aside, the American Values Party is flying high, causing both Republicans and Democrats to scratch their heads and wonder what they can do to slow down the erosion of their respective party bases before the mid-term elections.

"This is Kristen Connelly, reporting from Dallas for PNN."

She continued to stare at the red light of the camera until it blinked off and Mitch raised a clenched fist, indicating the broadcast was over. She removed the earphone and mike and handed the apparatus to Mitch. "I'm going inside to find a ladies room, and then I'm going to see if I can reach somebody in the Martinez inner circle who can give us an idea of what they hope to accomplish in Chicago later this week. I'll take a cab back to the Sheraton later."

Mitch nodded. "Sounds good. Wanna grab some dinner tonight?"

"No, I think I'll just order room service and watch Ron's show. I'll meet you in the lobby at seven-thirty tomorrow morning and we'll head for the airport." She tapped his camera with her finger. "Get this sent in pronto, okay?"

Receiving his assurances, she turned and walked into the lobby of the hotel. But she didn't look for the ladies room. Instead, she headed straight for the bar, where she found a small, secluded table and ordered a glass of Chardonnay. She hadn't lied to Mitch about her intention to watch the broadcast that would start in another ninety minutes. She just wouldn't be back in her room at the Hilton. She'd be upstairs in the Masters Suite, watching it with the man himself.

And then she would get her grade.

Chapter 5

THE MONTH OF JULY seemed to drag by for Miriam. Watching Peter's body grow weaker every day was nerve-wracking. Although his oncologist had assured them that Peter had another four to six weeks, Miriam couldn't stand to be away from his side, even for a few minutes, for fear of coming back into the room and finding he had died in his sleep. She wasn't worried about him when he was awake. His mind was still crystal clear, and he knew what to do. He just needed to be awake to do it.

Eugenio, the full-time home health nurse, had been given very explicit instructions. Under no circumstances was he to leave the room—not even to walk into the adjoining bathroom—without the young woman he knew as Julia sitting at Peter's side. He slept on a cot by his patient's bed, within arm's reach, and was required to check Peter's vitals every two hours. All of his meals were served to him in the room. When he needed to go to the bathroom or step outside for a few minutes to stretch his legs, he was required to summon Julia to cover for him. It had been exhausting until he'd gotten into the rhythm. Then it had just become tedious and boring. But he was being paid handsomely, three times the going rate for private nurses.

They had lucked upon Eugenio after an exhaustive and disappointing search for the position. The placement service had sent over a dozen men—it had been made clear that no female candidates, no matter how qualified, would be considered—and could not understand why every single one was rejected. What difference did it make if a male nurse was young, as long as he was strong enough to do whatever was required? And so what if he had brothers and sisters living nearby who were also in healthcare? That should be a plus, not a negative. And one was turned down for no reason at all…but the placement agent got the impression that the young man simply wasn't handsome enough.

Miriam had begun to panic. They were running out of time. On the evening of Independence Day, she had argued vehemently with Peter, but to no avail.

"We need a new host, and we need to find him quickly," she had said. "We have to broaden our search. He doesn't have to be your nurse. He could be a handyman. Or another student intern."

"We still have time," he protested. "We planned this carefully, every detail. It doesn't make sense to throw all of that out the window just yet."

Miriam was fighting to control her temper. "It doesn't make sense to just sit here and watch you die either!"

Peter took her hand and squeezed it. "That's not going to happen."

Miriam was trembling with a combination of anger and fear. "You can't be sure of that. The cancer is taking more of a toll every day."

"But other than that, my body is strong."

"*Other than that? Other than that?*" She was almost shouting now. "Other than that, Mrs. Lincoln, how was the play?"

Peter laughed, which brought on a coughing spell, but it all served to lower the tension meter a point or two. "Okay, how about this," he said. "Let's give it one more week. It's early July, and we have the real estate closing on August first. This diseased old body should make it well into August. We can afford to give our original plan one more week. If we don't have someone on board, or at least hired, one week from today, we go to Plan B. Deal?"

She sighed, and wiped a tear from her eye. "I still think we're taking a risk by not having someone right here, by your side, every day. If push comes to shove, we use someone temporarily and then find a suitable long-term host."

Peter studied her for a moment before whispering, "You know we don't do that. We don't take a human life for short-term use. Not unless we absolutely need to."

She put her hand on his chest. "I know. But I have no greater need than to have you with me. Don't you understand that?"

He smiled wearily. "Yes, darling. I understand."

The problem was resolved the following morning when the placement service agent called to say that she had one more candidate they should see. Eugenio Alessi, a twenty-seven year old former medic in the Italian army, had arrived in New York the previous week. He had entered the military right after finishing secondary school, and after eight years of service—three in Afghanistan as part of a NATO team—he wanted to start a new life in America. He had no family in Italy, and the medical system there paid poorly anyway. He had a little money saved, but was looking for a part-time or temporary job to generate a little income while he searched for a more permanent position.

He sounded perfect, and he was. Six feet tall, dark brown hair, blue eyes, and the toned physique one would expect of a soldier. He was a non-smoker, a moderate drinker, and the blood tests—which Julia insisted on, saying Eugenio would be in close physical contact with an immune-compromised patient, although the actual purpose was for Miriam's protection—came back negative for any infectious disease.

If the young man was confused about the amount of control wielded by a graduate student intern in her mid-twenties, he kept his questions to himself. He had interviewed with Julia and Peter on July fifth, and had moved in and assumed his duties two days later. He adapted to the situation quickly, and the days passed with little variation to the melancholy and monotonous routine of watching a man die.

Finally, the end of July arrived. The evening before closing day was somber. The following morning would officially close a long and wonderful chapter of Peter and Miriam's epic love story. For forty-six years, this beautiful home on small, idyllic Manitou Island had been their sanctuary. They had enjoyed the peaceful years they had spent there more than any other place they had lived, and they'd lived in some truly special places. But neither the charm of Budapest, the vibrancy of Paris, nor the natural splendor of Aspen had kept them as content as had this quaint little lake community in northwest New Jersey. Which is probably why they had remained there longer than in any other location.

But now it was time to move on…to start a new chapter. And as invigorating as youth was, they would miss the serenity that had accompanied middle age and beyond. They now understood why these were often referred to as "golden years."

Miriam and Peter were in the bedroom, where she was feeding him spoonsful of her homemade tomato bisque. Eugenio had been sent downstairs to eat his dinner and watch a little television, but had received and acknowledged the usual instructions to stay within earshot should he be needed. Miriam spooned more soup into Peter's mouth, wiped his lips with a napkin, and held a water bottle with built-in straw for him to drink.

"There's plenty more soup downstairs if you feel like eating it," she said.

He took a long sip of water and then turned to look at her. "No, that's enough. It was delicious, as always."

She smiled. "I'm glad you enjoyed it. Just a couple more days, and you'll be able to eat solid food again. I bet you're looking forward to that."

He returned her smile. "That's not the only thing I'm looking forward to."

She leaned over and kissed him gently. "I've noticed the way you've been looking at me. Anxious to explore this twenty-five year old body, are we?"

"Don't be so judgmental, darling," he said, with a slight chuckle that sounded more like a cough. "I've seen you checking out our young Italian a time or two."

"Well…" She cocked her head to the side and smiled coyly. "I do look forward to taking him for a test drive. I'll be interested to find out what's under the hood."

"Just be sure you wait for me," he said.

She gave his shoulder a playful swat. "I'm going to pretend you never said that."

They sat in silence for a few minutes before she whispered, "I still feel like we're cutting it awfully close."

"Don't worry," he said. "I'm weak, but I haven't experienced any of the symptoms that the doctor said I could expect at the end. Two more days won't be a problem."

"You keep saying that, but I can't help but worry. Every cancer patient is unique. You may not have all of the typical symptoms. I'm scared out of my wits that you could just pass unexpectedly."

"It'll happen exactly as we planned," he said. "In two days. No sooner."

That had been their plan, and it looked as if it was indeed going to work out perfectly. Peter Ebersole would expire two days after closing on the house. It would be a little sooner than the doctors had expected, but not enough to arouse suspicion. The house would already be sold, and the money—a certified check—deposited into Peter's PNC Bank account and then immediately transferred to an offshore account in Grand Cayman. An estate sale would be conducted, starting the day after his death and concluding the day after that, with the proceeds being deposited at PNC and then being transferred to a numbered account in Geneva. Exactly one week after the closing—five days after Peter Ebersole's death—the new owners would take possession and start their renovation project. On that same day, Peter's accountant would give Julia Crutchfied and Eugenio Alessi their final pay checks, and the two would simply disappear without a trace.

"So," Peter said, anxious to change the subject before Miriam started fretting again, "you really think I'm going to like Birmingham?"

"Yes, I do," she said, a small measure of excitement momentarily outweighing the sense of fear and uncertainty that had dictated her mood for the past month. "It's perfect for a young, wealthy couple. Up-and-coming food and music scene, lots of college sports, and a pretty decent symphony orchestra. Big enough to allow anonymity, but small enough to get around easily. I think we'll like it."

"It's always hard with a new location we aren't familiar with," he said. "Especially finding a place to live. You want to plan on just renting for a while until we learn our way around?"

"We can do that if we need to, but I've already been checking out some real estate on the internet. There's an affluent community called Mountain Brook on the south side of Birmingham that has some beautiful old homes for sale." She smiled. "It would be the natural location for a spoiled, rich-kid day trader living on a large trust fund."

"And what would you do? You're pretty young to be an arts matron like you were here."

"Actually, I think I want to get a job. You know, work with people my age so I can keep up with the jargon and the interests of our generation. It'll help us maintain our cover."

"We can talk about that later," he said. Peter had never really liked her working outside the home, although she had done it several times before. As close as they were, and as alike as they were in so many aspects, that was one area where they differed. He preferred isolation, whereas she craved social interaction. It had always been a bit of a balancing act.

"I'm anxious to get down there and check things out," she said. "I always get excited when I'm starting a new adventure with you."

He sighed wearily. "Let's just get through the next week. When we leave here, we'll need to spend a few days in New York while our new documentation is completed."

"And I'll need to go to a women's health clinic to get my tubes tied," she murmured, a hint of regret in her voice. They both loved children, and would have loved one of their own. But they were unsure a child would be like them, and the risk of watching their child die of old age was one they wouldn't take. So they had always been careful, having employed tubal ligation as their method of birth control for the past three generations.

He looked at her and smiled weakly. "Yes, that too. And then we can head down south. But right now, just thinking about all of this wears me out. I feel so damned tired."

Her momentary rush of excitement was now displaced by the more familiar sense of apprehension. She would not rest easily until Peter was in a new, healthy body. She leaned over the side of the bed and rested her head on his shoulder. She closed her eyes, fighting tears. The next seventy-two hours were going to be torture for her. They had been together for so long, and had been through so much. It couldn't stop here. She wouldn't be able to bear it.

"Stay strong, *kochanka*," she whispered. "We're almost there. Please stay strong for me."

Chapter 6

THE CITY STILL reeked of burning flesh. The distinctive odor of mass cremations was nothing new. For months, dozens of bodies had been burned every day, but always well outside of the city. Depending on the direction of the wind, the smell and the smoke hung in the air like a fetid fog of death. But the burning of over a thousand Strasbourg citizens two days earlier had been different. For one thing, the massive pyre had been constructed right on the edge of the city. And for another, those burned had still been alive.

Miriam pulled a foul-smelling piece of deer hide—it had been used as a dog bed for years—around her shoulders and piled more straw on her legs and lower torso in an effort to get warm. She was hiding in a barn about two miles south of the city that had been her home since she was born, fifteen years earlier. But it was home to her no longer. In fact, no Jew could call Strasbourg home now. On February 14, all of the residents of the Jewish quarter had been ordered to gather in the center of town. Once again, as had happened numerous times over the past two years, they had been condemned as the cause of "the Pestilence" that had consumed most of Europe. They were accused of poisoning wells and spreading disease so they could eradicate Christianity. But this time, the new city council—now populated with an alliance of nobles and artisans who had successfully displaced the ruling master tradesmen a week earlier—did not stop with insults and threats. This time, they were out for blood.

The assembled Jews were given an ultimatum—they would consent to be baptized as Christians, after which they would be allowed to leave the city, or they would be burned to death. Miriam's father was a rabbi, so there was no way he would trade his faith for his life. He and Miriam's mother were among the first to be pummeled, bound and dragged away. Miriam tried to follow them, but was physically restrained.

It quickly became evident that children and attractive young women would be spared the burning, and sent away with those who acquiesced to baptism. Miriam was certainly attractive—tall and slender, with dark brown hair and hazel eyes, and full lips that her mother had always teased made her look like she was pouting. Over the past two years her body had transformed from that of an awkward, gangly girl to the shape of a voluptuous young woman. She was aware that the Christian men in town had started to stare whenever she walked by, and it always made her nervous. On that day, once she realized she would be spared from the fire, she feared the men had other plans for her. But after a few hours of being shoved, taunted and spit upon, she was forced to leave town with the blasphemous cowards who had turned their backs on their God and His chosen people. She staggered along in a daze, wondering if this was all just a bad dream, until the screams of the burning shocked her back to the hideous reality of the pogrom.

As darkness fell and the only light in the clouded sky was that of the human bonfire behind them, Miriam had slipped away from the wailing crowd of exiles. She couldn't stand to be with them, and she had no one to look after but herself. She had no siblings, her younger sister, Sarah, having died of the Pestilence in December. Shivering from the cold, she found her way to the small farm of a Jewish family her parents had known. The family, of course, was gone, and the tiny two-room house had already been looted. Afraid more Christians might show up, she sacrificed the relative comfort and warmth of the house and hid herself in the cold, drafty barn. There were no animals remaining, unless you counted the rats that scurried constantly across the dirt floor and into the straw, sometimes brushing against her legs and causing her to bite her fist to keep from screaming. Even Samson, the large but gentle mongrel who had always licked Miriam's face when she had visited with her father, was gone. It was his deer hide bed that she now wrapped tightly around her shoulders and arms.

This was her second day in the barn. She hadn't ventured out on the day after her arrival—the day after the murder of her parents—too frightened and suffering from too much despair to even move from her freezing, makeshift bed. But this morning, her aching hunger and parched throat had forced her to summon enough courage to search the house for food and water.

She was terrified that she'd be seen and that death, or worse, would be her fate, but she managed to creep across the yard and sneak a peek through a torn parchment window. Seeing no signs of life, she had slipped inside and frantically searched the small larder. She found nothing but some spilled corn meal—which she scooped, along with a considerable amount of dirt, into the pocket of her frock—and a half rotten potato. She quickly ate the part that wasn't rancid before hurrying outside to the well. The wooden bucket was still there, so she filled it and drank as much water as she could hold, and then filled it again and took it back to the barn.

She kicked the straw around to scare out any rats hiding underneath before sitting on the dirt floor and piling straw on her legs. After a few minutes she shook the straw back off when she felt something crawling along her left leg. At first she was afraid it was a rat—she shuddered as she remembered the one that had crawled under Sarah's bed covers a couple of nights before she got sick—but was relieved to see it was just fleas. She had several bites on her inner thigh and they itched, but she could tolerate that.

She drank some more of the water from the well. It was icy cold and caused her to shiver, but she continued drinking so that the raw potato in her stomach would swell and create a sense of fullness. She pulled the deer hide tighter around her shoulders and, despite her best efforts, started crying again. She was so hungry, and so dirty, and so grieved by the loss of her parents, that she found herself wishing she'd been burned with them. At least her misery would have ended. Now it would continue as long as God cursed her by keeping her alive.

She stayed that way the rest of the morning and into the afternoon. She must have dozed off at some point, because she was not aware of the barn door opening until a shaft of late-day sunlight hit her eyes, temporarily blinding her and filling her heart with paralyzing terror.

A FORM WALKED slowly toward her. Shrouded in bright sunlight, it looked to Miriam like an angel of God. Or Satan. It was only when the form moved to the side, out of the direct path of the sun's rays, that Miriam could see it was a woman. A girl, really; about her age, perhaps a year younger, with golden blond hair and fair skin. She approached cautiously, looking from side to side as if expecting to find someone else in the barn. When she spoke, her voice was hardly more than a frightened whisper. "Who…who are you?"

Miriam whispered also, afraid the girl—obviously a Christian—might have others with her. "My name is Miriam."

"Where did you come from?" the girl asked.

"Strasbourg," Miriam answered.

"Why are you here?"

"I'm hiding."

"Are…are you a Jew?"

Miriam's immediate inclination was to lie, but she realized she had no other story to explain why she was hiding in a freezing, rat-infested barn, so she just nodded her head.

The girl inched closer. "Are you alone?"

Again, Miriam responded with a nod of her head.

"Where is your family?" the girl asked.

At first, Miriam couldn't answer. She hadn't spoken to anyone since leaving Strasbourg, so she had not yet said the words. But now she did, and the pain of actually saying them out loud was greater than anything she had ever felt. "My family is dead."

Unable to control herself, she began to cry—a whimper at first, and then her shoulders shook, her gut heaved, and she fell on her side, sobbing so hard her entire body convulsed as if she were having a seizure. When she was finally able to lift her head and wipe her eyes, she saw that the girl had knelt in the straw a couple of feet away.

"Are you hungry?" she asked.

Miriam nodded her head vigorously, hoping the girl wasn't just curious, but actually had something to offer her.

The girl reached into a sack by her side and removed a large slice of bread. "It's stale, but it's all I have." She handed it to Miriam, who bit into it immediately. It was indeed stale, but Miriam could not remember ever having anything that had tasted better. She fought to slow down her chewing, knowing it would be wise to save some for later.

"Papa sent me here to see if any of the chickens had come back," the girl said. "The family who lived here was taken away a couple of days ago. People from some nearby farms took the animals and a lot of stuff from the house, but some of the chickens got away. Papa said they might have come back, so I was to use pieces of bread to attract them and then tie this string around their necks and take them home with me."

Miriam swallowed a mouthful of bread and washed it down with a gulp of water. "Where do you live?" she asked.

"About two miles west of here," the girl said. "It's a long walk, but I didn't have anything else to do this afternoon so I told Papa I could come over here and look for the chickens. The man that lived here had lots of chickens. We sometimes bought eggs from him."

Miriam had come here several times with her father for the same purpose, although the man would not allow the rabbi to pay him. "Just put in a good word for me," the man would always say with a big, toothless grin.

"What is your name?" Miriam asked.

The girl smiled. "Elizabeth."

"Thank you for the bread, Elizabeth," Miriam said. "I'm very grateful."

Elizabeth stood. "I'd better start home. It'll be getting dark soon, and Papa will come looking for me if I'm not home before sundown."

Miriam stared up at her. "What would he do if he found out you were helping a Jew?"

Elizabeth laughed. "He'd skin me alive!" She then whispered, "So I don't intend to tell him."

Miriam managed a smile, although it felt unnatural—totally removed from what she was feeling. Still, there was something special about this girl. "In addition to being very pretty, you are very brave."

Elizabeth beamed. "I'll try to come back on Wednesday, and will bring some food in case you're still here. Papa said there are snow clouds forming, so I won't be able to come tomorrow. But maybe Wednesday. Thursday for sure."

Miriam realized it was Monday. Two days after the massacre on the Sabbath. How could some Christians be so sadistic, and others, like Elizabeth, so kind? "Well, thank you again."

"You're welcome. Goodbye, Miriam." And she disappeared back into the sunlight.

Were it not for the bread she still clutched in her hand, Miriam might have thought she had imagined the entire encounter. Elizabeth had suddenly appeared out of the sunlight and just as suddenly disappeared back into it. Maybe she was an angel after all. Maybe there was hope.

THE SNOW STARTED during the night. When Miriam woke up the next morning and peeked out the barn door, there was already a three or four inch blanket of white covering the ground, and it was still falling steadily. She knew she would need more water for the day, so she grabbed the bucket and hurried to the well. This time, she wasn't worried so much about being seen. Nobody would be out wandering the countryside in a snowstorm like this. She drew some water and decided to take one more look through the house for food and something to help keep her warm. She found no blankets or clothing, but there were a few pieces of wood left by the fireplace. She was sorely tempted to build a fire, just to try to thaw out her hands and feet, but knew that smoke curling out of the chimney would announce her presence to anyone who happened by, especially once the snow stopped. She couldn't take the chance.

Reluctantly, she turned from the fireplace, and that was when she spied a small clay jar lying on its side behind the open door. She picked it up and removed the lid, nearly squealing with delight when she saw that it contained several dried apple slices. They had obviously been dried and put up in the fall, and had somehow been overlooked by the looters. Shivering with both cold and anticipation, she clutched the jar in one hand and the water bucket in the other as she ran back to the barn.

She allowed herself one of the apple slices for her breakfast, along with another piece of the stale bread and a paste she made of dirty corn meal and water, which she mixed on a wooden shingle. It was certainly not the kind of meal she would've been served by her mother, but it was reasonably filling, and that was all that really mattered. She would have liked to watch the snow fall—she'd always loved watching it from the warmth of her bed—but knew she wouldn't be able to stand the cold wind blowing in through the open barn door. So she spent the day napping in the straw, constantly scratching the flea bites that now covered both thighs.

The chills started that night. At first Miriam thought it was just the frigid night air, but then realized the coldness seemed to originate from inside her body, as if her bones were made of ice. She shivered violently through the night, praying for morning to come and for the sun to shine through the slats and create some warmth. But when dawn finally arrived, she could tell it was still snowing. There would be no sun. No warmth, and precious little light. She briefly considered going to the house and risking a fire, even if just for an hour or two, but didn't have the energy to get up from her bed of straw and walk across the yard.

She tried to get up to walk to the barn door for a quick look outside, but the itching on her thighs had been replaced by a deep, dull ache. She pinched a small piece of the bread and tried to nibble it, but it almost made her retch. She had the same result when she tried to sip some water. Although her throat felt dry and scratchy, she abandoned the attempt to drink and lay back on the straw. She slept off and on throughout the day. At one point, probably late afternoon, she realized it was still snowing and that Elizabeth would not be coming today. Maybe tomorrow. Not that it mattered. She couldn't think of anything the girl could bring that she would want to eat.

That night, she dreamed of her parents being led off to their fiery death. Only this time, Miriam went with them. They tied her down between her mother and father and threw a torch into the kindling at their feet. Her mother started to scream first, and then her father, but Miriam didn't scream. It felt so good to be warm… so very, very warm. And then she looked to her side and saw her mother's eyes explode from the heat, and she woke up screaming. It had been a nightmare—a horrid nightmare—but the heat was real. She was drenched in sweat.

She kicked the straw from her legs and unfolded the deer hide from her shoulders. Leaning on one elbow, she dipped a hand into the water bucket and splashed a handful of cold water onto her face. Then another. Exhausted by the effort, she lay back down and fell asleep.

When she woke up, there were rays of sunlight stabbing through the spaces between the slats of the barn wall, but she was freezing again. She pulled the deer hide back around her shoulders and sat upright to push straw back over her exposed legs. The pain in her thighs had lessened somewhat, and she pulled up her frock to look at the flea bites. They weren't itching now, but when she touched the area she could feel that her thighs were swollen. With a feeling of dread mixed with desperation, she ran her hand further up her thigh and around her groin. And there at the hairline she felt them.

Knots under the skin. Large ones. Just like Sarah had…two days before she died.

MIRIAM KNEW THAT Elizabeth would try to come back today. She had said she would return after the snow and bring more food. The girl had a kind heart, unlike most other Christians Miriam had known. Because of that, Miriam could not let Elizabeth enter the barn. She couldn't allow her to risk exposure to the Pestilence. For some reason, Christians were more susceptible to the disease, which was one reason they blamed it on the Jews. Her father had said at dinner one night that maybe it was because Jews bathed every day, whereas Christians believed bathing opened up the pores and thus increased the likelihood of disease. But, Miriam reasoned, Sarah had bathed regularly and she still got sick. Miriam herself had not bathed in nearly a week, so maybe that was why she now had the disease. Whatever the explanation, the fact was that she had it and, based on what she knew about it, would probably not live until the next Sabbath, two days away.

She did her best to stay awake so she'd be able to shout a warning to Elizabeth as soon as the barn door opened. But she was so tired, and so sleepy. And when she awoke in the early afternoon, the girl was sitting by her side, holding a bundle that could only be food she had smuggled from her home.

Miriam tried to speak, but it was more like a croak. "You…can't…be…here. Get away. Right now."

"I brought you food," Elizabeth said. "Just like I promised."

Miriam tried to focus on the pretty blond girl, but her eyes felt as if they were nearly swollen shut. "I'm sick," she muttered. "You…must go."

"The tip of your nose is all blackened," Elizabeth said. "Did you fall down on your face?"

She was dipping a patch of cloth in the water bucket and bathing Miriam's forehead. It felt so good. So refreshing. Perhaps this girl really was an angel sent from God.

Miriam opened her eyes again, and this time managed to focus on the young face mere inches from her own. *If only I had a chance at life like she does,* Miriam thought. *If only I could start all over and...*and then she knew. Somehow, inexplicably, she was consumed by the belief—no, the absolute certainty—that she could change places with the girl in front of her. It made no sense. Perhaps it was near-death delirium. In fact, everything was becoming hazy, as if she were looking through a dense fog. The light in the barn seemed to be dimming, Elizabeth's face fading slowly into the encroaching darkness.

And then, for just an instant, Miriam had a vision of looking down at herself, as if she was seeing what Elizabeth was seeing. And she knew, as much as she had ever known anything in her young life, that if she reached out and touched the girl, she would become her. That she would leave this dirty, half-starved, Pestilence-riddled body behind, and walk out of this barn as a vibrant and beautiful young woman. But what would become of Elizabeth? Where would she be? When her father came looking for her, would he find nothing but the cold, lifeless body of a dark-haired Jewish girl?

There were so many questions, and no answers that made any sense at all. It was beyond comprehension. There was no reason, and no time, to debate it. She must either act or die. With no further thought, other than pausing to beg God's forgiveness, Miriam reached out and grabbed Elizabeth's hand.

THE EARLY MORNING sun shone down from a cloudless sky. The warming rays felt good on her shoulders. It had been a long, cold night. But Miriam had kept moving, not wanting to take the time to rest or eat any of the food in the parcel she carried. And certainly not wanting to take the time to think about what she had done.

It had been mid-afternoon when she ran from the barn. She was panicked, like a murderer fleeing the scene of the crime. And she supposed that was indeed the case. Only it was unlike any murder she had ever heard of. The body of the killer was lying cold and still inside the barn. The body of the victim was running through the snow.

At first, she hadn't been able to decide which way to go. She knew she was south of Strasbourg, so she couldn't go north. And Elizabeth had said her family's farm was west, so she couldn't go in that direction. That left south or east. For no other reason than the anticipation of feeling the sun on her face the following morning, she had headed east.

Throughout the long night she had plodded on through the fresh snow. If there was a path, she hadn't been able to see it. But the moonlight reflecting off the white landscape had allowed her to see where she was going. And the brilliant, guiding presence of the North Star had helped her stay on course.

Sometime after midnight, she began to hear occasional sounds behind her, like snapping twigs, and had feared she was being stalked by wolves. But she had never seen anything, and whatever it was had kept its distance.

Still, she was glad when the sun climbed over the hills ahead of her, bathing the snow-covered forest in its warm glow. She crested a ridge and was almost blinded by the sparkling water of a small pond, fed by a narrow, rock-strewn brook. She was thirsty, having had no way to carry water, and the location looked perfect to stop for a rest and eat some of the food Elizabeth had brought to the barn. *Poor Elizabeth!* But she couldn't think about her now. She needed water and food, and then she needed to keep going, to put as much distance as possible between herself and the nightmare of Strasbourg.

She laid her parcel of food on a rock and walked to the edge of the pond. The water was crystal clear, its surface as smooth as glass. She knelt in the grass and leaned over the water, preparing to bend forward to take a drink, when she froze in shock. The reflection in the pond was not a blond-haired, blue-eyed German girl, but a dark-haired, hazel-eyed Jew. She was in the body of Elizabeth, but the reflected image staring back at her was Miriam. How could this be? Would others be able to see who she really was? Or was this all in her mind? Had she escaped that freezing, rat-infested barn and left behind a body rotting from the Pestilence only to go insane?

She slapped the water with her hand, praying that when the ripples settled and the surface smoothed back out she would find herself looking at the face of Elizabeth. But as the water calmed, the shimmering reflection was again the face of Miriam. She was staring at it so intently, trying to make some sense of it, that it took a moment before she noticed the other reflection. Standing behind her was a man. He was young, perhaps in his early twenties, with curly red hair and green eyes. She hadn't heard him approach, so he must have intentionally snuck up behind her. Frightened and angry, she turned her head to face him, ready to fight if his purpose was malevolent.

"What do you want?" she shouted, just before her eyes rested on his face and all of the air rushed from her body, leaving her gasping for breath like a fish out of water. The face looking back at her was that of a boy, not much older than herself, with straight brown hair, olive skin, and chestnut eyes. She looked back at the reflection in the pond, then back at him, certain now that she'd lost her mind.

He kept his eyes focused on her reflection, as if the girl on the shore was not even there. Miriam also settled her gaze on their reflections in the pond, and the two of them seemed to study each other for a minute or two, trying to reconcile what their eyes could see but their minds couldn't comprehend.

"Who are you?" she whispered.

When he answered, he spoke to her reflection, his eyes never wavering. "I am Peter," he said.

Chapter 7

PETER WALKED INTO the bathroom, where Miriam stood in front of the mirror applying her makeup. "Excuse me," he said. "I have to pee."

She looked at him and smiled. "Go ahead. I've seen you pee thousands of times."

He laughed. "I know that. It's just that I have to get used to exposing myself in front of a twenty-five year old blond."

"You didn't seem to have any problems with that last night," she said, batting her eyes playfully.

He flushed the toilet and studied her reflection in the mirror as he washed his hands. That beautiful young face with those pouty lips, the hazel eyes and lush, dark brown hair. Neither of them understood why their reflected images appeared to the two of them as their original faces. But of all the blessings he had—wealth, near-immortality, the love of the same woman in over a dozen exquisite forms—the one Peter cherished most was still being able to see that face he'd first seen staring back at him from the surface of a pond nearly seven centuries ago.

"You are so beautiful," he whispered.

Miriam looked at his reflection, focusing on the emerald green eyes staring back at her. "That me?" she asked, pointing at the mirror. "Or this me?" she said, pointing to herself.

He pulled her to him and kissed her gently. "Both," he said. He brushed back a strand of her short blond hair from her forehead and looked into her blue eyes. "I have absolutely no problems with this body."

She smiled. "Again, that was apparent last night."

"But," he continued, "that's because I know that the other you, the original you, is inside. And that is the woman I have always loved."

"And always will, I hope," she whispered.

"Forever," he said, and kissed her again.

She turned back to the mirror, giving her eye shadow one more glance. "Okay, I'm ready," she said. "Let's go downstairs and get some breakfast, and then I have some shopping to do. You can tag along or you can come back to the room and hang out."

They were staying at the Hyatt Regency in Hoover, Alabama. Miriam had chosen it for two reasons. One was that Hoover was south of Birmingham, a short drive to Mountain Brook and the other communities she wanted to consider for a new home. The other was that the hotel was attached to The Galleria, a huge shopping mall with several department stores that she figured would offer most anything they would need for the next week. They had just arrived in the area by car the previous afternoon, and tomorrow she had a job interview with a PR firm downtown. They had traveled light—just a couple of suitcases—and she knew that, among other things, she needed some new outfits more suited to a savvy young professional than the ones she'd brought with her from Lake Mohawk. The job sounded perfect for her, and she intended to make a solid first impression.

"I'll come back up here after breakfast," Peter said. "The realtor we talked with sent me about two dozen listings to review. I'd like to go online and narrow down the list before we meet with her this afternoon."

They left the room and walked, hand-in hand, to the elevators. Miriam leaned into him the way she always did when getting ready to ask for something, and said, "Since this is just a *get acquainted* meeting today, would you mind terribly much if I skipped out? I'd really like to spend a little more time preparing for my interview tomorrow. It's been a while since I was in the job market, you know."

Peter pushed the down button and turned to her. "Are you sure you want to do the job thing again? I really loved having you around all day when we lived in New Jersey."

She smiled and gave his hand a squeeze. "I know, and I loved it too. But I really think it's best. We can't learn all the millennial nuances just by watching TV. "

The elevator doors opened and they stepped inside. "Besides" she added, "it'll be a good test for our new documents. If there's a problem with any of them, we need to find out sooner rather than later, don't you think?"

"Yeah, I suppose. But this guy was supposed to be good. Simon gave him his highest recommendation."

One of the problems of becoming a new person every fifty years or so was the need for documentation. Social Security cards, driver's licenses, birth certificates, marriage certificates—all were essential to buying a home, getting a job, opening new bank accounts, or even paying taxes. Prior to moving from Aspen to Lake Mohawk in 1970, they had engaged the services of Simon Metzenbaum, a master forger who had spent most of World War II in a concentration camp, where he was forced to create false documents for the Nazi SS. It had been galling for a Jew to provide assistance to the Third Reich, but it was better than manual labor, and it kept him alive. He had moved to New York after the war and had set up a very lucrative forgery business in the back of his print shop. He had trained a young immigrant from the Czech Republic who had married Simon's youngest daughter, and had turned both businesses—the legal one and the illegal one—over to Sergei when he retired in 1992 and moved to Miami. In addition to having a knack for forgery, Sergei was a computer whiz and a master hacker. Claiming there were no government files he couldn't gain access to if needed, he had told Peter, "There's nobody I can't find, and nobody I can't hide." Peter took the brash young man at his word, and it was Sergei who had done the work for them the previous week.

They had always used their own first names. It was too confusing, and therefore too dangerous, to change those. But now they were Peter and Miriam Hoffman, both born in Albany, New York. Sergei had assured them that their background records were inserted everywhere it was feasible to do so without setting off alarms. As long as they didn't apply to the FBI or take a job that required a high level security clearance, they'd be fine.

They exited the elevator and walked across the lobby to the restaurant. To their right they could see that the lobby opened right into the second level of the mall. "Convenient," Peter said.

"Should be able to get whatever clothes and sundries we need until we get more settled," Miriam said. "First and foremost, I need an outfit for the interview tomorrow. Something nice, but not so nice that I don't look like I need a job."

Peter smiled. "Good to know you won't be hitting those expensive boutiques where you usually shop."

"Oh, I will, dear," she said, patting his hand. "I know just where to find them. I'm always thorough with my shopping research."

Peter grimaced. "Great."

It was already after nine so there was plenty of seating available in the restaurant. After being shown to their table and quickly perusing their menus, they placed their orders so Miriam could be finished and ready to hit the stores as soon as they opened at ten. Miriam ordered the warm berry quinoa, saying she had to be careful about eating too much before shopping for new clothes. Peter ordered the shrimp and grits, saying he needed to develop a taste for grits so he would "fit in" in the Deep South.

"You don't have to worry about fitting in," Miriam said. "You're young, handsome and rich. With that Mercedes you bought and a big house in Mountain Brook, you'll be able to do anything you want and people will think you're wonderful."

"Except cheer for Notre Dame," he said, smiling. "That might not go over so well down here."

She leaned across the table and whispered, "Why would a nice Jewish boy cheer for Notre Dame?"

"Hey, I was raised a Catholic."

"That was seven hundred years ago. And when you got the sickness, and realized you could jump into someone else, you had the good sense to pick a nice Jewish boy."

Peter looked down at the table. "It wasn't so much that I picked him. He was just there at the time. His bad luck, I guess."

She reached across the table and took his hand. "No, his good luck. If he had lived another day, he would've faced the fire."

They sat in silence until their food was brought out. Miriam ate all of her quinoa, but Peter mostly picked the shrimp off his plate, merely pushing the grits around. "Looks like I'll really have to work on my enthusiasm for grits," he said.

"Remember—young, handsome, rich. And rich is what really carries the day."

Peter nodded and smiled. They had been living in Poland after escaping Strasbourg, him working as a tanner and her as a seamstress, when it finally occurred to them that they could jump to a rich body as easily as a poor one. They always did their homework, and after a few generations had amassed all the wealth they would ever need. Like anyone else, they were impacted by recessions, depressions and wars, but they always had enough of a cushion to last until it was time to find new hosts. They never did that until it was necessary—they were very strict about that—but it was always comforting to know that they could "inherit" more capital with their next jump.

He looked at Miriam. She had certainly made the most of Julia Crutchfield's natural assets. With her chic hair style, tinted contacts, perfect make-up and tastefully tailored clothes, she was stunning. He raised his orange juice in a toast, and they clinked glasses. "To new lives."

"New lives," she echoed.

"I just hope they're as peaceful here as they were on Lake Mohawk."

"Oh, I don't know," Miriam said. "I loved it there too, but I think I'm ready for a little more excitement."

MIRIAM COULDN'T believe it. She was going to be late for her 9:00 AM interview. It was already 8:45, and she was creeping along I-65 at a snail's pace, caught in a morning rush hour that she had seriously underestimated. The hotel concierge had told her the previous afternoon that it would be less than a thirty minute drive. But apparently he'd meant at two in the afternoon, not eight in the morning, when thousands of "over the mountain" commuters converged to create a logjam that rivaled the entrance to the Lincoln Tunnel in Manhattan. She'd allowed an hour for the drive, planning to arrive in time to find a ladies' room and freshen up before going to the fourth floor, but that was clearly not going to happen.

She saw a sign that indicated her exit was another two miles. At her current pace, that would take ten minutes or more, and she'd still need to cover several blocks and find a place to park. So much for favorable first impressions. She supposed she should at least call and give them a heads up that she was running late, rather than just walking in at 9:15 as if nothing was wrong. She pulled her cell phone from her purse and hit the speed-dial button she'd had the foresight to enter before she left the hotel. Her call was answered on the first ring.

"Good morning. Sheffield and Associates. This is Abigail."

"Good morning, Abigail. This is Miriam Hoffman. I have an interview with Mr. Sheffield at nine o'clock, and I'm afraid I'll be a few minutes late. I didn't anticipate this much traffic."

"Stuck on 65?" the woman asked.

"Yes. I'm about two miles from University Boulevard."

"Okay, you should be here in about twenty or twenty-five minutes. I'll let Mark know. Take your time and drive safely. And thank you for calling."

Miriam disconnected the call and let out an exasperated sigh. Abigail sounded nice. And efficient too. Like a lot of administrative types, she probably ran the show. She hoped the woman had some pull with Mark Sheffield and would keep him calm until she got there.

Abigail's time estimate was spot-on. Miriam stepped off the fourth floor elevator at 9:12 and hurried through the glass door into the firm's reception area. A petite, attractive woman who appeared to be in her mid-forties stood up immediately. "You must be Mrs. Hoffman."

"Miriam," Miriam said, extending her hand. "And you must be Abigail."

"Yes." She smiled, showing off perfectly matched dimples. "Welcome to Birmingham. The traffic can be a little challenging, but otherwise it's a great place to live. You're from New York, right?"

"Right. Originally from Albany, but I've lived in Manhattan for the past seven years."

"Well, everyone here is looking forward to meeting you. Mark's in the conference room. Are you ready to go in?"

"Of course. I've kept him waiting long enough."

Abigail smiled again. "Oh, don't you worry about that. Fifteen minutes late is actually early in the PR business."

She led Miriam through a door and down a narrow hallway. They passed a series of small offices on the right and then entered a door on the left. Miriam was surprised, but tried not to show it, to find five people—two men and three women—spread out around a long polished oak table. The room was sparsely decorated, with no art work, just a long sign on one wall that said, *Sheffield & Associates, A Personal Approach to Public Relations.* Under the sign was a long sideboard with a coffee service, orange juice, and bottled water.

Everyone stood as Abigail announced, "This is Miriam Hoffman. Mark, you can introduce the team while I get Miriam some coffee or juice. What would you like, dear?"

"Oh, no," Miriam protested. "Thank you, but I'm fine."

"Then I'll get back to my desk and let you all get started," Abigail said, and walked out of the room.

The man at the head of the table walked over to Miriam and extended his hand. He was handsome, with a lean, athletic build and thick dark hair, graying at the temples. He looked to be in his mid-to-late forties, and exuded an air of confidence, but not arrogance. As Miriam shook his hand, he said, "I'm Mark. I've enjoyed our phone conversations, and I'm glad to finally meet you face-to-face."

"The pleasure's all mine," Miriam said, immediately regretting the comment as not fitting the image of a twenty-five year old. She'd have to be more mindful of things like that.

"Let me introduce you to my staff," Mark said, first leading Miriam to a slightly chubby but attractive young woman with short black hair and large, tortoise shell glasses. "This is Stephanie Mullins, Senior Associate. She manages our political accounts. We represent the current mayor, the state Lieutenant Governor, several members of the State House, and the home office of U.S. Senator Richard Carson."

Seated next to Stephanie was a wiry young man with long blond hair pulled back in a ponytail. "This is Allen Trammell," Mark said. "Allen manages public relations for the Alabama Ballet and the symphony orchestra." He slapped the young man on the back and added with a smile, "Allen knows pretty much everything there is to know about the art of fundraising."

Allen smiled and said, "So true, so true." Miriam picked up a trace of an effeminate affectation, but the man's handshake was firm as he looked her squarely in the eyes, as if trying to determine how open-minded she was.

Mark continued around the table, stepping over to a tall, slender redhead wearing a miniskirt that bordered on indecency. Miriam felt she may have dressed a little too maturely for this crowd, but reminded herself it was better to err on the side of caution. "This is Courtney Pruitt," Mark said, "our resident foodie. She's responsible for our clients in the food and beverage industry, which is our fastest growing segment. We represent the city's largest craft brewery and several upscale restaurants, including those owned by Master Chef John Stark. Maybe you've seen him on *The Today Show*?"

"Absolutely," Miriam said. "My husband and I have reservations at *The Twilight Grill* tonight."

"That's his flagship restaurant, but not really his best," Courtney said. "When we talk later, I'll give you a better option."

"And last but certainly not least," Mark said, stepping next to the only woman in the room who looked like she'd celebrated her thirtieth birthday, "is our Operations Manager, Claudia Meeks. Claudia's in charge of HR, including payroll and benefits, as well as accounting."

Mark gestured to a chair for Miriam and returned to his seat. "These talented people, along with Abigail and myself, comprise Sheffield and Associates. We're a small firm—I prefer to just say we're very selective about who we represent—and, as our sign states, we provide a personal touch for our clients that just can't be found in the big PR houses. Having said that, we're continuing to grow, so we're adding a new position, the one we talked about on the phone. We're not quite at the stage where Stephanie, Allen and Courtney each need to hire assistants, but they could all use some help. So, we're looking for someone who can take on projects in all three areas, which from time to time overlap anyway. It wouldn't involve actually managing relationships with clients—at least, not to start—but would be more of a support and integration function. Sound interesting?"

Miriam looked him in the eye and nodded affirmatively. "It sounds exactly like the kind of work I'd like to do."

Mark smiled. "Excellent. I'd like to have you spend about forty-five minutes with each member of the team, starting with Claudia, and then you and I will go grab some lunch and see where we stand. That approach work for you?"

"Perfectly," Miriam said.

Claudia stood. "Well, let's go to my office and get started," she said. "I assume you brought names and contact information for references and school transcripts?"

"Of course," Miriam said with a smile, but inside she was anxious. Claudia gave the impression of being all business. And very thorough. *Okay, Sergei,* she thought, *you said background records would be in place everywhere they needed to be. Let's see if you earned your money.*

Chapter 8

"**I**T'S PERFECT," Miriam whispered to Peter. "We'll need to do a little updating before we move in, but it has everything we're looking for."

It was late Saturday afternoon and they had just completed their fifth house tour of the day. They'd also seen five houses on Friday, Peter having worked with Marcia, their real estate agent, to narrow the original field of twenty-three down to his "top ten." As luck would have it, the one Miriam liked the most was the last one on his list, but that was okay. They'd accomplished a lot in the four days they'd been in Birmingham. Miriam had secured a job, and now they'd found a place to live.

Miriam had gotten the call from Mark Sheffield during lunch on Friday. He'd told her that the team was unanimous in wanting to bring her on board, and that her references and background check, including her college transcripts, had been impeccable.

"You didn't mention you were on the Dean's List every semester at NYU," Mark had said.

"Well, I didn't want to sound like I was bragging," she replied, surprised to learn that herself. Apparently, Sergei had earned every penny of his rather hefty fee for preparing their new documentation. "Besides, I've been out of school for three years, so that's ancient history."

He laughed. "It's hard to associate the word *ancient* with someone so young. Anyway, I'd like to email the offer letter and would love to hear back from you before the end of the day, if possible. A big project just came our way, and we could use some help, pronto."

"I'm out house hunting with my husband, but I can read it on my phone. Send it to me as soon as it's ready and I'll respond within an hour."

Her phone had buzzed five minutes later. The salary was a little less than she'd been hoping for, but the job description was perfect. He had included a modest signing bonus if she could start the following Monday, which she agreed to do. Everything was falling into place.

She and Peter walked back into the foyer and waited for Marcia, who was locking the doors that led from the kitchen and family room onto the patio. "So, what do you think?" she asked the two as she approached.

"Tell me the asking price again," said Peter.

He whistled when she told him, although it was a third less than the price they'd gotten for the Lake Mohawk home. "I don't know," he said, looking at Miriam. "It needs a lot of work, don't you think, hon?"

Miriam recognized the negotiating ploy, and realized that Marcia probably did too. "Yeah, it definitely needs a makeover," she said.

Marcia gave them an earnest look. "Well, like I said earlier, this house has great bones. You could turn it into a showplace with a little paint and some new light fixtures."

"And a new kitchen, and new hardwoods, and some major landscaping," Miriam said, playing her role of the nitpicking, spoiled, rich man's wife.

"Tell you what," Marcia said. "My office is five minutes from here in Mountain Brook Village. There's a nice little tavern right across the street. Why don't I drop you two off there so you can discuss it some more, and I'll go into my office and call the seller's agent. Let me do a little negotiating for you. I'm betting we can get this price into a range you can work with."

"That's fine with me," Peter said, and then smiled. "I'm always more agreeable once I've had a couple of beers."

Two hours later they arrived back at the Hyatt, proud owners of a six thousand square foot manor in one of the most desirable areas of Mountain Brook. It sat on a two acre lot, and was across the road from a park that appeared perfect for jogging, walking or biking. It would be a fairly short commute to Miriam's job downtown, and provided Peter with the relative seclusion he desired. It was as close to ideal as they could imagine.

They celebrated the job and the house over a dinner of lobster tails and champagne at Shula's Steakhouse, owned by the legendary former coach of the Miami Dolphins. The restaurant was housed in the hotel, making it easy for Peter and Miriam to sit back and relax after a tiring day and very busy week.

After the champagne had been poured and their dinner orders placed, Miriam raised her flute in a toast. "Here's to us. We're official *Brookies* now."

"*Brookies?*"

"Yeah, apparently that's how the locals refer to residents of Mountain Brook."

Peter took a sip of champagne and smiled. "So do I have to start acting snobby?"

"Well, yeah, but in an easy, down home kind of way. You'll need to be more subtle about it than the rich folks in Aspen. You're a smart guy. You'll figure it out."

"And what about you?" he asked. "Do you have your new role figured out?"

She laughed. "Mine's easy. I'm just a working girl. My husband's the one with all the money."

"Speaking of which, what am I supposed to do all day while you're at work? It'll probably be two months before we can move into the house. This hotel is going to start closing in on me."

"Why don't you get Marcia to find a furnished apartment we can rent for a couple of months?" She smiled coyly. "Then I can look forward to a nice home-cooked meal after a hard day at the office."

His expression turned serious. "I'm still not crazy about this job thing. It's not too late to back out, you know. Just call this Sheffield guy and tell him you changed your mind."

She reached across the table and took his hand. "Let me give it a try, okay? We're on a roll. Our documentation worked out, we found a great house, and the job actually sounds fun. Everything just feels right. It feels…I don't know…safe."

HAVING LEARNED FROM her experience with Birmingham traffic the previous week, Miriam allowed more than an hour for her commute on Monday morning. Ironically, traffic was lighter and she made the trip in forty minutes. She'd been asked to show up at nine, but arrived at 8:30, and was pleasantly surprised to find the door to the office suite unlocked and Abigail already at her desk.

"Good morning," the brightly smiling woman said. "So, did you decide to leave earlier this morning or was traffic just a little lighter?"

"Both," Miriam said with a laugh. "I'm glad you're here. I was afraid I might have to sit in the parking lot for a half hour."

"No, Mark and I are always here by eight," Abigail said. "It's good to have a little time to get organized for the day before the phones start ringing."

"Well, I want to thank you again for smoothing things over with Mark when I was late last Wednesday. If he was aggravated with me, he didn't show it." She then whispered in a conspiratorial manner, "You must hold a little sway around here."

Abigail laughed. "You could say that. I suppose I didn't fully introduce myself last week." She stood and extended her hand. "Abigail Sheffield."

"Oh," Miriam said, trying to mask her surprise. "You're…"

"Mark's wife." Abigail shook Miriam's hand and then folded her arms across her chest. "I've been calling the shots for twenty-four years. A young thing like you wouldn't understand the art of keeping a man in line for that long, but I bet you'll master it."

Miriam couldn't help smiling. *If you only knew, lady. I might be able to teach you a thing or two about that.* "Peter and I have only been married two years. I may need to seek your counsel from time to time."

"I'd be happy to share my secrets with you," Abigail said, with a wink. "Well, let's see. The first thing on your agenda today is to meet with Claudia and fill out a few forms. She's not here yet, but should be soon. Let me show you to your office and you can wait for her there."

"Office? I didn't realize I'd get an office right off the bat."

Abigail laughed as she opened the door to the hallway. "Don't get too excited. It's a closet…literally. We just moved the office supplies out of there last week. But you have a brand new desk and a bookshelf, which leaves just enough room for you to squeeze in if you turn sideways."

She led Miriam down the hallway they had traveled the previous week, past the other offices and the conference room. At the end of the hall they turned right, passed a nameplate which indicated Claudia's office, another one for Stephanie, and then stopped in front of a closed door. "Here we are," Abigail said as she swung the door open. It was indeed a closet, no more than eight by eight feet square, with no windows, and nothing on the walls but a coat of fresh paint that Miriam could still smell. "You might want to keep the door open until the paint fumes dissipate," Abigail said. "It was just painted Friday afternoon, right after you accepted the job."

Miriam stepped inside and looked around. As Abigail had said, there was a new desk, small but made of pretty, cherry-stained oak, facing the door. To the right was a matching bookshelf, narrow but functional, with cabinet doors enclosing the bottom half. There was a black leather desk chair and opposite the desk, placed caddy-cornered so it would fit in the narrow space between the desk and the wall, a straight-back chair for visitors. "This will be just fine," Miriam said. "Thank you for having it ready for me."

Abigail turned to leave. "I ordered you a laptop and a printer which should be delivered this morning. And I'll help you get stocked with office supplies. Meanwhile, get yourself settled in, and I'll let Claudia know you're in here when she arrives." She nodded back in the direction they'd come from. "Down that way is a little kitchen area. I just put a fresh pot of coffee on, so help yourself. Right past the kitchen are the restrooms. Make yourself at home, and I'll see you a little later."

Claudia arrived a few minutes later and they sat at a small round table in her office and completed all the necessary on-roll formalities. At one point, Claudia mentioned that she'd never gotten such prompt responses from references and college transcript requests as she'd gotten for Miriam, but she didn't sound particularly suspicious, so Miriam didn't worry about it. By ten o'clock she was back in her tiny office, unpacking the laptop and color printer that had just been delivered.

A few minutes later there was a rap on her door and she looked up to see Stephanie smiling at her. "Welcome aboard," she said, pulling her glasses down to the tip of her nose as she studied the cramped space. "Good thing you're skinny. I'm afraid if I managed to fit behind that desk they might have to call a rescue team to pry me back out."

Miriam laughed. "Good morning, Stephanie." She looked around. "It's really not that bad."

"First of all, call me Steph. And secondly, yes it is. I hope you're not prone to claustrophobia."

"I'll keep the door open," Miriam said with a smile.

"Well, if you can squeeze out of there without the help of a bottle of Mazola, I need you to come with me. We've been summoned."

"Mark?" Miriam asked.

"Nobody else has the power to summon," Stephanie said, and then whispered, "but if Abigail ever makes a suggestion, you might want to give it a lot of consideration."

Miriam extricated herself from behind her desk and joined the other woman in the hall. "I just found out today that she's Mark's wife. She seems really nice. Are you saying she has a bad side that I should avoid?"

"Not at all," Stephanie said, sotto voce. "And Mark's very nice too. But if he thinks you show even a hint of disrespect to Abby, he'll cut you off at the knees. She's the one who pushed him to stop working for somebody else and open up his own PR firm five years ago. He's been very successful, and apparently never happier, and he says he owes it all to her."

"I'll keep that in mind," Miriam said. "Where's his office, by the way? I've been up and down these halls, and didn't see it."

"It's on the other side of the lobby. Abby guards the door like a tigress protecting her cubs. Mark's very open and approachable, but if you need to see him, go through Abby. She'll make it happen."

They passed through the lobby, slowing down at Abigail's desk for Steph to ask, "Okay if we go on in, Abby?"

"He's expecting you," she replied.

"Thanks," Stephanie said, opening the door and holding it for Miriam to pass through.

Mark's office was the opposite of Miriam's in every way. First, it was massive. A huge, glass-top desk was centered on the opposite wall, in front of a window that provided a panoramic view of the vast UAB medical complex. On either side of the large window, floor-to-ceiling bookcases were tastefully filled with a perfectly balanced combination of books, bric-a-brac, and a collection of framed pictures of Mark with various celebrities, including one with him standing between Peyton and Eli Manning. Two stuffed leather chairs sat opposite the desk, with a small glass-top coffee table between them. To the left of the desk was a seating area, with sofa, wing chairs and another coffee table. To the right of the desk was a conference table with eight leather chairs. Behind that, Miriam saw a door that she assumed led to his private bathroom.

"Welcome to the inner sanctum," Stephanie said with a smile.

"Reminds me a lot of my office," Miriam said.

Mark laughed as he rose from his chair and walked around the desk to shake Miriam's hand. "It's just for show," he said, sweeping the room with his other hand. "Like I told you, we're a small firm. When I meet with prospective clients here, it presents an image of success. Makes us look bigger than we really are." He released her hand and headed back toward his desk chair. "Anyway, welcome. We're delighted to have you join our team. Please, have a seat."

The two women sat in the leather chairs facing him, and Miriam marveled at the comfort. She'd have to make note of the manufacturer so she could order a couple for the new house.

Mark looked at Miriam. "I really appreciate you being willing to start right away. I know you and your husband just arrived in Birmingham and haven't gotten settled yet, but like I mentioned on Friday, we have a new project and need all the help we can get, starting right now." He glanced at Stephanie. "Steph, have you had a chance to brief Miriam yet?"

"No, she was with Claudia earlier and I just got a chance to see her right before we came in here."

He tilted his chair back and folded his hands under his chin. "Okay, let me lay it out for you. Steph got a call from Senator Carson's chief of staff on Friday. You may remember that Carson made quite a bit of news when he renounced his membership in the Republican Party in protest over Donald Trump's nomination. To say that Carson is a staunch, purist conservative would be the understatement of the year. Anyway, he's still been caucusing with the Republicans in the Senate, despite his official status as an Independent, but in recent weeks has been quite vocal in his support of the new American Values Party. Apparently, he and Robert Martinez have known each other for several years, and now he seems to want to align himself with the AVP. Over the weekend he offered to host a fundraising dinner for the AVP here in Birmingham. The good news is that Martinez accepted. The bad news is, it's in three weeks."

"Wow, that's big," Miriam said. She turned to Stephanie and smiled. "I guess I know what's going to be occupying your time for the next three weeks."

"Not just her time," Mark said. "Everybody's time, including yours. Remember when I said your position here would be assisting all three of the associates, and that sometimes their projects overlap?"

Miriam nodded.

Mark leaned forward, resting his elbows on his desk. "Well, this is a perfect example. The dinner will be prepared by John Stark, Courtney's biggest client, and a chef whose culinary talent is surpassed only by his ambition. This could lead to some huge publicity for him, maybe his own show on the Food Network. And music for the dinner and for dancing afterwards will be provided by an ensemble from the Birmingham Symphony Orchestra, so Allen also has a big stake in this. You'll be supporting all three of them, but Steph has the lead on this, so you'll take most of your direction from her."

"This is exciting," Miriam said. "I wasn't expecting to be involved in such a big project starting on day one. How will I know what to do?"

"Don't worry about that," Mark said. "Steph, Allen and Courtney know what to do; there're just so many things that need to be done by all three, there's no way they can do it all. That's where you come in. Each one will let you know what's needed, and Steph will coordinate all of the assignments and make sure you don't get overloaded. We don't have much time, so we can't afford for any little detail to fall through the cracks."

"I'll do whatever's needed," Miriam said, trying to mask her uncertainty. She didn't have all of the experience listed on her resume—including the degree in business communications from NYU— and a huge assignment like this, before she had a chance to learn the ropes, could expose her gaps. She'd just have to give it everything she had and hope for the best. She'd probably be working seven days a week until the event was completed, and Peter wouldn't be crazy about that, but she'd make it up to him somehow.

"I knew you would," Mark said. "That's why you're here." He leaned back in his chair again and smiled. "And just so you don't think Abby and I won't also be in it up to our necks, she and I will be working the phones and calling in every favor we can. We've got to find five hundred people who are willing to spend $10,000 apiece to have dinner and shake hands with the man who many in this part of the country think could become the next President of the United States."

Thank goodness, Miriam thought. *Here's something I know I can do.* "Make that four hundred and ninety eight people you need to find, Mark. You can count on Peter and me being there."

Chapter 9

"ARE YOU KIDDING me?" Stephanie exclaimed when they walked into her office after their meeting with Mark. "You and your husband can afford to drop twenty grand in one night?"

"Well," Miriam stammered, "I certainly can't, but Peter can. Family money...a trust set up by his parents before they died. And Peter's a pretty savvy investor. He's almost doubled the value of the portfolio in the last four years."

Stephanie was not to be placated. "I had no idea you had that kind of money. None of us did. I think Mark was as shocked as I was, although I'm sure he's glad to have a start on the guest list. The firm will cover the cost of him and Abby going, but I seriously doubt he thought anyone on his staff could afford it, especially his newest, entry-level associate. Is there anything else you're hiding?"

Miriam couldn't help but smile. If Stephanie was shocked by her and Peter's wealth, their age would absolutely blow her mind. "No, I think that's pretty much it."

Stephanie plopped into the chair behind her desk, practically falling into it, as if her legs could no longer support her. "Here I was, thinking I had some anxious, eager-to-please gofer at my beck and call, only to find you could buy and sell all of us, including Mark, without missing a beat."

"Not quite true," Miriam said. "Peter could, but not me. I could barely afford to buy you lunch."

Stephanie leaned across the desk toward her and smiled. "Oh, but you will, Lady Miriam. You are absolutely picking up our lunch tab today. No pimento cheese sandwich from the food truck for me today. I'm having the lobster tacos…two of them."

Miriam laughed. "Fine. Lunch is on me. Meanwhile, how do we get started on this monster project?"

Two hours later, Miriam was wishing she hadn't asked. Stephanie had apparently devoted her entire weekend to sketching out a detailed to-do list, much of which she unloaded on her new assistant. She found herself doing everything from selecting typeset for the invitations—which needed to be printed that afternoon—to reserving blocks of rooms at four different downtown hotels. Stephanie was working with Allen and Courtney to compile a massive spreadsheet with critical task headings and an ever-growing list of details under each. Many of those details would be assigned to Miriam. Mark had called for project meetings every afternoon at 5:00 PM, starting today, and the spreadsheet would serve as a working agenda and status update. Miriam wanted to show up for the first meeting with as many items completed as she possibly could.

Around one-thirty, Stephanie stuck her head into Miriam's office. "Hey, if you're going to buy me lunch, we'd better get going or we'll miss the food truck."

Miriam looked up from the preliminary mailing list Mark and Abby had assembled—four hundred names and still growing. "Food truck? You're serious?"

"Best tacos you've ever tasted. I guarantee it. Come on. It's probably going to be a late night. We'd better grab something while we have the chance."

They rode the elevators to the lobby, exited their building and turned left. The food truck was on the next block. Despite their relatively late lunch break, they still had to wait in line. True to her word, Stephanie got a double order of lobster tacos and a large sweet tea. Miriam thought she could understand why the perky young woman, although only a year or two older than her own claim of twenty-five years, was at least thirty pounds heavier. Miriam settled for a single order of the *tostadas de ceviche*, made with tilapia and shrimp, and a bottled water. It was a typical August day—much too hot to sit outside—so they carried their food back to Stephanie's office.

After just one bite Miriam agreed with Stephanie's assessment of the food truck. "Wow, you weren't kidding," she said. "This really is the best taco I've ever tasted."

"Told you," Stephanie said, wiping guacamole from the corner of her mouth before taking another big bite. "One day when we get this Martinez dinner behind us, I'll take you to lunch at *Post Office Pies*. Best Margherita pizza in the world."

Miriam laughed. "Good thing I'll be living across the street from a park. I'm gonna need to increase the distance of my morning run if you're going to start taking me to places like that. My typical lunch is peaches and cottage cheese."

Stephanie started in on her second taco. "Beautiful, rich, and a health nut. Tell me again why you want to work here? I don't know what Mark's paying you, but I know what he pays me, and it ain't gonna keep you in *Dior*, sweetie."

Miriam smiled. "My tastes aren't quite that expensive but you're right, I don't have to work. But I'm twenty-five years old. What am I supposed to do, spend every day shopping and going to the spa?"

Stephanie picked up a chunk of lobster with her fingers and popped it in her mouth. "See, that's the irony. People like me work their asses off so they *can* go shopping and occasionally splurge on a visit to the spa, and people like you want to get a job because you're bored with doing the things the rest of us can only dream about."

So there it was, out in the open. Miriam had suspected that once discovered, her and Peter's wealth would be an issue. She had actually regretted the impulsive commitment to attend the Martinez fundraiser—she reminded herself that she needed to call Peter and tell him about that—but had decided that her financial position would come out sooner or later, so why not take advantage of the opportunity to help out the firm? She hated to have this discussion on her very first day, but figured now was as good a time as any.

"Stephanie, is my financial status going to be a problem here?"

Stephanie looked at her as she continued to chew her taco. She wiped her fingers with a napkin, slurped the last of her tea through her straw, and leaned back in her chair. "That'll be up to you."

"Up to me? I don't know what you mean."

Stephanie looked up at the ceiling, as if her cues for this awkward discussion were written on the tiles, and then stared back at Miriam. "Look, I worked all weekend on this project, and it's highly unlikely I'll take a single day off for the next three weeks. I work that way because I care about Mark and Abby and believe in what they're trying to accomplish with this firm, but also because I need this job. I'll always do everything that's expected of me, and then some, because I need them to need me. I don't have anything else to fall back on. But you do."

Miriam locked eyes with the other woman. "So you're questioning my commitment?"

Stephanie held the stare for a few seconds and then looked down at the remnants of her lunch. She began wadding up the trash and dropping it into the waste basket by her desk. "No, I'm not questioning your commitment. I have no reason to…yet. I'm just saying that I don't understand it. What's going to keep you working like Courtney, Allen and me? Big projects like this don't come along often, but when they do, we put our lives on hold and give the job everything we've got. Why would you do that when you don't really have to?"

"So what you're really saying is that you're concerned about me carrying my own weight?" Miriam asked.

Stephanie smiled, and the mood lightened a bit. "Carrying *your* own weight wouldn't be much of a contribution, sweetie. What are you, a size zero?"

Miriam returned the smile and said, "A size two, actually. But seriously, you have to understand something about me. I wasn't wealthy before I met Peter. I don't come from money. I know what it means to struggle." She thought back to a week she'd spent in a freezing barn just outside of Strasbourg. "You're right; I don't need this job for the money. But I need it. For myself…to have a reason to get up in the morning. To accomplish something worthwhile."

She paused a moment to take a deep breath. "I may not be here for the same reasons you are, Steph. But as long as I'm here, you'll be able to count on me. No matter what it takes."

Stephanie studied Miriam's face a moment before saying, "I believe you. So let's get back to work. We have three more hours before we have to report our progress to Mark."

Miriam rose from her chair, gathering her own lunch trash and dropping it in the waste basket. "Okay. I'll be in my closet around the corner if you need me."

Stephanie laughed, and then, as Miriam walked out the door, said, "Miriam."

Miriam turned. "Yeah?"

"Thanks for lunch."

DESPITE THE LINGERING paint fumes, Miriam closed her office door before dialing the number for Peter's cell phone. He answered after two rings.

"Hi handsome," she said. "What are you up to?"

"I just got back in the room," he said. "Marcia picked me up and took me to see a couple of apartments. There aren't very many available for short-term leases."

"Any luck?"

"One was a dump, but the other may be okay. A bank executive is doing a six-month assignment in Shanghai, and wanted to rent his place out for as much of that time as he could. Marcia's going to see if he'll go for a two month lease. If he will, we'll go see it one evening this week."

"Sounds good."

"So how's the first day on the job? Everybody being nice to you?"

"Well," she said, hesitantly, "pretty good overall, but this one woman I'm working closely with on a big, urgent project may be a little uncomfortable with the fact that we're not your typical working class citizens."

"I guess that's to be expected," Peter said. "If it gets uncomfortable, you can just quit and stay home with me. We can drink champagne and count money all day."

She laughed. He always seemed to know the right time to ease the tension by making a wise-crack. "Good to know I have a back-up option. So, listen, I have a question for you."

"Uh-oh. Whenever you tell me you have a question rather than just coming right out and asking it, it either means I'm going to have to do something I don't want to do or spend money I don't want to spend."

"Oh, don't be so cynical. Who was the last president you met?"

He paused a moment and then said, "That's your question?"

"Actually, I have two questions. That's the first one."

"Well, Eisenhower, I think. When he came to Aspen and those friends of ours threw him that dinner party and invited us."

"So, how would you like to meet another one?" she asked.

His response was quick and definitive. "I am *not* interested in meeting that idiot. I think the whole country is beginning to understand we made a huge mistake."

"That's not who I'm talking about. I'm talking about someone who could be a real contender in the next general election. Robert Martinez."

"Martinez? Really? He's a little further to the right that I am, but a hell of a lot more acceptable than what we have now. So how would I meet Martinez?"

She told him about the fundraiser dinner she was working on, and he was all for it until he heard the price. But after a few minutes of half-hearted bickering, he acquiesced, as she'd known he would. She offered to pay for her own ticket with her salary, although it would take three months to net that much, but he laughed and told her not to worry about it. "I may let you buy your own dress for it though," he said. She readily agreed.

"Listen, sweetheart, I have to go," she said. "I think I'm going to be here until at least seven or so. I just finished a late lunch, so I won't need anything for dinner. Why don't you go down to the tavern in the lobby and have a burger or something, and then we'll have a glass of wine when I get there."

He hesitated so long before responding that Miriam was afraid he was angry. When he spoke, his voice was soft, almost a whisper. "I have something I need to tell you about. I was hoping I could do that at dinner."

His tone alarmed her. "Is something wrong?"

He was suddenly trying to be light again. "I don't know. It's probably nothing. We'll discuss it over a glass of wine tonight."

"No," she said. "Tell me now."

"It can wait."

"Tell me."

He sighed. "You left so early this morning I didn't get a chance to mention it." He paused a few seconds before saying, "I had a dream."

For most couples, the discussion of a dream would be a light-hearted, half-serious interchange on the mysterious workings of the human brain. *Where did that come from? Why would that have been on my mind? What could that mean?* But with Peter, dreams were treated seriously. On more occasions than Miriam could remember, the grim scenes in Peter's dreams had foretold the coming of trage-dy—walking through a field of mass graves shortly before the Polish cholera epidemic in 1831; streets littered with mutilated bodies two nights before the Warsaw pogrom of 1881; burning buildings and a sea of broken glass a week before *Kristallnacht* in Berlin, in 1938. And there were other examples specific to the two of them, such as the night Peter had awoken screaming for Miriam to get out of the water. Less than a week later, she had nearly drowned in a canoeing accident on the Colorado River.

Miriam suppressed a shiver. "What was it?"

"I don't know, exactly," he said. "It wasn't all that clear. I just know I was looking for you, and was panicked that I couldn't find you. There was a lot of smoke…and broken furniture…and bodies everywhere. And I was looking at them, scared crazy that one of them would be you."

She shuddered. "And then what happened?"

"And then I woke up. And you were right there beside me. I put my arm around your waist and nestled my face against your neck for a long time, telling myself it'd just been a dream. It took forever for me to get back to sleep. I guess that's why I didn't wake up when you left this morning."

"You're right, it's probably nothing," she said, trying to convince herself as much as him. "We'll talk about it tonight, and see if there's anything we can think of that would minimize the risk if it really is real."

"Okay," he said. "Give me a call when you're heading this way. And be careful."

"I will."

"I love you."

She sighed. "And I adore you, *kochanka*."

THE FIVE O'CLOCK staff meeting lasted over an hour. Stephanie's spreadsheet was reviewed in detail, and everyone—especially Mark—had additions to the list of tasks. Stephanie captured them on her laptop as they were discussed, and said she'd clean it up and forward a copy of the revised document to everyone before she left for the evening.

Mark seemed impressed by the progress Miriam had made on her first day, which pleased her. And everyone made a big deal out of the fact that Miriam and Peter were filthy rich and would attend the event, which did not. Still, it got the money thing out in the open and Miriam hoped the "shock and awe" would be short-lived. She couldn't help but feel that Allen and Courtney probably shared Stephanie's belief that Miriam would cut and run the first time the going got tough, but she would just have to wait for the opportunity to prove them wrong. She had faced much more challenging situations than this job could ever provide, and she'd never backed down before. And she never would.

By the time she finished proofing the printed invitations and the names and addresses on the final guest list, it was seven thirty and her eyes were dry and burning. Time for that glass of wine with

Peter. Past time, actually. She grabbed her purse and computer bag and walked around the corner to tell Stephanie she was leaving, but her office was empty. Rubbing her eyes again and deciding it might be a good idea to remove her contact lenses and put on her glasses for the drive to the hotel, she headed to the restroom.

She walked into the ladies room and set her purse on the counter by the sink and her computer bag on the floor at her feet. Fishing out her lens case and cleaning solution, she washed her hands and proceeded to remove her contacts. She took a paper towel and was drying her hands and dabbing her eyes when she heard a toilet flush behind her. She looked into the mirror and saw a blurry figure emerge from one of the stalls. The figure took a couple of steps toward her and stopped.

"You told me you weren't hiding anything else," Stephanie said, her voice quivering.

Miriam froze, still facing the mirror. "What...what do you mean?"

Stephanie took another two steps, stopping right beside her. But she didn't look at Miriam. She was focused on the new associate's reflection. When she spoke, it was barely a whisper. "There's another one of you here."

Chapter 10

"IT'S ALL ABOUT message consistency," Arthur Stephenson said. He and Martinez were seated around a table with their four regional campaign managers in the Gold Coast Suite of the Drake Hotel in Chicago. The view of Lake Michigan was stunning and the room décor impeccable. Martinez would have preferred the Presidential Suite, but Stephenson had convinced him that it would be better not to appear too ambitious until the American Values Party occupied a few House seats, and possibly a governor's mansion or two.

Candidates backed by the two major parties usually had their own local campaign teams, but the American Values Party could not yet afford that. Therefore, the AVP regional management team—three men and one woman—handled all of the campaigns in their assigned geographic areas. It was a grueling job with a ridiculous travel schedule, but seemed to be working well so far. One of the advantages of the structure was that it provided more control over messaging, which was the topic of this particular weekly team meeting.

Stephenson locked eyes with each team member in succession before continuing, making sure he had everyone's undivided attention. Whenever he spoke he expected eyes on him and pen in hand, ready to write down anything of significance. Which, as far as he was concerned, was just about every word he uttered. "The differences between us and the other two parties on our three core issues are crystal clear, so keep your candidates on script. If any of your guys have to be called in for another meeting like the one we just had in Dallas, you will be held accountable. *Comprendes?*"

Everyone nodded. Two even wrote it down.

Stephenson continued. "As of this morning, polls have us in the lead in six House races, and running a close second in eight others. In addition, the Pennsylvania race is getting closer. The latest poll shows our guy only five points behind Ed Wilkes, the mayor of Scranton, who two weeks ago was ahead by over twenty points. Definitely going in the right direction."

He leaned back in his chair and consulted the notepad in front of him. "Okay, regional updates. Sally, you're up."

Besides being the only woman in the inner circle, Sally McDaniel, at twenty-nine, was the youngest. Tall and blond, with the figure and seductive smile of a Victoria's Secret model, she was a Vanderbilt graduate and the daughter of one of Nashville's biggest record producers. She was bright, articulate, well-connected with the country music industry, and she routinely slept with Martinez when they were in the same city. She was responsible for the campaigns in the southern states, stretching from the Carolinas west to Texas. With the possible exception of North Carolina, and even it was starting to lean their way, every state in her region looked promising for the AVP candidates. Those being the reddest of the red states, they were especially receptive to the far-right positions of the American Values Party, but Sally got the credit anyway. The other three campaign managers, aware of her special relationship with Martinez, certainly knew better than to suggest otherwise.

"Yes, we have a five-day sweep through the Bible Belt starting in two weeks," she said.

Martinez looked up from his iPhone. Although he relished the idea of five straight nights with Sally sharing his bed, he felt the need to ask, "Why spend five days in states where our candidates are already in the lead?"

"Two reasons," Stephenson interjected. "One is that we'll have huge, enthusiastic crowds. The news footage all week long will make it look like we're bigger than we really are. And the other reason is money."

"I have fundraiser dinners scheduled in Charlotte, Atlanta, Birmingham, Nashville and Little Rock," Sally said, "with you making press-the-flesh stops with the candidates in a dozen other locations. It'll be a PR bonanza."

Stephenson leaned toward Martinez, but spoke loudly enough for everyone to hear. "Sally believes the fundraisers will net twelve to fourteen million in five days. That'll buy a lot of TV ads." He glanced around the table and was glad to see that the other three managers were writing feverishly on their notepads. He smiled. Message delivered, loud and clear. He expected he'd see fundraising proposals from all three within the next day or two.

"Thanks Sally. Try to have the schedule fleshed out by the time we meet in Dallas on Friday." Stephenson looked around the table. "We're about out of time. Anyone else with anything critical?"

They all knew from experience that when Stephenson used the word "critical," he meant just that. Anyone throwing out fluff in an attempt to score brownie points would be publicly humiliated. But Mike Flaherty, the campaign manager for the northeast, wasn't going to walk out of the meeting without putting at least something on the board. "One thing," he said.

Stephenson cast him a warning glance. "Make it quick, Mike."

Flaherty took a deep breath, hoping to get it all out in a sentence or two. "I'm meeting with George Blankenship in Scranton tonight. He says a friend of his in City Hall has evidence that the mayor made a little side money on the bid to construct three new fire stations."

Stephenson raised an eyebrow. The Democratic mayor of Scranton was Blankenship's main opponent for the open congressional seat, the incumbent finally retiring after thirty-two years in Washington. "Side money...you think Wilkes took bribes?"

Flaherty nodded. "Looks that way. If the evidence is real and we can leak it to the press, George should be able to take the lead in the polls. I'll have an update for you in the morning."

"That's good, Mike," Stephenson said. "Just make sure nothing can be traced back to us. We have to be the clean guys. Everything must be…" Before he could complete his sentence, the cell phone on the table by his notepad buzzed. He gave it a quick glance and picked it up. "Excuse me a minute," he said, as he rose from the table and walked into the adjoining bedroom.

Less than a minute later he walked back to the table but remained standing. "Are we all done here?" he asked, with a tone that made it clear that, indeed, they were. Everyone except Martinez rose and Stephenson brusquely walked the four out, nodding at the private security guard outside the door before returning immediately to the dining room.

Martinez looked up from a text message on his cell phone. "Who was that call from? Once you took it, you seemed in a helluva hurry to get everyone out of here."

"It was our girl, letting us know she'll be on the air in ten minutes."

Martinez pushed back from the table and stood, still focused on his cell phone. "More good polling news, I hope."

Stephenson shook his head. "It's not about polls. And it's damn sure not good news."

"THIS IS KRISTIN CONNELLY, reporting live from Millennium Park in downtown Chicago, where American Values Party founder Robert Martinez will be appearing at a rally in support of congressional candidate Roy Spencer in just about two hours. But this time, the crowd may not be made up entirely of enthusiastic supporters. I've been informed that a fairly sizable contingent from *Brigada de Proteccion Hispana*—The Hispanic Protection Brigade— will be on hand to continue their increasingly vocal protest against Martinez and the AVP platform.

"The Brigade, as they are commonly called, was formed late last year, they say in response to the 'hard line' immigration policies proposed by Martinez. They point specifically to a speech Martinez made last November in which he said that if the federal government couldn't plug the holes in our southern border, it was up to American patriots to do it. The Brigade claims that immediately after that speech, self-appointed border militia, armed with everything from hunting rifles to military grade weapons, began to spring up in every one of the border states, and a few other states as well. Tensions rose even higher in December when a young Mexican man, allegedly trying to sneak across the border into Arizona, was shot and killed. The local police claimed they couldn't identify the shooter. The Brigade alleges they just covered up the shooter's identity.

"With no suspects to prosecute, the episode quieted down after a few weeks, but then some of the militia started raiding job sites and apartment complexes populated by undocumented immigrants. That created quite a stir in the Hispanic community, and the Brigade gained more support and stepped up their protests. With cells in over twenty southwestern cities, they so far have been peaceful, but loud and incessant in their opposition to Martinez, who they view, in the words of Brigade founder Carlos Guerra, as 'a traitor to our Hispanic heritage.'

"Security will be tight at the rally this afternoon, with Mayor George O'Malley reported to be increasing the number of police in the park to ensure that the confrontation between the Brigade and the AVP supporters continues to be nothing more serious than a war of words.

"Kristen Connelly, PNN, reporting from Chicago."

MARTINEZ ROSE from the sofa and began pacing back and forth across the hotel living room. "I thought she was supposed to be on our side," he exclaimed, pointing angrily at the television.

"She is," Stephenson said. "That's why she called to warn us that this report was about to be aired. She said the presence of the Brigade at the rally is news, and she has to appear to be unbiased in her reporting of it. But she also assured me she'll start putting a negative spin on some of her reports about them."

Martinez plopped back onto the sofa with a loud sigh. "So how do we shut these crazy bastards up?"

"That won't be easy," Stephenson said. "They're holding press conferences nearly every day. The militia raids are starting to back-fire from a PR standpoint. They were generally applauded in the border states, but now they're being debated in some areas where our candidate's position is more tenuous, such as here in Illinois. The press hasn't come right out and linked the raids to our campaign, but their implications are clear. If the Brigade keeps making noise, it's only a matter of time before the AVP will be portrayed as the party that caters to the lunatic fringe."

Martinez smiled. "I might be offended if it wasn't true."

"Keep in mind what I told the team this morning. We have to be consistent with our message, but we also have to manage our image. Having said that, it's clear that the Brigade is getting more aggressive. We need to find a way to muzzle them."

Martinez nodded his head toward the door, where a member of their detail from Arrowhead Security Services, a private global security service made up almost entirely of military and FBI veterans, stood in the hall. "Think any of those guys could be trusted to take on some *special assignments*?"

Stephenson leaned across the coffee table and spoke in a hushed voice. "Arrowhead may be a little too much on the up and up for the kind of work we need to get done. Remember that small security outfit we used last year during the employee satisfaction survey?"

Ten months earlier, just about the time Martinez was becoming well known nationally, there had been some negative reports in the press about working conditions at Liberty Toys, Inc.. Stephenson had decided that the best way to nip the story in the bud was to discredit it, and the best way to do that was to conduct an employee satisfaction survey that would portray Liberty as one of the most desirable workplaces in America.

An independent security company was hired to oversee the survey process, which was presented as being "100% confidential." In reality, it was anything but. Hidden cameras and same-time access to computerized inputs allowed Stephenson to match every single employee with his or her responses. Workers who had given negative responses were visited by the security company and told there had been a computer glitch with their input, and they would need to vote again. It was strongly implied that their survey input was being monitored, and that continued employment—and the physical safety of them and their family members—would depend on the nature of their votes. Even after the incredibly positive results were published in major newspapers and business magazines across the country, several of those workers were fired. Second visits by the outside security team ensured no complaints were lodged.

Martinez nodded. "Yeah, they did a good job. Wycliff Security, right?"

"Right," Stephenson said. "Maybe they could visit a couple of the Brigade leaders, see if they could be persuaded to tone down their rhetoric a bit."

"They're pretty fired up. They might need a lot of persuading."

"That can be arranged. And Wycliff knows how to be discreet. If any of the Brigade's people are crazy enough to talk to the press after being visited, there won't be any connections back to us."

"I like it." Martinez paused and smiled. "Arthur, you are a PR genius."

Stephenson returned the smile. "It's just a matter of knowing which buttons to push…and how hard to push them."

Chapter 11

MIRIAM CHECKED HER rearview mirror as she turned onto the entrance ramp for I-65 south. Stephanie was still behind her in a white Camry. They were on their way to the Galleria Mall. Specifically, to the Hyatt Regency. They had a lot to talk about.

Miriam took her cell phone from her purse and dialed Peter. He wasn't going to like this. Not one bit.

"Hi babe," he said. "Finally on your way?"

"Yeah," she said, trying to think how she should present this to him.

"Good. Want to come up to the room and get into something more comfortable before we head downstairs for that glass of wine?"

"No, meet me in the tavern. Traffic looks light. I should be there in about twenty minutes." She paused a beat before adding, "I won't be alone."

His voice tensed. "What's going on? You don't sound right. Is everything okay?"

She took a deep breath. "Not really. Remember me mentioning the woman I'm working with on this big American Values Party event?"

"Stephanie, right? What's wrong? Does she still have her panties in a wad because you're rich?"

Miriam didn't feel like playing twenty questions, so she just blurted it out. "She has the gene."

The other side of the call went completely silent. Peter was probably just as shocked as she had been in the restroom twenty minutes earlier. After fifteen or twenty seconds, he finally spoke. "I knew this job thing was a bad idea."

"Don't start with that, Peter," she said, her anger momentarily rising to the same level as her fear. "This could happen anywhere. All it takes is a mirror or a reflecting pool."

In reality, it had happened only twice before. Once in Warsaw in 1580, and another time in Milan in 1792. Theirs was apparently a very rare condition. Exceedingly so when considering they'd only had those two episodes in their nearly seven hundred year history together. Until now.

"What are the odds?" Peter muttered. "So, this Stephanie…how many hosts has she ridden?"

"None. She obviously carries the gene, but she's never been sick, so she hasn't converted."

"Dammit, we need to leave Birmingham and find another place to live. We'll back out of the house deal and I'll get Sergei started on new identities."

"I don't think that will be necessary," Miriam said. "At least, not yet. Let's talk to her tonight, both of us, and then decide what to do."

Peter's voice started to rise. "We have no choice, Miriam! We have to go. We can't take the chance."

"I believe we can trust Steph to keep her mouth shut," Miriam said.

"And what makes you believe that?" he demanded. "You just met her last week. How can you possibly think you can trust her with something like this?"

Miriam paused to take a deep, shuddering breath before answering. "Because another of the associates is a rider, and she hasn't told anyone about him. Until tonight, when she saw me."

Peter's response was so low she was barely able to make it out. "Holy shit," he said.

MIRIAM AND STEPHANIE walked into the lobby of the Hyatt. Neither had spoken when they'd emerged from their cars, parked side by side in the lot outside the door. Despite the hot, humid night air, Miriam had felt a chill as they traversed the parking lot. She had a million questions, but didn't want to have to repeat things for Peter, so she said nothing. Stephanie apparently had reasons for her own stony silence. Miriam could only guess what they were.

"In here," Miriam said, pointing to the entrance to Merck's Tavern.

It took a moment for her eyes to adjust to the dim light, but then she saw Peter sitting in an isolated area in the back corner. She headed that way, Stephanie following timidly. Peter saw them coming and stood.

Miriam took a few seconds to study them both, as if she wasn't sure what kind of behavior to expect from either of them. Finally, she spoke. "Stephanie, this is my husband, Peter. Peter, Stephanie Mullins."

"Call me Steph," Stephanie muttered.

"Call me stunned," Peter said, and all three of them smiled tentatively as they pulled out their chairs.

"At the risk of being rude, I started without you," Peter said, holding up a glass of amber liquid, neat. He looked at Miriam. "You said you needed a glass of wine. I decided I needed a double scotch."

The tavern was nearly empty and a waiter appeared quickly. "Ladies?" he said.

"I'll have a glass of Pinot Noir," Miriam said. "How about you, Steph?"

"Same for me," Stephanie said.

"Might as well bring us a bottle of the Meiomi," Peter suggested. "We may be here a while."

The waiter nodded and hurried toward the bar. Immediately, Stephanie reached her hand into her purse and pulled out a compact, which she opened and placed on the table. She looked at Peter, who nodded, and slid it across so it was directly under his chin. She studied his reflection a few seconds, noting the curly red hair and emerald-green eyes, and then pulled it back, closed it, and returned it to her purse. "Sorry," she said. "I just wanted to see who I was really talking to."

Peter offered a weak smile. "That's okay. I'm sure you had quite a shock tonight."

"Not as big a shock as when I saw Allen's reflection," she said. "That absolutely blew my mind."

"Allen?" Peter said.

"Allen Trammell," Miriam said. "One of the other associates at the firm." She turned to Stephanie. "How did you discover him?"

"Allen is gay," Stephanie said, as if that explained anything.

"I suspected that," Miriam said.

"Well, did you also suspect that he's really a forty-seven year old black man?" Stephanie said. "I let him talk me into going to a gay bar for drinks one night after work. It was about a year ago. We were seated near a mirrored wall, and it took me several minutes to get my head around the fact that the guy in the mirror was the same guy sitting across the table from me. I actually thought someone had put a hallucinogen in my drink. I began freaking out, and Allen got me out of there pronto. We walked around town and talked all night. We both showed up for work in the same clothes we'd worn the day before." She smiled. "If Allen wasn't living with the artistic director of the Alabama Ballet, it probably would've started some serious rumors."

"So who is he really?" Peter asked.

"His name was Marvin Douglas. He contracted AIDS in Houston in the early eighties and moved into to a hospital orderly when he was nearly dead. He told me he just suddenly realized he could do that. So he left an emaciated corpse in the hospital bed and walked out the door. He used the other guy's identity and made his way to Key West. He lived down there until he developed liver cancer and was told he had only a few months to live. That was in 2009, I think he said. He met a kid from New Zealand who had come to America to explore his sexuality far away from the judgmental eyes of his family, and Marvin became Allen Trammell."

Miriam was nodding as she listened. "That makes sense," she said.

Stephanie gave her a hard look. "To you, maybe; not to me. What the hell…"

She stopped as the waiter delivered their wine. They remained silent while it was presented, opened, sampled and poured. When the waiter was finished, he confirmed they all had everything they needed, and walked away.

Stephanie resumed her question. "What the hell is going on with you two, and with Allen, and why am I the only person who can see it?"

Miriam looked at Peter. "You want to answer that?"

Peter took a big gulp of his scotch and let out a long sigh. "I'll try." He turned to Stephanie. "We don't have a complete answer, but we have the makings of a good theory."

"That's more than Allen was able to provide, so let's hear it," Stephanie said.

"Do you know anything about the Human Genome Project?" he asked.

Stephanie thought for a few seconds before answering. "Just what I remember from a high school biology class. My teacher was fascinated by it. They had just completed the project and he said it was one of the greatest achievements in modern science. That was my sophomore year, so it must have been sometime in 2003 or 2004."

"That's right," Peter said. "It was an international research effort to sequence and map all of the genes—together, they make up what is called the genome—of human beings. Well, in a place Miriam and I lived previously, I got to know a neighbor who was a retired geneticist from Princeton University. He actually worked on the project."

"So you were living in New Jersey?" Stephanie asked.

"Yes, Lake…" Miriam started to say, but stopped abruptly when Peter shot her a stern look.

"It doesn't matter where we lived," Peter said. "The important thing is that this guy…"

"What was his name?" Stephanie asked.

"Again, that doesn't matter," Peter said. "What matters is that he loved talking about his work on the project. He called it HGP and, like your high school biology teacher, thought it was a monumental achievement. It gave me the opportunity to pick his brain over the course of several discussions…"

"And several bottles of Bordeaux," Miriam added.

Peter smiled and nodded. "Yes, the good professor did like his French wine. Anyway, I asked him a bunch of questions about some people having immunity to certain diseases, and some having a genetic predisposition for cancer, and stuff like that. And from his responses, I've been able to construct what I consider to be a fairly reasonable hypothesis for our…our *condition*, for lack of a better word."

"Go on," Stephanie urged. "I need to hear this, so I won't continue to think I'm insane."

"Whether our hypothesis is valid or not, you're definitely not insane," Miriam said. "We're real. And Allen sounds real."

"So, here goes," Peter continued. "We know that all human beings have the same genome. It's what makes us human. There are some differences, obviously, or we'd all be exactly the same. But there are also genetic mutations. Some are fairly common, some are extremely rare. And sometimes, a catalyst is required to manifest a mutation."

"A catalyst?" Stephanie asked. "Like what?"

"Like a disease," Peter said. "My friend had several examples of gene mutations that weren't activated until the person was exposed to some deadly disease, oftentimes a disease that attacks the autoimmune system."

"Like HIV/AIDS," Stephanie said.

"And Bubonic Plague," Peter said.

Stephanie's eyes widened and she looked from Peter to Miriam, and back to Peter again. "*Bubonic Plague*? That's what triggered it for you two?"

They both nodded.

"But that would've had to be five or six hundred years ago!"

"Closer to seven," Peter said. "But let me finish. So, we know that there can be extremely rare gene mutations, sometimes affecting less than one-tenth of one per cent of the population. So if Miriam, Allen and I have such a mutation, and we all had serious diseases to trigger it, that may be an explanation."

"But what about me?" Stephanie asked, a bewildered expression on her face. "The most serious disease I ever had was measles, and maybe a couple of cases of the flu. Nothing like AIDS, and certainly nothing like the Black freakin' Plague!"

Miriam put her hand on Stephanie's arm to silence her as the waiter came back to the table to see if Peter wanted another drink, which he did. When the waiter left, Miriam said, "My thinking is that you have the gene mutation, but it hasn't been triggered. You can see our original faces in a reflection, just like we can, and just like Allen would be able to do. But your ability to jump hasn't been activated."

"Jump?"

"That's what we call it," Miriam said. "The ability to move from one body to another."

Stephanie stared off in the distance, as if pondering the possibilities. "So I guess Angelina Jolie is safe from me."

Miriam smiled. "You want her body?"

"And her husband. Somebody else can take all those kids though. Brad and I can make some new ones." She paused for a moment, a look of confusion causing her brow to crease, and then said, "But if this ability to *jump*, as you call it, is genetic, how do you maintain it in the new host? I mean, you're in a new body with a totally different genetic make-up."

"That's a good question," Peter said. "One that I don't have any plausible answer for. I guess there are some aspects of human beings that reside in the soul, not just in our DNA. Like memory, for instance. When we jump, we retain our own memory but don't have any memories of the new host. Their mother could walk up to us right after the jump and we wouldn't have a clue who she was. So, even though we construct completely new identities every time we make a jump, we try to learn as much as we can about a prospective host beforehand."

Stephanie nodded. "Make sense, I guess. As much as any of this could make sense." She looked at Peter, and then back at Miriam. "So you two really met during the Black Plague?"

Miriam told her the story of the Strasbourg Massacre, her living in a barn, getting sick, and then jumping into the body of a young Christian girl. She paused when the waiter delivered Peter's drink, and then resumed the story, recanting her encounter with Peter by a pond in a German forest. She told how Peter had gotten sick in Strasbourg and had jumped into a Jewish boy who worked at his father's tannery.

Stephanie looked at Miriam. "So you were a Jew who jumped to a Christian, and Peter was a Christian who jumped to a Jew? All in the midst of this bloody, barbaric pogrom? And now you've been in love for seven hundred years. That's ironic."

Miriam grasped Peter's hand and gazed into his eyes. "Yes it is, isn't it, *kochanka*?"

"*Kochanka*?" Stephanie asked, a puzzled expression on her face. "What does that mean?"

Miriam smiled. "It's Polish. The literal translation is *lover*."

"That's a rather racy nickname for an old married couple," Stephanie said. "And by old, I mean six or seven hundred years."

"Actually," Miriam said, "we've never been officially married. At first we just didn't want to take the chances with getting the license, and all that. And we would've needed to get married again every time we jumped to new hosts. After a couple of centuries, we decided there just wasn't a point to it."

"Wow, this is incredible," Stephanie said. "So what did you two do after you met in the forest? Just go set up house somewhere?"

"We went to Poland," Miriam said. "A little town called Lubin. We had heard that the Pestilence was uncommon in Poland. To this day, we don't know why. But we went there, posing as husband and wife."

"How did you support yourselves?" Stephanie asked.

"I'd been an apprentice tanner in Strasbourg," Peter said, "working for my father. And hunting game for the skins was part of the job. I actually stalked Miriam through that entire night in the forest without her knowing I was there. Anyway, we always had meat that I killed, and I sold my goods to others in town, and Miriam worked as a seamstress."

"And you just jumped from host to host whenever you wanted?"

Peter's expression changed from smile to scowl in a heartbeat. "We've never done that!" he exclaimed. "We've never jumped until it was absolutely necessary. And we went to great pains to pick hosts who had minimal family ties so that we disrupted as few lives as possible."

"I'm sorry," Stephanie said. "I didn't mean to imply you were cavalier about it. But what did you do when it was time for a change? Like when you got old?"

It was Miriam who answered, glancing at Peter to make sure he'd calmed back down. "We'd select new hosts, make the jump, and then move to another location to establish new identities. From Lubin we went to Warsaw, where we stayed for three generations because it was a big enough city to provide anonymity. From there we moved all over Europe—Budapest, Milan, Geneva, Paris, Munich, Berlin. We left Europe right before the start of World War Two. We came to America, and have moved around in this country ever since."

Stephanie smiled. "And somewhere along the way, picked up a boatload of money."

"We figured that out in Warsaw," Peter said, his smile returning. "It's as easy to jump into a wealthy host as a poor one."

Stephanie leaned back in her chair and took a sip of wine, which she'd largely left untouched during their discussion. "This is all so unbelievable." She turned to Miriam. "But I'm glad it happened. You two have answered so many questions I've had ever since I discovered Allen's secret."

Peter leaned across the table and locked eyes with her. "Miriam and I have done our best to answer every question you've had. Now

I have one for you, and I cannot overstate the monumental importance of it."

Stephanie held his gaze. "You want to know if I can keep this to myself."

"Can you?" Peter whispered.

Stephanie lifted both hands, palms up, in a gesture of perplexity. "Who am I going to tell? What would I say? Most of all, who would believe me? There's no way to prove any of this. I'd be declared insane and locked away in some asylum!"

"She has a point, Peter," Miriam said. "Think how ridiculous this would sound to someone who can't see our original faces."

Peter appeared to be wrestling with it, but finally nodded and said, "So this stays just between the three of us?"

"And Allen," Miriam said. "All it takes is one reflective surface and he'd see for himself. It's better if we're proactive with him. He has as much of a reason to stay quiet as we do. It's better that he knows about us, and realizes that we know about him."

Peter slumped in his chair and sighed. "I can't believe this. We go over two hundred years without seeing another human being with this apparent gene mutation, and now we move to Birmingham, Alabama and find two in one day."

Miriam placed a hand on his shoulder. "Don't worry, *kochanka*. It'll be two hundred more years before we find another one. We're still safe."

Chapter 12

DESPITE DRINKING TWO double scotches before helping Miriam finish off the bottle of Pinot Noir after Stephanie left, Peter had trouble getting to sleep. He lay in bed for hours, his mind racing with scenarios of where these new developments could lead. None of them were good. He'd always been more concerned than Miriam was with secrecy and security—he actually viewed them as two sides of the same coin—so it hadn't surprised him when she took the position that the situation with Stephanie and Allen could be managed. If it had only been one other person involved, he might have been able to get comfortable with it. But, in his mind, a second person didn't just double the risk; it increased it exponentially.

He finally fell asleep sometime after two o'clock, but bolted upright when Miriam's alarm clock buzzed at six-fifteen. He called room service while she was in the shower, and they promised they could deliver coffee, orange juice and cereal within twenty minutes. It ended up being closer to twenty-five, but it was there by the time Miriam emerged from the bathroom looking as refreshed as if she hadn't a care in the world. Her hair was freshly shampooed and styled, her make-up was perfect, and she smelled faintly of *Tresor*, her favorite fragrance. She was ready for work except for one minor detail—she was naked. He watched every move as she walked across the room and pulled a terry cloth robe from the closet.

She caught his gaze and smiled as she slipped into the robe. "Not enough time this morning, sweetheart. But tonight we'll have some fun."

He poured them both a cup of coffee. "It won't take much to make it more fun than last night," he said. "My head's still spinning."

She accepted the cup of coffee and sat on the bed next to him. "From the alcohol or from everything Steph said?"

"A little of both," he said, "but mostly the latter."

"It's going to be okay," she said quietly.

"How can you know that?" he asked, skepticism evident in his voice. "You haven't even discussed this with Allen yet. You have no way of knowing how he'll react."

"Steph and I will meet with him this morning. I'll grant that I've spent very little time with Allen, so I hardly know him at all, but I'm very confident that we'll be able to trust him."

Peter shook his head, totally unconvinced. "And what is the basis of that confidence?"

She rose from the bed and stepped over to the room service cart. As she poured skim milk on a bowl of Wheaties with sliced strawberries, she said, "What possible reason would he have to say anything about us? He's in the same situation we are. He's taken lives in order to save himself, just as we have. We've been doing it a lot longer, but that's hardly relevant from either a legal or a moral perspective. He can't tell anyone about us without betraying himself. There's just no reason to do that."

"I don't know..."

"Besides," she interrupted, "he'll probably see us as a resource. Certainly not a threat."

"A resource? What do you mean?"

She carried her cereal back to the bed and sat beside him again. "Think about it. We can provide him with a plausible explanation of how his *condition*—that's the term you used last night—evolved. He may have come to terms with it over the past thirty years, but that's a lot different from understanding it. I'm sure our hypothesis is better than anything he's come up with on his own. Plus, I would think it's lonely being the only person you know of that is like that. I've had you from the beginning, and you've had me. He's had to deal with this by himself."

"He has Steph," Peter protested.

"Not the same," she countered. "Steph has the gene, and therefore the ability to recognize us, but she's not actually *like* us. Not yet, at least."

"But she will be one day. She'll find a way to convert."

Miriam nodded as she took another bite of cereal, using the spoon to scoop up a stray drop of milk from the corner of her mouth. "It wouldn't be all that hard to do. Fortunately, there's no more Bubonic Plague. But there's still HIV, Legionnaire's Disease, Ebola. Even malaria. Any of those would probably catalyze the mutation. And then she's practically immortal. Well, maybe *immortal* isn't the right word. *Open-ended.* At least, a lot more open-ended than just about every other human being on the planet. And her potential for achieving that is what will keep her quiet. So I really don't think we have to worry about either one of them."

Peter got up and refilled his coffee cup, and then sat back down. "Okay, I'll concede that neither of them have a motive—at least, one we can think of— for purposely betraying us. But we also have to worry about inadvertent slips of the tongue. You and I have had a long time to develop our mental discipline with respect to what we say out loud. Those two, not so much."

"We'll teach them," she said, patting him on the leg before standing up to place her empty cereal bowl back on the cart. "In fact, that's an advantage for all of us. Having someone else who understands our situation and helps look after us. We'll have their back, and they'll have ours. We've never had that kind of support before."

"And yet we've managed to survive for nearly seven centuries," he said.

She looked at him solemnly. "Let's just give it a try, okay? First sign of a problem, we can disappear and they'll never find us. We know how to do that."

He followed her when she went into the bathroom to brush her teeth. "You're assuming that if there's a problem, we'll have the opportunity to escape. Depending on the problem, we may not get that chance."

She turned to face him. "What kind of problem are you talking about where we wouldn't have a chance to get away?"

He leaned against the door frame and let out a long breath. "I don't know. Just some danger resulting from our secret being revealed. I can't help wondering about the timing of all of this…so soon after that dream I had."

She put down her tooth brush and stepped over to him, wrapping her arms around his waist and resting her head on his chest. "Come on, sweetheart. You know I take your dreams seriously, but you said you saw wrecked furniture, and smoke, and bodies. That has nothing to do with us, Steph and Allen. Your dream and this development are totally disconnected."

But when she left for work twenty minutes later, Peter still wasn't convinced that that was the case.

"I CAN'T BELIEVE IT," Allen muttered, as if talking to himself. "I'm not the only one. I thought I was some kind of freak of nature."

"Oh, you're a freak, alright," Stephanie said with a grin. "Don't even try to deny that."

"Well, by definition, a freak is abnormal…a rarity," Miriam said. "The three of us, along with Peter, definitely meet the criteria. I've just never thought of using that term to define us."

The three of them had been sitting in the conference room, huddled close and speaking in low voices, for almost an hour. Ostensibly, they were working on the music arrangements for the AVP fundraiser, and had the event spreadsheet and an assortment of Birmingham Symphony pamphlets strewn across the table. In reality, they'd gotten no work done at all, using the time and privacy to inform Allen of Stephanie's discovery and subsequent meeting with Miriam and Peter. At first, Allen had been alarmed and angry that Steph had shared his secret with others. This actually pleased

Miriam, because it showed that he shared her and Peter's security concerns. But then, as she had expected, he started to see the benefits of having others like him nearby. In fact, once he got over the shock, he seemed relieved to no longer be facing his secret life alone.

He looked at Miriam. "So you and your husband believe we have some kind of gene mutation that's triggered by certain deadly diseases. In my case, HIV/AIDS."

"And in their case," Stephanie interjected, "the freakin' Black Plague. I'm still having trouble getting by brain wrapped around that."

Miriam ignored Steph's comment and addressed Allen's question. "Yes, that's our hypothesis. It's pretty well vetted by a world-renown geneticist from Princeton. Peter obviously had to be careful with what he asked and how he asked it, but over the course of five or six discussions with the professor, he was able to fit the pieces together. It makes sense to us."

"So there could be others like us?" Allen asked.

"I'm sure there must be," Miriam said. "But having that specific gene doesn't necessarily mean the carrier will become a rider. It's likely that most people who have it live their lives and die without ever realizing there's anything different about them. Like Steph. If she hadn't seen your reflection, and later mine, she probably would've never known she had it. Unless she contracted one of those diseases."

"Maybe I'll get lucky and develop cancer someday," Stephanie said with a wry grin.

"I don't think cancer would trigger the mutation," Miriam said. "Not from what the Princeton guy said. It sounds like the disease needs to be infectious in nature, and only certain ones of those fit the bill. And it has to be deadly. He said there are certain biological mechanisms that are unique to the death process. And those mechanisms, at the genetic level, can vary based on the cause of death. So, the presence of the gene is probably rare to start with, and the death-bed circumstances required for activation are rarer still."

Allen smiled. "Makes me feel kind of special."

"You *are* special," Stephanie said.

He looked at her. "A few minutes ago you said I was a freak."

She patted his arm. "You are…but you're a very special freak."

"Okay, okay," Miriam said. "I hate to interrupt this Hallmark moment, but we have to decide how we're going to handle this."

"What do you mean, *handle* it?" Allen asked.

"All four of us have a vested interest in keeping this secret," Miriam said. "I hate to be blunt, but when you get down to it, you're a murderer."

She noted his visible recoil and then added, "And so am I. And so is Peter." She shifted her gaze to Stephanie. "And you're an accessory to murder."

"And a murderer-in-waiting," Allen said.

"What?" Stephanie exclaimed.

"Oh, come on, Steph," he said. "You know that the day will come when you'll find a way to convert. No matter how strong your moral fortitude, you won't be able to resist. Everybody wants to live forever. Most religions are based on that desire. If the means are available to you, you'll take advantage of them. Trust me."

Stephanie stared off into space, her brow wrinkled in concentration, as if she were trying to see into her future. "I don't know," she murmured. "I'd certainly like to have a more attractive body." She looked at Miriam. "Like you. And to be rich like you."

Miriam locked eyes with her. "But neither of those goals justify taking someone else's life."

"What does justify it, then?"

Miriam thought for a moment, and then asked, "Do you own a handgun?"

Stephanie stared at her, bewildered by the question. "What's that got to do with anything? But to answer your question, no, I don't."

"But if you did," Miriam said, "would you just go out and shoot someone for the fun of it?"

"Of course not. That's ridiculous to even…"

"But if someone broke into your home with intent to rape or kill you, would you use the gun then?"

"Yes, but that's not the same. That would be self-defense!"

"Exactly," Miriam said. Nodding toward Allen, she continued. "In our case, it's self-preservation. Maybe that's not as justifiable as self-defense, but it's clearly different than killing because of envy or greed. We didn't ask for this ability we have, but we have it, and we use it. But believe me, the first time you use it, and every time thereafter, it weighs on you. Heavily. And I hope that never changes, for me or for Peter."

"You two are lucky to have each other," Allen said. "If Russell and I stay together, I dread the thought of continuing to live—maybe for hundreds of years—without him." He paused and grinned. "Russell is my significant other. This may surprise you, but despite my rugged appearance and manly ways, I'm actually gay."

"No!" Miriam exclaimed, feigning shock. "Next you'll be telling me that Steph eats lobster from a food truck."

"Okay, enough of this nonsense," Stephanie said. "We have work to do. Mark will be expecting to see a lot of progress when we meet this afternoon. So let's put all of this out of our minds and get to it."

Miriam smiled amiably at the two of them before gathering her files and heading to her tiny office. The former closet didn't even have its own air conditioning vent, but she shut the door anyway. As the morning wore on, the room got stuffy and warm, but that didn't bother her. For some reason, she couldn't stop shivering.

Chapter 13

MIRIAM CALLED PETER as soon as she got in the car. She was anxious to get back to the hotel so she could fill him in on the details of her discussion with Allen. She had sent him a text that morning, but it was careful and cryptic, simply saying they had talked and everything looked good. But she knew he would have a lot of questions, and she wanted to put them to rest. Remembering the way he'd been looking at her when she'd emerged from the shower that morning, she also wanted to make good on her promise of a night of "fun."

"I'm on my way," she said when he answered.

"Good, you got away fairly early," he said. "Got any plans for tonight?"

"Actually, I do," she cooed. "Starting with room service and ending with you."

He hesitated a few seconds before saying, "Oh yeah, I forgot about that."

"What? You *forgot* that I promised you a night of passion? Since when did we become a typical old married couple?"

"No, wait," he stammered. "It's not so much that I forgot, as much as there's something I thought we could take care of tonight."

She tried to sound irritated, but couldn't quite pull it off because her curiosity had been aroused. "Oh? And what's more important to take care of than your horny wife?"

"Well, just a reminder…technically we're not married, you know."

"Listen buster, we've met the common law requirements about a hundred times over, so we're married. Don't ever think otherwise if you know what's good for you."

He laughed. "Okay, okay. I surrender."

"That's better," she said. "So what's so important that you have to abdicate your husbandly duties?"

"Not abdicate," he objected. "Just delay a couple of hours. Marcia called. She just got an email back from the banker that owns the apartment. He didn't want to do a two month lease. He was holding out for three. Finally, she countered with ten weeks and he accepted. If we go see it tonight and you like it, we could move in tomorrow. That would start the clock with the last week of August, so we'd be able to move into our house the second week of November, which should be just about perfect."

"Yeah, that sounds good. It's just temporary, so if you like it okay I'm sure it'll be fine with me. Do we really even need to go over there tonight?"

"I'd feel a lot better if you saw it before I signed a lease," he said. "I can have Marcia bring the paper work just in case, and then we could get that wrapped up, grab a quick bite of dinner, and I could be performing my husbandly duties by ten."

"Just like you to make a girl wait," she said coyly. "Okay, call Marcia and tell her we're on. I'll pick you up at the hotel entrance in twenty minutes."

Two hours later they were seated in a quaint little wine bar behind a popular Italian restaurant in Homewood. Owned by the people that owned the restaurant, it offered the same menu, but was much more casual and didn't require reservations. Best of all, it was only five minutes away from the apartment they'd just leased.

Sipping on glasses of Montepulciano while they waited for their bruschetta and salads, they discussed their logistics for the next day. Peter would drive Miriam to work and would then move their clothes from the hotel to the apartment. He'd stock their kitchen and, time permitting, start shopping for a second car. Everything was coming together, and Miriam was excited.

"This will cut my commute in half," she said. "Plus, it'll be nice to be in a place that feels more like home. I'm getting a little weary of hotel life."

"You and me both," he said

"And the apartment is probably only ten or fifteen minutes from the house," she said. "That'll make it easier for you to oversee the renovations."

He took a sip of wine and studied her face. "So you still think we're okay to move forward on that? It's not too late to get out of it if we have any concerns about being able to stay here."

She smiled at him. He was so cautious, perhaps overly so, but she knew it was because he loved their life together—no matter how many iterations it took—and would do everything in his power to protect it. "It's going to be fine," she said softly. "We're going to have a wonderful life here. And for the very first time, we'll have friends we can trust."

"So you think I'll like Allen?"

She grinned. "I do. And I can guarantee he'll absolutely *love* you."

"I thought you said he was in a relationship."

"He is," she said. "But anyone who's interested in men is bound to go *gaga* over my handsome Italian thoroughbred."

He smiled. "Oh really? I'll remind you of that when we get back to the hotel."

She kicked off a shoe and ran her bare toes up the side of his leg. "You won't need to remind me, sweetheart. Just get that waiter to hurry up with our food so we can get out of here."

PNN EVENING ANCHOR Ron Archer glanced quickly at his producer to make sure the live feed from Los Angeles was ready. He got an affirmative nod and thumbs up, and turned to look at the screen behind his broadcast desk. There stood Kristin Connelly, blond hair shining under the lights and green eyes sparkling with their usual intensity. She was a petite woman—a couple of inches over five feet, although her bio claimed five foot five—but Archer knew she stood tall in the eyes of the viewers. He'd tried more than once to get her out for drinks when she was at their Chicago headquarters, but she'd always made polite excuses. Rumor had it she was interested in bigger fish than the evening anchor of a small political news network.

He looked back at the camera. "And now we have an update from our own Kristen Connelly, traveling with the leadership of the new American Values Party in Los Angeles. Kristen, what can you tell us about these new allegations?"

Kristen stared into the camera and raised the mike to her lips. "Well, Ron, as you just reported, political mudslinging has risen— actually, a more apt term might be lowered—to new levels tonight with allegations surfacing that American Values Party founder Robert Martinez has for years carried on sexual relationships with prostitutes. Statements have been issued from the campaigns of several Democratic and Republican candidates for Congress who are running against AVP challengers that these allegations show that the AVP is not about perpetuating American values at all, but rather about taking advantage of the dissatisfaction voters have been expressing about both major parties.

"A source within the campaign of New Mexico's incumbent Republican governor, Roy Baker, who is virtually tied in the polls with AVP challenger Joseph Garner, said these rumors have been swirling around for several years, but have never been spoken of because, until now, there has been no proof."

Archer interrupted. "Kristen, you just said *until now*. Is there proof of these allegations?"

"No, Ron, at this time there is nothing to substantiate these claims. However, the Baker campaign source I spoke with says he has it on good authority that one woman has indicated she is willing to make a statement in return for immunity from prosecution, and a second woman is purported to be willing to do the same. It's important to note that both women are Hispanic.

"I had a brief phone conversation with Arthur Stephenson, Martinez's chief of staff, and he said that this is simply another—and I quote—'outrageous, totally unfounded allegation perpetuated by the Hispanic Protection Brigade because they oppose Martinez's courageous stand against illegal immigration. The Republican and Democratic Parties are threatened by the American Values Party's attacks on the status quo, so they're giving credence to these ridiculous lies in an effort to halt the erosion of their own political bases.' End quote.

"So right now, it appears that the Martinez campaign is just dismissing these allegations as an example of dirty politics by the Hispanic Protection Brigade in concert with desperate candidates from both major parties."

"Thank you, Kristen," Archer said, swinging his chair back around to face the camera. In his opinion, her report had come across a bit biased in favor of Martinez. But most of the PNN viewers were conservative, so he supposed that was a smart move on Connelly's part. Plus, she did look great tonight. That sea-green sleeveless dress looked great on her. It would look even better on his bedroom floor.

IT WAS A HOT night in El Paso, humid and still. Ben Wycliff, founder and president of Wycliff Security Services, took off his Stetson and wiped the sweat from his bald pate with a handkerchief. He'd been standing in the parking lot of *El Vaquero Cantina* for nearly two hours, having followed Hector Ramirez and another man to the restaurant when they had left the construction site where they'd worked as roofers until sundown. Ramirez was second-in-command of *Brigada de Proteccion Hispana*, managing the Brigade's activities all across Texas. His longtime friend Carlos Guerra had come to him the previous year and pleaded for his support in establishing a group to counter the growing threat to the Hispanic community, a threat in large part fueled by one of their own—Robert Martinez.

Whereas Guerra was the face and voice of the Brigade, holding press conferences almost daily to criticize Martinez and the increasingly violent actions of the dozens of Anglo "militias" inspired by the AVP's policies, Ramirez was the master organizer. Despite working forty-plus hours a week in construction, he managed to travel all over south Texas setting up and directing new cells. He'd started getting quite a bit of press coverage himself, and was frequently recognized in public by both friends and foes. Fortunately, his notoriety was not a problem at work, since the owner of the construction company was a second-generation Mexican-American and a generous financial supporter of the Brigade.

It was Ramirez that Wycliff had driven to El Paso to see. More specifically, he was there to deliver a message. Arthur Stephenson had called him the previous weekend and enlisted the services of Wycliff Security Services, offering a substantial fee and the promise of more work in the coming weeks. Doing a job the previous year for Liberty Toys Inc.—one of the largest companies in Texas—had been quite a thrill for Wycliff. Having a working relationship with a future President of the United States made him practically giddy.

It was almost ten o'clock and the parking lot had thinned out considerably in the time Wycliff had been waiting by Ramirez's rusty old pick-up truck. He was beginning to wonder just how many beers and enchiladas the two Mexicans could consume when he heard voices coming from the direction of the restaurant. He stepped a few feet away from the truck, positioning himself between two parked cars. As the men passed by him, hardly noticing his presence, he called out, "Hey, amigo, don't I know you?"

The two men turned to face him. They studied the short, thick man in the cowboy hat, unable to see his face in the darkness. Ramirez answered, "I don't think so."

"Sure I do," Wycliff said, taking a step toward them, but remaining several feet away. "You're that Brigade organizer I've seen on the news. Ramirez, right?"

Ramirez glanced at his companion and then back at Wycliff, as if sizing up a possible threat. But there were two of them and only one Anglo, and the cowboy didn't appear to be armed, so he visibly relaxed. "Yes, I'm Hector Ramirez. Is there something I can do for you?"

"Well, yes there is," Wycliff said, nodding. "You can quit driving all over my state stirring up trouble. That'd be a big help."

Ramirez shook his head and started to turn around toward his truck. "Look, I'm just trying to help my people, that's all."

"There's a whole bunch of your people down in Mexico. Why don't you go help them down there?"

Ramirez raised his hands. "We don't want any trouble, mister. We just want to go home and get some sleep. We have to be at work in the morning."

Wycliff raised his tone but didn't move. "Yeah, work that ought to be done by U.S. citizens, not some green card toting Mexicans."

The second man took a step toward Wycliff, but Ramirez grabbed his arm. "No, Carlos, let it go. Let's get out of here."

They gave Wycliff one more look and turned to leave. They hadn't heard the approach of the two large men now blocking their path to the truck, their baseball bats already in full swing.

PETER PULLED THE Mercedes up to the front entrance of the office building. It was eight-forty, a few minutes later than Miriam liked to arrive, but they had taken the time to load their clothes into the car and check out of the hotel. Peter would head straight to the apartment to get them moved in before proceeding with his other errands for the day. After ten days in a hotel in New York and another week at the Hyatt, Miriam was excited about having more than one room to move around in at night.

She leaned over to kiss Peter's cheek. "Good luck today. I'll call you a half hour before I'm ready to leave tonight."

"Hopefully I can find us a second car today so you won't need me as your driver much longer."

She smiled and stroked his cheek. "Oh, I don't know. I've always loved those romance novels where the lady of the house carries on a sordid affair with her chauffeur."

He laughed. "In that case, I won't shop for another car. I'll just go buy one of those caps they always wear in the movies."

"If that's all you're wearing when you come to bed tonight, you've got a deal." She opened the door and got out of the car. Leaning back in, she blew him a kiss and said, "Love you."

"Love you, too," he said, and drove off.

As always, Abby was at her desk when Miriam entered the office suite. "Good morning, Miriam," she said, cheeks dimpling with her ever-present smile.

"Morning, Abby. Sorry I'm a few minutes later than normal. We finally checked out of the hotel and Peter is moving us into an apartment today."

"No problem," Abby said. "But Mark and Steph are waiting for you in his office."

Miriam frowned. "Uh-oh. No problems, I hope."

"I don't think so," Abby said. "Just some new developments."

Miriam opened the door to Mark's spacious office and found him and Stephanie sitting at his conference table. "Hi Miriam," he said, "come on in. Want some coffee?"

She actually did, but felt bad about being a few minutes late on a day that she was needed first thing, so she declined and pulled out a chair. "Everything okay?" she asked.

"Yeah, fine," Mark said. "Just a new wrinkle with the AVP fundraiser."

Miriam opened up her computer bag and removed a notepad and pen, ready to jot down any new assignments coming her way.

Mark took a sip of his coffee and leaned back in his chair. "I got an email last night from Sally McDaniel, the party's southern regional campaign manager. She requested a face-to-face meeting with whoever is in charge of planning for the dinner. She said she just wants to be aware of all the details, including a review of the guest list. I imagine these new rumors about Martinez are making them all a little jittery."

Miriam's brow furrowed. "Rumors? What rumors?"

"You didn't watch the news last night?" Mark asked.

"No, Peter and I were out renting an apartment." She didn't add that when they returned to the hotel they had interests other than television to occupy their time.

Mark smiled. "Well, we've known it was just a matter of time before the midterm campaigns turned ugly. Now we have both Democratic and Republican candidates slinging mud at the American Values Party. Apparently, *un-named sources* are calling Martinez's marital fidelity into question."

"Really?" Miriam said. "But his wife is absolutely beautiful."

"As if that matters to an egotistic male," Stephanie laughed. "And trust me, I've been around enough politicians to know that those without a huge ego don't win elections."

"Okay, so he has a girlfriend on the side?" Miriam asked. "Kind of a Bill Clinton-Jennifer Flowers deal?"

"Worse than that," Mark said. "The rumors are that Martinez has a long history of hiring prostitutes. And since many are purported to be Latino, the Hispanic Brigade is thought to be behind the allegations. Maybe some of the women feel betrayed because of Martinez's anti-immigration statements and want to get back at him."

Miriam shook her head. "Hell hath no fury like a woman scorned."

Mark nodded. "And politicians have been known to carry a grudge as well, so it'll certainly get interesting. Anyway, we've been summoned by our client, so we need to do everything we can to allay any fears they have about the event we're planning. I'm sure Ms. McDaniel will want to make sure we have some prominent religious leaders and family values types there, and that they have visible roles that evening. It's all about image, and we're a PR firm, so image is supposed to be our specialty."

"Okay," Miriam said, "so when is the meeting?"

"She suggested this Friday in Dallas," Mark said.

Miriam turned to Stephanie. "Just tell me what all you need and I'll get it ready for you."

Stephanie locked eyes with her. "I told Mark that I'd like for you to go with me."

Miriam couldn't mask her shock. "Me? I've only been here a couple of days. This McDaniel woman will see right through me. She's probably been working political campaigns since before I was born."

"Actually, she's about our age," Stephanie said. "So I doubt she'll have an age bias. But we'll need to be buttoned down. You'll have all the details in front of you, so I can focus on talking. And you can take notes. If she's anything like the other campaign managers I've dealt with, she'll want to make a lot of changes to our plans, if for no other reason than to show she's the one in charge."

"Okay," Mark said, pushing back his chair, signaling that the meeting was over. "We have today and tomorrow to get ready. I'll ask Abby to book your flights." He paused and winked at Miriam. "Sorry, but this trip is on the client's nickel so you'll have to fly coach. Anyway, let's start constructing an executive summary of the plans—two or three pages tops—with all the details as an attachment. Get Allen and Courtney involved, and I think we can present Ms. McDaniel with a plan that'll make her comfortable. Let me know if you need anything from me."

Miriam and Stephanie rose and headed toward their own offices. After they had crossed the reception area and closed the other door behind them, Miriam whispered, "Are you sure you want me to go along? I'm afraid my lack of experience could be painfully evident."

"You mean you've never worked on a presidential campaign before?" Stephanie asked.

"Whose campaign would I have ever worked on?" Miriam said with a dismissive wave of her hand.

"Oh, I don't know," Stephanie said, grinning widely. "Maybe Washington's or Jefferson's?"

"Smart ass," Miriam muttered as she continued down the hall.

Chapter 14

MIRIAM LOOKED UP from the jumbled pile of paper in front of her as Courtney walked into the conference room sporting a micro-mini that showed off nearly every inch of her extraordinarily long legs. "Hmmph...nice belt," she quipped to Stephanie, who was seated next to her, pounding furiously on her laptop as the team provided updates on the status of their assignments for the AVP fundraiser.

"Yeah, maybe I should contract Ebola and then jump to her," Steph whispered with a sly smile. "With my brains and her body, I could rule the universe."

Allen, apparently noticing the attention Courtney had generated, leaned over and said, "Hey, think she'd let me borrow that sometime?"

Stephanie shook her head. "You're a cute guy, Allen, but I don't think it would be a good look for you."

"No, but Russell would look fabulous!" he said. "Dancer's legs, you know."

Seeing she was the focus of the murmuring on the other side of the table, Courtney frowned and said, "What?"

"Just admiring your skirt," Stephanie said.

"Oh, you like it? I borrowed it from my little sister."

Miriam smiled. "And she's what, about six?"

"No," Courtney said, feigning irritation, "she's eighteen and a freshman at Auburn."

„War damn eagle!" Allen said.

"She went out for rush and wants a bid from Chi Omega, but a friend told her she wouldn't get one if she was seen on campus wearing skirts this short," Courtney said, her tone indicating how ridiculous she thought that was. "So she sent it home for me to wear. She sent another one too, but it might be a little too risqué for the office."

"I...but...oh, never mind," Stephanie said, shaking her head bewilderedly. "Back to business. Is the dinner menu finalized yet? For ten grand a plate, people aren't going to be happy with mac and cheese."

"Oh, you've obviously never had John Stark's lobster macaroni with Bleu d'Auvergne," Courtney said with a sigh. "Trust me, it's to die for!"

"If they ever start carrying that on the food truck, I'll give it a try," Stephanie said. "So, what's the status of the menu?"

"Not quite finalized," Courtney said. "John and his head chef from *The Twilight Grill* toured the kitchen that the Westin will make available for the event, and they say it's inadequate for preparing five hundred crème brulees at one time. So, dessert's still an open issue, but just about everything else is nailed down. Some of the appetizers for the cocktail hour will be prepared at the *Grill* and then trucked over, which didn't please the hotel management, but they finally agreed. So, except for dessert, and one white wine that appears to be in short supply and may have to be replaced, I'll have a detailed menu for you to present on Friday."

"Great," Stephanie said. "If you get those resolved by tomorrow afternoon, let Miriam know and she'll update our presentation. Now, let's move on to..."

She stopped in mid-sentence as Mark entered the room. "Good," he said, "everyone's here together. Sorry to interrupt, but I just got a call from Sally McDaniel, and now they have some new security concerns."

"I thought Arrowhead would be responsible for all the security arrangements," Stephanie said.

"Ordinarily, that would be the case," Mark said. "And they will manage everything inside the hotel, as well as all of the entrances. But now the campaign is worried about crowd control outside the hotel. Apparently they're expecting some protest activity."

"Here?" Stephanie asked. "Who would protest a conservative movement in Birmingham, Alabama?"

"There's a new development that has them a little worried," Mark said. "The news story just broke a couple of hours ago. Last night one of the main organizers of *Brigada de Proteccion Hispana* was attacked and beaten half to death. He and a friend of his were assaulted in a restaurant parking lot in El Paso. The Brigade is blaming Martinez and the AVP—if not directly, at least indirectly due to their rhetoric, which has fired up all of these border-control militias. Sally fears that, with two weeks to prepare, the Brigade could organize a massive and potentially dangerous confrontation here and in some of the other southern cities Martinez will be visiting on his fundraising swing."

"What does Sally want us to do?" Stephanie asked. "We're a PR firm, not a security outfit."

Mark smiled and raised his hands in a *mea culpa* gesture. "Well, Sally was just calling to express her concern, but she sounded so worried I was afraid she might want to cancel the event. So I just casually mentioned that you were in charge of the planning for the dinner, and one of the clients you manage is the mayor, and she may have put two and two together and concluded that you could pull some strings."

"Oh, great," Stephanie sighed. "So now I get to put one of my most important clients on the hot seat. If anything happens to the man who may one day be the President of the United States, he'll be the one they blame."

"If it happens on his turf, he'll get the blame anyway," Miriam interjected.

"Exactly," Mark said. "And if everything goes smoothly, he'll get the credit. Even a Democratic mayor would be happy to have an AVP president beholding to him, don't you think?"

"Yeah, I guess that's true," Stephanie said. "I'll get on it. I'm sure we can have something to say to Sally on Friday that will calm her down. Especially if it's in the form of guarantees from the mayor."

"I expected nothing less," Mark said with a sly grin. "See you guys at the update meeting in a couple of hours."

When he had left the room, Stephanie leaned back in her chair and rubbed her eyes. "This task list just keeps getting longer and longer." She looked around the table. "Courtney, see if you can get John to finalize the dessert and the wine list. I want everything to be as complete as possible when we meet with Sally on Friday. Miriam, add a 'security' heading to our plan summary, and I'll get us some details to include. Everybody know what they need to be working on?"

Everyone nodded affirmatively.

"Good," Stephanie said, pushing her chair back from the table. "I'll go call Hizzoner."

PETER WAS WAITING outside the office building in a white Lexus SUV when Miriam walked outside at seven-fifteen. Not recognizing the car, she walked right past him. He hit the horn and laughed uncontrollably when she jumped a foot into the air and dropped her purse.

"That was not funny," she fumed as she opened the passenger door and climbed in. "You almost made me pee my pants. Where did you get this? Is it a rental?"

"Nope, it's mine." He noted the look on her face and corrected himself. "I mean, it's ours. I bought it today. We're back to being a two-car family again."

She looked around, rubbing the leather upholstery and admiring the elaborate dashboard. "Very nice. Mine or yours?"

"Your choice," he said. "But you really seem to like the Mercedes, and you aren't the soccer mom type, so..."

She smiled. "So what you're saying is that you want to drive this one?"

"I just want to make you happy, sweetheart."

"Well, you can do that if you take me home and feed me. That cup of yogurt I had for lunch is all used up."

He pulled out of the parking lot and merged into light traffic. "I'll have you home in fifteen minutes. Dinner is ready and in the warmer, and the wine is open and breathing."

She patted his hand. "Looks like you've been a busy little boy. Everything all unpacked?"

"Not quite," he said. "Your hanging clothes are put away, but I didn't have time to tackle your suitcases. We can finish all that after dinner." He glanced at her tired expression and said, "How was work?"

She reclined her seat a little and closed her eyes. "I'll fill you in over dinner. Right now I just want to close my eyes and veg out for a few minutes."

He smiled and turned the radio up, letting her relax to the soft strains of cool jazz—Miles Davis and John Coltrane collaborating on Davis' *Flamenco Sketches*—watching as she appeared to be asleep until they pulled into the parking space of their temporary home. They got out of the car, which she gave another appraising look, and headed for the apartment door.

"Um, something smells good," she said, stepping inside and sniffing the air in the foyer.

"You change clothes and I'll pour the wine," he said.

"Deal," she said, kissing his cheek.

She appeared in the kitchen a few minutes later wearing shorts and a tee shirt. He handed her a glass of wine. She took a sip and nodded appreciatively. "Where's that food that smells so good? I'm famished."

"The salad is on the table," he said. "Have a seat and I'll bring out your plate."

A few seconds later he walked into the dining room and, with a grand flourish, set a plate down in front of her. She looked at it and then at him. "Frozen pizza?"

"Spinach and garlic thin crust, your favorite."

"And salad right out of the bag. You went all out, didn't you?"

He laughed and sat down beside her. "Hey, it was a very busy day. First I moved us in, then went car shopping, then on to the Piggly Wiggly to buy groceries. I barely had time to fit in my afternoon nap."

She took a big bite of pizza and then said as she chewed, "No complaints. I'm the one who wanted to get a job." She took another sip of wine and said, "And, boy, did I get one. It's interesting, fun even, but I hope the pace slows down once we get this fundraiser behind us."

"Yeah, I couldn't believe it when you called and said you have to fly to Dallas on Friday to review the plans. Are they trying to micro-manage the thing?"

"I don't think it's that so much as they're just worried about the PR hits they're taking."

Peter raised his eyebrows. "What PR hits?"

She took another bite of pizza and looked at him as she chewed. "You haven't caught any news today?"

"Like I told you, I've been pretty busy," he said.

She waved her hand dismissively. "Yeah, yeah, I heard you. Shopping, napping, cooking dinner. I'm sure you're exhausted."

"I'll ignore the sarcasm. Just tell me what I missed on the news."

"Well," she said, finishing off her wine and extending her glass for a refill, "it seems Mr. Martinez has a weakness for ladies of the evening."

"So? Who doesn't?"

Miriam kicked him under the table. "Anyway, it appears that some of the women who allege they've been hired by Martinez over the years are Latino, which the Martinez camp is saying indicates that these are nasty lies fabricated by the Hispanic Protection Brigade."

"And that prompted them to have you and Steph fly to Dallas? I don't get it."

"There's more," she said. "Last night one of the Brigade organizers was attacked and almost killed by men wielding baseball bats. Fingers are being pointed at the AVP for that too, so they're not only worried about image, they're concerned about the possibility of organized protests disrupting some of their campaign events."

"Like the fundraiser here," he said.

"Exactly. So, Mark feels like they'll want to organize the dinner in a way that demonstrates the trust Martinez garners from evangelicals and family value groups, and also minimizes the exposure and credibility of any protestors."

Peter set her refilled glass back down and topped off his own. "That's a pretty tall order. Can a small firm like yours do that?"

"We'll certainly try," she said. "I think it's just a matter of getting them to believe that we'll be controlling everything that can be controlled. Steph is close to the mayor, and he promised he'll make sure that no large protest group gets close enough to disrupt the event. There would obviously be news coverage of any protest, but as long as a riot doesn't break out it shouldn't be too big of a story."

He sighed. "You gotta love politics. Things may get sordid, but they're rarely boring."

They spent the rest of the evening talking and unpacking as they polished off the bottle of wine. Both were tired after a busy day, so they went to bed early. Peter kept thinking about the fundraiser, and was beginning to wish he'd never agreed for them to attend. It wasn't just the money, although twenty thousand dollars was a sizable investment in a new party whose leader might end up being deemed unsuitable to hold public office. There was something about the overall situation—and Miriam's involvement in it—that made him anxious. Like her, he'd be glad when it was over.

That night, when he finally fell asleep, he had the dream again.

Chapter 15

"I DIDN'T KNOW you wore glasses," Stephanie said as she plopped down in the seat next to Miriam.

"I wear contacts most of the time," Miriam said. "I'll put them in while we're on the plane."

It was five-thirty on Friday morning, and they were sitting at the departure gate for their 5:58 American Airlines flight to Dallas. Miriam had already been awake when her alarm clock buzzed at four o'clock and, thanks to laying everything out the night before, had been ready to leave the apartment forty minutes later. The drive to the airport had taken less than twenty minutes and very few other travelers had been crazy enough to book such an early flight, so the security line was minimal. Having arrived at her gate with time to spare, she now just wanted caffeine. Unfortunately, the coffee shop in their terminal didn't open until six, so it would be airline coffee instead of Starbuck's. Still, she wouldn't complain, lest Stephanie start the "spoiled rich girl" talk again.

"A crack-of-dawn flight on a Friday, the busiest air travel day of the week. It doesn't get any better than this," Stephanie muttered, her voice reeking of sarcasm. "Oh well, at least Sally is sending a car to pick us up, so we won't have to navigate the Dallas rush hour on our own."

"How far is the hotel from DFW?" Miriam asked.

"Turtle Creek is about twenty miles, I think," Stephanie said. "Unless traffic is particularly bad, we should be able to make it in thirty or forty minutes. Sally said she'd expect us around nine, but said she could flex either way, depending on our arrival. We should be done by noon. That'll get us back to the airport in plenty of time to grab a late lunch and make our four-forty return flight."

"Let's hope she likes our plans," Miriam said with a smile. "Then we can drink on the flight home instead of working."

"I think we have a pretty good plan. We've gotten an amazing amount of work done in one week. I'm sure she'll want to exercise her authority by making a few changes, whether they're needed or not, but she certainly won't be able to criticize our effort."

Miriam studied the face of her new friend. "I have to tell you, Steph, you're the most organized twenty-eight year old woman I've ever met."

Stephanie smiled. "And you're the hardest working seven hundred year old woman I've ever met. I guess that makes us quite a team."

"Absolutely," Miriam said, nodding. "We'll handle any surprises the Martinez folks throw at us."

Stephanie laughed. "Don't get too cocky. Just when you think you have everything figured out, you get hit with something you've never even dreamed of."

"WELCOME TO THE Rosewood Mansion on Turtle Creek," the desk clerk said with a broad smile. "Are you checking in?"

"No, we're here for a meeting with one of your guests, Sally Mc-Daniel," Stephanie said.

"Ah, yes. You must be Ms. Mullins and Ms. Hoffman?"

"I'm Stephanie Mullins, and this is Miriam Hoffman."

"She said you'd be here around nine," he said, glancing at his watch. "You actually got here a few minutes early. Let me call and let her know you've arrived."

After a short phone conversation he smiled again. "She's sending a gentleman down to escort you to her suite." He looked around and then whispered in a conspiratorial tone, "Security detail."

"I hope he doesn't have to frisk us," Miriam muttered as they stepped away from the check-in desk.

"Speak for yourself," Stephanie said with a wry smile.

A couple of minutes later a tall, lean young man with a dark suit and a coiled wire protruding from his left ear approached from the direction of the elevators. Stephanie elbowed Miriam and whispered, "I'll take a pat-down from him any day."

If the young man heard the comment, he didn't acknowledge it. Instead he said, "Ms. Mullins?"

"That's me," Stephanie replied, raising her hand shyly, like a first grader. "And this is Mrs. Hoffman."

Miriam couldn't help but smile when she heard how Stephanie emphasized the word *missus*, as if to make sure the handsome security guard knew which one was married.

"Ms. McDaniel is waiting for you in her suite," he said, extending an arm to show the way. "Would you follow me, please?"

"Anywhere," Stephanie muttered as they headed toward the elevators, where they were met by a stern-looking woman brandishing a metal detection wand.

"I apologize, ladies," the man said, "but I can't let you on the elevator without screening you first."

"Not quite what I was hoping for, but I'll get over it," Stephanie said, smiling at the man as she extended her arms from her sides. After the woman had scanned both of them and inspected the contents of their purses and computer bags, she turned and walked away and the man pushed the button for the elevator.

They emerged onto the third floor and walked halfway down the hall, where the agent stopped in front of a door and knocked once, then twice more. The door was opened almost immediately by a stunning blond woman who was almost as tall as the security guard, and looked to be no older than Stephanie. "Hi, I'm Sally McDaniel," she said, thrusting her hand at Stephanie, then at Miriam.

They both introduced themselves and Sally said, "Please come in." She then looked at the guard and said, "Thank you, Lance. I'll call you when we're done."

He nodded and she closed the door, gesturing at a dining table just beyond the foyer. "We'll meet here. I had a coffee service and some croissants sent up. I'm sure you left Birmingham too early to get breakfast."

"Thank you," Stephanie said. "As delicious as that stale muffin on the plane was, I could use a little something."

Sally threw her head back when she laughed, golden hair cascading down her shoulders. She then looked at Miriam, seeming to study her for the first time, as if sizing up the competition. "Ms. Hoffman?"

"Just coffee for me," Miriam said.

Once they were seated, pleasantries were cast aside and Sally was all business. "I cannot stress enough the importance of this series of fundraisers. Not just from the perspective of raising money, but also because of the PR potential. If that week goes the way I expect it to, the AVP will emerge as the most popular, well-financed third party organization in decades. There are no details too insignificant to be scrutinized. I realize you've only had a week to start planning, but I should let you know that I expect to see a pretty well-defined outline this morning."

"Ms. McDaniel…" Stephanie said, but was promptly interrupted.

"Sally." The campaign manager was smiling, but it was a cold smile.

"Sally," Stephanie continued, "we could pull this dinner off tomorrow if we needed to. Fortunately, we have two weeks, which is more than enough time to execute a flawless event. You will certainly have some changes you'll want to make, but I think you'll see that we've paid a lot of attention to details in every area. We intend to make the Birmingham fundraiser the most successful one of the tour."

Sally smiled and nodded. "That's a tall order, but I like your attitude. Let's see what you've got."

Three grueling hours later, Sally put her copy of the planning document on the table and smiled. Despite the fact that it had enough red-inked comments to make it look like it was hemorrhaging, she smiled broadly and said, "Well done. You thought of almost everything."

Stephanie returned the smile, although Miriam noted that she looked drained. "We appreciate your input, Sally. Miriam, do you think you captured all of the changes?"

Before Miriam could answer, Sally pushed her copy toward her. "Here, take mine. Hopefully you can read my hen scratching."

Miriam reached for it, and then paused. "Do you want to make a copy to keep so you'll remember all your changes?"

Sally smiled her cold smile. "Don't worry. I'll remember them." She then turned to Stephanie and said, "Why don't you give me a call around the middle of next week, just to touch base? I'll be especially interested in the status of the invitation responses."

"Mark is working his invitation list very hard," Stephanie said, "and he's plugged in pretty well across the state. He'll make sure every seat is filled."

Sally hesitated, as if considering whether she should say more, and then lowered her voice slightly and said, "It's not just filling the seats, it's filling the seats with the right people. Although the AVP is doing well in several polls, it's still early in the campaign season and the Democrats as well as the Republicans are getting pretty desperate, and pretty dirty. There are a lot of absolutely crazy, totally unfounded lies being thrown at us, and we're not going to stoop to their level of mudslinging, so it's critical we show the American public that religious leaders and those with traditional American values are still with us."

"We understand," Stephanie said. "I think you'll be pleased with many of the high-profile attendees Mark will deliver."

Sally looked from Stephanie to Miriam, briefly staring into the eyes of each one. "It's not only a matter of who we see there, it's also a matter of who we don't see."

Stephanie lowered her voice as well. "If you're referring to any protesters, the mayor has given me his assurance that they won't get within a block of the Westin."

"We'll hold him to that," Sally said, again flashing that cold smile.

She dialed a number on her cell phone and said, "Lance, we're done." As she was rising from her chair, her phone buzzed. "Hi Arthur," she said. "Yes, we're just finishing up. I'll be there in five minutes."

She then cut her eyes to Stephanie and Miriam. "Yes, I'm sure they would. Hold on a sec."

"Are you ladies in a big hurry to get to the airport?"

"Not really," Stephanie said. "Our flight isn't for another four hours."

Sally smiled. "Then how would you like to meet the founder of the American Values Party, and quite possibly the next President of the United States?"

MIRIAM WASN'T SURE which gave Stephanie a bigger thrill—meeting Robert Martinez, or being escorted to his suite by Lance, the Arrowhead Security agent. When they arrived, Sally knocked on the door, which was opened by a gray haired, middle-aged man Miriam didn't recognize.

"Hi Arthur," Sally said. "These are the two representatives from *Sheffield & Associates* that I told you about. Based on what I saw this morning, the Birmingham event should be a great success."

The man extended his hand. "I'm Arthur Stephenson, Mr. Martinez's chief of staff."

Stephanie and Miriam introduced themselves in turn as they shook Stephenson's hand, and then followed him into the suite. Miriam noticed the disappointment on Stephanie's face when Lance remained outside. But her friend's expression brightened considerably when the imposing and instantly recognizable form of Robert Martinez strode in from the bedroom and thrust out his hand.

"Good morning, ladies. I'm Robert Martinez."

Stephanie shook his hand. "It's an honor, sir. I'm Stephanie Mullins."

Miriam noticed that he looked directly into Stephanie's eyes as he grasped her hand, and did the same with her. She also noticed that he held onto her hand a second or two longer than he had Stephanie's, and a quick glance at Sally told her that the campaign manager had noticed too.

"Sally told me that everything looks to be in good shape for the Birmingham event," Stephenson said.

"These two are almost as anal about details as I am," Sally said with a smile.

Martinez laughed. "That's good, because I'm more of a big picture guy. That's why I surround myself with people who are detail-oriented. Arthur here happens to be good at both strategy and execution. I wouldn't be here without him." He glanced at Sally. "And don't let the young age of this one fool you. She can stand toe-to-toe with people who've been in the political arena for decades."

He focused on Stephanie. "So you're going to help me spread the message of the American Values Party in the great state of Alabama?"

Stephanie shook her head and smiled. "You're message has already been heard and pretty well received in the state of Alabama. Which is why we appreciate you making a big appearance in Birmingham. The whole city is buzzing about your visit."

Martinez grinned. "That's what I like to hear. So, I'm assuming you'll both be there that night to make sure everything goes according to plan?"

"I'll be working on site, and will make sure everything goes perfectly," Stephanie said, and then nodded toward Miriam. "Miriam and her husband will actually be attending the dinner as guests."

Martinez gave Miriam another appraising look. "Representing the firm?"

Miriam felt herself blushing. "No, sir. Representing ourselves. It's a wonderful opportunity for us to contribute to your movement. My husband is very excited about the prospect of meeting you."

Martinez smiled again. "That's not a prospect," he said. "That's a guarantee. I look forward to meeting him as well."

"Thank you, sir," Miriam said. "I'll tell him that tonight."

Martinez pointed to a buffet table set up with soft drinks, ice and glasses. "Arthur and I were about to take a soda break. Would you ladies like something to drink before you head back to the airport?"

"No thanks," Stephanie said. "Sally took good care of us."

"I'm fine too," Miriam said.

The two men stepped over to the buffet and started putting ice into their glasses. "I'm sure Sally told you we're going to be particularly diligent about security at these fundraisers," Stephenson said over his shoulder.

Miriam looked at Sally and smiled as the campaign manager, obviously comfortable in her role, joked, "Oh, no, Arthur, that never came up."

Miriam was momentarily focused on Sally, so she was taken by surprise when she glanced back at Stephanie and saw her friend, wide-eyed and open-mouthed, staring in the direction of the buffet. And then she turned and saw for herself the cause for alarm, and her blood seemed to turn to ice.

Martinez and Stephenson were chatting quietly between themselves as they poured Diet Coke into their glasses. Both men's faces were reflected in a mirrored surface on the top of the buffet. But only one of the reflections looked like the man standing over it. The other had the dark, wrinkled skin, thin lips and broad, hooked nose of an elderly Egyptian.

Chapter 16

ANWAR STUDIED HIS reflection in the bathroom mirror. They had seen him, he was sure of it. And he'd seen them. The odd thing was, when he had noticed their dumbfounded expressions he had quickly glanced back at the mirrored surface of the buffet table and looked at their faces, and the pudgy, dark-haired one looked the same. The pretty little blond, on the other hand, was different. The reflection he saw of her was a brown-haired, teenaged Jewess. Still pretty—beautiful, in fact—but obviously a Jew nonetheless.

He didn't understand the whole reflection thing. Didn't understand any of it, really. And didn't care to. All he cared about was that he had the ability to move freely from one living body to another, and this ability had made him rich. And immortal. He knew there were others with this power—the Jewess his most recent example—and ordinarily they were of no concern unless they discovered him. And then they were a problem. And, to Anwar, problems had to be eliminated. He had come too far over too long a period to stop now. True power—the power of the highest office of the mightiest nation on earth—was within his grasp. And he *would* grasp it. And he would use it. And God help any poor soul who tried to stand in his way.

He continued to study the face looking back at him. It was not a handsome face—far from it—but it was *his* face. A face weathered by age and hardship, a face that had been ignored by the people of his day. Almost as if he'd been invisible. A non-entity. Well, he was damn sure an entity now. Sometimes he wished that the snobby bastards who had looked down on him when that was his face could see him today. But they'd all been worm food for almost two centuries now, so he supposed he'd won by a long shot. But he'd love to be able to rub their noses in it. Oh, how he would love to be able to do that.

He remembered every detail of that fateful day. A day when it had seemed his life was at its end. But it wasn't. It was just beginning.

IN 1831, CAIRO was a bustling metropolis, home to a quarter of a million people. Most of them, like Anwar, were poor. There were only two classes of Egyptians for the most part—the rich and the poor. Certainly there were shop owners and skilled craftsmen who enjoyed comfortable, albeit hard-working, lives, but they were certainly not considered to be part of the elite. Except to a street merchant like Anwar. To the likes of him, they were fabulously wealthy.

He had been born in 1768 to a papyrus peddler. Afflicted with a club foot, Anwar was too handicapped to play sports and do many of the things the other school children could do—for which they teased him unmercifully—so he discontinued his education when he was twelve years old and worked full-time with his father. Every morning they slogged through the swamps along the Nile, gathering the papyrus shoots, which they carried back to their outdoor shop on the edge of the city. There they performed the dirty, smelly work of stripping the rinds, cutting and stacking the fibrous pith strips, and soaking the strips until they were ready to be hammered into sheets, dried in the sun, and then polished with smooth, round rocks. It was a laborious process, and not a very lucrative one. Their product was crude, nowhere near the quality required for use as writing paper, so they sold it to craftsmen who used it to make baskets, fish traps, and door mats.

When his father died in 1797, Anwar realized that, by himself, he couldn't manage to collect and process the papyrus on the same scale. So he started making baskets and floor mats himself, and peddling them on the streets of Cairo. He devoted five days a week to producing the papyrus and weaving his wares, and two days each week to selling them. He made no more money than he and his father had made, but the work was less demanding physically—he could at least sit while he was weaving—and there was one less mouth to feed. Two less after his mother died in 1802, leaving Anwar alone, but self-sufficient. He never married. He was never aware that he even attracted the attention of a woman unless it was for her to giggle at his deformity. Otherwise, he was just another haggard face in a city teeming with the downtrodden.

That was how he lived and worked until everything changed in 1831 with the arrival of four thousand pilgrims from Mecca. By then he was sixty-three years old, an old man still working seven days a week because the alternative was starvation. He was tired and weak, and was among the first to succumb when the cholera struck.

His initial symptom was the sudden onset of crippling diarrhea. Fortunately, it was a day when he was working at home, completing an order of two dozen baskets for a German shop owner who exported certain handmade items back to Hamburg. Anwar was barely able to work, the interruptions so frequent and severe. By that evening, the nausea started, followed by vomiting so forceful it felt as if his stomach would come up through his throat. That night, he hardly slept due to the muscle cramps in his legs that constricted so tightly he thought his bones might snap.

He finally fell asleep for a short while, awakening just as the sun was coming up. He had never been so thirsty in his life, but when he tried to drink a cup of water he immediately threw it up all over his bed mat. Too tired to even try to clean it up, he lay there and prayed that the rumbling in his stomach would cease. But it didn't. He managed to make it outside, where he left a pale, milky puddle of waste by his door. It was then that he heard the clatter of a wooden cart, and looked up to see Ammon, the sixteen year-old boy who worked for the German, approaching his door. He was coming to collect the baskets.

Anwar staggered back into the house to gather his product. If he was too sick to work, at least this sale would finance his food costs for a few days. Not that he was interested in food at the moment. The very thought of swallowing anything, even water to cool his parched throat, made him gag with revulsion. His one room house was tiny, but the distance to the far wall where the baskets were piled seemed like a mile. The next thing he knew, he was lying on the dirt floor, his head throbbing from its contact with a wooden chair on the way down.

"Anwar, are you alright?" It was Ammon, standing in his doorway.

Anwar lifted himself to a sitting position. "Yes, I'm okay," he lied. "I saw you coming and was hurrying to get the order ready. I tripped and fell."

The boy rushed to his side. "Your head is bleeding. Just sit here a minute and let me get some water to clean it."

Ammon grabbed a rag off the table and poured some water from the pitcher by the bed mat. "I was afraid you had the sickness," he said as he swabbed the old man's head wound.

"Sickness?" Anwar said, his tongue so thick and dry it was sticking to the roof of his mouth, making speech difficult.

"Yes, there is some kind of disease spreading through the city. I have heard that over a hundred people have already died. Many of them are pilgrims who just arrived from Mecca. But now others are getting it too. The people are starting to panic."

"I've been working here at home for the past three days," Anwar said. "I wasn't aware of a sickness."

"Oh, it's terrible," the boy said. "Diarrhea, nausea, vomiting. Some people, especially the elderly and small children, die within a day or two. When I saw you on the floor here I was afraid you had it, and wasn't going to come in. But then I saw the blood on your head and knew you had fallen. Otherwise, I would have had to tell the authorities, who would put you in quarantine with the others. They are saying the disease is highly contagious."

Anwar was not concerned with infecting others. He just knew that if he was quarantined with hundreds of people infected with the disease, he would surely die. Better to take his chances here alone. Which meant he could not let Ammon know he'd been bedridden for the past day and a half with the very same symptoms the boy had described.

"Those who are able are leaving Cairo," Ammon was saying. "My boss, Herr Richter, is leaving tomorrow to sail back to Germany." The boy was beaming now. "And this time he's taking me with him as part of his work crew. I will finally get a chance to leave Egypt. Even if I have to come back when he returns next year, it will be a great experience!"

It was at that precise moment that Anwar realized two things. One was that, inexplicably, he could leave his tired, sickly, deformed old shell and jump to the strapping sixteen year-old body kneeling next to him. The other was that he would leave Egypt and never return.

THE TRAIN TRIP to Alexandria had been uneventful. Herr Richter had barely spoken to the boy before boarding his first class coach as the four man work crew climbed into an open boxcar. But the large seaport city had also been struck by the disease, and everyone, including Herr Richter, was quarantined for three days before being allowed to board the ship. For the first few days of the voyage, Anwar feared he might have again contracted the disease, but eventually realized the nausea and vomiting were due to sea sickness, not cholera. There was no work to do on board, so he used the free time—when he wasn't retching—to learn some basic conversational German from Ernst, the only German boy on the crew.

Other than for the sea sickness, the three week voyage was like a holiday for Anwar. Three meals a day, a relatively clean bed with an actual mattress, and no work to do. And when he finally got his sea legs and climbed up to the deck of the ship where there was a limited area for his lowly travel class, he was awestruck by the expanse and bright blue color of the ocean. The only body of water he'd seen in his entire life had been the muddy Nile, and he felt this was just the first example of the wide new world awaiting him.

When they disembarked in Germany, he was amazed and delighted by the coolness of the air and the fact that everything was so green. Other than fields of hay, he saw no scenes dominated by the dull brown hues of Egypt. He felt he had arrived in Paradise.

Herr Richter did not actually live in Hamburg, as Anwar had thought, but on a farm about twenty kilometers north of the city. He would come to realize that the stone farmhouse was not extravagant by European standards, but with four bedrooms for only one man and a house servant, it seemed like a palace to Anwar. His quarters were in a small bunk house that he shared with Ernst and the other two workmen. They often complained about their accommodations, but he never did. Nor did he complain about the work. Farm labor was actually the easiest work he'd ever done, and he had a strong young body with which to perform it. But he had his sights set on the house servant position. To live in that grand house—and have daily access to Herr Richter—became his goal, and he was relentless in its pursuit.

The house servant was a middle-aged man named Franz Wolff. Anwar always addressed him as *Herr Wolff*, in deference to the older man's elevated job status. He always finished his assigned chores before the other farm workers, and started hanging around the kitchen, offering his help with washing and peeling vegetables, cutting meat, and other menial kitchen tasks. Anwar used their time together to further improve his language skills and to learn how to cook Herr Richter's favorite foods. After three months of voluntary kitchen servitude, he felt he was ready, and started using his kitchen access to sprinkle gradually increasing doses of rat poison from the barn into Herr Wolff's food.

It took only a few days for Herr Wolff to start complaining of headaches and diarrhea. A few evenings later Anwar walked into the kitchen to find the older man asleep at the kitchen table, a knife and a heap of unpeeled potatoes by his head. When Anwar tried to awaken him, the man seemed confused and disoriented. Anwar immediately alerted Herr Richter and, after helping Wolff to his bed, offered to complete the preparations for dinner.

The soup which Anwar fed to the house servant over the next week was laced with increasing doses of the poison. When Wolff began suffering convulsions and soaked his bed with bloody urine, a country doctor was summoned, but he attributed the symptoms to a severe stroke and internal hemorrhaging. Ten days after the start of the arsenic regimen, Herr Wolff died, and Anwar—who had by now aptly demonstrated his cooking abilities and diligent work ethic—was promoted to the position of house servant.

Now it was just a matter of waiting for the right opportunity, which presented itself three months later. Herr Richter instructed the three farmhands to drive a herd of sheep to auction a few kilometers south of Hamburg. Because of the travel distance and the entire day devoted to the auction, they would be gone for two nights. That was all the time Anwar needed.

On the morning of their departure, Anwar waited four hours before gathering an ample supply of silverware, along with the contents of the wooden petty cash box kept in the back of a supply closet, stuffing them into a burlap sack and hurrying out to the pond behind the barn. Filling the sack the remainder of the way with rocks, he tied the end of the bag securely and hurled it out to the middle of the pond. On the way back to the house he stopped in the barn for a coil of rope, and then hurried back to the kitchen to complete preparations for lunch.

Precisely at twelve-thirty, as was customary, he called Herr Richter from his study into the dining room, where a steaming bowl of potato soup and a small loaf of fresh baked bread awaited him. Anwar did not tell his master that he had not baked the apple strudel for dessert as he'd been instructed. The man would not be needing dessert today.

As soon as Herr Richter was seated, he bowed his head in prayer, as he did before every meal. Anwar used that opportunity to strike a measured blow to the back of the man's head with a pewter candle holder. He had been careful not to inflict permanent damage, but Richter was out cold for several minutes. When he came to, he was tied securely to his chair with a strand of rope, and found himself staring at the tip of a large kitchen knife positioned an inch from his left eye. He looked back and forth from the tip of the blade to the face of the boy poised mere inches from his own, seeming to have great difficulty processing the terrifying scene.

"Ammon...*Mein Gott*...what is the meaning of this?" he sputtered. "Have you gone mad?"

Anwar glared at him, an evil scowl on his youthful face. "Perhaps. But that doesn't matter. What matters is that you answer my questions...quickly and truthfully. If you don't, I'm afraid the next two days will be the most painful you've ever experienced."

Richter stared at him disbelievingly, fear raging in his eyes. "And if I answer your questions, will I live?"

At that, Anwar smiled. "Yes, you will. This body has many more fruitful years remaining. I promise you that."

Richter seemed confused by the answer, but no more confused than he was by the entire situation. "What...what is it you want to know?"

"We will start with your bank accounts. Where are they, how much money is in them, and how do I access them?"

Richter's eyes went even wider and he shook his head violently. "This is absurd! I demand you untie me and leave my home immediately. I'll give you until tomorrow morning before I notify the authorities."

Anwar positioned his thumb about an inch from the tip of the knife and jammed it into Richter's shoulder. The damage was minimal but the pain was immense, causing the man to howl in agony. It was the beginning of a horrific afternoon and night.

BY THE TIME the sun filtered through the windows the following morning, Richter was soaked in blood from over two dozen puncture wounds to his arms and legs. Despite repeated threats to the contrary, his eyes had been spared. But perhaps the most agonizing times of the entire ordeal were the multiple times he'd been strangled with a two foot piece of rope until he lost consciousness. Each time he was slapped awake, the most recent question was repeated, and the blade of the knife inflicted yet another excruciating cut. The man was only in his mid-forties and had always been of robust health, but the shock, pain and blood loss were taking their toll. Anwar gave it until noon, and then decided he should not risk further damage. Richter may have withheld some information, but Anwar had gained enough to suit his needs.

Richter had come to terms with the fact that his Egyptian house servant had ruthlessly betrayed him and stolen access to his wealth, and had already assumed that he would die soon from either the rope or the knife. He was therefore completely unprepared when the boy sat down on the floor at his feet, smiled, and brandished the knife once more before thrusting it deeply and forcefully into his own abdomen. The wound, which must have been more painful than anything Richter had endured, was not immediately fatal, but Richter knew the boy would bleed out in a matter of minutes. He was thoroughly confused and horrified by this turn of events, but started to harbor the hope of surviving the ordeal. And then the boy grasped his leg tightly, looked up at him, and smiled. And everything faded away.

ERNST AND HIS two companions were horrified with the scene that awaited them when they returned the following afternoon. Their master, still bound to a dining room chair with rope, had been tortured nearly to death. Ammon, the young house servant, had been brutally murdered. The constable made note of the stolen silver and surmised that cash had been taken from the wooden box found on the kitchen floor, and his team scoured the countryside looking for the murdering thief. But no arrest was ever made, and the case remained unsolved.

Herr Richter recovered fully from his wounds, except for the damage to his vocal cords that had been inflicted with multiple strangulations. As a result, he spoke in a hoarse whisper, and used as few words as possible because of the discomfort caused by talking. This, of course, had all been part of Anwar's plan. Simple sentences disguised his limited German vocabulary, although he continued to master the language by listening and reading. He hired an attorney to handle the sale of his business in Cairo—he had no intent of ever again setting foot on Egyptian soil—and settled into the simple, comfortable lifestyle of a moderately wealthy German landowner.

Life was good until about twelve years later when he began to develop painful arthritis. At first he managed his way through it with analgesic prescriptions from his doctor, but then concluded there was no reason for him to suffer continuous discomfort. He deposited the majority of his money in bank accounts in Geneva, and started spending more time in Hamburg, where he frequented the social haunts of the wealthy. He befriended an unmarried thirty-year-old heir to a coal mining fortune, and poor Herr Richter died of unexplained, but by all appearances natural, causes, and the wealthy playboy heir moved to Berlin.

That worked well for over twenty-five years, and then it was on to a diamond merchant, a move that virtually doubled his already extensive financial portfolio. That ended up being the longest time he had ridden a single host, but human bodies aren't designed to last forever and he'd been forced to make a drastic unplanned move into the body of a young nurse. But that had indeed been a fortuitous move, because it resulted in his introduction to a strange yet charismatic army corporal in Pasewalk at the end of the Great War.

Leading the creation of the Third Reich was the most exhilarating thing Anwar could have imagined. He knew from the beginning it was doomed, but he also knew he would live to walk away from it and couldn't resist the fun. Despite what the historians would come to say, he accomplished great things, not the least of which was the extermination of over six million Jews. He didn't know why he hated Jews so much—he supposed it was deeply engrained in his Arabic heritage—but he always had. And still did. He also hated and refused to tolerate anyone who criticized him openly. Dr. Edmund Forster, the psychiatrist at Pasewalk Military Hospital who had sullied the reputation of the young corporal with his blatantly irresponsible diagnosis—*a psychopath with hysterical symptoms*—had learned that lesson some fifteen years later.

On April 30, 1945, Anwar had moved into the body of a young army lieutenant as Berlin lay in smoldering ruins above his bunker. A carefully placed bullet into the head of the Fuhrer's corpse, followed by the burning of the body in a courtyard as the Russians closed in, was the stuff of which legends are made. It still made Anwar smile.

Twenty years in Brazil, followed by thirty more raising cattle in Honduras, had finally led him to America. And now, standing in front of a bathroom mirror at the Rosewood Mansion on Turtle Creek in Dallas, he was on the verge of parlaying his quarter of a century in the United States into his greatest achievement ever. Everything had been planned perfectly, executed perfectly. There were threats to his plans—there always were threats to the plans of the great—but the only threat he perceived to be significant was that posed by the unexpected appearance of a Jewess and her pudgy young associate. But that threat would be eliminated. Within the week, he'd been promised. And people didn't break promises to Anwar.

Chapter 17

MIRIAM AND STEPHANIE barely spoke during the ride back to the airport. Whether it was the shock of their discovery or the fear of being overheard by the driver—or both—Miriam couldn't be sure, but she kept her mouth shut until they were out of the car and walking through the entrance to Terminal B. Then she exploded.

"Peter's going to go nuts!" she exclaimed. "This is exactly the kind of thing he fears most. He's probably going to insist I quit my job. And frankly, I'm inclined to think that would be wise."

Stephanie's response was immediate. "If you're gonna quit, you can do it two weeks from today, and not one day sooner. You are going to help me get through this dinner. Remember what you said on Monday, that I'd be able to count on you *no matter what it takes*?"

Miriam stopped and turned to face the woman she'd known just a week, but who she was quickly coming to consider a friend. "To be fair, Steph, I said that in response to your concerns about my financial status."

"I don't care if it's your money or your secret that you're really a seven hundred year old woman in a twenty-something year old body, you are *not* deserting me at this stage of the game! Especially after what we've just seen."

Miriam took a deep breath, glancing around to make sure no one was close enough to hear their conversation. "Okay, you're right. I owe it to you to see this through. But Peter was seriously considering backing out of the house deal and moving somewhere else just because of you and Allen. When he hears about this, there may be no stopping him. He's absolutely paranoid about protecting our identities."

"Then don't tell him," Stephanie suggested.

"That would never work," Miriam said, shaking her head. She smiled, "One of the downsides of living with the same man for almost seven centuries is that he gets to the point where he can read you like a book."

"Let's hope I never get to test that theory," Stephanie said. "I've yet to meet a man I could stay with for seven *weeks* without considering a bullet to the head." She grinned. "His, of course. Not mine."

Miriam sighed. "I'll still need to tell Peter. Tonight."

"Need moral support?"

"I'll probably need help restraining him from packing our bags and loading the car," she said, knowing the comment was not entirely in jest. "So yeah, why don't I call him and tell him you're stopping by for a glass of wine on your way home from the airport?"

Stephanie thought for a moment, and then said, "What do you think about getting Allen to stop by too? We might as well get all of us immortals in the same room at the same time."

"You're not immortal until your gene mutates," Miriam corrected.

Stephanie smiled. "Then find me a man with a dozen STDs. If I need to get a deadly bug, I might as well have some fun doing it."

FORTUNATELY, THEIR FLIGHT landed right on time at six-thirty, and by seven-fifteen Miriam was pulling into her parking space outside the apartment. Stephanie was right behind her. Peter had seemed a little suspicious when Miriam had called from DFW and asked if it would be alright for Steph and Allen to stop by for some wine and cheese to debrief about their big day in Dallas— including a face-to-face with Robert Martinez himself— but he'd agreed to make a run to Piggly Wiggly to get what they needed. He was always so intent on pleasing her, and Miriam felt guilty knowing he was in for some very distressing news. And that it was all because of her insistence on getting a job, despite his now somewhat prophetic protestations. But at least it would give him a chance to meet Allen and to get to know Stephanie a little better. Maybe being in the presence of other riders would instill a sense of calm. Or maybe that was just wishful thinking.

She got out of her car and was waiting by the door for Stephanie, only to see Allen emerge from a black Audi a few spaces down. "Been waiting long?" she asked as he approached.

"Just ten minutes or so," he said. "I've been listening to the news on NPR."

"You had the apartment number. Why didn't you go on in to meet Peter?"

He cocked his head and smiled. "You'd actually trust me alone in an apartment with your man?"

She laughed. "Good point. Peter's always played for the other team, but then again, he hasn't met *you* yet."

He pointed a finger at her. "Precisely. Never trust a man to resist temptation from a diva." He bowed with a flourish. "And I, sweetheart, have had my share of curtain calls."

"You're not doing that *diva* shtick again, are you?" Stephanie said, joining them.

"Listen, dearie," Allen said, "just because my balls are employed in a different manner than the ones to which you've been exposed, doesn't mean you must feel compelled to bust them all the time."

Miriam pointed the palms of both hands at them. "Okay, okay. Can we clean it up before we go inside? My poor Peter is in for a rough night."

"Ooh," Allen cooed. "Wish I could say the same for mine."

Miriam shook her head as she inserted the key in the door and pushed it open. "Peter," she called, "the gang's all here."

He met her in the foyer with a kiss, and then turned to his guests. "Hi Steph," he said before thrusting a hand at Allen. "You must be Allen. I'm Peter."

"My pleasure," Allen said. "Thank you for throwing this impromptu soiree."

Peter laughed. "I don't know if wine and cheese qualifies as a soiree, but come on in. I set up a tray in the living room. The cheeses are Italian, so I can offer Pinot Grigio and a Barolo."

Allen elbowed Miriam in the side and whispered, "Well, didn't you just win the grand prize of husbands? *Congratulazione.*"

She smiled. "Yeah, he's a keeper, alright."

They took seats in the living room and Peter proceeded to pour the wine. "Nice apartment," Stephanie said.

"Yes," Allen said, looking around, "but it could use a little feminine touch. Let me know if you'd like for me to stop by this weekend and fluff it a little."

Stephanie looked at Peter. "He's talking about the apartment...I think."

They all laughed and Peter said, "So, tell us about your visit with the man who you think might someday be the leader of the free world."

"Actually," Stephanie said, "we met both Martinez and his chief of staff, Arthur Stephenson. I got the impression that if Martinez was ever elected president, they'd be sharing the power...*a la* Bush-Cheney."

"Interesting," Peter said. "But if that's the case, you might want to tell Martinez to never let Stephenson take him quail hunting."

There was more joking and casual chatter as everyone sampled the cheeses and took their first sip of wine. But when Miriam and Stephanie began sharing the details of their day, the joking and chatter ceased. Within minutes, there wasn't a smile left in the room.

AS MIRIAM HAD expected, Peter was extremely distressed by the discovery of another rider. At first he simply sat staring at the two women, apparently stunned speechless. But then he recovered enough to put voice to his concerns, which were numerous.

"This is bad on so many levels," he said. "First and foremost, for the country. This man, who isn't at all who he appears to the rest of the world to be, is poised to possibly gain immense power. And you say he looked to be Middle Eastern?"

"Yes," Miriam said. "I'd say Egyptian, but he could be from a neighboring country. It was hard to tell exactly, and I was trying not to stare."

"Well," Peter said, "at the expense of being politically incorrect, the prospect of someone from that region of the world secretly gaining even partial control of this country scares the hell out of me. We have no way of knowing how long he's been a rider, so I suppose he could be a third or fourth generation American who's loyal to our way of life, but I wouldn't bet three hundred million lives on it."

"I agree," Stephanie said. "I mean, the three of you are honorable"—she glanced at Allen and winked—"or, at least, two of you are, but your main focus is on keeping a low profile. Here we have someone who is doing the exact opposite, and you really have to wonder about his motivations."

"And then there's the personal risk to the two of you," Peter said, looking back and forth between Miriam and Stephanie. "If he realizes you saw him, he'll conclude you pose a great risk to him achieving his goals, whatever they are."

Stephanie shook her head. "I don't think he saw us."

"But you can't be sure," Peter countered. "And if he did, how far do you think he might go to protect himself?"

"But what can we do?" Miriam asked, her own frustration mounting. "We can't go to Mark, or the police, or the FBI, or anywhere else and tell them about this. First, anyone we tell will probably want to have us institutionalized. And even if someone did believe us—and that's a huge *if*—it puts all four of us at risk. Peter's always been extremely focused on protecting our secret. We've only been compromised twice by other riders in almost seven hundred years. And one of those was minimal risk, if any at all. Just a passing glance at our reflections, which we noticed and, seeing hers as well, we simply disappeared into a crowd. But even then we changed locations and identities, just to be safe."

"And the other time?" Allen asked.

"The other time was a little more involved," Peter said. "Let's just leave it at that. The point is, Miriam and I could leave Birmingham tonight and be in a different country with all new documentation by the end of next week. And that's what I'm seriously considering right this minute."

"No!" Stephanie exclaimed, almost shouting. "Please, let's think this through. I can't pull this fundraiser off without your help, Miriam. Especially under these circumstances." She turned to Peter. "And there's a lot I need to learn from you. Allen and me both. Our day will come when we'll need to disappear. And even if one day I have the ability to jump to another body, I won't take someone else's life just to get away from a threat. Not unless it's a last resort, at least. I need to know how you do it. I need to be prepared."

"Me too," Allen said. "I've been lucky these past thirty years, but I can't depend on luck forever. I need to learn what seven centuries of subterfuge has taught you."

Peter sighed, drained his glass of wine and poured another before leveling his eyes on his two guests. "Please try to understand. I've known the two of you an extremely short time. You both seem to be good people, with pure intentions. But I have to put Miriam first. And that means putting me right beside her on the priority list, because nothing on earth is more important to me than being there to protect her. So I'd like to help the two of you; I honestly would. But unless you're willing to receive that help in another city, if not another country, I don't think I'm going to be able to do anything for you."

"But he may not have even seen us," Stephanie said, her voice fraught with desperation. "And if he didn't see us, he wouldn't have any reason to expect we saw the real him. There may not be any risk here."

"So what do you do?" Peter demanded. "Wait around and see what happens, just assuming everything will be okay? I tried that once, and it almost destroyed us. I won't let that happen again."

Stephanie slumped back on the sofa as she fought back tears. "I understand; I really do. It's just that, until I saw Miriam in the mirror at work and then met you and heard your story and your hypothesis on the gene mutation, I didn't know what the hell was going on. I just knew that Allen's reflection was that of a black man, and nobody other than me seemed to be able to see that. I thought I was going crazy. And then you two come along and it makes sense to me. It's surreal—bordering on fantasy—but it makes sense. I don't think I could handle losing the two of you so quickly. I don't think I could make…" She suddenly started sobbing, her whole body convulsing as she buried her face in her hands and wept uncontrollably.

Miriam moved to the sofa beside Stephanie and put her arm around her shoulder, pulling her tight to her and stroking her hair. Looking up at Peter she mouthed the word *Please*.

Peter finally gave a slight nod, the movement of his head almost imperceptible. He allowed Stephanie another minute to regain her composure, and then said, "If I gave you four or five days, what do you think you'd be able to find out that would indicate whether or not he realized you saw him?"

Stephanie lifted her head and wiped her nose with the napkin she'd been using to hold cheese and crackers. Her eyes, although reddened and swollen, suddenly looked hopeful. "I'll be talking to Sally McDaniel next week. I'll check in with her at the beginning of the week instead of the middle, as I'd promised. If anything is different about her attitude—even the tone of her voice—I'll tell you. I promise."

She blew her nose and then continued. "I'll also have Senator Carson call Martinez or Stephenson, whichever one he can reach. He's actually the host of the dinner, so it would be a natural courtesy for him to call and make sure the PR firm he employed is meeting their expectations, especially since they met us in person today. I'll come up with some reason as to why I might be worried, so that he'll do a little fishing. Again, if either of them says anything to him that indicates nervousness or *anything* out of the ordinary, I'll tell you."

Peter sighed. "Okay. I don't like this at all, but okay. See what you can find out, over the weekend if possible. We'll meet again next week, Tuesday or Wednesday, and do another risk assessment. But

I want to be clear—if there's so much as a hint of evidence that you two were exposed, Miriam and I are out of here. And believe me, you'll never find us."

Stephanie nodded. "That's fair. Thank you."

Peter inhaled deeply and downed the rest of his wine. "I just hope this doesn't turn out to be Milan all over again."

PETER WAS GLAD it was a Friday night so that neither he nor Miriam would have to get up early the next morning. He had a feeling both of them were in for a restless night. He could hardly believe what had transpired in the ten days since they'd arrived in Birmingham. So much for the slow, easy pace of life in the Deep South. Things were happening faster than he could process them, and that scared him. He missed the solitude and serenity of life on Lake Mohawk.

At one point, about two hours after Stephanie and Allen had left, he walked into the bedroom where Miriam was getting undressed and said, "I want you to pack a bag before you go to bed."

Her eyes bore into him. "What? Peter, you promised."

"Not for tonight," he said, holding up his hands as if to stave off a verbal attack. "I just want to be ready. Pack a bag with essentials, including your passport, and a few days of clothes. Keep it in the closet. If we need to, I want us to be ready to walk out this door with a minute's notice. I'm flexing more on this than my brain tells me I should, so support me on this, okay?"

She walked around the bed and put her head on his shoulder, her arms encircling his waist. "I know you think we should leave tonight. And I know you aren't convinced that we're not in danger. I appreciate your willingness to flex a little." She looked up into his eyes and kissed him. "And I appreciate your concern for me. More than you could ever know."

As he expected, sleep did not come easily. And, as he expected, when he finally did fall asleep, the memories of Milan two and a quarter centuries earlier haunted his dreams.

Chapter 18

PETER AND MIRIAM settled back in their box seats in *Teatro alla Scala*, known locally as *La Scala*, and by most of Europe simply as the Milan Opera House. The magnificent house was packed, the crowd drawn by a much anticipated revival of Monteverdi's *L'Orfeo*, considered by many music aficionados to be the first true opera ever composed. If not the first one, certainly the first truly great one. It was based on the legend of Orpheus, the ancient Greek musician, poet and prophet, who descended into Hades in a fruitless attempt to bring his dead bride, Eurydice, back to the living. The production had been billed as sensational, both visually and musically, and the audience was rapt with anticipation.

Miriam leaned over to Peter as the curtain started to rise and whispered, "Would you venture into hell to bring me back?"

He smiled and lifted her hand to his lips. "Don't be ridiculous. You would never be in hell in the first place. Angels belong in heaven."

"Don't dodge the question," she said, arching her brows.

"Then yes," he said, giving her hand a squeeze. "I'd follow you to hell or anywhere else. You should know that by now."

"I do," she said, smiling warmly. "I just like hearing it from time to time."

They'd been in Milan almost twenty years and loved the Lombardy lifestyle, especially the cuisine. Peter had to work constantly to keep the risotto and Panettone from beefing up his sixty-year-old frame. He had jumped to the body of Janos Szabo, a wealthy Hungarian railroad owner when he and Miriam were preparing to leave Budapest, after spending two generations in that grand city. Their liquid assets, the bulk of which resided in banks in Geneva, had now grown to considerable proportions. Still, they lived somewhat modestly in a brownstone on Via Spadori, a short walk from *La Scala*.

Miriam inhabited the body of Szabo's housekeeper who, although ten years younger than her employer, had been rumored to be his lover. Whether their bodies had actually connected in their former lives would never be known for sure, but they had certainly connected over the past twenty years as Peter and Miriam Lengyel, a handsome, quiet Hungarian couple permanently residing in Milan.

The first two acts of the opera were everything Peter had expected, and he applauded enthusiastically as the curtain closed for intermission. He stood to stretch his legs for a moment before leaning down to Miriam and saying, "I think a glass of champagne would be nice."

She readily agreed, and they joined the slow moving exodus to the lobby. Once they had their wine and were strolling between the columns in the grand foyer as they admired the paintings and sculpted busts, Peter noticed a man who seemed to be following them. He was a younger man, mid-forties perhaps, with dark, wavy hair and a thin moustache. Despite his young age, he carried a cane, which he didn't appear to use for support, but simply as an accessory. He kept looking at Peter, studying his face as if he thought he was familiar. But he kept his distance, and looked away whenever Peter tried to make eye contact. It made Peter nervous, fearing that it could be someone who had known Jonas Szabo twenty years earlier. If that were the case, the man would have been no more than a boy at the time, which could explain his reluctance to approach Peter.

But the man was definitely following them, never letting them out of his sight. Finally, as a bellman walked through the foyer ringing a chime to signify that the opera was about to resume, the young man with the moustache appeared to overcome his reluctance and strolled up to Peter, his head cocked quizzically to one side. "Pardon me," he said, "but aren't you Jonas Szabo from Budapest?"

Peter did his best to express confusion, not fear, and said, "No, I'm afraid you're mistaken. I've never been to Budapest."

"So sorry," the man said, slowly backing away, but still studying Peter's face. "The resemblance is remarkable."

Miriam's eyes also reflected alarm, but she said nothing as she took Peter's arm and the two of them walked casually toward the staircase. As they ascended the stairs and turned the corner on the first landing, Peter glanced back and saw the man was still behind them, and still looking at him. The handle of the cane was hooked over his right arm, differentiating him from the hundreds of other men who were all dressed in similar formal evening attire. Wanting to keep an eye on the man without being obvious about it, Peter kept his gaze forward and used a wall mirror on the landing to scan the crowd behind him. But the young man no longer seemed to be there, although there was a man carrying a cane—an older man with straight gray hair tied back in a ponytail, revealing a jagged scar on his left temple. Confused, Peter turned and looked, and there was the young face with the thin moustache. Panicking, he quickly turned back to the mirror, and locked eyes with the gray haired man, who smiled knowingly as he nodded at Peter's reflection.

FOR SEVERAL DAYS following the encounter with the other rider at the opera, Peter was painfully cautious whenever he went out, and didn't allow Miriam out on the street unless he was by her side. Despite the frequent feeling that he was being watched, he never saw anything out of the ordinary, and began to think he was being paranoid. So what if another rider recognized him as the former Janos Szabo and knew from the reflection in the mirror that he was no longer that man? The other man was likely protective of his own true identity as well—he'd be crazy not to be—so what would he stand to gain by trying to expose Peter? The smile and nod of recognition were probably just a discreet way of saying *I see you and you see me; we share the same secret.*

One morning, after a week of guarded vigilance, Miriam finally persuaded him to let her venture out to the butcher shop and the bakery without him. "I'll get some veal and make Picatta Milanese for dinner," she said. "And I'll pick up a loaf of the Tuscan flatbread you like so much, so you can sop up the sauce like a peasant."

"That sounds wonderful," he said. "Just be careful. If you see anyone that resembles our friend from *La Scala,* I want you to come straight home, okay?"

"The shops are only two blocks from here," she said. "And it's broad daylight. No one is going to accost me on a busy street. Don't worry."

"I can't help but worry." He smiled. "It's my nature."

"I know you're just being protective of me, *kochanka,*" she said, rising on her toes to kiss his cheek. "But we can't live in constant fear, or we'll become reclusive hermits."

"I don't want that either, but when we encounter a threat…"

"If it's a true threat, then we should leave Milan," she said, impatiently. "But we both love it here. Neither of us wants to do that."

He put his arms around her and kissed her forehead. "No, we don't. I know I tend to be overly cautious, so just humor me and be very careful. Please."

"I'm always careful," she said. "Now, I'm off. I'm getting the food, so you're in charge of finding a wine that will do my veal justice. I'll be back in an hour."

Peter knew she was right, that he was attaching too much significance to a one-time, random encounter, but he still couldn't stop himself from worrying the moment she walked out the door. He decided he should keep himself busy to make the time pass more quickly, and went into the kitchen to clean up their breakfast dishes. When there was a knock on the door a half hour later, his first inclination was to ignore it and pretend no one was home. But a moment later there was a second knock, this time louder and more insistent, so he sighed and went to the door.

When he opened it, he was surprised to find a small boy, no more than nine or ten, standing at the door with his cap in his hand. He was breathing heavily, as if he'd been running. "Signore Lengyel?" he panted.

"Yes," Peter said, surprised to hear his name spoken by someone he was certain he'd never seen before. "Who are you?"

"I'm Benito," the boy said, looking around nervously. "My father owns the bakery where your wife shops. She was talking to my father and she said she felt ill, and then she fainted. My father sent me for you."

"Oh, my God!" exclaimed Peter, grabbing his coat from a hook behind the door and rushing out into the street. "Hurry! Take me there!"

The boy took off running, with Peter on his heels. After one block the boy turned right. This surprised Peter, because the bakery he had been to with Miriam was one street over to the left, but he supposed she may have gone to a different one for the flatbread. The boy ran another block and was halfway down a second one when he abruptly turned into a long alley.

"Where are we going?" Peter yelled, nearly out of breath.

"My father took her to the back so she could lie on a cot until you got there," the boy said, as he stopped in front of a large wooden door. "In here," he said, opening the door and pointing inside.

Peter rushed into a dark, cavernous space, apparently a storage room. Or at least, what used to be a storage room. Now it was almost empty, except for some old barrels caked in dust, and some links of heavy chain hanging from the rafters, garlanded with cobwebs. He stopped and turned back to address the boy, but the door to the alley slammed shut with a loud bang, plunging the room into near-total darkness.

Peter stood still, trying to adjust his eyes to the diminished light, when he heard the scuffle of feet and turned to see a figure emerging from the darkness to his right. The figure was about his height, and perhaps a bit slimmer, and it was carrying something long and narrow. A cane.

"I cannot tell you how delighted I was to see you again after all these years, Mr. Szabo," the man said cheerfully. "Or, I guess it's Mr. Lengyel now."

Peter's mind was racing as fast as his pulse, but he managed to calm himself enough to ask, "You've been following me?"

"Of course," the man said. "It was such a shock to see a face from the past, I just had to investigate. Following you and your lovely wife home was no problem, and it was then just a matter of watching your house and waiting for an appropriate time for us to have a little chat."

Miriam! Had he done something to Miriam? "Where is my wife?" he demanded.

The man chuckled. It was a sinister sound. "The last time I saw her she was entering a bakery a few blocks from here. I have no idea where she is now. She's not my concern. You are."

Peter took a deep breath. At least Miriam was alright, if this strange, disturbing man was to be believed. "What is it you want?"

"I knew dear Janos twenty or so years ago," the man said. "He was very wealthy, and my host at the time was approaching fifty, so I thought he'd be worth a short ride. Just a year or so…long enough to get the money secured. But, lo and behold, poor Janos suddenly disappeared from the face of the earth. You can't imagine my disappointment. I had to spend another six months in a worn out old body searching for another suitable replacement—and, by suitable, I mean young, handsome and rich—which, as you can see, I did. But he was not as wealthy as Szabo, and my lifestyle sometimes can border on extravagant, so now I find myself in need of additional financing. And then, miraculously, I go out for a night at the opera and *voila*, there you are."

Now Peter understood. "So it's money you want."

"Precisely," the man said.

"How much?"

The man, now slightly more visible since Peter's eyes had adjusted to the darkness, shifted the cane to his right hand and held it by the tip. "All of it."

He started to circle to his right, as did Peter, matching him step for step. He knew he was at a severe disadvantage. Not only was the other man younger and undoubtedly stronger, he had a weapon. Peter flexed his empty hands. He'd had a few fights through the years, but he certainly wasn't a brawler, and with his fists alone was no match for a man brandishing a heavy baton. He needed a weapon. And he needed some time to think.

"Killing me won't get you what you want," he said, trying to buy some time before the battle began.

"I have no intention of killing you, Mr. Lengyel. I intend to *become* you."

Peter was confused. "How will you do that? I'll fight you. My will is as strong as yours; maybe even stronger. I won't let you jump into me."

The man continued to circle to his right. "Well, you won't have any fight in you if you're unconscious, right? I'll have to explain my injuries after I wake up, but I'll just say I was the victim of a mugging."

Peter continued to dart his eyes from side to side, looking for either a weapon or a means of escape. "Even jumping to me won't automatically put you in possession of my money," he said, still trying to buy time.

"No," the man said, with an edge to his voice, "but it will put me in possession of your wife. And once I'm through with her, I'll have the money. You can be sure of that."

If Peter needed an incentive to act, that was it. He feinted a step forward and, noticing the way the other man positioned his feet, ducked just as the heavy cane whizzed a mere inch above the top of his head. The man had put his full weight into the swing and was off balance after missing his target, giving Peter the opportunity to throw a kick, which landed solidly on his attacker's thigh. Peter heard a groan, but the damage appeared to be minimal as the man whipped around and raised the cane back over his head, poised to attack again.

Desperate to find something to use to defend himself, Peter suddenly remembered the heavy chains hanging from the rafters. He backed up slowly, keeping his eyes on the cane waving menacingly back and forth.

"You can try to make a run for the door if you want, but it's barricaded from the other side," the man said, breathing heavily. "And you can scream if it'll make you feel better. I doubt anyone will hear you, and even if they do, they won't get back here before my work is done."

Peter kept backing up until he felt a length of chain brushing his right shoulder. Quickly he moved to the other side of it, grasping it firmly in both hands. If nothing else, it limited the other man's attack options, making another roundhouse swing less likely. Hitting the taut chain instead of Peter's head or body might possibly break the cane. Peter felt the more obvious move would now be a vertical swing, which the man attempted, but missed by a foot or more when Peter jumped to the side.

"Rather light on your feet for an old man," his assailant snarled. "Or maybe just lucky. But now you have a dilemma." He raised the cane straight over his head, holding it with both hands. "My next swing may be to the left of the chain, or it may be to the right. If you guess correctly and duck in the opposite direction, I'll just swing again. If you guess wrong, our little game of chase will be over."

Peter knew he was right. In that way, the chain was working against him. But it still felt better to have something in his hands. And then it occurred to him how he could use the chain more defensively. He slowly lowered his left hand as he raised his right, until there were about two feet of chain between them. Tightening his grip so much his hands ached, he waited for another swing.

He didn't have to wait long. The other man took a long step forward and swung violently, aiming to the left of the chain. But it didn't matter which side he attacked. Peter had no intention of dodging the cane. Instead, he stepped into it, raising the two foot length of chain above his head and using it to absorb the impact. As soon as he felt the cane connect, he charged the other man, both falling to the floor in a tumble of sweat and dust. Fueled by visions of the man hurting Miriam, Peter drove his fist into the man's ribs repeatedly, certain he heard a crack after several blows. The man screamed in pain, but kept fighting, trying to use the cane to beat Peter away. But with Peter on top of him, he couldn't get enough leverage in his swing, and finally let go of the cane so he could use both hands to protect his body from Peter's savage pummeling.

Finally, the man managed to get a knee up between the two of them and use his leg to push Peter away. Peter stumbled backwards, reaching out for the chain to keep from falling to the floor. As he straightened his legs, he saw the man scurrying across the floor to recover the cane. Peter lurched forward, still grasping the chain, and wrapped it around the man's neck. He gave it a vicious tug, snapping the man's head back, and then wrapped the chain around again. Now he could use his heavier frame to his advantage. He threw his body atop the other man's head as he held firmly to the chain. The man thrashed and heaved, but the makeshift gallows did its job. After about thirty seconds, the man ceased to move. Peter stayed on top of him another two minutes before rising and hurrying to the door. A barrel had been rolled up against it on the other side, most likely by the boy who had lured him there. He put his shoulder against the door and pushed his way out into the alley. He was temporarily blinded by the sudden bright sunlight. Even before his eyes could adjust, he was running toward home.

That night, Peter and Miriam Lengyel boarded a train to Geneva. They were never heard from again.

Chapter 19

"RUNNING AWAY WHENEVER we imagine a threat is not a sustainable strategy," Miriam said, her frustration mounting.

"Why not?" Peter countered. "We have the resources to go wherever we want, whenever we want. To not use them when we need to is reckless and irresponsible."

"But we don't even know for sure that a threat exists. Steph and I saw him, but he might not have seen us."

Peter took a deep breath, fighting to control his temper as they continued the debate that had occupied their entire weekend. It was Sunday afternoon and they were sitting in their living room, one of the owner's Norah Jones CDs playing in the background but doing little to mellow the combative atmosphere. Miriam was drinking a rare afternoon cup of coffee. Peter, feeling he was already nervous enough without adding caffeine to the equation, had opted for a beer.

"We should always consider it a threat when there's a possibility of exposure," he said. "We never know the motivations of another rider. Don't forget the lesson we learned in Milan. We knew he knew about us, and that we knew about him, and we let our guards down. We got complacent, and it almost got us killed."

"But the woman in Warsaw saw us, and all she did was smile at us and continue along her way," Miriam said. "Her intentions weren't malicious."

"We don't know that for sure," Peter argued. "We left for Budapest two days later. For all we know, she spent the next year trying to track us down."

Miriam threw up her hands in a gesture of exasperation. "You are so...so...cynical."

"I am not cynical, Miriam. I'm cautious. There's a difference. And that caution has kept us alive and together for a very long time."

She leaned back on the sofa and covered her face with her hands. "I know...I know. It's just that we finally have two allies. Steph and Allen understand us, and I think they really care about us. They need us, and I need them."

Peter reached out and took her hand. His voice was low and measured. "Don't you see, sweetheart, that's our dilemma. You believe that finding two other riders is a blessing. I believe that having someone else know our secret is a risk. Having two people know it increases the risk exponentially. And the possibility that a third person now knows...well, that just sends the risk factor off the charts."

She looked at him through wet eyes. "So you believe we should just pull the plug on our Birmingham lives, back out of the real estate contract, and disappear?"

He squeezed her hand. "Yes, I do."

She sniffed and then wiped her nose with her other hand. "And just leave Steph and Allen to fend for themselves?"

"I don't think Allen is at risk," Peter said. "Nobody has seen him. And frankly, the risk for Steph is not so great. If he saw her in the mirror, her reflection looked no different than her in the flesh. But you're a different story. If he saw your reflection, he knows what you are. And is fully aware that you know what he is. And given what he's trying to achieve, he may feel that he can't accept the risk of you knowing."

"But that's what makes me wonder if he saw me. There was no change in his demeanor or behavior. If he had seen me as a fifteen-year-old girl, he would've reacted in some way. So either he didn't see me, or he's the coolest, most unflappable man I've ever met."

"You don't survive at that level of politics if you can't keep your cool," Peter said. "You have to be prepared to keep your wits about you even if a hundred nukes are flying in your direction. I don't think we can assume anything about what he may or may not have seen."

Miriam looked down at their intertwined hands and sighed. "So that's it? I just don't show up for work tomorrow and we leave Steph to sort this all out by herself?"

Now it was Peter's turn to sigh. He loved her so much. It was breaking his heart to break hers, but people usually survived broken hearts. He knew, deep down inside, that the logical thing to do was to cut their losses and get out of Birmingham right away. But Miriam had been so excited about their new lives—the house, the job, the new friends, and the city itself. He hated to rip it all away from her, but he had to balance her desire for stability with his desire for security. He didn't know if he could actually achieve that balance…but he knew he had to try.

"Call Steph," he said. "See if she's been able to reach Senator Carson over the weekend. We need him to speak with either Martinez or Stephenson tonight, if possible. Tomorrow at the latest. And tell Steph she needs to call Sally McDonald tomorrow morning."

"McDaniel," she corrected, but he could see the edge of a smile.

"Whatever. She needs to call Sally tomorrow instead of waiting until Tuesday. We need some tangible evidence that the AVP campaign is continuing to roll along as before; that there have been no sudden changes in actions or attitudes since your encounter on Friday. Even if this guy is as cool as a cucumber, seeing your reflection in the mirror and knowing you saw his would have to change something. We just have to hope and pray we can recognize what it is."

Miriam nearly jumped across the sofa to throw her arms around his neck. "Thank you, sweetheart. It's going to be alright, I know it is. I'll call Steph right now."

He kissed her. "Okay. I hope I don't live to regret this."

"You won't. Everything's going to be fine."

"Tell Steph that I'll drive downtown after you finish work tomorrow and meet you, her and Allen for a drink. We'll debrief, and if everything looks normal—and I do mean *everything*—we'll figure out some additional security measures. If we stay, we'll be on heightened alert, at least until after the fundraiser is done and the AVP team is out of Birmingham. Okay?"

Miriam was already reaching for her phone. "Absolutely. I love you so, so much!"

Once she had relayed Peter's instructions to Stephanie, she lowered the phone and said, "Steph is asking where you want to meet for drinks."

"Anywhere is fine with me," Peter said. "Let her and Allen pick the place."

Just as she was about to repeat that to Stephanie, Peter called out, "But not the gay bar!"

WENDELL HARRISON—known as *Doctor Dubya* to his fellow gang-bangers—patted the left pocket of his low-riding Tommy Hilfiger jeans, just to reassure himself that the thick wad of hundred dollar bills was still there. Fifty of them, to be exact. Five grand. And that was just the down payment. He'd get another fifty Benjamins when the job was done. This had to be the easiest money he'd ever made. Certainly the quickest.

The man he'd met with was quite mysterious. He was a thick, squatty white dude with a New Orleans Saints ball cap pulled low and tight on his head. He wouldn't say anything about how he found Wendell, except that he'd been "highly recommended" by some friends in the Big Easy. Doctor Dubya had a few friends there alright. He'd lived there until Katrina. Then he'd spent a few years in Memphis before moving on to Birmingham. He'd settled in nicely in *the Ham*, finding a crew that could use his particular expertise. Running drugs and guns was risky, but profitable if you knew how to keep your head down and stay under the radar screen of the police. Which he did. No big scores, just lots and lots of little ones. Steady eddy, that was the ticket. Keep that profile low and the money rolling in.

In a typical month, Wendell would net about ten grand after acquisition costs and a few distribution fees, not to mention the occasional bribe. To make that much for just a couple hours of work was like a dream come true. It would make a nice little nest egg, to be sure. Unlike some of the other guys he worked with, he wouldn't run around throwing out cash and calling attention to himself. Hell no, he was too smart for that. In fact, nobody would ever know he'd done this job. They'd hear about it—it'd be the talk of the town for a day or two—but nobody would be able to connect him to it. He'd talk no different, act no different, look no different. Unless somebody happened to notice the bulge in his pants caused by a big-ass wad of cash.

He'd gotten the phone call on Saturday morning. Caller ID was blocked, but that wasn't terribly unusual in Wendell's line of work. But the guy on the other end was all cloak and dagger, like he was some kind of secret agent or something. Wanted to know if Wendell could meet him at Avondale Park at noon on Sunday.

"Why would I want to do that?" Wendell had asked.

"To make a shitload of money," Mystery Man had said.

"What's your definition of a shitload?" Wendell had asked.

"Probably the same as yours," the man said. "Trust me, it'll be worth your while. I'm willing to pay well for good talent, and your friends in New Orleans tell me that's what you've got. Be there at noon tomorrow. You won't be sorry."

"I don't know you, man. How will I find you?"

"I'll find you," the man said. "Just be there."

Wendell had gotten to the park right at noon. He'd found a bench off by itself and had parked himself on it and waited. And waited. At twelve-forty he was beginning to think he'd been played, when suddenly the dude had come out of nowhere and plopped down on the bench next to him. He was eating a grape snow cone, which he kept near his mouth, further blocking a good view of his face. His New Orleans Saints cap was pulled down tight, the brim covering mirrored Ray-Bans. Although Wendell couldn't see the man's hairline, he got the impression the dude was bald. Bald people just have a certain look.

The man wasn't much for small talk, or answering questions, so Wendell just let him get to the point. Which he did very quickly. He told Wendell what he wanted, and how much he'd pay him. And then, apparently to show he wasn't pulling some kind of scam, he slid a white envelope across the bench. Wendell picked it up, glanced around to make sure they weren't being observed, and looked inside. His heart literally skipped a beat when he did a quick count of the bills.

"So," Wendell said, "once I'm done, how do I get the other half?"

"I'll meet you here next Sunday, same time," the man said. "That gives you a full week to get the job done."

Wendell looked at him, but all he could really see was ball cap, sunglasses and snow cone. "How do I know you'll show up? I could do the job and then you could just decide to keep the other five grand."

The man kept his face pointed straight ahead. He took another lick of the snow cone and said, "And how do I know you won't just walk away with what I just gave you and never do the job?"

"Hey, you can trust me to do what I say I'm gonna do," Wendell said indignantly.

"And you can trust me," the man said. "Looks like we've got ourselves a deal."

He stood to leave, but after a couple of steps, turned and walked back to lean in close to Wendell's face. "Are you sure you don't have a problem shooting two women?"

What Wendell said was, "I can handle it." But what he was thinking was, *Shit, man, for ten grand I'd shoot the damn president!*

Chapter 20

STEPHANIE FINALLY MADE contact with Sally McDaniel on Monday morning. She tracked her down at her home in Nashville just as the campaign manager was leaving for a meeting to review the details of the AVP fundraiser at the Opryland Resort and Convention Center, which was scheduled for the night following the Birmingham event. Stephanie had a list of fabricated questions, nearly all of which she already knew the answer to, and then resorted to the tried and true *woman-to-woman* approach to fish for any signs of concern about her or Miriam. Not only did she come up empty on concerns from Sally, Martinez or Stephenson, she received very positive feedback and an expression of great confidence in the work being done by Sheffield & Associates.

Miriam was sitting across the desk in Stephanie's office, listening to her side of the conversation. "Sounded like that went pretty well," she said as Stephanie hung up the phone.

"Extremely well, actually," Stephanie said, smiling. "If anybody has expressed any worries or changed their attitude as a result of our meeting in Dallas, Sally doesn't know about it. When she took us to Martinez's suite to introduce us, she was about to sit down with them for a two hour meeting. Not only did she talk as if everything was okay, she said both men were very complimentary after she reviewed our plans for the Birmingham fundraiser. They even indicated they might use us again for other events in Alabama, especially if their candidate here wins."

"He didn't see us," Miriam said as she exhaled the breath she'd been holding during the entire phone conversation. "There's no way he would've been able to conceal the shock of seeing two other riders—well, me at least—for the duration of a two hour meeting. I don't care how cool of a cucumber he is; he would've shown something."

"I agree," Stephanie said. "If I get the same kind of feedback from the Senator, I think we can feel pretty confident that we're in the clear."

"I think so too," Miriam said, nodding. "The bigger issue is how confident Peter will feel. When he dropped me off this morning he was still setting the stage for an abrupt departure from Birmingham if we got anything less than an *all clear* from Sally or Senator Carson. He's really pushing his normal boundaries about situations like this. He's trying so hard to accommodate my wishes, but unless he can get his confidence level up to the ninety per cent range, he'll still force the issue and we'll be gone."

Stephanie frowned. "Ninety per cent? Can't he flex just a little?"

Miriam shook her head. "You don't understand, Steph. That *is* flexing. Peter has always operated on one hundred per cent certainty when it comes to our security. As far as he's concerned, he's already being flexible to the point of carelessness."

"Well, let's hope we can move his confidence meter further up with Carson's feedback," Stephanie said. "I'll let you know as soon as I hear from him."

"Okay," Miriam said before rising and heading to her own office. She spent the rest of the morning working in the tiny room, unable to stop herself from wondering if it would be her last day there. If only they could hear from Senator Carson, and the news would be as favorable as it had been from Sally.

Finally, after what seemed an interminable amount of time but which had actually been only three hours, Stephanie stepped through the door, her face beaming. "Just got off the phone with the Senator."

Miriam looked up, noting the smile. "Good news?"

"Couldn't be better. Carson got a return call from Stephenson a little while ago. He was in the back seat of a limo with Martinez, and turned on his speaker phone. Carson talked to the two of them together for about five minutes. He fished and fished, but all he got back was glowing reviews. From both of them."

Miriam let out a sigh of relief. "That's fantastic! I'll call Peter right now."

"Let's go hit the food truck first," Stephanie said. "I'm buying today."

"It won't take me but a minute," Miriam said. "I'm sure he's anxious to hear."

"I know, but let's grab lunch and bring it back up here and you can call him then. I need to fill you in on the details of my conversation with Carson. I think we'll be able to allay any fears Peter has."

"I wouldn't bet on that, but let's go. Suddenly, I'm ravenous."

A few minutes later they exited the building and turned left, heading for the food truck's usual location on the next block. They chatted excitedly as they walked, both reveling in the relief of a crisis passing them by. When they were standing in line waiting their turn to order, Stephanie said, "Tell Peter to meet us at O'Brien's on Sixth Avenue South, just off Twenty-second. Let's say around seven. I'll tell Allen when we get back to the office."

"Sounds perfect," Miriam said. "A couple of stiff drinks are exactly what I need."

They both laughed, neither paying attention to the tall, skinny black man standing in line behind them. Nor did they notice that, despite the humidity and temperature both being in the nineties, he wore a hoodie pulled up over his head, hiding his face in shadow.

PETER WAS WAITING for Miriam and Stephanie when they arrived at O'Brien's Pub. The plan had been for him to drive Miriam to work so they'd both be in one car for the drive home. It had also served to give the two women more time to polish up their case for moving forward without fear that they'd been exposed in Dallas. Miriam had called Peter while eating lunch in Stephanie's office and, while he had seemed encouraged by the comments from Sally McDaniel and Senator Carson, he still seemed far from convinced.

"I see you decided to start without us," Miriam said, giving him a peck on the cheek before they sat down.

He held up a half empty pint glass of dark, foamy beer. "Guinness. Hardly seemed appropriate to order anything else in an Irish pub."

"Well, at the risk of being geopolitically incorrect, I'm going for something a little stronger," Miriam said. She turned to Stephanie. "Think they make a good vodka martini here?"

Stephanie smiled. "They certainly did when I was in here last week." She raised a hand and flagged down a waiter.

"Where's Allen?" Peter asked.

"He was right behind us," Stephanie said. "Probably still looking for a parking space. I got lucky and found one just two doors down."

Peter drained the last of his beer. "Yeah, I'm a block and a half away. This neighborhood has a pretty active bar scene."

"That's why I like it," Stephanie said. "My apartment is only three blocks from here. I walk here a lot of nights." She lowered her voice to a whisper. "Safer for me and everybody else on the street. Especially when it's been a day like today."

"Well, since your car is here tonight, Miriam or I can drive it home if you're overserved," Peter said, grinning.

"Speak for yourself, dear," Miriam said. "I intend to get hammered."

"Hammered? Ooh, I love that game!" The three of them looked up to see Allen pulling up a chair. He sat down and immediately began looking around the room. "What's a girl got to do to get a drink in this establishment?"

Apparently the waiter heard him, because he immediately appeared beside their table. "I'll have a glass of Pinot Grigio," Allen said, and then patted Peter's arm. "Ever since the wine and cheese at your place, I've been obsessed with everything Italian. Wine, food, clothes..."

"Men?" Stephanie said with a smile.

"I'm spoken for, sweetie," Allen said with a playful smirk. "Russell is Scotch-Irish, which is ethnically boring, but he does have his charm, so I am blissfully monogamous." He looked around the table and then added, "For now."

They chatted casually until the drinks were served and Peter had ordered his second beer, and then Stephanie leaned across the table toward him and whispered, "So, are you feeling better about things now?"

Peter leaned forward as well. "Better is a relative term, but yes, I certainly feel more comfortable than I did when you first told me about all of this on Friday night. But not as comfortable as I was before that."

Stephanie's forehead wrinkled in a quizzical frown. "Meaning?"

"Meaning," Peter said, "that I'm still not convinced we're not at risk." Noting the look of alarm on everyone's face, including Miriam's, he quickly added, "But I feel that if we are at risk, we should be able to manage it, at least until we get this fundraiser next Thursday behind us. If that goes well, without setting off any alarms in my head, we'll reassess and go from there."

"So then you'll be willing to believe he didn't see me?" Miriam asked.

"Either that, or that he doesn't want to incur the risk of doing anything about it," Peter said. He took a sip of his beer, and then studied the foam on its surface, like he was reading tea leaves, searching for a clue to their future. "But I'm still not feeling completely secure. In fact, I've never felt this exposed in all the years we've been together."

For once, Allen was serious. "So your unease is not just based on him. It's also because of Steph and me, isn't it?"

Peter looked from one to the other and said, "It's nothing personal. Please understand that. I like you both, and Miriam certainly does. It's just that we've been operating for a very long time with the two of us being the only people on earth who knew our secret." He paused a moment. "Well, there have been a couple of exceptions, and one of those didn't end so well. But the point is, I'm not sure I'll ever be able to get comfortable with someone else knowing. I just believe it increases the danger of exposure significantly."

"You don't trust us?" Stephanie asked, a pained expression on her face.

"Of course I do," Peter said. "But there are a lot of moving parts in a situation like ours. None of us knows what we could slip up and say inadvertently. Or what we would say if someone used force to make us talk." He studied their faces. "And we don't know the lengths to which someone might go to shut us up."

WHEN THEY FINISHED their third round of drinks, Peter said it was time to go. Despite the hearty protestations from the other three, he signaled the waiter to bring the check, which Allen promptly grabbed. "Tonight's on me," he said. "You can buy next time when we go somewhere more expensive."

Peter laughed. "That's fine. Thank you."

The men shook hands and Miriam gave Allen a kiss on both cheeks before they left him to settle the bill. Now that she was standing, Miriam could feel the effect of the three martinis, and she held tightly to Peter's arm as they walked out. The three of them strolled leisurely to Stephanie's car, parked between a bakery and a dress shop, both closed. They stood there chatting for a minute, and then Peter said to Miriam, "Why don't you wait here with Steph while I get our car? It's a bit of a hike."

Miriam turned to Stephanie and lowered her voice to a hushed whisper. "That's just his gentlemanly way of saying I'm too drunk to walk that far."

"I'm saying no such thing," he laughed as he started to walk away. After three steps he turned back to Miriam and said, "Wait right here. And try not to throw up on Steph's car."

They both giggled and watched as he walked back past the pub and turned the corner. Miriam was just about to say something about Peter seeming a bit more relaxed, when a dark figure emerged from the shadows by the dress shop and grabbed the shoulder strap of her purse. She reflexively resisted, pulling it back toward her, when the figure's other hand came into view a few inches from her face. It was holding a gun.

She cried out faintly, too frightened to create much sound, but Stephanie shouted in a loud, shrill voice, "No, don't!"

The gun suddenly swung in her direction as another voice cried "Stop!" and Allen's skinny form rushed between Stephanie and the weapon. Allen was raising his hands to push the gun away when it fired—three times in rapid succession—and he fell back against Stephanie before bouncing forward into their assailant. Both men went down in a tangle of flailing arms and legs, and the two women bolted for the entrance to the pub, screaming at the top of their lungs. At the door, Miriam looked back at the hooded man as he pushed Allen off him and tried to point the gun in her direction. She gasped, thinking she was about to die, when an arm grabbed her from inside and pulled her into the pub. She looked up to see it was Stephanie, wide-eyed and shaking uncontrollably as she tried to speak.

Miriam found her voice first. "Call the police!" she shouted at the approaching hostess. "And an ambulance! Our friend's been shot!"

Less than a minute later, Miriam saw Peter's Lexus SUV screech to a halt in front of the pub, and watched as he jumped from the vehicle and ran toward the spot where Allen had been shot. Afraid the shooter was still outside, she screamed "No, Peter, stop!" She wrenched her arm free of Stephanie's grip and bolted outside to see Peter kneeling beside Allen. She raced toward them, scanning the street for signs of the man with the gun, but saw no one else.

When she reached them, her knees almost buckled at the sight. She'd never seen so much blood in her life. The sidewalk looked like a shimmery reflection pool, except where Peter's pants leg was soaking blood up like a sponge. She felt like she was going to be sick, but managed to stifle the nausea when she heard the reassuring sound of a rapidly approaching siren.

Peter was ripping off his sport jacket. Miriam reached out and took it from him, rolling it up and putting it under Allen's head, which was raised in a feeble attempt to see the damage that had been inflicted on him. "Be still, Allen, help is almost here," she said.

He looked at her and tried to speak, his voice a ragged croak. "Steph?" he said, his eyes imploring.

"I'm here, Allen," Stephanie cried over Miriam's shoulder. "I'm right here."

Just then a police car lurched to a stop on the other side of Stephanie's Camry. A young officer ran to them, his hand on his service revolver, as his partner emerged from the car and spoke into a microphone on his shoulder. The first officer knelt and glanced at Peter. "How many shots?"

Miriam answered for him. "Three," she said.

"Did they all hit him?" the officer asked, now looking at Miriam.

"Yes, I think so," she said, her voice quivering with fear.

"Joe, where's that ambulance?" the officer shouted over his shoulder.

"Two minutes," the other officer called back.

"Okay buddy," the kneeling officer said, applying pressure to the area on Allen's chest that seemed to be bleeding the most profusely. "You've got to hang in here with me, okay? Just two minutes, and then we'll get you taken care of. Can you do that for me?"

Suddenly, the shocked silence was shattered by a single word, shouted by Stephanie. "Jump!"

The officer looked up at her. "What?"

"Jump, Allen!" Stephanie shouted. "Do it! Right now!"

"Ma'am, do you mind backing up a little?" the officer said, his eyes staying on Allen as he tried to stem the flow of blood.

Allen darted his eyes toward Steph, and then back to the officer. "Are you married?" he whispered.

The policeman seemed surprised by the question, but answered quietly. "Yes, sir, I am. Now you just stay quiet, okay? Just a minute more, and the ambulance will be here."

"Jump, Allen!" Stephanie was screaming.

"Kids?" Allen asked, his voice now a weak whisper.

"Yeah, yeah," the officer said. "Two girls. Just stay quiet and hang in there, okay?"

"Jump, Allen!" Stephanie continued to scream. "Jump, damn you!"

Miriam watched as Allen again turned his gaze to Stephanie. His eyes burned fiercely as he shook his head slowly from side to side. And then they glazed over, and he was gone.

Chapter 21

PETER GLANCED at his watch. Ten forty-five. They would have to get going soon. They were in a separate dining room at the back of O'Brien's, a room normally reserved for private events like company Christmas lunches, or bachelor parties, or birthday celebrations. Happy events, with music and laughter and—it being an Irish pub—free-flowing beer. But for the last two hours the management had allowed it to be used for a much more somber purpose—for the Birmingham Police Department to question the witnesses to the mugging-gone-wrong that had occurred right outside the restaurant entrance.

Lieutenant John Greene, a slender, crew-cut homicide detective with a soft voice and gentle but probing eyes, had just left. He had questioned Miriam and Stephanie separately and together, and had chalked up the tragedy to a purse snatching and car-jacking attempt—and possibly even a kidnapping—that had been thwarted by Allen's heroic intervention. "Unfortunately, I've seen a lot of these types of attacks over the years," Greene had said, "and I really don't think murder was the objective. But if your friend"—he referred quickly to his notepad—"Mr. Trammell, had not charged the perpetrator, anything could have happened. He was a very brave man."

That had started Stephanie sobbing again. Miriam wrapped her arms around her friend's heaving shoulders and Peter just stared into space, unsure what to do next. The pub closed at eleven, and he knew he had to get them out of there, but also knew Stephanie was in no condition to drive herself home, even if it was only a few blocks. The effects of the alcohol had worn off, burned away by adrenaline and emotional shock, but now her mind was numbed by grief. Peter waited until Steph calmed back down and then said quietly, "They're going to be closing in a few minutes. We need to go. Steph, we'll drive you home."

Stephanie looked at him with swollen, wet eyes and nodded, but Miriam shook her head. "We're not just driving you home. We're going in with you so you can pack an overnight bag. You're staying with us tonight."

"N-n-no, that's okay," Stephanie stammered. "I'm alright."

"No, you're not alright," Miriam said forcefully. She paused and then continued, in a softer voice. "And I'm not either. We need you nearby tonight as much as you need us. We'll all feel better if we're under the same roof." She looked at Peter for affirmation, which he granted with a solemn nod.

"Okay, then," he said, standing. "Let's get going. Miriam, you drive Steph in her car. I'll be right behind you."

He thanked the pub manager on the way out, promising to return soon, and to not bring trouble with him on his next visit. He made the two women wait inside the entrance while he brought Stephanie's Camry to the curb right outside the door. They thought he was being overly cautious, but that wasn't the case. He had no serious concerns about the possibility of the shooter still lurking around outside. He just didn't want them staring at the dark blood-stain on the sidewalk beside Stephanie's passenger door.

They got into the car, Miriam behind the wheel, and waited while Peter jogged to his Lexus, a few spaces back. He then followed them to Stephanie's apartment building, which took only three or four minutes. Once they were inside her third floor unit, he and Miriam waited in the living room while Stephanie went into her bedroom to pack a bag. She'd been in there less than a minute when she walked back into the living room, a pained look on her face.

"Oh, my God," she said, choking back tears. "I have to call Mark and Abby. How could I have not thought of that until now?"

"I'll call them," Miriam said, stepping forward and putting her hand on Stephanie's shoulder. "You finish packing."

"No...no, I should do it," Stephanie said, reaching for a phone on the table beside the sofa. She punched in a number and waited, not making eye contact with Miriam or Peter. After a few seconds, she spoke into the receiver. "Hi Mark, it's Steph. I'm sorry to be calling so late, but something terrible has happened. Allen was...Allen is... oh God, Mark, Allen is..."

Peter reached for the phone just as Stephanie began to emit a long, plaintive wail, a pained and sorrowful moan that left her gasping for air as she looked around the room as if suddenly bewildered by her surroundings. Peter glanced at Miriam and nodded his head toward the bedroom. She took Stephanie by the arm and led her there.

When they were out of the room and the bedroom door had been eased shut, Peter lifted the phone to his ear. He could hear the sound of a man's voice saying, "I don't know, Abby. Something about Allen."

"Mark, this is Peter Hoffman. We haven't had the chance to meet yet, and I'm afraid that when we do, it will be a very sad occasion."

He proceeded to narrate the events of the night, emphasizing that Allen's heroic intervention might very well have saved the lives of Stephanie and Miriam. He went on to say that they wouldn't be able to find out until the next day when Allen's body would be released for burial, but that he would be happy to assist—both physically and financially—with any funeral arrangements. Mark's silence was so prolonged that Peter finally had to ask if he was still there.

"Yes, I'm here," Mark said. "Sorry, I'm just stunned. I can't believe this has happened."

Peter could hear Abby in the background, pleading for information from her husband. "Mark, I'll drive Miriam and Steph to work tomorrow and I'll come in and see you then. Maybe we'll know more, and can start making some plans."

"Okay," Mark said. "No need to get them there early. Let them get some sleep if that's even possible. I'll try to track down Russell. He's in Houston working on some ballet project. I have his cell number on my computer." He sighed. "Man, that's one call I dread making."

"I'm sure," Peter said. "I'm so sorry this happened. It seems more like a nightmare than reality. I'd give anything to wake up right now."

The two men disconnected just as Miriam walked back into the room. Peter was seated on the sofa, and she walked up behind him and wrapped her arms tightly around his neck. "How is Mark?" she whispered.

"About what you'd expect," he said. "Shocked, stunned, genuinely sad. I could hear his wife in the background going crazy trying to figure out what was going on."

"Poor Abby," Miriam said, releasing her strangle hold and walking around the sofa to sit next to her husband. "She's the quintessential Mother Hen. Losing one of her chicks is going to be devastating."

"I'm sure," Peter said. "Mark's going to track down Russell in Houston. I don't envy him having to make that call."

Miriam leaned her head on Peter's shoulder, tears rolling down her cheeks. "Steph is really upset. It was bad enough for her to watch him die, knowing he'd been shot trying to protect her…and me. But knowing that he could've saved himself makes it even worse for her."

Peter gently lifted her chin with a finger so he could look into her eyes. "But if he'd done that—saved himself—an entire family would've been destroyed. Allen knew that, and he made a very brave, unselfish decision."

She exhaled a long, uneven breath. "I know. I've jumped so many times I've kind of gotten used to the fact that it costs someone else her life. But we've always been mindful of family situations when selecting new hosts. We may have taken the hosts' lives, but at least we haven't destroyed families. For all his superficial vanity, Allen was a good soul." She stared into Peter's eyes. "Now we have to focus on helping Steph get through this horrible, senseless tragedy."

Peter took her hand and returned her stare. "It was most definitely a horrible tragedy, but it wasn't a senseless one. At least, not from the shooter's perspective."

Miriam's brow creased in a quizzical frown. "What do you mean?"

"This wasn't a random mugging. You and Steph were the targets. Allen just got caught in the crossfire."

Her face seemed to melt from a frozen mask of confusion into a molten pool of sad understanding. She wiped a tear from her eye. "You were right all along. This has to be connected to what we saw in Dallas. It's much too much of a coincidence that we just happened to be on the street in the exact spot and exact time that a street thug was looking for a victim."

He squeezed her hand tightly. "And you know what that means, right? For us?"

Miriam looked at their intertwined fingers, studying them for nearly a minute. "We can't run away this time, Peter."

He started to raise his voice, but mindful that Steph was in the next room and the apartment walls were probably thin, he lowered his voice to an urgent whisper. "What are you talking about? It's what we've always done. It's the reason we're still alive."

She raised her head and locked his eyes in a determined stare. "We've always run when we were in danger ourselves. But this is different. One of our own has been killed and another one is threatened. We can't simply disappear again. This time we stand and fight."

AS PETER HAD EXPECTED, it was a sleepless night. Miriam had finally drifted off somewhere around four-thirty, but would periodically shiver violently, as if freezing. He managed to nap a little, and finally climbed out of bed and tiptoed from their bedroom a little after eight. He put on a pot of coffee and set out English muffins and orange juice. Just as the coffee finished brewing, Stephanie emerged from the guest room.

"I thought I heard someone walking around in here," she said. "And then I smelled the coffee and knew either you or Miriam were up."

"Sorry to make so much noise," Peter said. "Did I wake you?"

She shook her head. "No, I'm not sure I ever fell completely asleep. I just couldn't stop replaying the attack and the sight of Allen lying on the sidewalk. And all that blood." She stared into space, as if visually reconstructing the horrendous scene, and shuddered. "My God, there was so much blood."

"Sit down," he said quietly and, he hoped, gently. "I'll pour you some coffee."

"Thanks. Black."

He filled two mugs and walked into the living room, handing her one. He studied her face as she stared into the rising steam, as if looking for answers in the whirling mist. She looked terrible. The frames of her glasses did little to hide the swelling and redness of her eyes, and her shoulders slumped as if she were carrying the weight of the world. He supposed that, in her own way, she was.

She took a sip of coffee and then closed her eyes to stay the emergence of more tears. "I just can't believe he's gone. I saw it unfold, watched him die, and yet I still can't believe it actually happened."

"I know," was all Peter knew to say in response.

"I just keep thinking…what if we'd stayed for one more round of drinks," she said. "Maybe the guy would've moved on by then."

"I don't think so," Peter said, studying her face, looking for a reaction. Actually, for a realization of what had really happened, and why.

She looked at him and said, "What do you mean?"

"What I mean is, he would've waited all night for you and Miriam to come out. The two of you were his targets. Allen just got in the way."

She continued to stare at him for a full minute or so before exhaling loudly and shifting her gaze to the floor. "I guess I already knew that. I just didn't want to admit it. I really don't know what would be worse—knowing that Allen was dead as a result of a completely random encounter with a mugger, or because he took a bullet that was meant for me. I suppose it really doesn't matter. Dead is dead."

Peter placed his mug on the coffee table and leaned toward Stephanie, his elbows on his knees. "No, it does matter. It matters a lot. Because if it really was a random attack, you and Miriam would be out of danger. But if the two of you were the intended targets of a hit, the danger is still there."

She continued to stare at the floor. "So you're convinced it was a direct result of what we saw in Dallas?"

"I am."

Stephanie looked up from the floor and locked eyes with him. "So, I guess that means you and Miriam will be leaving." She said it as a statement rather than a question.

"That was my plan, yes," he said, sighing. "But Miriam won't go. She says this time is different. And, as much as I hate to admit it, I think she's right."

She shook her head. "You two don't have to put yourselves in danger just so you can stay here to try and protect me."

"It's more than that," he said, then fearing he might have hurt her feelings, added, "although that's certainly a factor. We've never had any kind of relationship with other riders. There's a feeling of—I don't know—kinship, I suppose, that we've never dealt with before. Losing Allen, and knowing that you're still at risk, makes it harder for us to just run away like we've always done before."

The corners of her mouth turned up in a sad smile. "That's a rather noble sentiment."

He smiled back at her as he reached for his coffee and took another sip. "I suppose it is. But there's a bit of a selfish motivation mixed in there as well."

"Selfish? What do you mean?"

"In the past, we've taken new identities—and in some cases, new bodies—and simply moved to another area. It's not all that difficult, once you work through the mechanics and have the right resources lined up. But we've never had a reason to believe someone would still be trying to pursue us. Our documentation and background stories are pretty good, but if tracking us down was a priority of say, the FBI, I'm not so sure we'd be able to stay hidden."

Stephanie's eyes widened. "How would he be able to use the FBI to track you down?"

"All he'd have to do is concoct some story about us being a threat and relate it to the Bureau and, given the AVP's growing influence as a political force, maybe even the Secret Service. Our documentation resource is quite good, but there's sure to be some kind of paper trail. Or computer trail. New Social Security numbers or new passports showing up in the system would be like a red flag, leading them right to us. We'd never feel safe again."

"So, what can we do?" asked a voice behind them.

They both turned to see Miriam walking into the room, tying the sash of her robe. Her hair was disheveled and her eyes were red, but they burned with an intensity that had not been there the night before. She no longer looked shell-shocked. She looked determined. And pissed.

"Sit down," Peter said. "I'll fix you a cup of coffee."

Miriam sat on the sofa next to Stephanie and put a hand on her knee. "Did you get any sleep?"

"Not really," Stephanie said with an attempted, but failed, smile. "Every time I closed my eyes I saw Allen lying on that sidewalk and heard myself screaming at him to jump. I still don't know why he didn't do it."

"I do," Miriam said softly. "When you've taken lives to save your own, you can become a little hardened. You can rationalize that it's necessary for survival. But you always have that lingering doubt and guilt. Why is my life more important than the life of the host? Do I really have any conceivable right—by any moral code known to man—to make that jump? I'm sure that Allen asked himself that very question last night." She paused to take a deep breath. "And in that particular case, I believe he came to the right conclusion."

"I guess so," Stephanie muttered, once again fighting tears. "I heard him ask the cop if he was married, and if he had children.

He was thinking about making the jump, I'm sure of it. But he just couldn't make that one."

"He made the right choice," Peter said, handing Miriam a steaming mug of coffee before sitting in a leather chair next to the sofa. "It was a heroic choice. I'd like to think that I would've made it too." He looked down at his own coffee and whispered, "I just don't know."

Miriam reached out and squeezed his hand. "I heard what you told Steph about fearing we might not be able to disappear and establish new identities this time. That the FBI could possibly be used to track us down. So what do we do? It's obvious we're still at risk."

Peter thought for a moment and then shook his head slowly. "I don't know. Simply disappearing doesn't seem to be a viable option. Doing nothing damn sure isn't. So I think we have to work off the assumption that he's as scared of us as we are of him." He looked from Miriam to Stephanie. "I think we have to confront him. Face to face."

"How are we going to do that?" Stephanie asked. "He'd see us coming and never let us get past security."

"He'd see the two of you coming," Peter said. "He doesn't know about me."

Chapter 22

ARTHUR STEPHENSON pushed his coffee cup aside and spread the note cards in front of him on the dining room table. He had reviewed them over a dozen times, and had discussed them nearly that many times with Martinez. He still was not completely satisfied with the response to the question about the allegations of infidelity. He thought the use of the term "marital bliss" came across as glib, almost condescending, and was thinking out loud about possible alternatives while the founder and face of the American Values Party gazed out the window at Pittsburgh's afternoon rush hour traffic sixteen floors below. They were in Stephenson's suite at the Omni William Penn Hotel, waiting for the television interview with PNN's Kristin Connelly, scheduled to start in Martinez's suite in another half hour.

Stephenson looked up from the table and waved the note card as if trying to dry the red and blue ink that covered it. "What if you said that rumors like this are indicative of the opposition's envy of your strong partnership with Maria rather than them being jealous of your 'marital bliss?' That still sounds a bit pretentious to me. Like you consider it a joke or something."

Martinez turned from the window to face his chief of staff. "That's what I was trying to do...dismiss the allegations as if they were a joke. I don't want to give the impression that I take them seriously."

"I get that," Stephenson said, nodding. "I just don't want any of the viewers to misconstrue your comment and think you don't take your marriage vows seriously. Also, there are the other network commentators to consider. Fox and CNN are both pretty pissed that we're giving PNN an exclusive one-on-one interview, so they'll dissect every word you utter."

Martinez laughed. "Well, neither Bill O'Reilly nor Anderson Cooper are as attractive as Kristen Connelly. And I certainly don't think they would've given us all the interview questions two days in advance."

"Exactly. So could we please stick to the script? I've given a lot of thought to these answers, and if we make this last change on the marriage thing I believe this interview will be a big plus."

"I suppose. But if you ask me, she sounds like a shark on the attack with a couple of her questions."

"That's by design," Stephenson said. "If she comes across as too soft, she loses credibility as a hard-hitting journalist. On the other hand, if she looks like she's on the attack, but you counter with solid, logical, unemotional answers—like the ones I've written on these cards—you'll both look stronger and more credible. A definite win-win." He suddenly glanced down at his cell phone on the table. "Hold on a sec."

He picked up the phone and hit the receive button. "Hi Sally. We're about to go back to Robert's suite for his TV interview. Can this wait an hour?"

He listened for a moment and then cut his eyes over to Martinez and waved him over to the table. "Hold on, Sally. I'm putting you on speaker phone."

He hit a button and placed the phone on the corner of the table, between him and Martinez. "Okay, Sally, you've got us both. Start over."

"I just got off the phone with Mark Sheffield of Sheffield and Associates in Birmingham," Sally said, breathing heavily into the phone as if she'd just run up several flights of stairs.

"Back away from the phone a bit, Sally," Stephenson said. "You sound like you're out jogging or something."

"Sorry," Sally said, her voice nervous but the breathing less audible now. "You remember the two women you met last Friday… Stephanie and Miriam?"

"Of course," Martinez said. "What about them?"

"They were out for dinner in downtown Birmingham last night and they were mugged."

"My God," Stephenson exclaimed. "Were they hurt?"

"No," Sally said, "but one of the other associates, a young man named Allen Trammell, was shot while trying to intervene. He died from his wounds."

"What about the shooter?" Martinez asked. "Did they catch him?"

"No, he got away," Sally said. "But Steph and Miriam were obviously traumatized. Their friend bled out on the sidewalk, right in front of them."

"So do they want to cancel the event in Birmingham next week?" Stephenson asked.

"No. Mark told me they'll still get it done. He just wanted us to be aware of the situation."

Martinez leaned down toward the phone. "I appreciate their commitment Sally, but do we still want to go there? Birmingham doesn't sound as safe as I was led to believe it was."

"As tragic as this shooting was, it actually works in our favor from a security standpoint," Sally said. "The Westin is only a few blocks from where this occurred. Mark has already met with the mayor and the chief of police. With the possibility of a Brigade protest, on top of this apparently random incident, the city will be on high alert from now until you've been there and gone. They're not going to let anyone get near you."

"Unless they've paid ten grand a plate," Stephenson said with a grin. "And then, all bets are off."

TWENTY MINUTES LATER Robert Martinez was seated in the living room of his suite, which over the past hour had been converted into a television soundstage. Three lights were erected on poles around the room and cables crisscrossed the edges of the Oriental rug. A soundman monitored a keyboard with an array of lights, knobs and switches, and Mitch the camera man had replaced his usual hand-held camera with a tripod mounted unit. The total result was an atmosphere that was the polar opposite of what the viewers were intended to see—an intimate, casual setting where the founder of the most visible and successful third party in decades would be conversing openly and without notes with a member of the press.

Martinez obliged the request for another sound check as a woman applied a last touch of make-up to his face before removing the towel that had been protecting his crisply starched powder blue shirt and red, white and blue striped tie. Mitch did a final adjustment on the lavalier microphone attached to the candidate's coat lapel and stepped back behind the camera. "Everyone set?" he asked, glancing first at Martinez, then Kristen Connelly, and finally Arthur Stephenson, who stood two feet to Mitch's right—easily in view of Martinez should any directive gestures be required during the interview.

Everyone nodded affirmatively and Mitch swung the camera for a close-up of Kristen. Satisfied with the clarity of the image, he lifted his left hand and began counting down to one finger, which he pointed at her before giving a thumbs-up sign. It was show time.

CONNELLY: Good evening. This is Kristen Connelly. Tonight PNN is bringing you an exclusive interview with San Antonio business executive and founder of the American Values Party, Robert Martinez. Mr. Martinez has graciously accepted our invitation for an open and candid discussion of several issues that are of critical importance to his party. Mr. Martinez, thank you for taking the time from your busy campaign schedule to sit down with us.

MARTINEZ: My pleasure, Kristen.

CONNELLY: Let's start with the voter polls. In the past couple of weeks you've seen a slight decline in the position of several of your congressional candidates, particularly in California and a couple of Midwestern states, as well as the Arkansas gubernatorial race. Are you concerned that this could be the start of a downward trend in the popularity of the AVP?

MARTINEZ: Not at all. I believe what we've been seeing is the typical up and down fluctuations that you see in any campaign, especially when one party is new and relatively unknown. The more our party positions gain traction, the more our opposition attacks them. This creates temporary confusion in the minds of the voters until they can sort out fact and fiction and conclude which side is really providing viable solutions to the problems our country is facing.

CONNELLY: Several political analysts have stated that your party's poll numbers have been impacted in the past month by two specific issues. First, there is the vehement opposition to the AVP platform by *Brigada de Proteccion Hispana*—The Hispanic Protection Brigade—which their leaders claim was formed as a direct response to your stance on immigration. As our nation's first Hispanic political party leader, and possibly even a future presidential candidate, how does it feel to see fellow Hispanics comprising your most vocal opposition?

MARTINEZ: Heh heh, if you're asking has it hurt my feelings, let me just say that I have a pretty thick skin when it comes to political criticism. Anyone who doesn't shouldn't be in this business. But, if I had to describe my feelings about the Brigade in one word, it would be "disappointed." I'm disappointed that my views and the thoughtful, logical policies of the American Values Party have been distorted by a loud, uninformed minority of Hispanics, many of whom are in this country illegally.

CONNELLY: You used the term "uninformed." What exactly do you mean by that?

MARTINEZ: It's simple. The Brigade is trying to paint our views as *anti-immigration*, and nothing could be further from the truth.

CONNELLY: So, for the record, what are your personal views on immigration?

MARTINEZ: I am as pro-immigration as any political figure this country has ever seen. Look, the United States is a nation of immigrants. People have come here from every region on earth, and we've assimilated and worked together to become the most successful, most affluent, and most powerful nation in history. My own parents came here from Mexico and built a life, and raised a family, and educated their son. And now that son is a successful businessman and the leader of a movement that could literally redefine the political discourse in this country. Where else on earth could that happen? I'll tell you. Nowhere. Not in Europe, or Asia, or Africa, or South America, or Central America. Nowhere but here. So why would I, a beneficiary of this country's hospitality and boundless opportunity, be anti-immigration? It's illogical. In fact, it's preposterous.

CONNELLY: And yet your party's proposed policies would dramatically reduce the influx across our southern border.

MARTINEZ: Kristen, let me be perfectly clear. Our concern is not with people from Mexico, Central America and South America coming to the United States. Our concern is with them coming here *illegally*. We have a border that is broken, and that is an issue of national security. That is why securing the border and revamping our immigration policies is one of the three critical issues our candidates discuss consistently. Once we have our borders secure and have the systems in place to accept and process applications for work visas, education visas and citizenship, I believe the number of immigrants coming into this country each year will actually increase, not decrease.

CONNELLY: So you don't consider yourself to be anti-immigration?

MARTINEZ: No more than a man who wants to fix a hole in his roof would be considered "anti-rain."

CONNELLY: At a recent AVP rally in Chicago, there was a pretty large Brigade protest. Do you expect more protests of this kind and, if so, how will you respond to their presence?

MARTINEZ: First of all, let me say that as long as their protest is civil, peaceful, and not disruptive to those who are there to hear what we have to say so that they can cast their votes in an informed manner, then the Brigade has just as much of a right to be there as anyone else. Not everyone who shows up at one of our campaign events is an AVP supporter. But just as their right to be there is respected, they must respect the rights of others who attend. Again, peaceful and civil. That's not asking too much.

CONNELLY: So far the Brigade's protests have been peaceful, but some of the actions against them have been anything but. There was the fatal shooting of a young Mexican man trying to cross the border into Arizona several months ago, followed by numerous reports of militia raids on predominately Hispanic apartment complexes and business establishments, and then the brutal beating just last week of Brigade organizer Hector Ramirez. How do you respond to Brigade claims that these violent episodes are the natural outcome of anti-immigrant sentiment fueled by your party?

MARTINEZ: I respond by saying that is an absolutely absurd claim. The response to our calls for lawful immigration is violent, unlawful behavior? That doesn't even make sense. Look, it was a terrible tragedy when that young man was shot while attempting to enter this country illegally. No responsible leader at any level of the United States government would advocate firing upon people who unlawfully trespass our borders unless they present a clear, unequivocal threat. And, regarding those alleged raids on Hispanic communities, I was told those raids were for the purpose of rounding up illegal immigrants who were involved in criminal activities. But even if that were the case, that's the job of the police and border authorities, not self-appointed militia groups. And finally, the attack on Mr. Ramirez was an act of criminal violence, and the perpetrators should be identified, arrested and prosecuted to the full extent of the law. We don't fight unlawful activities with more unlawful activity. This is America, and the rule of law is sacrosanct.

CONNELLY: Moving now to the second issue that has garnered a lot of media attention in the past week. There have been allegations of marital infidelity; specifically, the use of prostitutes on numerous occasions. To whom do you attribute these rumors and how do you respond?

MARTINEZ: I'm glad to hear you use the word "rumors," Kristen, because that is exactly what they are. This is just dirty politics at its dirtiest. I don't know how many of your viewers have seen my wife, Maria, but those that have will understand why I'll quote the late, great Hollywood icon, Paul Newman. As you know, he was married to the beautiful and accomplished actress, Joanne Woodward. When asked about rumors of marital infidelity, Newman responded by asking why a man would go out for hamburger if he had steak at home. That's the best response I can think of for these ridiculous allegations, which I believe are being spread by sick individuals who are envious of the strong partnership Maria and I have.

CONNELLY: Two of the women who have made claims about engaging in sex-for-hire relationships with you are purported to be Hispanic. Has that led you to suspect that the Brigade is behind these allegations?

MARTINEZ: I won't go so far as to say I specifically accuse the Brigade, but I will also say that it wouldn't surprise me if evidence was discovered that linked them to these sordid lies. After all, they've totally misrepresented my views on immigration, so it wouldn't be a big stretch to believe they'd misrepresent my personal life as well.

CONNELLY: You said you wouldn't go so far as to accuse the Brigade of spreading these allegations, but would you be more inclined to suspect them than your party's Democratic and Republican opposition?

MARTINEZ: Look, the Democrats, the Republicans, and the Brigade all have a vested interest in derailing the American Values Party train. I'm not going to speculate on which of the three would be more likely to fabricate such an unscrupulous smear tactic. All I'm going to do is publicly defend my honor, and the honor of my beautiful wife, and the honor of our AVP candidates who are working hard every day to provide our country with a viable alternative to the status quo and restore our country to its rightful position as the greatest nation on earth.

CONNELLY: Back to the Brigade protests for a moment. Does the increasing size and frequency of their protests create additional concerns for security at your campaign events?

MARTINEZ: You'd have to ask my security detail about that. I'm not letting security threats deter me or any of our candidates from doing what the American people expect us to do, which is to meet as many of them as possible and present a clear, compelling case for why they should entrust us with their most precious gift as a United States citizen—their vote. We will not allow ourselves to be shut off from the American people.

CONNELLY: Even if it puts your personal safety at risk?

MARTINEZ: A man who hides from the American people—for security reasons or anything else—does not deserve the honor of serving as an elected official.

CONNELLY: Well, Mr. Martinez, thank you for sitting down with me and addressing these issues in such a candid manner.

MARTINEZ: I appreciate the opportunity, Kristen. The citizens of the United States have an important decision to make in the midterm elections, and everyone involved in the American Values Party is totally committed to doing everything within our power to make their choice as clear and unambiguous as possible.

CONNELLY: And that concludes our exclusive interview with the founder and leader of the American Values Party, Texas businessman Robert Martinez. From Pittsburgh, this is Kristen Connelly, PNN.

Everyone in the room remained still and silent, Martinez and Connelly both smiling at the camera, until Mitch signaled that the recording had been completed. He then proceeded to disconnect the lavalier mikes from both of them before switching off the three pole lights.

Connelly leaned toward Martinez and extended her hand, which he took. "Thank you again, Mr. Martinez. I hope you feel comfortable with the interview."

He smiled and chuckled softly. "I feel a lot better now that it's done. You hit me with some pretty hard questions, but you were fair and you gave me ample time to respond. I appreciate that."

"I wasn't here to do a hatchet job, sir," she said, returning the smile. "I just wanted to provide you the opportunity to give your side of the story on these particularly contentious issues."

"And again, I appreciate that. So, this will air this evening?"

"Yes. Ron Archer is including it as part of the evening news at six."

Martinez glanced at his watch. "That's just an hour and a half from now. Arthur and I will watch it before we leave for our dinner in the ballroom downstairs. You'll be covering the dinner, I suppose?"

"Yes, of course."

"Then why don't you hang out here and watch the interview with us? As soon as that segment is done, you can get back downstairs to meet up with your crew."

"Well, that would be an honor, Mr. Martinez," she said, glancing back and forth from the candidate to his chief of staff. "Are you both sure I won't get in the way?"

"Not at all," Stephenson interjected. "If we see something we don't like, it'll save us the effort of having to track you down to complain."

She laughed. "Understood." She turned to her camera man. "You okay with that, Mitch? This will be Ron's lead segment, so I should be able to watch it and still get downstairs by six-thirty, which would give us an hour before Mr. Martinez's arrival at the dinner."

"No problem," Mitch said. "I'll send this video to Chicago and then grab a sandwich. I'll meet you in the ballroom."

Once Mitch and the sound technician had disassembled their equipment and carried it from the room, Stephenson headed for the door as well. "I have a bunch of phone calls to make, so I'm heading back to my suite. I'll be back a few minutes before six. Call if you need me."

"I'm sure I'll be fine, Arthur, even with a member of the press watching my every move" Martinez said, walking to the door and opening it for Stephenson. "See you in a bit. We can review tonight's speech one more time after we watch the interview."

He watched Stephenson walk down the hall before shutting the door and stepping over to Kristen. "So, you think it was believable?"

"The interview? Of course. I think you were very convincing."

He smiled and shook his head. "I'm not talking about the interview. I'm talking about the ploy to get the two of us alone in this room."

"Yeah, well, about that," she said, smiling coyly. "I'm not so sure I like being compared to hamburger."

He brushed a strand of hair back behind her ear and kissed her neck. "Didn't you hear what I said?" he whispered. "I don't go out for hamburger. But chateaubriand is a whole 'nother story."

Chapter 23

THE OFFICE SCENE—exactly one week before the AVP dinner at the Westin—contrasted sharply with the morning before, when Miriam, Stephanie and Peter had been greeted by a staff that was alternately dazed and overwhelmed with emotion. Mark had convened his small team in the conference room, giving Steph a chance to relate the horrible events of the previous evening just once. She told the story in a somber but stoic voice until she got to the point where Allen took his last breath, and then erupted into uncontrollable sobbing, with Miriam and Peter kneeling on either side, each squeezing a hand. Afterward, Mark invited Peter to his office for a brief discussion of funeral logistics while Abby remained in the conference room to console Stephanie, Miriam and Courtney.

Today the atmosphere had a semblance of normalcy by all outward appearances, but with a melancholy pall permeating the air, weighing down everyone's movements as if the pull of gravity had somehow doubled. Mark had sent everyone home early the previous day, so their daily update on the Martinez fundraiser had been held this morning. They were still on track to execute an elaborate, well-planned event, with Courtney taking over Allen's responsibilities with the symphony. Miriam had also received several new assignments that had previously been managed by Allen, but when she returned to her office she didn't even glance at her notes. Instead, she stared at the wall, as if it were a screen upon which she could project an image of a plan to address their dire situation.

"You do realize there's nothing on that wall, don't you?"

The unexpected sound of a voice startled Miriam back to reality, and she turned to see Stephanie standing in her doorway.

"Just trying to come up with some ideas," she said, smiling weakly.

"Ideas on how to make the fundraiser better?"

"No. Ideas on how to use it to address our problem."

Stephanie stepped inside the tiny room, pulling the door closed behind her before sitting in the chair opposite Miriam's desk. "How have you and Peter managed to do this for so long?" she whispered. "I've only known about Allen for a few months, and didn't have any understanding at all of what it meant for me until you explained it last week. Now we're dealing with Allen's death, an apparent attempt on our lives, and the knowledge that unimaginable power could one day be in the hands of a rider with clearly evil intentions. And yet, we can't tell anyone about any of it."

"Not unless we want them to think we're bat-shit crazy," Miriam said, nodding.

Stephanie stared across the desk, her eyes magnified behind the thick lenses of her glasses, giving her an owl-like appearance. "So, again, how have you done it for so long?"

Miriam leaned back in her chair and closed her eyes, reliving over six and a half centuries of deception in a matter of seconds. "I have to give most of the credit to Peter," she said. "He's always been fanatical about secrecy and flexibility. If he had his way, we'd never go out in public and would move every few months whether we needed to or not. It's been hard...emotionally. We have each other, but you're the first person other than ourselves that we've ever trusted with this knowledge." She looked at Stephanie and blinked back tears. "You're the first real friend I've had since I was a little girl. I didn't realize how much that meant to me until faced with the prospect of running away and leaving you behind."

Stephanie wiped her own eyes and took a moment to regain her composure before speaking. "Thank you for saying that. Real friendships are hard to come by under any circumstances, and—well, let's be honest—our circumstances are pretty damn rare. And I'd never do anything to put that friendship at risk. But what's giving me so much trouble is being unable to go to anyone for help. A man whose power and influence is growing daily wants us dead, and there's absolutely no one we can tell. It's not just us at risk…if his political plans are successful, it's the whole damn country. Hell, the whole damn world!"

Miriam leaned across the desk and put her hand on Stephanie's arm. "I know. Peter and I have never had this much at stake. I'd give us up in a heartbeat if I thought it would make a difference. Peter would too. But that's the problem. All that would be gained by us divulging this to someone else would be us getting put away somewhere, and that would change nothing. Nobody would ever believe us, and there's no way to prove anything." She paused a moment, studying the face of her friend. "And if the three of us are locked up in some institution undergoing psychiatric evaluations morning, noon and night, it would be that much easier for him to get to us. Our only hope for survival is to remain free to move about, hiding if necessary. Because if we don't survive, who's going to stop him?"

Stephanie's eyes were even wider now. "So it's up to the three of us to stop him? How in God's name do we do that?"

"I don't know," Miriam said, exhaling a long, shuddering breath. "But we've got one week to figure it out."

AT FIVE O'CLOCK they resumed their routine schedule for end-of-day briefings. Miriam, Stephanie and Courtney were in their usual positions at the conference room table—each trying to not be obvious as they continuously glanced at Allen's empty chair—when Mark walked in and took his seat at the head of the table. "Okay, team, this shouldn't take too long since we just met this morning, but there are a couple of things we need to discuss."

He looked at each of the three women in succession, as if searching for cracks in their emotional armor, before saying, "Before we start the updates, I wanted to tell you where we are in the funeral planning for Allen." He took a deep breath. "I spoke with Russell this afternoon, and he told me Allen's body has been released by the coroner and is scheduled for cremation tomorrow. Neither he nor Allen were ever affiliated with any church, and he plans to hold onto the ashes for the time being, so he wants to just have a small memorial service in his apartment on Saturday afternoon. Allen didn't have any family, and not that many friends other than us, so it'll be a pretty intimate gathering. Just Russell, us, and perhaps a half dozen people they socialized with. It'll be at four. Can everyone make it?"

Everyone nodded, and Miriam said, "I'll check with Peter, but I'm pretty sure we can be there."

Mark looked at her and smiled. "I know for a fact you will. I just got off the phone with Peter, who had wanted to help with any arrangements, and he has graciously offered to pay for catering, including a bartender. Courtney, we were hoping you could recommend someone."

She nodded. "I'll take care of it, Mark. I know just who to call."

"Perfect, thanks," Mark said. He turned to Miriam. "And thanks to you and Peter, Miriam. For someone who's been here less than two weeks, you're doing a lot."

Miriam didn't know how to respond, so she simply nodded.

"Okay," Mark said. "Back to business. I assume everyone got a chance to watch the Martinez interview on PNN last night?"

"Yeah," Courtney said. "Is it just me, or did Martinez seem to be undressing that hottie blond reporter with his eyes during the whole interview? If I were Maria Martinez, I'd be more worried about her than any prostitutes."

Mark laughed, but simultaneously shook his head. "We can joke about things like that in here, but never outside of this room to anyone else, okay? Having a remark like that about one of our clients—even one made in jest—coming back at us would be a death knell for a PR firm."

"I know, Mark," Courtney said. "I'd never make a comment like that around anyone else." She leaned forward and smiled, lowering her voice to a mischievous whisper. "But it wasn't in jest."

"Well, we're not required to love and respect our clients," Mark said. "We just have to make sure everyone else does. So, back to the interview. Martinez threw a few more jabs at the Brigade, and seemed to be a little concerned about the prospects of more demonstrations at his appearances. Steph, how are we doing on security arrangements?"

"I spoke to the mayor again this afternoon. He said he can't enforce a two-block safety zone around the Westin like we requested, but can deliver a one-block zone in each direction. Any protest permits issued will require demonstrators to stay on the opposite side of Richard Arrington Boulevard. Barricades will hold back anyone not going to the hotel or one of the adjacent restaurants. Crowds of four or more will not be allowed to loiter outside the barricade."

"What about 23rd Street, where it runs between the Westin and the Uptown restaurants?" Mark asked.

"It'll be blocked off about half a block from the hotel entrance," Stephanie said. "That should be enough to keep anyone from throwing anything at any of the arriving guests, including the candidate and his entourage."

"It's close enough for a gun," Courtney said.

"Maybe, but that's for Arrowhead Security to worry about," Stephanie said. "The mayor is in charge of crowd control, so that's what he's focusing on. Besides, there's no evidence that the Brigade is interested in any violence. They just want to be seen and heard."

Mark looked at Stephanie. "Have you briefed Sally McDaniel on this?"

"I'm calling her in the morning. We have just about everything else buttoned down. I'll review it all with Sally to make sure she's comfortable with all the arrangements."

Mark looked around the room. "Okay, everyone make sure Steph has everything she needs for that call. At this stage, I don't think Sally is as concerned with food and music and décor as she is with security, but she seems to have a keen eye for detail, so let's be prepared. She's nervous, and understandably so. The loss of Allen is a great personal tragedy to us, but we have to convince Sally that it was a random crime that has absolutely no bearing on the city's ability to host a safe and secure political fundraiser. Right?"

Miriam and Stephanie both nodded in agreement, but the look they surreptitiously exchanged said they believed otherwise.

TWENTY MINUTES LATER Miriam was sitting in Stephanie's office, waiting for Peter to call and let her know he was waiting outside. The two of them would follow Steph to her apartment and make sure she was safely inside the building before driving home. It was a precaution Peter had insisted on until the fundraiser was behind them. Whatever precautions he had in mind for after the event, he was keeping to himself, but Miriam couldn't help but believe that disappearing was at the top of the list.

Stephanie was searching through her desk drawers for files and cramming them into her computer bag. "I have way too much work to do to be leaving at six o'clock," she said.

"You can work at home," Miriam said. "It's a lot safer."

Stephanie stopped packing and sat down in her chair. "Is it possible that we're overreacting? Is it possible that Mark's right; that Allen's shooting is totally unrelated to the campaign? To what we saw in Dallas?"

Miriam shook her head. "We can't take that chance. It would be one hell of a coincidence that we were involved in a mugging by an armed gunman just three days after Dallas. Peter doesn't believe in coincidences. Frankly, in this case, neither do I."

"But we still don't have a plan for resolving this," Stephanie protested. "If there really is a threat to us, it won't necessarily go away when Martinez and his crew leave town next week."

"Peter and I are trying to come up with a plan," Miriam said. "But I have to be honest; so far we don't have much. Which means we have to take precautions like this."

Stephanie smiled. "Prepare for the worst, but hope for the best, huh?"

"Pretty much," Miriam said before looking at her phone as it emanated a soft buzz. "Okay, Peter's downstairs. Ready to go?"

"Yeah, I guess. I just know that as soon as I get started working tonight I'll remember something that I need from the office."

"Well, it'll just have to wait until tomorrow," Miriam said, her voice stern. "Once you are locked safely inside your apartment, you stay there for the rest of the night."

"Okay," Stephanie sighed.

"Promise?"

Stephanie nodded. "Promise. But not going to a bar for a whole week is going to be a record for me." She picked up her computer bag and walked out the door, flicking off the office light before turning back to face Miriam.

"So you really think the shooter is still out there? Still looking for us?"

"We have to assume so, yes," Miriam said solemnly. "To the guy that hired him, we're loose ends. And I don't think he got to where he is by leaving loose ends lying around."

DOCTOR DUBYA couldn't believe it. He'd waited until dark to venture out of his small but expensively appointed apartment—compliments of his lucrative, tax-free occupation—and who should he find standing in the hallway but the squatty white dude with the New Orleans Saints ball cap? How the hell did this guy find out where he lived?

"Can we chat a minute?" the man said, by way of greeting.

"Uh, sure," Wendell said. "Where you wanna go?"

The man nodded toward the apartment door. "In there."

"Hey, listen man," Wendell said, "I don't do no business here. This is, like, my sanctuary, know what I mean?"

"It won't take but a minute," the man said, his tone indicating it was non-negotiable.

And he was right. Fifty seconds later, he was closing the apartment door behind him and heading back toward the stairs. One more loose end all tied up.

Chapter 24

REMEMBRANCES WERE SHORT and sweet, with heartfelt comments delivered by Mark, Abby, Stephanie and Russell. It was over in about ten minutes, but the food and drink had been flowing for the next two hours. The urn with Allen's cremains rested on a small table adorned with flowers and several framed pictures, mostly shots of him and Russell at various landmarks they had visited while traveling together. Although they had been a couple a little less than two years, Allen had apparently accompanied Russell on several ballet tours in Europe. Peter noticed one snapshot of the two of them standing in front of *Teatro alla Scala*, and couldn't help thinking about his and Miriam's narrow escape from Milan two and a quarter centuries earlier. In retrospect, the threat there was nothing compared to what they faced now.

Sipping his fourth glass of red wine, he walked over to a large window offering a view of the famous Vulcan—the largest iron-ore statue in the world—that stood guard over Birmingham from its perch atop Red Mountain. Miriam and Stephanie joined him a couple of minutes later and Miriam followed his gaze to where Courtney stood talking to the one attending friend of Allen and Russell who wasn't gay. She was dressed in appropriate funeral attire, if "appropriate" could be defined as a black micro-miniskirt, dark grey semi-transparent blouse, and black stiletto heels.

"You shouldn't stare, you know," Miriam whispered. "It's quite uncouth."

He smiled at his wife's uncharacteristic display of jealousy. "I'm not staring," he said. "I'm thinking."

She positioned herself directly in front of him, blocking his line of sight. "Well, if you're thinking what I think you're thinking, you're in deep trouble, *kochanka*."

He leaned to the side to peer around Miriam's head. "I'm thinking how I could use her."

"Oooh," Stephanie said with a feigned grimace, "I should leave you two alone to sort this out."

"No," Peter said. "I'm talking about my plan for next Thursday night. Courtney will be there, won't she?"

"Yeah, she'll be with me," Stephanie said, smiling. "As part of the hired help, not sitting in the ballroom with all you rich folks."

"Well, we know that Robert Martinez has an eye for the ladies, right?" Peter said.

"We know that it has been *alleged* that he has an eye for the ladies," Stephanie corrected.

"Yeah, but you know the old saying; where there's smoke, there's fire." He turned his gaze back to Courtney. "And if those legs can't kindle a man's flame, it can't be kindled."

"You're not making me feel any better, sweetheart," Miriam muttered.

Peter ignored the remark and turned to Stephanie. "Is there a way we can arrange for her to meet Martinez at the event?"

"I guess so," Stephanie said. "There'll be a receiving line where all the guests will be able to shake hands with him and Senator Carson before being seated for dinner. For ten grand a plate, people expect to press flesh with the main attraction. So maybe Courtney and I can tag along with you and Miriam when you meet him. I can justify being there since I've met him before and I'm in charge of the event, and Courtney could be introduced as my star-struck assistant who's there to help me make sure the evening goes according to plan."

"What do you have in mind, Peter?" Miriam asked. "We can't ask Courtney to do anything dangerous...or immoral."

"Well...." Stephanie said, wagging her head from side to side. "She might be open to..."

"No, no, nothing like that," Peter said. "I really haven't figured out exactly how we could use her. But if our plan calls for separating Martinez and Stephenson from the crowd for a few minutes, all we'd have to do is send Courtney wherever we want Martinez to go and he'll follow."

"But there'll be security guys there watching his every move," Miriam said. "And if one of them isn't attached to Martinez at the hip, Stephenson will be. Do you think he'll let Martinez out of his sight?"

"That's why I'm thinking about using Courtney," Peter said. "I can't come up with any other way to separate the two for a few minutes than to use the lure of a romantic dalliance. Martinez wouldn't want Stephenson around for that. That would be..."

"Sick," Stephanie said. "The word you're searching for is *sick*."

Miriam stepped in close to Peter and turned so that she too could observe Courtney. "You plan to separate Martinez and Stephenson. So you can do what, exactly?"

He drained the last of his wine. "I don't know. I haven't gotten that far yet. But I'm thinking that a one-on-one conversation, rider to rider, will be part of the equation, so I've got to find a way to get him alone. And I've got to figure out what I'll say when I do. "

Miriam managed a weak smile and said, "How about *Please don't have us killed?*"

Peter returned her smile. "It probably needs to be a little more forceful than that, but I'll try to work that into the conversation."

IT WAS GOOD to be home. Robert Martinez had decided to take the first half of the Labor Day weekend off from the frenzy of the campaign trail and spend a couple of nights in his own bed—and with his own wife—for a change. He was scheduled to attend a cocktail reception at a neighbor's ranch in San Antonio on Sunday evening, and a Labor Day barbecue and rodeo event the following afternoon in Houston. His swing through the southeast would start Tuesday morning and, although quite lucrative, would be exhausting. Appearances and press conferences every day, fundraiser dinners every night, followed by midnight travel to the next city to grab a few hours of sleep before starting the process all over again. It would be a grueling schedule, but Sally McDaniel had promised that every day with the voters—and every night with her—would be worthwhile.

Unfortunately, what had been planned as a Deep South political lovefest was starting to shape into a week-long confrontation with *Brigada de Proteccion Hispana*. The PNN interview a few nights earlier had not succeeded in terms of painting the Brigade as a disorderly band of lawless rabble-rousers. Their support base appeared to be growing daily, and their organizational and planning capabilities were far better than previously thought. It was looking like Martinez and his candidates would be confronted with large and vocal demonstrations in each of the five states he would be visiting.

He'd hoped that a Saturday afternoon and evening with no public appearances would be restful and rejuvenating, but that had unfortunately not been the case. He and Arthur Stephenson had sat in the large and lush family room of his sprawling San Antonio mansion, sipping scotch as they flipped back and forth between Baylor's season opener against SMU and PNN's continuing coverage of the scandal that had rocked the Pennsylvania congressional race. The anonymous leak to the press that the front-runner, Democratic Scranton mayor Ed Wilkes, had accepted cash and gifts totaling over sixty thousand dollar in exchange for a city construction project had exploded into a major national news story. The story had provided a welcome diversion from the prostitution rumors about Martinez and the AVP's alleged use of border state militias to terrorize Hispanics. Not seeing anything new from the reports that had aired earlier in the afternoon, Martinez turned back to the football game just in time to see his alma mater lose by a fifty-two yard field goal as time expired.

"Shit!" Martinez muttered as he rose from the sofa and walked over to the bar to pour his third double. He turned to Stephenson and asked, "Ready for a refill?"

"I'm good for now," Stephenson said. "Thanks."

"What a shitty day this turned out to be," Martinez said, returning to his seat and lifting his feet to rest on the antique oak coffee table. "At least I made the right decision when I turned down the tickets to the football game. You know good and damned well there would've been a dozen TV cameras zooming in on me right as that field goal was kicked. Better to be here where I could cuss and drink privately."

"Yeah, this may end up being your last day out of the public eye for a while," Stephenson said. "This next week is gonna be pretty taxing."

Martinez smiled and took a sip of his drink. "Don't use the word *taxing* in the presence of a conservative politician. That's the dirtiest of dirty words."

Stephenson chuckled. "Nice to see you still have your sense of humor."

"Yeah, well, I don't know why," Martinez grumbled. "I'm used to being the lead news story. Now, my coverage isn't about what I'm saying, it's on what is being said *about* me."

"How's Maria handling all these stories?"

"Let's just say I didn't get the warm welcome I'd hoped for when I got home this morning," Martinez said. He took another gulp of his drink. "What are we going to do about these bastards, Arthur? We've threatened them, strong-armed them, and tried to turn public opinion against them. Nothing works. They just keep getting stronger. And louder. We've got to find a way to shut them up."

"Well, remember that *free speech* thing in the Constitution?" Stephenson teased. "As long as they remain peaceful, there's not an awful lot that can be done to muzzle them."

"I know, I know," Martinez sighed. "Makes me wish they'd start a riot or something. Anything to show they aren't a bunch of saints with Spanish accents."

IT WAS ALMOST MIDNIGHT when Anwar strode across the marbled foyer entrance to answer the soft knock on his door. He paused before reaching for the doorknob and gazed into a framed mirror hanging above an antique rosewood lowboy. The reflection staring back at him differed from the face everyone else saw except for one feature—the eyes. It wasn't just that they were the same color. Anwar had ridden hosts with eyes of every conceivable color over the past one hundred and eighty-five years. But they always took on the cold, unfeeling depth and fierce, penetrating stare of the original being. If the eyes truly were the window to the soul, then his opened into a dark, empty pit.

He opened the door to Ben Wycliff, whose Wycliff Security Services was now almost totally committed to jobs for the American Values Party. He had a couple of junior guys working on a long-standing contract helping to guard the grid of the power company serving most of south Texas, but his more experienced—and more ruthless—men were working directly with him on whatever was asked by the man who stood before him.

Wycliff stepped through the door into the much cooler air of the house. He removed his Stetson and wiped sweat from his bald head with a red handkerchief, which he then returned to the back pocket of his jeans. "Must be something important for us to be meeting this late," he said.

"Everything I call you about is important," Anwar said as he turned and walked to the kitchen.

Wycliff followed, marveling at the size of the rooms and the obvious lavishness of the décor. "Well, we could have saved you some time if you'd just called, you know. It's an hour drive for me to get here from my place."

"Too many ears on the phones," Anwar said. "And I couldn't take a chance of being seen, so meeting in the middle wasn't an option. Don't I pay you enough to make a two hour round trip to get your next assignment?"

"Absolutely," Wycliff answered quickly. "I'm available to you 24/7. I was just saying I hated for you to have to wait up so late for me to get here."

"I'm moved by your concern for my rest, but I don't require much sleep," Anwar said with a notable touch of sarcasm. He noticed the visible flinch of his guest and smiled, knowing he'd put his hired help back in his place.

He walked to the kitchen side of a granite-topped bar separating the kitchen from a white oak paneled keeping room. The opposite wall was dominated by a large, stacked stone fireplace, which was certainly not needed on such a hot and humid early September night. He retrieved his Reidel Vinum scotch glass from the counter and pointed to a stool on the other side of the bar. "Have a seat. Can I offer you a drink? I have plenty of beer if you'd like one."

"I'll have whatever you're having," Wycliff said as he perched his squatty form on a stool.

Anwar was drinking 30 year old scotch, which he hated to waste on a man whose palate was certainly not as developed as his own, but he nodded and reached for a glass. "Ice?"

"Yeah, just a couple of cubes, thanks," Wycliff said.

At least that gave Anwar an excuse to select a sturdier glass than the delicate one he was using. "I'll give you a tumbler then" he said. "These Reidels are really for drinking it neat. They don't leave much room for ice."

He quickly plopped a couple of ice cubes into the tumbler before his roughneck guest could change his mind. He put the drink on the bar and walked around to the other side, sitting on the stool next to Wycliff. "I'm still disappointed that you couldn't take care of those two women. You're sure your local talent—and I use the term loosely, given his abysmal failure—has been silenced?"

"Permanently," Wycliff said after swallowing a gulp of the best scotch he'd ever tasted. "Took care of it myself."

"Good," Anwar said, his look menacing. "We can't afford any more screw-ups."

- 203 -

"I'll drive back to Birmingham and take care of those bitches tomorrow night," Wycliff said. He didn't scare easily, but the look his employer was giving him caused him to shiver, despite the warm weather.

"No," Anwar said. "Too risky. You had a chance to make it look like a random mugging. Another attack in less than a week will make it clear that they're being specifically targeted."

"So we're gonna just forget about them?" Wycliff asked, more than a little confused. If the two women were not that much of a concern, why had he been tasked with killing them in the first place?

Anwar fixed him with another ice-cold stare. "I'm not going to forget anything. They still have to die. And soon. We're just going to have to go about it differently."

"I'll do whatever you want, whenever you want," Wycliff said, anxious to get back in the good graces of the man who paid him extravagantly and scared him shitless.

"Fine, but this time, I need a hell of a lot more than your good intentions. I need results. It's going to take thoughtful planning and flawless execution. And we don't have much time."

"Just tell me what you need," Wycliff said, even more nervous now that his expertise was being challenged. Not only did he want to keep the money coming in…he seriously did not want to piss this guy off.

"We've gotten word that the Brigade will be staging demonstrations at every campaign stop in our southern tour this week," Anwar said. "The one in Birmingham on Thursday night will be especially big, given the migrant farmhand population in the state. If it turned violent, the group would be exposed as the criminal instigators they are. And then all of their nasty accusations would be discredited in the minds of a lot of the voting public."

"I see," said Wycliff, nodding slowly as his mind began to wrap itself around the assignment. "But what about the two women? How do they fit in?"

Anwar took a sip of the scotch, savoring the rich, smoky burn on his tongue. "Well, as you know, whenever there are violent confrontations, innocent victims can get caught in the cross-fire."

"I see," said Wycliff, nodding knowingly. "We'll kill two birds with one stone."

Anwar smiled his cold smile. "Oh, I imagine there will be a lot more dead birds than that. But civilian casualties are an unfortunate by-product of war. Such is the cost of victory."

Chapter 25

IT WAS THE WARMEST Labor Day that Miriam and Peter had experienced in quite a few years. In New Jersey, early September usually brought the cooler, drier air that promised the imminent arrival of autumn. Before that, Aspen had been the scene of more than two dozen Labor Day celebrations, a couple of which had even featured snow flurries. But Labor Day in Alabama was just another summer day—hot, humid and still. In spite of this, Peter was manning the gas grill on the condo patio, braving the heat and smoke as he tended three mammoth hamburger patties and a half dozen cheese Brats. He heard the sliding glass door open behind him and turned to see Miriam smiling as she stuck one arm out the door to hand him another beer.

"You wouldn't be any wetter if you were standing in a rainstorm," she said. "Want a hand towel?"

He took the beer and held it to the side of his face. "No, that's okay. Just bring me the mushrooms and the cheese. These will be done in another few minutes."

"Okay, stay right there," she said. "I don't want you dripping on the kitchen floor."

She returned a few seconds later with a platter, which she placed on the wrought iron patio table. "Everything else is ready. Steph made a beautiful fruit salad and I just took the baked beans out of the oven."

"Why'd you turn on the oven?" he said, spooning sautéed mushrooms and onions on the burgers before topping them with blue cheese. "You could've put them out here and they would've cooked just as fast."

"God, it does feel like it," she said. "When you bring those in you can hop in the shower while we set the table." She fanned her face with her hand. "I feel awful that you've been sweltering out here while we've been inside drinking margaritas. I'll make it up to you, I promise."

"Well," he said, grinning, "You could always join me in the shower."

She stepped to him and rose on her toes to kiss his sweaty cheek. "Behave, *kochanka*. We have company. But I think there could be some Labor Day fireworks tonight if you're not too worn out from slaving over a hot grill all afternoon."

She turned to head back into the condo, but when she reached the door she took a quick peek inside before sliding it shut and whispering, "I really do appreciate you letting me invite her over for the day. She's a lot more overwhelmed by Allen's death—and everything else, for that matter—than she lets on. And knowing that in three days she'll be face-to-face with the one responsible for it all really has her on edge. I don't think she would've made it through this holiday weekend without us."

"She's not the only one on edge," Peter said. "Our world is going to change on Thursday night. I don't know exactly how, and I don't know what we'll need to do in response, but it will be very different. You need to be prepared for that. And so does Steph."

"I know," she said, looking down at the flagstone patio floor. She then lifted her head, and her eyes were brimming with tears. "I so much wanted the life we were building here. The job, the house we bought, finding a friend who I can actually be myself around. I'm just so damned…mad."

He nodded and then turned back to the grill, starting the process of transferring the burgers and Brats to the platter. "It's okay to be angry. That's natural. You just need to focus that anger on something positive."

She wrinkled her brow, a confused frown creasing her sweaty forehead. "Something positive? Like what?"

He picked up the platter and turned to face her. "Like staying alive."

"THIS IS KRISTEN CONNELLY, reporting live from Houston, where American Values Party founder Robert Martinez and AVP congressional candidate Martin Roebuck are attending a traditional, Texas-style Labor Day campaign event. Nearly two thousand contributors were invited to a private rodeo, followed by a massive barbecue, featuring beef brisket, pork ribs and chicken. But not everyone who showed up at NRG Park was here to cheer on their fellow Texans. This eight foot fence, erected just for the occasion, separates the contributors from an equally large group of protestors from *Brigada de Proteccion Hispana*—The Hispanic Protection Brigade.

"The protestors started arriving at noon, just as the 90-minute rodeo performance was getting underway. As a result, the vast majority of invitees were completely unaware of the demonstration until they left the arena to walk over to this field behind me, where the barbecue pits, dining tents and stage were set up. Just on the other side of the fence, a large group of demonstrators was singing the old Woody Guthrie anthem, *This Land is Your Land, This Land is My Land,* so loudly that a country western band was unable to perform on the stage. The size of the protest group and the timing of their arrival indicate a higher level of organization than has been seen in previous Brigade demonstrations.

"At one point, Robert Martinez took the stage to address his party's supporters, but the protestors made so much noise booing and blowing air horns that he was unable to continue. Martinez gave up on the speech and has since been moving continuously through the crowd of supporters, shaking hands and posing for pictures in an apparent attempt to salvage the event. When I got close enough to ask him for a comment, all he said was, 'Just show America what is going on here today.'

"A few minutes ago I was able to speak briefly through the fence with Brigade founder Carlos Guerra. Mr. Guerra refused to appear on camera, but told me that he will be shadowing Martinez and the AVP team all week, and has demonstrations organized in every city where they will appear. I asked him what he hoped to accomplish with his demonstrations. He said, and I quote, 'I want voters to see that we are peaceful, law-abiding people who are simply trying to live the American dream. For some reason that I cannot understand, Robert Martinez wants to prevent that.' End quote.

"AVP organizers were hoping this week in the Sunbelt would galvanize their support in the southern states so their campaign organization can focus the majority of the next two months on more contested races in New Jersey, Ohio, Pennsylvania, and Michigan. They expect large crowds of supporters everywhere they stop over the next five days. However, it looks like they can expect equally large crowds of detractors, as the Hispanic Protection Brigade pulls out all the stops in their bid to derail the AVP train.

"From Houston, this is Kristin Connelly, PNN."

PETER TURNED OFF the television and rose from the leather recliner. "You ladies ready for a refill?" he asked, holding up his own empty margarita glass as he headed to the kitchen.

"Sure," Miriam said. She turned to Stephanie, seated beside her on the sofa. "How about you, Steph?"

"Oh, why the hell not?" Stephanie said. "Based on that report, this damned fundraiser dinner has moved from bad dream to total freakin' nightmare status. I mean, it was bad enough that we have to pull off a complex extravaganza for someone who just tried to kill us—and, in doing so, killed one of my best friends—now we have to do it in the middle of what could very well turn into a riot. Talk about being caught between a rock and a hard place."

"I imagine Martinez feels the same way," Miriam said. "If he softens his comments on immigration, he and his party lose support from a lot of right-wing conservatives. But if he doesn't, he's going to be shouting down large crowds of Brigade protestors everywhere he goes."

Stephanie leaned her head back against the sofa and closed her eyes. "Oh, God, I wish we'd never been hired to plan this damned fundraiser. I wish we'd never gone to Dallas. I wish we hadn't seen what we saw, and that Allen hadn't paid the price for it. I just wish…I just wish all of this would go away."

"We'll get through it," Miriam said.

"How?"

"I don't know," Miriam said, and then flashed a forced smile. "But we'll worry about that tomorrow. We promised ourselves we'd just relax and have fun today. So let me refill these empty glasses."

Miriam stood up and reached for Stephanie's glass, but her friend held onto it and said, "I'll help you clear the table. You two have waited on me enough today." She paused and then added, "It's good to have friends like you."

Miriam said nothing as she led the way to the kitchen. She and Peter had not yet figured out their course of action for Friday morning—assuming they made it through Thursday night unscathed. But she knew it was unlikely that they would stay in Birmingham. And equally unlikely that, wherever they went, they'd be taking Stephanie with them. The two of them knew how to disappear without a trace. They'd never had to concern themselves with anyone else, and didn't have the processes in place to create a new identity for a third person. Also, if the possibility of being recognized became too risky, they could—if absolutely necessary—find new hosts. Stephanie didn't have that option. Her ability to alter her appearance was limited to conventional means like hair dye, make-up or, in the most extreme circumstances, plastic surgery. But surgery took time, and left a trail. And positive identifiers like fingerprints couldn't be changed. She would always be traceable. And if she could be traced, anyone with her could be traced too.

Stephanie set her glass on the kitchen counter. "You can top me off while I start cleaning up some of this mess in here," she said, gesturing toward the table, still covered with paper plates, napkins and leftover food. "Where do you keep the trash bags?"

"Under here," Miriam said, reaching under the sink for one and handing it to Stephanie, who headed toward the dining room as she shook the trash bag vigorously to open it up. Leaning close to her husband, she whispered, "We have to tell her what our plans are. We can't just leave her stranded."

"I don't know what our plans are myself," Peter whispered back. "And even if I did, I wouldn't get into them with her right now. She's been drinking and would probably be overly emotional, which wouldn't help at all. We'll be spending a lot of time together over the next two days, finalizing our plan for Thursday night. When I've figured all of that out, and what you and I will do afterward, I'll think about sharing it with her."

Miriam looked down and fought back tears. She felt Peter's hand under her chin, lifting her face. She looked at this man she had loved so dearly for over six and a half centuries, and then buried her face in his chest. "Can't we take her with us?" she pleaded for probably the hundredth time in the past forty-eight hours.

"We've talked about this, Miriam," he whispered, his voice soft, but forceful. "It would increase the risk for her and for us. But I'll have a plan for her too. And the financial means to execute it. It'll be up to her to follow it or not. That's all we can do."

"Hey, you two, save it for after I leave," Stephanie said, walking into the kitchen with an overstuffed bag of trash. "Which will be shortly. Unless there's more cleaning up I can help with, I should probably get going."

Miriam wiped her eyes with the back of her hand, hoping her friend wouldn't notice that she'd been crying. "But we were just pouring you another margarita," she said. "You can stay a little longer."

Stephanie smiled and shook her head. "This is something I don't say very often, but I think I've had enough. One more margarita and I won't be in any shape to drive home." She cut her eyes at the two of them and added, "And you two need to get back to what you were doing before the buzz wears off. Tequila sex is the best!"

Miriam laughed, relieved that Stephanie had misread the scene in the kitchen. She agreed with Peter that now wasn't the time to have a serious discussion about their plans for the future. It had been a good day—a holiday respite from the stress of the situation they would have to face in three days. And the stress of knowing that even a successful plan for their confrontation on Thursday night would dramatically change their lives. Better to wait until tomorrow when their heads—and hopefully, their plans—would be clearer.

The three of them spent a few more minutes putting away the remnants of their holiday meal and then gathered at the door as Stephanie fished through her purse for her car keys. "Sure you're okay to drive?" Peter asked. "You can stick around a little longer and I'll put on some coffee."

"No," I'm fine. "I'll take it slow, and there won't be any traffic. I should be home in fifteen minutes."

"And you will call me the minute you're inside your apartment and the door is locked," Miriam said, the sternness of her voice covering the ache she felt at seeing her friend leave the condo for what could very well be—unbeknownst to her—the last time.

"Yes, Mom," Stephanie said, smiling. "I just don't want my phone call to interrupt anything, you know."

"I think we can wait fifteen minutes," Miriam said.

"Or, we could be done in fifteen minutes," Peter said.

"I think you'd better go with her plan," Stephanie said, nodding in Miriam's direction. "Seriously, though, thank you both so much. For taking care of me on Saturday, for having me over today, for... well, for everything. I really don't know what I'd do without the two of you."

Miriam knew she'd break down if she didn't get Stephanie out the door quickly. "Go," she said. "And I expect this phone to ring in fifteen minutes, okay?"

She and Peter watched as Stephanie got into her car and drove away. She pushed the door shut and leaned back against it, the tears starting to flow again. "I hate this. I...just...hate...it."

Peter took her into his arms and squeezed. "I know, sweetheart. But you have a target on your back. And so does Steph. And after Thursday night, so will I. It's just too risky trying to keep the three of us together. After some time, once we're resettled, we may be able to reach out to her. We'll just have to wait and see."

She didn't respond. She didn't know how to. She'd never been in this situation before, where anyone other than the two of them mattered. But Steph did matter. Maybe it was simply because she was—like them—a rider. Or maybe it was that she was the first person in six hundred and sixty years, other than Peter, who seemed to truly care about her. It was too much to give up. There had to be a way. There just had to be.

She pulled away from Peter's embrace and looked into his eyes. "Do you think there's any way, when we confront him, that we could convince him that it would be in everyone's best interest to just leave us alone?"

He shook his head slowly. "I don't see how. He has too much at stake. We'd never be safe. The risk is just too great."

"And there's no way to eliminate that risk?"

"Just one," he said, thinking back to the confrontation with the other rider in Milan.

She put her hand to her mouth, as if to block the question she had to ask. "You mean…?"

"Yes," he said. "I'd have to kill him."

Chapter 26

TUESDAY MORNING STARTED OUT to be a fairly routine day at the office. Mark had convened a comprehensive review of the fundraiser plans at nine o'clock. It took two hours to cover all the details, but at the end, he was satisfied that everything was in place.

"Great job, team," he said to Miriam, Stephanie and Courtney as the meeting closed. "In spite of the horrible tragedy we suffered last week, you pulled it off. I can't think of a single thing I'd change. I'm very proud of you, and also very grateful. This dinner will be a defining moment for Sheffield and Associates—the kind of event that could open doors we didn't even know existed."

Oh, if you only knew how true that statement is, thought Miriam. Their actions on Thursday evening might open doors that could not be closed again. Doors that once opened could potentially unleash the power and vengeance of the United States government to do the bidding of a being that no one in any government agency realized existed. It was a nightmarish scenario with unimaginable implications. How much havoc could a rider with a malevolent agenda wreak with the resources of the most powerful nation on the planet at his disposal? The possibilities were endless…and endlessly terrifying.

The only positive Miriam could see was that now that the PR firm's plans were nailed down, she, Peter and Stephanie could concentrate on their own agenda. At noon, Miriam was in Stephanie's office doing just that. Specifically, they were trying to decide the best way to approach Courtney about her task on Thursday night. Their concern over whether Courtney would be willing to play the role of seductress with Robert Martinez was not as troubling as their inability to come up with a plausible explanation of why they'd be asking her to do it. That was the topic of discussion when Stephanie's interoffice phone line lit up.

"Hold on, it's Abby," she said.

She listened for a moment before saying, "Okay," and hanging up the phone. She grabbed the thick Martinez file and pushed her chair back from her desk. "Mark needs us in his office. Right now."

"What's it about?" Miriam asked.

"Abby didn't say. She just said he wanted the two of us to stop what we're doing and head over there."

Miriam stood. "Should I get my Martinez file off my desk?"

"No," Stephanie said. "I have the master file here. Anything he wants to change, I'll make a note of it. Let's go. Abby implied he wanted us there ASAP."

Thirty seconds later they opened Mark's door and saw that he was sitting at his conference table. He wasn't alone. As Miriam walked toward the table she recognized Lieutenant John Greene, the detective who had interviewed them in the private event room of O'Brien's Pub the night that Allen had been murdered. He rose from his chair as the two women approached and shook hands with both.

"Ms. Mullins, Mrs. Hoffman," he said, looking intently, but not threateningly, at each.

Miriam and Stephanie pulled out chairs and sat, turning their gaze to their boss, who looked a little pale as he said, "Lieutenant Greene has an update on Allen's murder."

They turned back to face the detective, who had his hands folded on top of a manila envelope. "The Birmingham Police got a call on Saturday afternoon from the manager of a downtown apartment building. Tenants were complaining of a foul odor emanating from one of the units. When the responding officers couldn't get anyone to come to the door, the manager used his master key to let them in. They found a body. A suspected small-time drug and gun dealer named Wendell Harrison, aka Doctor Dubya. He'd been on our radar screen for a while, but had never been directly implicated in any of the busts we'd made.

"Anyway, he'd been shot twice in the head, execution style. The coroner estimated the time of death to have been sometime Thursday night or very early Friday morning."

"So, two nights after Allen was killed," Stephanie said.

"Yes," Greene nodded.

Stephanie locked eyes with the detective. "And you believe this is the man who attacked Miriam and me and killed Allen?"

"We do," Greene said, nodding solemnly. "We didn't connect him to your case at first. We thought his murder was just a gang thing, given his associations. So we processed the crime scene as a gang-related execution and began questioning known associates. But the next afternoon—that was Sunday—we were searching his apartment for drugs and weapons, and we found a loose board in the floor of the bedroom closet, underneath some boxes of old clothes. Beneath that board was an open space between two floor joists, and in that space was a small metal tackle box, with a combination lock. When we got the lock open, we found almost five thousand dollars in cash, and a .25 caliber semi-automatic with the serial number filed off. Late yesterday, on a whim, I had our lab run a ballistics test on the gun. It's a match with the bullets retrieved during Mr. Trammell's autopsy."

Miriam swallowed loudly and cleared her throat. "So you think the money you found was drug money?"

Greene looked at her, and then at Stephanie. "No, I believe it was hit money."

"What?" Stephanie said, her hands shaking visibly as she put them over her eyes, as if trying to block out the image she was most certainly reliving in her mind. "Why would you think that?"

Greene smiled. "Well, I hate to give away our investigative secrets, but here's why. Harrison was a small-time dealer. I'm sure he pulled in several thousand a month, but it would be in dribs and drabs. Wrinkled, well-worn bills of various denominations; whatever his buyers could scrape up. The cash we found was all twenties, and relatively un-worn, if that's a word. I'm sure the money had been laundered, as there were no sequential serial numbers or anything like that. They just weren't the kind of bills that a punk like Harrison would accumulate in his normal routine. So the fact that he had that kind of cash lying around, in that condition, within forty-eight hours of Mr. Trammell being killed with that gun…well, I think you'd agree, it's a logical conclusion."

They all sat looking at each other for a few seconds before Miriam broke the silence. "So you're convinced that this Wendell Harrison guy was *hired* to kill Allen? Who would hire someone to kill Allen?"

Greene held up one hand to stop her. "Let's not get ahead of ourselves. What we know is that we found five grand worth of neat, unmarked twenties in Harrison's apartment, along with the gun that was used to kill Mr. Trammell. We still can't be positive it was Harrison who pulled the trigger."

Miriam, obviously upset and frustrated, blurted, "Well, how will you ever be sure he pulled the trigger? He's dead now."

Greene turned to her. "Did you get a good look at him?"

"Well, yeah. I…I guess," she stammered. "Medium height, skinny black dude. But he had on a hoodie, and it was after dark, and there were shadows, so…"

"But you think you'd be able to recognize him?" Greene persisted.

Stephanie started shaking her head. "Oh no, oh hell no. You're not gonna make us go down to the morgue to identify his body, are you? I'm having nightmares already. Please don't make me do that!"

Greene spoke softly, gently. "Ms. Mullins, I can't *make* you do anything. And I'd never even suggest you go to the morgue to identify this body. Two shots to the forehead, two days of lying around in a fairly warm apartment…trust me, it's not a pretty sight." He sighed. "Having said that, I need your help."

He lifted his folded hands and tapped the envelope on which they'd been resting. "Would you and Mrs. Hoffman be willing to look at these morgue photos and tell me if this is the guy who accosted you and killed your friend?"

Mark spoke up. "Before either of you answer that, I want you to know that I asked Lieutenant Greene to show me the pictures before you came in here. They're…well, they're pretty gruesome."

Stephanie was still shaking her head slowly from side to side. It was obvious to Miriam that her friend was struggling with the detective's request. But she knew it had to be done, if for no other reason than to keep Lieutenant Greene from suspecting they were hiding something. "Will it really help your investigation?" Miriam asked. "I mean, Allen's dead; Harrison's dead. How will our looking at these pictures help at this stage?"

Greene leaned forward and spoke softly. "Look, I know this is difficult for you. You've both been through so much already. But we need to be sure that it was Harrison who shot Mr. Trammel. If it wasn't, if it was someone else using this gun we found in Harrison's apartment, it would likely mean that Harrison was involved in some way, but the killer would still be out there. Maybe Harrison was killed to keep him quiet. So we need to be sure who pulled that trigger, and the two of you are the only ones who can possibly resolve that."

"Fine," Stephanie blurted. "Show us the damn pictures."

Greene glanced at Miriam, as if to confirm that she was also agreeable. She nodded, and he opened the envelope and pulled out four photographs. "He'd been cleaned up a bit when these were taken," he said, "but they're still hard to look at. Just take your time. If you need to step out for a minute, that's okay. I'll wait."

He spread the photos on the table in front of the two women. Miriam pulled two to her and forced herself to study them. They were close-ups of Harrison's face. His eyes were not completely closed and his face looked a little puffy, but the main difference from when she had first met him was that he now had two small dark holes about an inch apart in his forehead. They were surprisingly neat, although she imagined the back of his head was a different story. She glanced at Lieutenant Greene, about to confirm that this was indeed the man who had attacked them one week earlier, but he met her gaze and shook his head. She realized he wanted Stephanie to have time to study the photos and reach her own conclusion as well. Miriam pushed her two photos back to the detective and waited.

A few seconds later, Stephanie looked up and said, "That's him. I'm almost positive."

Greene nodded and then looked at Miriam. "Mrs. Hoffman?"

"Yes, I'm pretty sure," she said. "Same nose, same mouth. It's him."

Greene gathered up the photos and reinserted them into the manila envelope. "Thank you both," he said. "I know that wasn't easy, but it was a big help to our investigation."

Stephanie took a deep breath and appeared to stifle a shudder. "Now what?" she asked.

"Now that we know Harrison was the killer, we find out who hired him," Greene said. He looked at both of them intently before adding, "And why."

Mark leaned back in his chair and shook his head. "But that's where this whole hired hitman theory seems to fall apart, Lieutenant," he said. "Allen worked here for two years, and was about as quiet and low-key as someone could be. He'd been involved in a stable relationship for almost that entire time, so a jilted lover scenario doesn't seem likely. Granted, I don't know an awful lot about his life before he moved here from Miami, but I just can't picture him being involved with anything that would get him killed."

Greene shocked them all when he said, "You're assuming Mr. Trammell was the target."

Mark leaned forward across the table, his face a mask of bewilderment. "If Allen wasn't the target, then who was?"

Greene didn't answer. Instead, he turned to Stephanie and said, "Ms. Mullins, you told me last Tuesday night that you and Mrs. Hoffman had walked out of the restaurant and down a few feet to where your car was parked, and the assailant—Wendell Harrison—stepped out of the shadows and pointed a gun at you."

Stephanie's eyes seemed to be dancing in her head. When she spoke, her voice was a barely audible whisper. "Yes."

Greene alternated his penetrating stare between Stephanie and Miriam. "So at the precise moment you were threatened, Mr. Trammell was still in the restaurant. Correct?"

"Well, I think so," Stephanie stammered. "It all happened so fast. I saw a hand grabbing the shoulder strap of Miriam's purse, and then I saw the gun, and I was thinking this couldn't be happening, and then all of a sudden Allen came running up, and the gun was pointed at him, and then it fired, and…"

"But when it all started, the two of you were the only ones out there, right?" Greene asked.

Stephanie looked like she was about to cry. "I don't know! I told you, it all happened so fast. One minute it was just me and Miriam, and then in a flash this guy with a gun was there, and then Allen stepped between us. Why is it so important to know whether Allen was still in the restaurant or already coming out the door when it started? The end result is the same."

"But it *is* important, Ms. Mullins," Greene said softly. "When we were working on the assumption of a street mugging gone wrong, Mr. Trammell's intervention and the subsequent shooting made perfect sense. But if we go on the assumption that Harrison was there to kill someone in particular, it makes no sense at all that his target was Mr. Trammell. Harrison would've gone straight for him. He wouldn't have complicated things by involving the two of you. So if this was a hired hit designed to look like a mugging or carjacking, the target wasn't your friend. The target was one of you."

He looked from one to the other. "Or both."

"THIS IS A NIGHTMARE," Stephanie whispered to Miriam as she pushed her office door shut. "I'd almost convinced myself that Peter was wrong, that Allen's death really was just the result of a random street crime. But having Lieutenant Greene come to the same conclusion pretty much cements it. That Harrison guy was there to kill us. Not just any women he happened upon that night. Us specifically."

"I know," Miriam said, dropping herself into the chair opposite Stephanie's desk. "I got really nervous when Greene started grilling us on where we'd been or who we'd met with out of the ordinary in the previous two weeks. I was afraid you'd crack and tell him what we saw in Dallas."

Stephanie exhaled a long breath. "I was tempted, believe me. But I remembered what you and Peter told me, and I caught myself. There's no way in hell we could convince anyone that what we saw wasn't a hallucination fueled by drugs, or psychosis, or…hell, I don't know. I wanted so much to blurt it all out before you could stop me; to put this threat to the country in the hands of people who might actually be able to do something about it. To put the threat to *us* in the hands of someone who might be able to protect us."

Miriam studied her friend's face. "So why didn't you tell him?"

"Tell him *what*?" Stephanie said loudly, almost shouting. She took a deep breath before continuing in a softer, more controlled tone. "I wanted to tell him the truth, but I realized I wouldn't even know how to start. Like…*Well, Lieutenant, see this pretty young blond sitting here? She's actually seven hundred years old!*"

Miriam smiled. "I'm really only six hundred and eighty. Please don't try to make me older than I actually am."

Stephanie stared at her as if she had just uttered the most ludicrous statement she'd ever heard and suddenly started to laugh and cry at the same time. "This is so crazy! I feel like *I'm* so crazy. This can't be real. *You* can't be real. That damned Egyptian we saw in Dallas can't be real. How have you been able to deal with this madness for…let me get this right…six hundred and eighty years? I would've been locked away in an asylum centuries ago!"

Still smiling, Miriam reached across the desk and touched Stephanie's arm. "You'll get through this. We'll all get through it. We'll do it together."

Stephanie's smile faded and the laughter subsided, leaving only the tears. "I don't know," she said softly. "I have this really ominous feeling. It's like some huge monster is heading this way—something too big and too dangerous to even imagine. And it's heading straight for us." She wiped her eyes and stared intently at Miriam. "And it won't stop until we're devoured."

"THIS IS KRISTIN CONNELLY, reporting from Bank of America Stadium in Charlotte, North Carolina, where American Values Party founder Robert Martinez and North Carolina congressional candidate Jerome Schumacher are holding a massive campaign rally this afternoon. Charlotte is the first of five Sunbelt cities the AVP bandwagon will be visiting in as many days, with rallies and fundraiser dinners scheduled in each. The AVP candidates are leading in all five of the states Martinez will be visiting, and his campaign staff has stated they are expecting large, enthusiastic crowds. If the crowd here is any indication, that is exactly what they will be getting. But not all of the attendees—or all of the enthusiasm—project support for the AVP platform.

"The plan was to use half of the stadium, which has a capacity of a little over seventy-five thousand people, for this rally. A large stage has been erected on the fifty yard line, with a local high school marching band on one side and a host of dignitaries, including the Republican governor of the state—who Martinez has been courting heavily—seated on the other. It is estimated that over twenty thousand people are crammed into the stands in the south half of the stadium. Only a select few with special passes are being allowed onto the field itself. I asked if this was for security purposes, but was told by one of the guards that it was mostly to protect the turf, where the Carolina Panthers will host their season opener on Sunday.

"I don't think this end zone could possibly be any louder this Sunday. A large contingency of the Hispanic Protection Brigade is here, as they promised they would be, and they came to be heard. The size of the Brigade delegation is small relative to the size of the AVP crowd, but what they lack in numbers they definitely make up in volume. At one point, a shouting match between Brigade protestors and AVP supporters got so loud that speeches had to stop as police moved into the crowd to break up several fights. There were no reported injuries, and no arrests, but tensions are high and tempers are hot on both sides.

"A large crowd of protestors is also expected tonight at the Charlotte Marriott City Center, where approximately five hundred party supporters will gather for an elaborate black tie dinner and an opportunity to meet Schumacher and Martinez. At that event, the Brigade will certainly have the larger crowd, by a significant margin. And although they will not be allowed to enter the hotel, they have vowed to make sure that everyone there is aware of their presence. Brigade leaders have promised to keep their protest peaceful. But if what we have seen this afternoon is any indication, that may be a promise that will be hard to keep.

"I had a chance earlier this afternoon to speak briefly with Martinez's chief of staff Arthur Stephenson, and asked him if he believes Brigade founder Carlos Guerra's promise to keep their protests peaceful. Stephenson said, 'The Brigade has lied about our party founder's record, his views, even his marital status. I hope they're not lying about this too, but frankly, I have trouble believing anything they say.'

"Mr. Guerra could not be reached for comment, so the country will just have to watch and see what happens this week as Robert Martinez and the American Values Party bandwagon, with *Brigada de Proteccion Hispana* in hot pursuit, works its way west across the Deep South.

"This is Kristin Connelly, PNN, reporting live from Charlotte, North Carolina."

THREE HOURS LATER Robert Martinez stepped out of the shower of his suite on the top floor of the Charlotte Marriott City Center and reached for a towel. Sally McDaniel gently took it out of his hands and not-so-gently pressed her wet body against his. "Feeling better now?" she cooed softly as she went up on her toes to nibble his ear.

He smiled and kissed her. "Yeah, nothing like a hot shower to wash a man's tension away."

She ran her fingers up and down the small of his back. "I'd like to think I had a little to do with easing your tension too," she said.

Martinez hated it when she was so needy, requiring verbal assurances that her sexual skills fulfilled his needs. But given what she'd done in the shower—he was already thinking about a repeat after the fundraiser dinner—it was better to placate her. "We could've used nothing but cold water, and you still would've steamed the place up," he said, eliciting a broad, seductive smile. He patted her taut buttocks. "But you'd better get going if you're gonna have time to make yourself all glamorous and beautiful for the dinner tonight."

She frowned and stepped back from him, holding her arms out as if to give him a big hug. "Are you saying I don't look glamorous and beautiful now?"

He studied the dripping wet, perfectly shaped body and wagged a finger at her. "You, young lady, had better get that perfect butt of yours out of here or we'll both end up being late. These people are paying good money to see me tonight, so I need to be ready to press the flesh."

She smiled. "I thought that's what we just did."

"You know what I mean," he said, picking his towel back up. "Now get going."

"Fine, fine," she said, grabbing a towel and drying herself as she walked into the bedroom. "There's a gift box on the dining room table," she called out as she pulled her dress over her head and ran her fingers through her wet hair. "Be sure you bring it when you come down tonight."

"What is it?" he said, stepping into the bedroom.

"A gift for the mayor," she said. "For being your host. It's a Mont Blanc pen with an engraved onyx stand. I got one for each of the mayors where you have dinners this week."

"Cutting into the profits a little, aren't you?" he said, not completely kidding.

"Believe me, it'll be worth it," she said. "These five guys will be displaying their *personal* gift from you for the rest of their political careers. Despite all the noise from these nasty protestors, you're going to be President of the United States in a few years."

He watched her as she blew him a kiss and walked out of the room. He knew the Arrowhead security detail out in the hall would know exactly what had been going on when they saw her leave his suite with wet hair and glistening skin, but he didn't care. It probably made him all the more enviable in their eyes. And powerful. Real men, especially men with dangerous careers like they had, understood that big jobs and big appetites went hand in hand. He was sure there wasn't a single one of them that would turn down a night with the likes of Sally McDaniel. He wouldn't be needing her much longer, but he knew he'd miss her and would think of her from time to time.

Especially when he was in the shower.

Chapter 27

THE ROOM WAS filled with smoke. It was difficult to see where he was going, even to see his own feet, but Peter kept moving. He wanted to close his eyes, to shut out the swirling haze that was burning them, causing them to water so much he couldn't make out any details of his surroundings. What he wanted even more was to be able to close his ears—to shut out the moans and the pleas for help. And the screams.

He was crouched low, crab-walking slowly through the large room so that he could move without bumping into pieces of furniture or tripping over bodies…or parts of bodies. But also so he could see the faces of the dead and injured. He was looking for Miriam. Every time he turned over a body and it wasn't her, he uttered a prayer of thanks. But every time he quickly scurried toward the sound of a voice and saw it wasn't her, his desperation and fear grew exponentially. Losing her would be incomprehensible. Continuing life without her would be meaningless. He knew that if she was gone he'd never jump to another host. What would be the point? He'd die like everyone else. Maybe of old age, but more likely by his own hand.

His legs were starting to cramp, but he realized that if he stood erect he'd probably be overcome by smoke. So he pushed onward, edging left and then right, trying to cover as much ground as possible before reaching the far wall, shifting a few feet to the right, and traversing the room again. Just as he reached the wall he found another body. It was a woman. A slender woman, probably young. All he could see was the back of her head. Short blond hair. With his heart about to beat out of his chest, he scrambled to her on his knees and hurriedly turned her over to see her face. But there wasn't one. Just a gaping hole, charred and smoking. And yet, impossible as it seemed, the edges of what had once been a face began to quiver and a voice, almost too soft to hear, said, "Peter."

He squeezed his eyes shut and screamed—a long, plaintive, terrified shriek that seemed to emanate from the depth of his bowels. He suddenly felt hands grabbing him, but he pushed them away, fighting to stay there beside the woman he cherished more than anything in heaven or on earth. But the hands persisted, restraining his arms and slapping his face.

"Peter! Peter!"

He opened his eyes and saw her face inches from his, her eyes filled with terror and confusion. "Peter! You were dreaming. It's okay now. Everything's okay."

He stared at her for several seconds, finally realizing that she really was there with him. That she wasn't dead. That she was safe. And then, for the first time in over two hundred years, he erupted into gut-wrenching sobs.

WEDNESDAY MORNING, eight-thirty. Less than thirty-six hours until the dinner at the Westin. Miriam studied her husband's face as he parked his SUV in a visitor's space near the office building entrance. As he unbuckled his seatbelt, she touched his arm. "Are you sure you're okay?" she whispered.

They'd both been awake since he'd shocked her out of a sound sleep around three AM with his scream of unbridled terror and grief. She'd held him tightly until it was time to get out of bed and dress for work. She had never seen him so distraught. Despite repeated pleadings, it was over two hours before he would give her any details about the dream. And when he did, the pain in his eyes and the tremor in his voice made it clear that the nightmare had seemed very real to him. And given his track record with dreams presaging calamity, it now seemed disturbingly real to her too.

He looked at her and nodded. "Yeah, I'm okay." He turned his head away and stared out his window. "Look, I'm sorry I got so upset. My behavior wasn't very manly."

She reached out and put one finger under his chin, turning his head to face her. "There's nothing unmanly about loving a woman that much," she said. "The way you put me above everything else in your life is about as manly as any woman could ever want. And I love you just as much. I've loved you for over six hundred years. And, God willing, I'll love you for six hundred more." She leaned over and kissed his cheek. "Stay strong, *kochanka*."

He took a deep breath. "I just wish we were already out of here. I understand the need to stand and fight, and I'm committed to our plan for tomorrow. But once that's done, regardless of the outcome, regardless of whether we feel we've made things safer, we have to leave here."

She blinked back tears. "I know."

"We'll stay in touch with Steph," he said, "and we'll protect her as much as we can. And once we get everything resettled, we'll see about reuniting with her. But only if we can convince ourselves that it's safe. Okay?"

She pulled a tissue from her purse and dabbed at her eyes, checking her reflection—a very different looking reflection—in the visor mirror to make sure her eye make-up was still intact. "Okay," she said. "Ready to go in? I see Steph's car, so she's already here."

"Yeah, let's go."

Abby looked surprised when the two of them walked into the office lobby. "Hi Peter," she said, dimples crinkling as she flashed her genuinely warm smile. "I didn't expect to see you here this morning. Do you need to see Mark?"

"No, I just need to ask Steph a couple of questions," he said. "But I'll stick my head in the door on my way out if he has time."

"He'll make time for you," she said. "I'll let him know you're in the building."

"Thanks," Peter said as he and Miriam opened the door that led to the other offices. They found Steph at her desk. She ushered them in and shut the door.

"Claudia doesn't get here until nine, so we don't have to worry about her hearing through the wall," she said. "But let's keep our voices down, just to be safe."

Miriam took her usual seat across from Stephanie's desk and Peter pulled over a chair that was positioned against the side wall, next to the bookshelf. When they were all seated and leaning forward across the desk, Stephanie looked at them both and said, "Pardon my manners, but you both look like hell. Rough night?"

Peter glanced quickly at Miriam and said, "Yeah, I couldn't sleep."

"And when Peter can't sleep, I can't sleep," Miriam said.

Stephanie threw up her hands, palms facing them—a classic *I don't want to know* gesture. "I don't need to hear details of how you two pass the time when you have insomnia." She cut her eyes at Miriam and smiled. "Well, actually I do, but you can tell me later." She zeroed in on Peter. "So, Miriam gave me an overview of your plan yesterday. You really think it'll work?"

Miriam noticed that Peter was blushing, undoubtedly a little embarrassed by Steph's assumption they'd spent the night making love, but also relieved that she didn't know the real reason for their sleeplessness. He seemed to recover quickly as he looked at Stephanie and said, "Well, obviously we have to fill in a few details. First, what time will you and Courtney be getting to the Westin tomorrow?"

"I'll pretty much spend the day there," Stephanie said. "At least, from noon on. The doors to the ballroom open at seven, and I've asked Courtney to be there by five. As we discussed, we'll have her manning our little 'command central,' which is basically just a computer and headphones for our on-site communication, in a small conference room two doors down from the ballroom."

"And no one else will be in there with her?" Peter asked.

Stephanie cast a sly grin. "Not unless she invites someone to join her for a few minutes."

Peter nodded. "I'll stop by and see her on my way out," he said. "Remember, I want her to think this request is just between me and her. So once she's gone through the receiving line and has met Martinez, give her some space."

"As long as we don't have any last-minute service problems, she should be free to do her thing," Stephanie said.

"And you'll get Stephenson out of the room?" he asked.

Stephanie shook her head. "No, I thought about it, but it's too risky for me to do it. Since Miriam and I have met them both, we have to give the appearance of everything being perfectly normal. We don't want to cause any suspicion that we're up to anything."

Peter looked slightly agitated. "I thought we'd already discussed this. The risk of arousing suspicion is less than that of involving anyone else. We're already involving Courtney. Adding other players starts making the whole plan a bit cumbersome. I don't like it."

"I have a guy we can trust," Stephanie said. "He'll be one of the servers. His name's Phillip. I've known him for a long time, and he owes me some favors."

"But this is the kind of thing that could cost someone his job," Peter said.

Stephanie flipped her hand dismissively. "Not a concern. He only works as a food server to make a little pocket money now and then. He's actually a senior med student at UAB. It'll make no difference to him if this is his last catering job."

"And you really trust him to come through for you?" Peter asked.

Stephanie smiled, and it was her turn to blush a little. "The poor guy is suffering from the delusion that I'll marry him once he finishes his medical training. He'd drop his pants and shit on Stephenson's plate if I asked him to."

Miriam reached across the desk and swatted Stephanie's arm. "What? Why am I hearing about this Phillip for the first time? We could have included him at our Labor Day barbecue."

Stephanie smiled as she shook her head. "Uh-uh. He's the one that's in love, not me. But I'll let you rich folks take us out to dinner one night when this is all over."

Miriam tried to keep her smile going, but it was very difficult to brazenly deceive her friend. She knew that Stephanie would figure it out when Miriam didn't arrive for work on Friday, and she knew she would be devastated…not just by the loss, but by the betrayal. Miriam would just have to find a way to win her trust back at some time when it was safe to contact her. Hoping that Stephanie couldn't see the sadness in her eyes, she said, "So, what else do we need to cover?"

Peter stood. "That's about it for now. I'll go see Courtney, and I told Abby I'd drop in on Mark before I leave."

Stephanie raised a hand. "Hold on a minute. There's one aspect of the plan we haven't discussed. The most critical aspect, actually." She stared intently at Peter. "So, when you get him isolated, what exactly are you going to say to him?"

Peter looked at both women and shook his head. "That's the one part of the plan I haven't completely figured out yet."

PETER LOOKED THROUGH the door of Courtney's office and saw her working on her computer, which sat on the credenza behind her desk. He tapped on the door frame. "Hi Courtney. Got a minute?"

She turned her head to look at him and smiled. "Hi Peter. Abby said you were here. You all set for the big extravaganza tomorrow night?"

"Yeah, that's what I wanted to see you about," he said, stepping into the room and easing the door shut behind him. "I wanted to ask if you'd be willing to do me a favor."

She swiveled her chair around to face him. Peter had to force himself not to stare at her long legs protruding from a very short hot pink miniskirt. He must have been focusing too intently on her eyes, because she tipped her head to one side and asked, "Does Miriam know about this favor?"

"Sort of," he said. "Well, she knows I'm going to ask you for something, but she doesn't know exactly what it is. And I'd kind of like to keep it that way."

She laughed. "How intriguing. So, what is it you need?"

He glanced at the chair opposite her desk. "Okay if I sit down a minute?" he asked, desperate to get those legs out of his field of vision.

"Sure," she said.

He sat down and got right to the point. "You're aware that Martinez and his candidate will have a receiving line before dinner tomorrow, right? And that Miriam and I want you and Steph to be with us when we meet them?"

"Yes," Courtney nodded. "I really appreciate you doing that. I've been watching Martinez on the news for months. He's pretty much achieved rock-star status in the media. As part of the service staff, I really hadn't thought I'd have a chance to get within ten feet of him."

"Well, you will," he said. "You'll be able to shake hands with him, chat for a moment, maybe even snap a selfie."

"That'll be so cool," she said. "I'm actually a closet Democrat, but my mom and dad are somewhere to the right of Genghis Khan politically, so this will give them country club bragging rights for the next year. But you still haven't told me the favor."

Peter leaned forward, folding his hands together and resting them on the edge of Courtney's desk. He supposed it was a posture that suggested begging, and that was somewhat by design. "As you know, I inherited quite a bit of money and property when my parents died. I have some development plans for one piece of property out in Texas, but I've run into some politically motivated roadblocks. I think Martinez putting in a good word for me could make a difference."

Courtney looked perplexed. "So you'll mention this to him when you go through the receiving line? What do you need me for?"

"That's the thing," Peter said. "There won't be time for a serious chat—even a thirty second elevator speech—in the receiving line. And this could be the only time I ever get anywhere near the man. To be right there with him, with him knowing I just dropped twenty grand to support his new political party, is about the best opportunity I could imagine."

"So you'll ask him to step outside for a brief one-on-one?"

He smiled. "No, I think my chances of success would be better if you did that."

The look of shock on the young woman's face almost made Peter laugh. "You want me to try to seduce Robert Martinez?" she asked in a voice laced with skepticism.

"No, no, no," Peter said, waving his hand. "I was just thinking that if you mentioned you would be in charge of the command center for the evening, just a couple of doors down, and it was going to be kind of boring in there all by yourself, he might decide to follow you there. You know, just to see it."

She shook her head. "Look, I know Martinez has an eye for women—that's been all over the news—but what makes you think he'd follow *me* anywhere?"

Peter smiled. "Have you looked in the mirror lately?"

She was still shaking her head, as if Peter were weaving the most ludicrous tale she'd ever heard. "So you think that Robert Martinez will just step out of a receiving line for wealthy campaign donors and walk down the hall so he can see a laptop computer and a headset switchboard?"

"That will be his excuse," Peter said, "but certainly not his intent."

She now stared into Peter's eyes, her own burning with what could be either anger or disbelief. "And if he does show up there, what do you expect me to do with him? Surely..."

"Nothing!" Peter exclaimed before she could complete the question. "If he does go to the room you're in, I'll walk in about thirty seconds behind him. I'll say something to the effect that Steph needs you in the kitchen for a moment, and then when Martinez and I are walking back to the ballroom, I'll mention my project."

"And you don't think he'll recognize this as the set-up it is?" she asked.

Peter paused before answering, as if pondering the question, and then said, "Maybe. Maybe not. I'll take that risk if it buys me thirty seconds alone with him. That's all I need."

"So, you don't actually expect me to do anything that would be, as my mom would put it, unbecoming of a lady?"

"Absolutely not," Peter said, trying to sound reassuring. "There won't be time for him to even get within arm's reach of you. I promise."

Courtney leaned back in her chair, deep in thought. Peter was doubly glad he didn't have a view of those legs now. No man with an ounce of testosterone would be able to resist a glance, and getting caught staring would destroy her trust and any chance of getting her to go through with his scheme.

"So, here's the way I'm understanding this," she said. "I get the chance to shake hands with Martinez. I say something about being so thrilled to meet him, so honored to be involved with planning the event…blah, blah, blah…and then just mention that unfortunately I won't be able to hear his speech because I'm headed to our *command center* two doors down, where I will be working alone for the rest of the night. And if he decides to come down to that room once he's done greeting donors—and, despite your conniving flattery, that's a very big *if*—you'll make sure that he's interrupted before he can make any kind of unseemly move. Do I have this right?"

"Absolutely right," Peter said. But he was lying. Courtney had the gist of the plan right, but the details would be slightly different from what he'd laid out for her. And far more dangerous. Not for Courtney; he wouldn't gamble with her safety. But for Stephanie, Miriam and himself, the stakes couldn't be any higher.

Chapter 28

"THIS IS KRISTEN CONNELLY, reporting live from downtown Atlanta. I'm standing outside of the Ritz-Carlton Hotel, where American Values Party founder Robert Martinez will be appearing at the second of five exclusive, black-tie fundraising dinners scheduled for this week in an AVP sweep across the southeast.

"Earlier today Martinez spoke on behalf of congressional candidate Roger Albritton at a rally at Centennial Olympic Park, just a short distance from here, where the Atlanta Police were largely effective in preventing protestors from disrupting the proceedings to the extent they did in Houston on Monday and yesterday in Charlotte. They did this by using barricades to direct people into two segregated areas. Anyone carrying a sign or a noisemaker, like a bullhorn or air horn, was directed into an area at the back of the cordoned area, farthest from the stage. Everyone else was directed into the front section.

"Campaign workers were out in large numbers, picking out supporters with pro-Albritton signs and urging them to leave their signs outside the entrance to the rally area, thus ensuring they would be directed to the front. They said nothing to anyone carrying noisemakers or anti-AVP signs, and by the time the protestors realized they were all being shepherded to the rear section, it was too late. The area closest to the stage was packed with supporters of the party, while the protestors—mostly from *Brigada de Proteccion Hispana,* the Hispanic Protection Brigade—were too far back to disrupt the speeches.

"Carlos Guerra, founder and leader of the Brigade, wasted no time in crying '*foul*.' He accused the Atlanta Police Department and Republican Mayor Brad Sweeney of being in collusion with the AVP to stifle their right to legal protest. 'This was a brazen, pre-planned maneuver to push us to the back where we could not be heard,' he said. He vowed that tonight would be different, and that anyone arriving at the Ritz-Carlton would see and hear the message of those who have been, in his words, 'unfairly and unlawfully singled out for repression by the so-called American Values Party and its hate-mongering leader, Robert Martinez.'

"Judging by the size of the protest group assembled on the sidewalk across Peachtree Street from the entrance to the hotel, I would have to say it looks like Guerra is delivering on his pledge. Mr. Martinez and Mr. Albritton, a former robbery and homicide detective with the Atlanta Police Department, are scheduled to enter the Grand Ballroom at seven-thirty, about an hour from now. Donors have already started to arrive—many by limousine—and they are being greeted by chants of '*You were immigrants too*' and '*God bless America*' from an estimated three thousand protestors already in place. Police are lining the street, and have threatened to start arresting demonstrators if automobile traffic is blocked. So far, the protest has been loud, but peaceful and orderly, and there have been no arrests.

"After the dinner tonight, the Martinez camp will travel via a specially equipped bus to Birmingham, the site of tomorrow's rally and fundraiser dinner. The two-and-a-half hour trip should give the Martinez and his advisors time to plan their strategy for dealing with what could very well be the largest Brigade demonstration they will face all week. The AVP team scored a victory today with their crowd-handling tactics at Centennial Olympic Park, but that approach is not likely to be as effective if employed a second time. So the two big questions for tomorrow are…what can Martinez and the AVP do to keep the demonstrators off balance? And even more critical, can Guerra continue to keep the Brigade protests peaceful?

"Kristen Connelly, PNN, reporting from Atlanta."

MIRIAM CLICKED THE REMOTE control, turning the television off. "Enough of that," she said. "If this has to be my last dinner in this apartment, I'd prefer to eat it without being reminded of why I have to leave."

She and Peter were seated in the living room, washing down Chinese takeout with ample quantities of Cakebread Cellars Chardonnay. They had just watched Kristin Connelly's report from Atlanta, and knew that by the time they went to bed the AVP tour bus, and the threat to their survival, would be speeding toward them at seventy miles per hour. They felt that their plan for the following evening was about as complete as they could make it, given the fact that unknown security precautions and a million other unforeseen circumstances could unravel it with little or no warning. Still, it was the only plan they had and they were committed to it. Even if successful, the exact outcome couldn't be predicted. The best they could hope for was to thwart an evil hijacking of the United States political system and escape with their lives. And even if they did that, their lives would change dramatically. That is what continued to infuriate Miriam.

"If that sorry-ass Senator Carson hadn't been so determined to butter up Martinez, or if he'd decided to host the event in Mobile, or…I don't know…if somehow this project had never come to Sheffield and Associates, none of this would've happened. I'd have my job, my friend, the house." She suddenly sat up straight and looked at Peter. "Oh God, I forgot about the house! Are you going to call tomorrow to back out of the closing?"

Peter shook his head. "No, I don't want to do anything to get anyone's radar activated until we're safely out of town. I'll call early next week and cancel."

"We'll lose our earnest money," she said.

"Pocket change," he said. "Whoever heard of holding a nine hundred thousand dollar property with ten grand? That's barely over one per cent. It would've been almost ten times that in New Jersey."

"Southerners are very trusting" Miriam said. "They tend to value a man's word as much as a legal contract. It's one of the things I like about living here."

Peter didn't reply. He studied his wife's face, noting the tear streaking down her cheek, and set his food down on the coffee table. He moved closer and put his arm around her. "I'm sorry," he whispered.

She put her food down next to his and leaned into him. "I know you are," she said softly. "I think you like it here as much as I do. We could've spent forty or fifty years here, really settled into a lifestyle that suits us. It's just so damned unfair to have to give this up. It makes me so mad!"

He squeezed her shoulder. "Fighting mad?"

She started to cry, and punched his chest with her fist. "Yes!"

"Good," he said, taking her clenched fist in his hand and raising it to his lips. "Because we're definitely in for a fight. A war, in fact. It will be declared tomorrow night, but it won't end then. In fact, it'll just get started. This could possibly ignite a fire that burns for a very long time. Decades. Centuries, even."

"I wish we could just walk away from it," Miriam said.

"We can. But even that wouldn't change the need to leave Birmingham. In fact, if we aren't going to go through with this, we should leave tonight. That would make it even harder for him to find us. Sergei is already working on new identities and documentation for us. He claims they'll be ready by the weekend."

"No, if we have to leave here, let's make it count for something. If I can't have what I want, then I'm damned sure not letting that murdering bastard get what he wants."

"Fair enough," Peter said. "You know, even after what you and Steph saw in Dallas, this was still avoidable. I mean, we would've had to leave here; it's just too dangerous to have someone with that much influence and who knows what kind of resources watching our every move. But we might have been willing to just go away and assume that having a rider potentially gaining hold on the reins of power was not in itself a bad thing. But he showed his true colors with the attempted attack on you and Steph."

"I know," she said, her voice tight. "He had a chance to continue on with his plans, whatever they are. But Allen's murder changed everything. Now that sonofabitch is going to have to pay. And he can't pay enough to satisfy me."

THE RENTED BUS, unofficially dubbed *The American Express* by the campaign workers, had originally been customized for a popular country western duo. As a result, it had two private compartments—one for Martinez and one for Stephenson—each with a sofa bed, desk, and private bathroom with shower. Up front there were two more bathrooms, plus seating for forty passengers. Campaign staffers, security, as well as carefully selected members of the press—including PNN's Kristen Connelly and her camera man—occupied just over half of those seats, giving everyone room to spread out for the two and a half hour ride to the Westin Hotel in downtown Birmingham. They would gain an hour by crossing into the central time zone, so they expected to arrive at the hotel by one AM local time. Early enough for everyone to get a few hours of much-needed sleep before starting another hectic day on the campaign trail.

Anwar was the last to board the bus. He strode briskly down the aisle, eyes straight ahead, a clear signal that he was not in the mood to stop and chit-chat with any of the staffers or members of the press. As he passed the last row of seats, he tapped the shoulder of the man seated on the left aisle. The man rose and followed him into his private compartment.

Anwar motioned for Ben Wycliff to take a seat on the sofa as he opened a desk drawer and retrieved a bottle of scotch and two glasses. There was a bucket of ice on the desktop. He picked up a few cubes and dropped them into one glass, then poured a generous serving into each. He handed the one with ice to Wycliff before joining him on the sofa.

He took a sip of his drink and kicked off his shoes. "The bus was swept this evening?" he asked.

"Twice," Wycliff said. "Once when they delivered it around eight, and then again right before we started boarding. It's bug-free."

"Good," Anwar said, although he still chose his words carefully, just in case. "Your extra men are in place?"

"Yep. They were in Charlotte yesterday and were here today, so they won't stand out in Birmingham."

"Good," Anwar said before pausing to take another long sip of scotch. "And you have what we discussed?"

"Right here," Wycliff said, patting his coat pocket before reaching in and pulling out a cell phone and a small box, slightly larger than a deck of cards. He handed the phone to Anwar. "The number is loaded on speed dial. All you need to do is hit five."

Anwar dropped the phone in his pocket and then rose from the sofa and stepped over to where his suitcase rested on a folding luggage stand. He dialed up the combination on the lock, which he then removed and zipped the case open. Sitting on top was a small, wrapped gift box. He picked it up and carried it back to the sofa. "This is a gift for the mayor of Birmingham," he said. "It needs to be put on the shelf under the podium, right next to a glass of water. Make sure you're the one asked to put it there before the receiving line gets underway, and give me a confirming sign when that's done."

Wycliff smiled. "Only, it won't be the mayor's gift." He lifted the box in his hand. "It'll be this."

"Right," Anwar said, standing back up and stepping over to the desk, where he placed the gift. "We have to make sure we wrap it exactly like it is now."

He carefully untied the blue and red ribbon, and gently unfolded the glossy white wrapping paper from the box. Opening the box, he removed the pen and onyx stand, and replaced them with the smaller box Wycliff held. "Look in the bathroom there and grab me a wad of toilet paper," he said. "There's too much wiggle room in here. I don't want this rattling around."

Four minutes later, the box was re-wrapped, looking precisely like it had before. He lifted it. The weight was similar enough that anyone who had handled the pen and stand set wouldn't notice the difference. "Perfect," he said.

"One problem, though," Wycliff said. "If this is scanned, it's not gonna look like a pen and a chunk of rock."

"It won't be scanned," Anwar said.

"I thought every item carried by anyone would be scanned before entering the ballroom," Wycliff said. "That's Arrowhead's protocol."

Anwar smiled. "Items carried by *almost* everyone get scanned. There's one person who I can guarantee won't be subjected to any inspection at all."

Chapter 29

IT WAS TIME. Miriam had spent just half a day in the office. When Stephanie left around noon to oversee the preparations at the Westin, Mark had told Miriam to go home and "rest up for the long night ahead." *If you only knew*, she had thought. But she was glad to have the afternoon in the condo with Peter. There was so much to do, and it helped to pass the time. For several days she had alternated between wanting time to speed up and get this over with, and wanting it to slow down to postpone the inevitable pain. It was like waiting to have major surgery. You dreaded what you would have to go through to make your life better. It was often the immediate aftermath, the pain of the healing process that caused more anxiety than the procedure itself.

Casual clothes were set out on the bed. All of their other clothes were packed into suitcases that were already loaded into the SUV. They would drive the Mercedes to the Westin. If everything went according to plan, they would drive back to the condo afterwards to change clothes and then hit the road, in two cars, heading northwest on I-22 to Tupelo, Mississippi, where Peter had reserved a room at a Holiday Inn under another name. The following day they would continue northwest to Memphis, then St. Louis, and arrive in Kansas City late that afternoon.

There, Peter had reserved a hotel room under yet another name for two nights. That would give them time to contact Sergei in New

York and have him overnight their new identities and documentation. Peter had already received a special delivery thumb drive with all the information he'd requested. There were no e-mail trails and there would be no phone trails. Sergei relied on "old school" methods of communication, leaving no records behind. Accessing supposedly secure records was how Sergei made his living, so he knew perfectly well how dangerously unprotected they sometimes were.

By Sunday morning, Peter and Miriam would have decided where to go. From Kansas City, they had the option of heading in any direction in the continental United States. Peter had even suggested it might be time to leave North America for a while. Miriam had briefly brightened at the prospect of going back to Budapest, her favorite European city, or maybe even trying out South America. She'd always thought Buenos Aires would be nice. They had the means to go anywhere—a mixed blessing, because Miriam wanted nothing more than to stay right where they were.

Now she stood in front of a mirror, marveling at the incongruity of the image staring back at her—the face of a dark-haired fifteen year old girl decked out in a black Valentino gown and a double strand of pearls. She was suddenly aware of movement at the bathroom door and turned to see Peter smiling as he studied her reflection.

"Is it a little creepy for a seven hundred year old man to get aroused looking at the face of a fifteen year old girl?" he asked.

Despite her somber mood, she returned his smile. "Ordinarily I'd say yes, but these are pretty unusual circumstances." She looked back at the mirror and gazed lovingly at his reflection—curly red hair, green eyes and a sprinkling of freckles on his cheeks. "Besides," she said, "I'm probably a little old for this twenty year old boy, but I just can't seem to get him out of my mind."

He stepped behind her and wrapped his arms around her waist. "We've come a long way," he whispered. "It's been a long time since we first saw each other reflected in that lake."

"Yes, but I remember it like it was yesterday," she said. "I was so scared and so confused by what had happened to me. I thought I'd gone insane. And then when I saw you, I was convinced of it."

"Two kids, living in one of the darkest times of history, struggling to comprehend the incomprehensible," he said. "But we managed to keep our sanity and build something very special."

She leaned back against his chest. "Not that there hasn't been difficult times. Like now. I don't know what is affecting me more, the fear of what we could be unleashing or the sadness of what it requires us to do."

He squeezed her and kissed her cheek. "We'll be fine…on both counts. There's just no way of knowing what we'll force him to do, but we'll deal with it. Leaving him alone and allowing him to proceed with his plans—whatever they are—just isn't an option. Living forever has no appeal if you can't live with yourself, and there's no way we could face each other if we let this go unopposed."

She released a long, nervous breath. "I guess we'd better get going. I told Steph we'd be there by six, and I don't know what to expect in terms of traffic. I know a couple of streets near the hotel will be blocked off."

"Lots of protestors?"

"That's what we've been told to expect. But maybe they've already accomplished their goal. Maybe it'll be a quiet night."

He released her from his embrace and headed into the bedroom, where his tuxedo jacket lay on the bed. "I wouldn't bet on it," he said. "I don't think a quiet night is in the Birmingham forecast."

"THIS IS KRISTEN CONNELLY, reporting live from the Uptown Entertainment District in Birmingham, Alabama. Ordinarily, this area would not be particularly crowded on a Thursday evening, but every bar and restaurant here has been packed all afternoon with people hoping to catch a glimpse of American Values Party founder Robert Martinez, who is immensely popular here. Earlier this afternoon Martinez and local congressional candidate William Chastain held a rally in the Legacy Arena, part of the Birmingham-Jefferson Convention Complex, right across the street from where I'm now standing. The arena has a capacity of nineteen thousand, and it looked like every seat was filled when Martinez followed the

University of Alabama marching band onto the floor and then spoke for over forty minutes to a wildly enthusiastic crowd.

"Because it was an indoor event and the attendees were pre-screened, there was very little disruption caused by protestors from *Brigada de Proteccion Hispana*—the Hispanic Protection Brigade—that has been following the AVP entourage from city to city since the beginning of the week. The Brigade demonstrators basically shut down a campaign event in Houston on Monday, and created quite a disturbance in Charlotte on Tuesday. But yesterday in Atlanta, the effectiveness of the Brigade protest was diminished significantly when the Atlanta Police Department—in a move that Brigade leader Carlos Guerra denounced as 'a blatant attack on the right to free assembly and free speech'—managed to separate protestors from supporters, relegating the demonstrators to a back section too far away from the stage to allow disruption of the proceedings. And today, Martinez had another trick up his sleeve.

"In what was apparently a planned leak, word got out this morning that at the conclusion of the rally at the arena, Martinez and Chastain would travel by car to the employees' entrance of the Westin, on the far side of the hotel. Hundreds of protestors, armed with signs and bullhorns, lined the likely route, a distance of only a city block. Instead, Martinez surprised everyone when, escorted by the marching band's drum corps, he walked right across Richard Arrington Junior Boulevard and entered the hotel through the main lobby. People who had already walked outside from the rally and were on their way to BJCC parking lots across the street behind me were joined by thousands of other supporters, including many who rushed out of several popular Uptown bars and restaurants, to form a cheering human tunnel for a political figure that, in this part of the country, has achieved virtual rock star status. By the time the protestors realized what was going on, Martinez was safely inside the hotel, leaving a delighted throng of supporters in his wake.

"I was invited to join Martinez and several members of the AVP staff in the hotel's concierge lounge immediately afterward, and I asked him what prompted the seemingly last-minute route change.

He told me that he'd been made aware of the large number of people that were here in the entertainment district today, and since both the rally and tonight's dinner had limited capacity, he wanted a chance to interact with the people of Birmingham. When I asked him if this change of plans upset his security detail, he said—and I quote—'Of course, but that's not my concern. My concern is that the people of this country understand that I don't hide from confrontation. I never have, and I never will. That's what they want, and what they deserve, in their political leadership.' End quote.

"He shouldn't have to worry about confrontation at tonight's event. Nearly five hundred wealthy donors will be standing in line to shake his hand and say a few words to him before entering the ballroom for a ten thousand dollar a plate dinner. Everything on the menu was either raised here in Alabama or caught in the Gulf of Mexico, and will be prepared under the supervision of renowned Birmingham chef John Stark. Co-hosted by Democratic Mayor Darnell Simpson and Independent Republican-caucusing U.S. Senator Richard Carson—who I've been told is seriously considering changing his affiliation to the AVP—the dinner will be packed with many of Alabama's wealthiest and most influential citizens.

"But that's inside. Out here, the atmosphere could be very different, as busloads of demonstrators continue to arrive. By the time the guests start arriving in another two hours, they will likely be greeted by the largest Brigade contingent to appear at any AVP event so far. That's one of the ironies of politics—what is arguably one of the country's most conservative states has one of the largest populations of Mexican farm laborers, and it looks like a sizable percentage of them will be here tonight.

"Reporting live from Birmingham, this is Kristin Connelly, PNN."

MARTINEZ AND SALLY McDaniel were walking down the hall from the concierge lounge to the elegant Presidential Suite. Arthur Stephenson followed behind, and they were surrounded by a phalanx of Arrowhead Security guards. Martinez was pleased that Stephenson had finally dropped the argument that staying in presidential suites appeared too presumptuous. They agreed that it looked better to appear confident that the mid-term elections were swinging their way, and that the allegations of womanizing and bias against immigration were simply examples of the dirty politics being waged by a desperate opposition. Everything was proceeding according to Martinez's plans. Except the conversation he was now having.

"Why did you have to invite her up here?" Sally whispered between clenched teeth. "We wasted almost an hour in there."

"Time well spent," Martinez said. "Kristen has always been in our camp. She can spin her news reports just enough to sway the minds of her viewers toward us. She's a master of subtle nuance."

"There's nothing very subtle about her behavior when she's around you," Sally hissed. "And I get the distinct impression that not only has she *been in our camp* as you put it, but that she's actually spent a little time in the inner sanctum."

Martinez stopped and fixed her with an admonishing stare. "The only woman who has a right to get jealous is my wife," he said. "Considering this is our party's first outing, we're running an amazing campaign, and you've done an excellent job." He smiled. "At times, an *exquisite* job. But you need to start thinking about what role, *if any*, you'll play in our party's future growth. I'd hate to think your emotions might make you a liability."

She smiled nervously. "I'm sorry, Robert. I was just hoping we'd get a little private time this afternoon." She batted her eyes at him. "Maybe a shower."

He continued walking as an Arrowhead escort unlocked the door to his suite and looked inside. He nodded to another guard who'd been waiting in the living room and stood aside as the man walked out into the hall. Seeing that it was now safe to enter the suite, Martinez turned back to Sally. "Why don't you run along and check on the preparations downstairs? Arthur and I have some work to do."

Appropriately rebuked, Sally broke eye contact with him and glanced down at the floor. "Sure. I'll see you down there at seven-thirty. Don't forget to bring the mayor's gift."

"It's on the table by the door," Martinez said. "I won't forget it. See you in a couple of hours."

As she turned to leave, he said, "Sally."

She looked back at him, and he detected a slight quiver in her chin. "Yes?"

He smiled. "I appreciate everything you've done this week." He glanced at the other men in the hall before adding, "And I do mean *everything*."

He turned and strode into the suite, followed by Stephenson. The leader of the security detail closed the door and took his post outside. The two men picked up bottled waters from the sidebar before settling into plush leather armchairs. "So," Arthur said, "what was that all about?"

"Oh, it's nothing," Martinez said with a dismissive wave of the hand. "Sally was just a little annoyed that I made time for Kristen this afternoon."

Stephenson chuckled as he shook his head. "Yeah, I thought we were going to have a good, old-fashioned cat fight for a while there. Each seemed determined to protect you from the other, like a lioness protecting her cub. I don't know how you manage all these women."

Martinez leaned back in his chair and put his feet on the coffee table. "Well, a man's gotta do what a man's gotta do. Thanks to those Brigade bastards I can't call in any of my regular girls. Besides, it's nice to get freebies. I do miss that professional touch, though."

Stephenson threw up his hands in mock protest. "More information than I need to know." His expression turned serious. "But at some point you're going to have to make a choice. These two now know each other. You won't be able to juggle them both for very much longer."

Martinez nodded. "You're right. And I don't intend to."

"So, who'll get the boot?" Stephenson asked.

Martinez took a long drink of water and looked out the window at the view of Uptown Park, already filled with demonstrators. "A politician always needs friends in the press," he said, his voice somber. "But he doesn't need a campaign staff when there is not a campaign going on. After the mid-term elections, Sally will be done."

IT WAS TEN PAST SIX when Peter and Miriam walked into the lobby of the Birmingham Westin. The lobby bar wasn't open for business but was bustling with activity as waiters and set-up crew made their last-minute preparations for the onslaught of fundraiser attendees. A rope barrier separated the bar area and ballroom from the rest of the lobby, and Miriam could see another one set up at the far end of the hall, preventing stragglers from cutting through the reception area when exiting the specialty coffee shop at that end of the building. Two men in dark suits, sporting wires running from left ear to coat breast pocket, were stationed at each barrier. Undoubtedly, they would be reinforced with more security once Martinez, Chastain and Carson were due to arrive.

"Nobody's getting through there without invitations," Miriam said to Peter. "You have ours, right?"

Peter feigned surprise. "I thought you had them."

For a split second she appeared to fall for the ruse. "What?" she gasped.

"Just kidding," he said, patting the pocket of his tuxedo jacket. "You think I'd leave two pieces of paper worth twenty grand at home?"

"Don't tease me tonight," she said, her voice stern. "I'm nervous enough already." She reached into her tiny purse and pulled out a laminated card that read, STAFF PASS, Sheffield and Associates. "I'm going to go find Steph. She should be in the ballroom. You're not on the staff list so you'll need to wait out here."

Just as she started to walk away, a man's voice called out, "Mrs. Hoffman."

They both turned to see Lieutenant John Greene walking briskly in their direction. He was not smiling.

"Hello, Lieutenant," Miriam said. "I didn't expect to see you tonight. Surely there hasn't been a homicide here."

"Not yet," Greene said, "but the night's still young." He nodded toward the hotel entrance. "As you undoubtedly saw when you arrived, we've got quite a situation developing outside. It looks like the size of the protest group has exceeded our expectations, and we expected a lot. So tonight it's all hands on deck, including me. We've got to make sure things don't get too exciting."

"I'm sure you'll keep things under control," Peter said, knowing that if his plan worked, there would indeed be a lot of excitement before the evening was over.

Miriam showed the detective her staff pass. "I was just going to check in with Steph. I'm sure I'll see you again sometime tonight."

Greene fixed her with a probing stare. "Mrs. Hoffman, I'm not just worried about the situation outside. I'm worried about something happening in here. Specifically, I'm worried about you and Ms. Mullins. Are you sure there isn't something you need to tell me?"

Miriam glanced nervously back and forth from the police officer to Peter. "What do you mean? I've answered all of your questions,"

"No, Mrs. Hoffman," he said, shaking his head, "you've *responded* to all of my questions. I still don't feel like I have very many answers. Not complete ones anyway."

"I'm sorry," she said, "I don't understand what you're looking for from me."

"Look," Greene said, "I'm convinced that when your friend was killed, it was no random mugging. I've studied all the evidence from every conceivable angle, and I just can't come up with any other conclusion except it was a hit, and you and/or Ms. Mullins were the targets. Now the only place the two of you had been together since you started working at Sheffield and Associates was your trip to Dallas. To meet Mr. Martinez and his campaign staff. I believe something had to have happened there. Something that either Martinez or one of his associates was so concerned about that they had to get you out of the way. Probably before tonight. So I'm worried about tonight.

And I'll do everything in my power to keep the two of you safe. But I can't do anything if I don't know what I'm up against."

Peter spoke up. "I really appreciate your concern, Lieutenant." He nodded toward Miriam. "We both do. But we just don't have anything else we can tell you."

Greene gave them both a long stare and then sighed loudly. "Okay, fine. But when you've done this kind of work as long as I have you develop a strong sense of intuition. I've been popping antacids like Tic-tacs all afternoon because, intuitively, I know something bad is going to happen tonight."

He turned his head to glance back outside. The crowd filling the park across the street was getting larger and louder by the minute. "Something very bad," he muttered, as if talking to himself.

Chapter 30

A NWAR STUDIED HIS REFLECTION in the mirror, giving his bowtie a little tug to the left. Perfect. He was wearing his favorite tuxedo shirt, handmade by a shirt-maker in London whose cotton—Egyptian cotton, of course—Marcella construction was the gold standard for men's formal wear. He'd brought two other tuxedo shirts on this trip, which he'd worn in Charlotte and Atlanta, and they were now in the hands of the Westin laundry and should be hanging in his closet when he returned to his suite after dinner. This one, though, was special, and he'd saved it for this special night. He wouldn't allow anyone other than his trusted dry cleaner in San Antonio to launder this one. He would deliver it to Arnold for cleaning this weekend, and then put it away for a really special event—like an Inauguration Ball.

He heard the knock he'd been expecting, but before turning to the door he shot one more glance at the face in the mirror. Dark, severely creased, with deep-set eyes that resembled chunks of coal. There was no light in those eyes. Just a cunning intelligence focused obdurately on self-preservation. He often marveled at how he had survived a life of handicap and poverty in Cairo for sixty-three years, long enough to be a victim of the cholera epidemic that had, ironically, saved his life. More than saved it—changed it forever, giving him access to tremendous wealth and authority. For twenty years, supreme authority, but even that was not as great as what he'd wield if he could bring the AVP to power. Winning decisive victories in the mid-term election was the first step to accomplishing that, and he would let no one—not the Brigade, and certainly not a couple of other riders—prevent that from happening. Tonight would resolve both problems.

He stepped to the door and opened it. He nodded to the Arrowhead Security guard posted outside and then stepped back, allowing Ben Wycliff to enter. The man was dressed in a dark suit, but still wore those damned high-heeled cowboy boots. Probably to give him some much needed height, stretching out that short, stocky frame so that he was at least as tall as most women he met.

"You needed to see me?" Wycliff asked.

Anwar nodded. "Just wanted to make a last-minute check on a few details before the show begins. Your men are in place outside?"

"Yep, all eight," Wycliff said. "We just did another test of their earphones and they're working perfectly. They'll be listening for my command."

"Good," Anwar said, glancing at his watch. "We'll be heading down in about forty-five minutes, precisely at seven-thirty. Make sure you're part of the security detail at the elevator. You'll be the logical one to hand the mayor's gift to. Put it under the podium and then station yourself just inside the middle door to the ballroom. Keep your eyes focused on that podium. We can't have anyone moving things around at the last minute."

"Got it."

"Who's the Arrowhead lead tonight?" Anwar asked.

"Brian."

"Okay. That's who you go to. When I give you the signal, give your guys outside the command, wait thirty seconds, and then go directly to Brian. He'll take care of things inside."

"And this will be somewhere between salads and entrees, right?"

"That's the plan," Anwar said. "But be ready to flex on that. I'll figure out when the right moment arrives and give you the sign. Just make sure you can see me clearly at all times."

"Got it," Wycliff said, nodding. "I think we're good to go."

"Excellent," Anwar said, and then locked eyes with the shorter man. "You know, Ben, if this goes according to plan, you'll be set for life."

Wycliff smiled.

"But if it doesn't," Anwar continued, "there will be no place in heaven, on earth, or in hell that you can hide."

Wycliff's smiled faded. He gave his boss a curt nod and left the room.

THE HOTEL LOBBY was packed. Fundraiser attendees had started arriving early, many no doubt concerned about navigating the congestion outside, where the massive throng of demonstrators looked like an invading army. The reception area was not scheduled to open until seven o'clock, with the candidate and Martinez arriving a half hour later, but Steph had just met with Sally McDaniel to suggest they go ahead and allow donors to start into the reception fifteen minutes early. This was after the hotel manager had pulled Steph aside and, in a voice quivering with agitation said, "Hotel guests are having to fight a mob outside and another one here in the lobby. They can't even get to the check-in counter."

Sally had agreed, but somewhat reluctantly, saying, "The sooner we start pouring champagne, the more costly this event becomes. But go ahead. We don't want to be seen as a problem for the hotel."

Now the crowd was progressing from the lobby to the lobby bar, albeit slowly due to their convergence into two lines to allow invitations to be checked. Moving along with the crush of people, Miriam whispered to Peter, "I don't know about you, but I'm ready for some of that champagne."

He smiled. "Actually, I'd prefer a beer, but I'll be sticking with sparkling water tonight. I need to stay sharp."

"Me too," she said, "but I also need to steady my nerves. I'll just have one."

A few minutes later they were inside the rope barrier and saw Steph talking to one of the waiters passing through the crowd with trays of hors d'oeuvres. When the young man had resumed his duties, Miriam and Peter stepped close to her. "Is that the doctor who's in love with you?" Miriam asked, grinning impishly.

"More importantly, is he the guy with the special assignment?" Peter said.

"Yes to both questions," Stephanie said. She looked at Peter. "He'll await my signal, which I told him will come sometime near the end of the receiving line. You tell me when you're ready, and I'll give him the secret sign."

"Perfect," Peter said. "I haven't seen Courtney. Is she still okay with her part?"

"Yeah, she's fine," Stephanie said. "A little excited about it, actually. Let's just make sure we hold up our end and get in there quickly. Anything more than thirty seconds alone with the man could get awkward."

"We'll take care of it," Miriam assured her.

"Take care of what?" a voice behind them said. "No problems, I hope."

They turned to see Mark and Abby, each holding a glass of champagne. Mark, in his tuxedo, was dressed like every other man there. Abby, on the other hand, was sparkling in a gold sequin gown that hugged her petite yet shapely frame. "Abby, you look beautiful," Miriam said. "Is that a Badgly Mischka?"

When Abby nodded, Miriam put a hand to the side of her face and laughed. "Oh my God, I almost bought that exact dress for this evening. How awkward would that have been?"

"I'd better not see anyone else wearing this one," Steph said. "The cashier at Walmart told me this was the only one they had in this color."

Mark laughed and put his hand on Stephanie's shoulder. "If that's your not-so-subtle way of saying I don't pay you enough, pull this evening off without a hitch and we'll talk about a raise, okay?"

"I'll definitely take you up on that," Stephanie said.

"So," Mark continued, "when Abby and I walked up you were talking about taking care of something. Is everything under control?"

"Absolutely," Steph said, nodding. "We just have a checklist of things we'll be going over throughout the night and we've divvied them up. Don't worry about a thing. This is your big night. Just enjoy yourself and leave the details to your loyal minions."

Mark laughed. "Fine. I'll leave everything in your capable hands. But let me know if you need anything. Abby and I are on duty tonight too, you know."

As they walked away, Miriam said, "How do you think he'd react if he knew we had a whole 'nother agenda tonight?"

Stephanie leaned closer and whispered, "Probably the same way he'd react if he knew the three of us held the key to immortality."

"Hey, listen," Peter said, his tone hushed but urgent. "Let's all remember something tonight. We are *not* immortal. Allen is proof of that. All three of us are vulnerable, especially tonight. Stick to the plan, and keep your wits about you at all times. No unnecessary risks, okay?"

The two women nodded solemnly and then Steph glanced at her watch. "Martinez should be coming down in about thirty minutes. Let me go check on things in the kitchen. Chef Stark was yelling at everyone a few minutes ago. If the cooks get mad and walk out, we'll all three be wearing aprons. See you back out here in a bit."

As Steph walked away, Peter released a long sigh. Miriam studied his face. "You okay?" she asked, taking his hand.

"Yeah, I'm fine," he said wearily. "Just ready to get this night behind us. This whole thing could be even more dangerous than we imagined."

She squeezed his hand. "It'll be fine. *We'll* be fine. As long as I have you looking after me, I know I'll be safe."

"THIS IS KRISTEN CONNELLY, reporting live from the Westin Hotel in Birmingham, Alabama, where the American Value Party leadership, including founder Robert Martinez, is in the middle of its five-day campaign swing through The Deep South. All week long their appearances have been encumbered to some degree by the presence of large gatherings of protestors, mostly representing the

Hispanic Protection Brigade, but tonight's demonstration is in an entirely different category.

"In just about twenty minutes, Martinez, Alabama congressional candidate William Chastain, and U.S. Senator Richard Carson are expected to appear in the reception area of the main hotel lobby, where supporters are enjoying champagne and canapes. Ostensibly, they are waiting for the opportunity to meet and speak with the candidate and their junior Senator, but it is obvious that it's Martinez they really came to see. They'll have a chance to do that, as there will be a receiving line at the entrance to the ballroom where the dinner will be held. Many supporters commented on their way in that they arrived earlier than they would have normally, due to television reports of the massive demonstration.

"The street right behind me is Richard Arrington Jr. Boulevard, a main thoroughfare in downtown Birmingham, feeding not only the Westin hotel but the Birmingham-Jefferson Civic Center and the Uptown Entertainment District, which boasts several popular Birmingham restaurants. Across the street from the entrance to the hotel is Uptown Park, consisting of a large grassy area and several BJCC parking lots. As you can see behind me, that park is absolutely brimming with protestors waving signs and shouting slogans such as "You were once immigrants too," and "We love America as much as you." At this moment they are singing the classic Woody Guthrie freedom song, *This Land is Your Land, This Land is My Land*, as they've done at several other demonstrations. Thus far, they've obeyed the terms of their assembly permit, which stipulates that they cause no obstruction to traffic on Arrington or 23rd Avenue North, which essentially bisects the park.

"But if my camera man can follow me for a moment, I want to show you something that was apparently not anticipated by the AVP staff or the Birmingham Police Department. The Westin actually sits back about fifty yards from Arrington Boulevard, on what is essentially a semi-circle that runs past the hotel entrance on the right and behind several restaurants before reconnecting with Arrington. But, as I hope you can see, there is a very large open area down at the far end, right where the street curves around the corner of the popular Southern Kitchen & Bar. That open area is now packed with demonstrators as well, resulting in the Westin being effectively hemmed in from both sides.

"A police officer informed me that no assembly permit was issued for that area—just for the park across the street—but it appears the police will not try to disperse the crowd gathered there. He told me that as long as the demonstration remains peaceful and orderly, traffic is not impeded, and the restriction requiring the protestors to stay fifty or more yards back from the hotel entrance is observed, the police will not intervene.

"But as someone who has covered Martinez and the rapidly growing American Values Party for several months now, I can tell you that the energy level of this demonstration, in addition to its unprecedented size, is different from anything we've seen so far. Brigade founder Carlos Guerra has reiterated his pledge to keep the protest peaceful, but with this many people, and so much angry rhetoric filling the air, that may be a difficult pledge to keep.

"We'll be staying here providing updates until the fundraiser dinner is completed and the protest crowd has dispersed. But the way things are looking right now, that could be several hours away.

"This is Kristen Connelly, PNN, reporting from Birmingham."

AT PRECISELY SEVEN THIRTY the elevator doors in the Westin lobby opened up and Robert Martinez emerged, carrying a small gift box. He was surrounded by his security detail, along with Arthur Stephenson, William Chastain, and Senator Richard Carson. The entourage was met by more Arrowhead Security staff, a smiling Sally McDaniel, and a very serious looking Ben Wycliff, who stepped in close to Martinez and said, "Sir, would you like me to put this gift behind the podium for you?"

Martinez looked at him and smiled, his affable graciousness on grand display in the event any cameras were nearby. "Thank you, Ben, I'd appreciate that," he said.

The group turned to their right and walked into the hotel lobby. They could have come down on a service elevator and emerged a short distance from the ballroom, the approach adamantly favored by the security detail, but Martinez would have nothing of it. Having to traverse the lobby before entering the roped-off reception area would, as he had put it, "Give me a chance to meet some people who couldn't afford ten grand to eat rubber chicken and hear me speak."

As he made his way across the lobby, he paused to shake hands and speak with every guest, desk clerk and bellman in the room. Every smile and every gesture projected empathy, energy, and un-affected love for people. Several members of the press—including Kristen Connelly, who beamed as Martinez graced her with a smile and a wink—covered his every move, as planned. By the time he paused to shake hands and share a laugh at the concierge desk, the crowd behind the ropes had seen him, and started applauding and cheering as he approached. As Martinez continued to move toward the opening in the rope barricade, the throng of admirers parted, as if he were Moses and they were the Red Sea. He smiled and nodded and raised one hand above his head, two fingers forming the classic victory V, and then leaned over to Sally and said, "This is the best crowd yet. I think it's going to be a memorable night."

Chapter 31

PETER AND MIRIAM watched the entourage approaching from their position in the back of the crowd, by the windows to the outside. They had purposely moved to that area several minutes earlier. It was part of Peter's plan for them, along with Steph and Courtney, to be among the last attendees to meet Martinez, who was at the end of the receiving line. As people met and shook hands with the candidate, the senator, and finally the charismatic founder of the AVP, they were directed to the open middle doors of the ballroom, where their names were checked off a list and they were escorted to their assigned table. The going was slow, but that had been anticipated. Steph had allowed forty-five minutes for about two hundred and forty couples to pass through, assuming an average of ten to fifteen seconds per couple. Some would try to hog more time than that, but Sally McDaniel and her assistants were focused on keeping the line moving as expeditiously as possible without creating the feeling of a cattle drive.

About twenty minutes into the process, when the crowd in the reception area had been reduced by approximately a half, Stephanie walked out of the ballroom and joined Peter and Miriam. "Looks like everything is moving along pretty much on schedule," she said. "Everything's in order in the ballroom, and the kitchen staff no longer looks like they'll walk out. The band will start playing at eight, and will be ready to start belting out *The Yellow Rose of Texas* at eight-thirty. That's when Martinez will make his grand entrance walking down the center aisle and then up the steps onto the dais."

"That was a clever move," Miriam said. "It means Martinez should have a few minutes to walk around the corner to the Camellia Room for his rendezvous with Courtney instead of having to get backstage."

Stephanie smiled. "I knew it was going to work the moment I pitched the idea to Sally. She loved the idea of the whole audience focusing on the stage and then suddenly turning around to see their newest political star walking right past them. Apparently, he loved the idea too. It seems the man's ego never takes a rest."

"Let's hope his libido doesn't either," Peter said. "Speaking of which, where's Courtney? Shouldn't she be out here too?"

Stephanie nodded her head toward the far corner of the reception area, next to the entrance to the coffee shop. "The Camellia Room is right there. "I'll get her when we get down to only a dozen or so people left in the receiving line. I want her to kind of catch Martinez by surprise."

A young woman carrying a tray of champagne appeared, but everyone declined. Stephanie's admirer, the medical student, arrived a couple of minutes later offering petite salmon mousse pinwheels. Stephanie took one and popped it into her mouth and then studied the tray. "Got anything a little messier?" she asked.

"There's another tray of the stuffed mushrooms in marinara sauce," he said.

"Perfect," she said. "Make sure you're out here with that in another five minutes."

The young man smiled and winked at her before turning and walking toward another couple near the end of the receiving line. They watched as he worked his way up the line until his tray was empty. He then headed briskly toward the kitchen.

"Wow, Steph, you've got that boy completely wrapped," Miriam said, laughing despite her nervousness. "Are you sure you're not interested in being a doctor's wife?"

Stephanie shook her head. "He's got an internship and three or four years of residency before he starts making any money. We'll see where things are then."

Peter grinned. "I didn't realize you were such a material girl," he chided.

Stephanie grinned back at him. "It's hard to take that comment seriously when it comes from someone who's amassed a fortune by hijacking the bodies of wealthy men."

"Ouch!" Peter said, raising his hands in mock surrender. "The material girl has a nasty streak too."

"Damned right," Stephanie said, the smile fading as she looked toward the front of the receiving line. "I've been known to carry a grudge. And tonight, I have a score to settle. Be back in a minute."

She walked along the receiving line before making a circle around the reception area and rejoining Peter and Miriam. "There are about sixty couples left. That should take another ten or twelve minutes, and then it'll be our turn. Let's give it another five, and then I'll go get Courtney. Phillip should be back out here with those mushrooms by then."

They passed the next five minutes chatting anxiously, all of them trying not to show the building tension that was driving their adrenalin levels to the stratosphere. Finally, Steph looked across the lobby bar and said, "There's Phillip. I'm gonna get Courtney now."

She abruptly turned and walked away. Miriam took a deep, quivering breath and leaned in against her husband. "So you think we'll be able to separate them?" she asked.

"We have to," Peter said. "I have to be one-on-one for this discussion. I won't have much time, and can't afford to have anyone else around to cause any distraction or interfere with me making my point."

"What if Martinez is too busy or wrapped up in his entourage to take the bait from Courtney?"

Peter's eyes widened as he stared over Miriam's shoulder. "Unless he's gay or brain-dead, I don't think that's a concern," he muttered.

They both watched Stephanie and Courtney approach. Courtney was wearing the black miniskirt she'd worn to Allen's memorial service, only this time with a sheer white blouse and—if it were possible—even higher stiletto heels. Her long auburn hair, sun-streaked to perfection, framed an audaciously sensuous face with sleepy hazel eyes and pouty red lips. By contrast, the winged models on the annual Victoria's Secret fashion show would be considered matronly. The other parts of the plan might be iffy, but having Martinez follow Courtney into the Camellia Room was as good as done.

THE FOUR OF THEM were next in line when another couple suddenly appeared from the direction of the restrooms, the woman probably insisting she check her make-up and hair before meeting the handsome Texas businessman who she declared would be the next President of the United States. They were probably hoping to be the last in line so they could steal an extra moment with the man, but Stephanie turned to them and ushered them ahead. "You folks go ahead. We're staff, and have a couple of things we need to review with Mr. Martinez."

The couple reluctantly nodded and stepped forward. Their ploy of being at the end of the receiving line worked, and Martinez spent a good thirty or forty seconds with them, but Peter noticed the man give a nod of recognition to Miriam and Steph, and a lascivious look of appreciation when his eyes then settled on Courtney. As the foursome stepped in front of Martinez, Stephenson moved in and said, "Robert, I'm sure you remember Ms. Mullins and Mrs. Hoffman from Sheffield and Associates."

"Of course I do," Martinez said, shaking hands with each before turning to Peter and saying, "You must be Mr. Hoffman."

Peter took the outstretched hand and shook it firmly. "Yes, sir. Peter Hoffman. It's an honor to meet you." He then extended his hand toward Stephenson. "And you as well, Mr. Stephenson."

"My pleasure," Stephenson said, glancing back into the ballroom as if preparing to announce they needed to get ready for their entrance.

But Martinez appeared to be in no hurry. His eyes settled on Courtney. "I haven't met you, though. I'm sure I'd remember if I had."

Courtney smiled and extended her hand. "Courtney Pruitt, sir. I work with Steph and Miriam."

"Ah, so you've helped pull this magnificent event together," Martinez said, smiling broadly as he clung to her hand. "So I suppose I'll be seeing you inside?"

"Actually, Courtney is manning the agency's command center tonight," Stephanie said. "So she'll be in there for the remainder of the evening. She just wanted to come out and have a chance to meet you."

"Oh, that's too bad," Martinez said, the disappointment visible on his face. "That's an important job, being in charge of the command center. I imagine it'll be a bee hive of activity."

"Not really," Courtney said, looking down as if embarrassed. "It's just a table with a laptop and a headset around the corner in the Camellia Room. It'll actually be pretty boring." She turned her head to gaze longingly into the ballroom. "All the excitement will be in here."

At that moment, Stephanie looked to the side at Phillip who'd been standing dutifully nearby with a couple of servings of the stuffed mushroom. She gave a subtle, almost imperceptible nod and Phillip stepped forward. "Mr. Stephenson, Mr. Martinez, you've both been so busy you haven't had time to eat anything," Stephanie said. "Try one of these mushrooms. They've been the favorite appetizer tonight."

Martinez nodded, obviously wanting to spend a little more time with Courtney, but Stephenson declined. "No thanks," he said, shaking his head.

Phillip waited for Martinez to lift a tiny plate holding the mushroom and marinara sauce, and then picked one up and held it out toward Stephenson. "Just one left, sir. You really should taste these. They're one of Chef Stark's…:

Before he could finish his sentence, he dipped the end of the plate just enough for a marble-sized drop of sauce to drip spill over the edge and land squarely on Stephenson's pristine white shirt. Stephenson just stared at the stain in apparent disbelief for two or three seconds, and then his face turned as red as the imported San Marzano tomatoes used in the sauce. "Dammit, I told you I didn't want one!" he muttered between clenched teeth.

Phillip was in full panic mode. Or, at least, was acting as if he were. "I'm so sorry, sir! I don't know how that happened. Please, let me help you with that."

"This shirt is hand-made!" Stephenson sputtered. "It cost more than you make in a month. Thanks for the offer, but I think you've done enough."

"Please, Mr. Stephenson, let me help," Phillip pleaded. "My dad owns a laundry. I've spent my summers working there since I was twelve. I know what to do." He started to walk in the direction of the lobby. "The lobby bar is right here. There's a staff only washroom right behind it. Let me get some club soda on that and treat it with lemon juice and a dash of vinegar. It'll be as good as new, I promise."

Stephenson glanced at his watch and then at Martinez. "Oh, what the hell. We don't need to go in for a few more minutes. I'll meet you back here in five."

His face still burning with anger, he followed Phillip behind the lobby bar, where the young man grabbed a small bottle of club soda, a sliced lemon and two white towels. The two men then disappeared through the door with a sign reading "Hotel Associates Only."

Stephanie looked at Martinez and let out a long sigh. "And everything had been going so well."

Martinez smiled. "Don't worry about it. Accidents happen. And the kid seemed to know what to do."

"Well, I'm sorry it happened." She looked at her watch. "I need to take care of a couple of things inside before you walk in, sir. Please excuse me."

As Steph hurried off, Courtney gave Martinez a dreamy-eyed smile and said, "I guess it's time for me to go too. I doubt anyone will be calling me, but I need to be there if they do."

Peter's heart soared when Martinez, still studying every inch of Courtney's nearly six-foot frame, said, "So where is this command center of yours?"

"Right at the end of this corridor, next to the coffee shop," Courtney replied in a whispery voice that created the distinct impression that she'd like some company.

Martinez made a show of glancing at his watch, as if the dinner might start without him. "Well, Arthur said he'd be five minutes, so I've got time to take a look at the brains of this operation if you'd like to show me."

It occurred to Peter that brains of any kind—human or electronic—were not what was motivating Martinez at that moment. Courtney had played her role to perfection. The man would follow her into a cesspool if that's where she led him.

"Okay," Peter said. "I'll go check on Mr. Stephenson and see how that's going."

"I'll wait here for you," Miriam said to Peter.

"Good, then we're all set," Martinez said, his smile now more of a lewd sneer. He turned to one of the nearby Arrowhead guards. "Brian, can you have one of your guys run down ahead of us and check out the Camellia Room? Courtney and I will follow."

"Yes, sir," the guard said, looking at another member of the security detail who nodded and hurried down the hall so he could check out the room and get back out of there before Martinez and his newest lady friend arrived.

Martinez and Courtney followed in the same direction, and Peter looked at Miriam. She offered a weak smile as he stepped over and gave her a quick but affectionate hug. "Wish me luck," he said. "I'm gonna need all I can get."

Her eyes began to swell and her hand trembled as she reached up to touch his cheek. "You'll do fine," she said. And then she lifted up on her toes and kissed him lightly on the lips. "Stay strong, *kochanka*."

SALLY MCDANIEL WAS feeling great. Despite the unexpectedly large demonstration going on outside the hotel, the night was going exactly according to plan. Martinez had seemed genuinely pleased by the reaction of the crowd when he appeared in the lobby. His whispered remark that this was the best crowd yet had been gratifying, but the one that followed—that tonight was going to be a "memorable night"—was the one that had shifted her imagination into overdrive. The campaign staff would be staying the night at the Westin and leaving early the next morning for the two and a half hour bus ride to her hometown of Nashville. She knew that after a night like this Martinez would be too keyed up to go right to sleep. Perhaps she could help him work off some of that nervous energy.

She glanced at her watch. Eight twenty-two. The receiving line should be finished now, or close to it, so she decided it was time to go out and make sure Martinez was ready for his triumphant entry into the packed ballroom.

She rose from her seat at the table right below the dais and started weaving her way toward the doors leading to the lobby bar. Only the middle set was open, guarded by that creepy private security consultant, Ben Wycliff. She expected the usual leer—after all, she figured that, with the possible exception of Miriam Hoffman, she was the youngest and most attractive woman there tonight—and was a little surprised when Wycliff hardly seemed to notice her. His attention remained focused on the dais, which was weird because neither Martinez nor Stephenson were up there, but she was glad to be spared the *Oh baby, what I'd love to do to you* look.

She turned her attention back to the empty-looking reception area as she rounded the last table at the back of the room and saw one of the Arrowhead guards hurrying down the corridor to the right. What was that all about? Was there some kind of problem? She was just about to pick up her pace so she could get out there and see what was going on when Martinez came into view. He was less than ten feet away, but he never even glanced at Sally. His attention was focused on a woman Sally had never seen before. A tall, slender, auburn-haired beauty wearing a skirt that bordered on indecent.

She looked very young; younger than Sally. And in those ridiculously high heels, she was tall enough to look directly into Martinez's eyes, which she was doing with an expression of lustful expectation.

Who the hell was this slut, and where had she come from? Sally had reviewed the guest list a dozen times, and didn't remember any single women on the list. Was Martinez back to hiring women again? At a campaign fundraiser? Even he knew better than that. Sally had to get to the bottom of this.

She exited the ballroom and looked to her right. Nothing that way except a coffee shop—the Octane Coffee Company. But Martinez and the woman were not headed there. They turned to the right of the shop where there was another conference room—the Camellia Room. Could that be where they were going? She got her answer a moment later when one of the Arrowhead guards stepped out of the room and gave Martinez a curt nod. He then held the door open as the two of them, still chatting and laughing, entered.

Burning with anger, Sally stormed in that direction as fast as she could walk.

PETER LEANED AGAINST the lobby bar and waited, his eyes focused on the "Hotel Associates Only" door behind it. He'd watched Stephenson and Phillip walk through it, and had been assured there was no other way in or out. Which meant the man he needed to speak with was inside. Unfortunately, so was Phillip, and this conversation was not for his ears, or anyone else's for that matter. So Peter had to steel himself and execute the most difficult element of his plan—he had to wait for the right moment.

And then it came. The door opened and there was Phillip, who looked back inside and said, "Wait right here, sir. I'll be back in less than a minute." He looked at Peter, his mind obviously racing with questions he knew better than to ask, and hurried around the bar and toward the kitchen.

This was it. Peter had needed a two minute window, with Martinez and Stephenson separated not only from each other but from their security detail. Two minutes. That's how long it would take to deliver his carefully rehearsed message and either end this threat or increase it exponentially. The clock was ticking. He didn't have much time. He walked quickly to the door, took a deep breath, and pushed it open.

Chapter 32

MIRIAM WATCHED as Courtney and Martinez entered the Camellia Room and an Arrowhead Security man assumed his position outside the door. She also saw Sally McDaniel follow them down the corridor. She observed the other woman slowing down, as if contemplating turning around and heading back toward the ballroom, and then suddenly accelerate her pace as she headed straight for the guarded door. *No, it was too soon!* Miriam had seen Peter preparing to enter the employees' washroom just a few seconds earlier. He was depending on having a minimum of two minutes alone with Stephenson, not much time when considering his goal was to dismantle a threat to the United States government. If Sally interrupted now and Martinez headed right back to the reception area, a security guard would probably be sent into the washroom to get Stephenson and the plan would be disrupted. That couldn't be allowed to happen.

"Sally!" Miriam called out as she started moving at a rapid pace toward the Camellia Room door. "Sally!"

On the second call, McDaniel turned around. Miriam caught up with her and said, "Is everything okay? I thought you'd be in the ballroom, waiting for Martinez's grand entrance."

Sally glanced impatiently toward the Camellia Room but stopped to engage Miriam. "I just came out to get him," she said. "It's time.

But I saw him go into that room with a young woman I don't know. Probably the daughter of one of the big donors."

"No, that's Courtney Pruitt," Miriam said. "She works with Steph and me."

Sally looked confused. "She works with you? Well, what would they be going in there for?"

"It's our command center for the event," Miriam said, counting off the seconds in her head as she stalled for more time. "He said he wanted to see it. Mr. Stephenson is in the restroom and they had a few minutes to kill, so..."

Sally again looked back at the door, obviously aware that Martinez had other reasons for going in there than learning how catered events were managed, and said, "Well, I have to get him. We need to have him ready to walk into that ballroom the second Stephenson comes back out."

"Sure," Miriam said, nodding knowingly. "I'll go with you. I need to check on a couple of things with Courtney anyway."

They approached the door. The stern-looking young man guarding it started to challenge them, but Miriam held up her staff pass and said, "This is my firm's command center. I need to go in there."

The guard nodded reluctantly and then held them back with one hand while he knocked once, then twice more with the other. He then pulled open the door and the two women entered to find Courtney and Martinez huddled in front of the computer screen. He was standing very close to her, his hand resting on the small of her back. They both looked up to see who was interrupting them. Martinez looked annoyed. Courtney looked relieved.

PETER WALKED INTO the washroom and found Stephenson hunched over by the sink, dabbing at the spot on his shirt with a wet towel. The man didn't look up. He just said, his voice rank with irritation, "Did you find some damned vinegar?"

Peter didn't respond. Instead, he took a moment to study the scene which he had known to expect, but which still seemed to test the boundaries of believability, even for him. The man bent over in front of him was quite clearly the wealthy businessman and political campaign czar Arthur Stephenson. But the reflection in the mirror was exactly as Miriam had described—a brown, deeply creased face with a broad nose and dark, cruel eyes. Mediterranean for sure; most likely Egyptian.

"So, who are you, really?" Peter asked.

Appearing startled and bewildered by an unexpected voice, Stephenson lifted his head slightly to glance in the mirror to see who had entered the supposedly private washroom. But instead of the clumsy waiter, he saw the reflection of a young man in a tuxedo. A pale, slightly freckled young man with curly red hair and bright green eyes. He turned around quickly and saw Peter's face—dark brown hair, blue eyes, the tanned skin of an Italian—and his lips slowly turned up in an amused smile.

"Well, Mr. Hoffman," he said. "I guess I should've expected Miriam to be married to another rider. Long-term relationships with ordinary people can be a bit depressing when you know their days are numbered."

"I repeat my question," Peter said. "Who are you, really?"

Stephenson stood up straight, thrusting out his chest and smiling proudly. "I am Anwar. I discovered my gift when I almost died in the Cairo cholera epidemic in 1831. And you?"

"My name really is Peter. And let's just say I've been at this a little longer."

"I see," Stephenson said, returning his focus to the barely visible stain on his shirt. He began dabbing it with the wet cloth again and said, "So why this obviously planned ruse to get me alone? Just wanted to meet a kindred spirit?"

Peter didn't respond. Instead he asked a question of his own. "Did you try to have my wife killed, getting her associate killed in the process?"

Stephenson looked up from his shirt. "Well, right to the point, I see. Now, I suppose I could deny your accusation, but I won't. For two reasons. One is that it happens to be true. And the second is that there's nothing you can do about it. Just consider it a lesson—you do not want to mess with me."

Peter stood erect, hoping he looked more menacing than he felt. "Well, I guess I must be a slow learner, because that's exactly why I'm here. To mess with you."

"Oh, really?" Stephenson said. "And why is that? Revenge?"

"Partly," Peter said. "But mostly because I can't allow someone like you to gain access to the power of a potential United States President."

Stephenson began to shake his head slowly as he appeared to study the young man who dared to challenge him. "So your intent is what, to kill me?"

"No," Peter said, softly but deliberately. "My intent is to expose you."

Stephenson laughed and waved his hand in a dismissive gesture. "Expose me? And how do you think you can do that?" He turned his head to the side, as if carrying on an imaginary conversation. "You see, officer, we're not really who we appear to be. We're actually several hundred years old, and we just jump from one body to another and ride it until we're ready for a change." He looked back at Peter and sneered. "Good luck with that, Junior."

"I don't plan to try to expose you as a rider," Peter said. "You're right; no one would believe that. But I can certainly bring some things to light that would derail your association with Martinez and the AVP."

"Like what?" Stephenson snarled. "He trusts me implicitly. He wouldn't be where he is today without me, and he knows it. He's not my superior. Not now, and not when he becomes president. We're partners. Equal partners. We will *share* the power of the presidency."

Peter held his ground. "Trust me, *Anwar*, after tonight, Martinez won't be able to distance himself from you fast enough. Like most politicians, he's a self-centered egotist. If he thinks you're a threat to his party, he'll drop you like a bad habit."

"You're crazy," Stephenson snarled. "You have no idea what you're talking about." He stared into Peter's eyes. "Or what you're up against."

Peter smiled. "I told you a minute ago that I've been at this a bit longer than you. Quite a bit longer, actually. And one of the things you learn to do over time is to identify resources that you need to survive. I have one now who promised me he could hide anyone, or find anyone. He's lived up to that promise. He's done some research on you, and he found proof that Arthur Stephenson isn't the self-made Texas multi-millionaire he claims to be. He found that most of your wealth wasn't made here in the U.S. at all. It's been around since the 1940s, residing in a tightly protected numbered bank account in Sao Paulo. It contains money, jewels and securities that can be traced, and they were. They were all pilfered from wealthy German Jews by the Nazis. And now, for some reason, that account belongs to you."

Stephenson cocked his head to the side and grinned maliciously. "So you'll do what—tell Martinez I'm the reincarnation of Adolf Hitler?"

In spite of himself, Peter felt his eyes go wide and his knees buckle slightly. He hadn't quite made that connection. And now that it had been made for him, he realized just what kind of demon he was dealing with. He tried to speak, but it came out as more of a choked whisper. "You...you were...?"

Stephenson's grin morphed into a sneer. "Kind of makes you want to reconsider threatening me, doesn't it? And the fact of the matter is, your threats are idle. So you found the account...big deal. I can have it moved with one phone call, and this time I'll make sure it can't be found again."

Now it was Peter's turn to smile, although it was a weak one. "Actually, you can't. My resource has been bombarding your account with bogus e-mail inquiries all afternoon. The bank has the account on lock-down, as a security measure. They won't let it be touched until you request it, and to do that you have to either appear in person or provide a thumb print matching the one on file. And you can't make either of those things happen faster than the FBI and Interpol can get there with a handful of warrants, which is probably happening as we speak. So the connection of that account to you is not erasable. I don't think Martinez will need longer than a second or two to denounce a man whose wealth was amassed as a result of Nazi crimes against humanity."

Stephenson's face had turned beet-red and Peter could actually see the veins on his temples pulsing rapidly. "You are going to die! You and that Jew bitch wife of yours, both."

"You'll have to find us first," Peter said. "And you won't be in a position to use the FBI or any other government agency to do that. Your political career ends tonight."

Peter turned and pulled open the door before the man could make any kind of aggressive move. But right before he walked out of the washroom, he glanced at the face of Arthur Stephenson standing in front of him and the face of Anwar in the mirror. Both were twisted in a grimace of rage. The expression on Stephenson's face was frightening, but Peter knew that the maniacal glare of Anwar would haunt his dreams for as long as he lived.

"THIS IS KRISTEN CONNELLY, with another live update from the Westin Hotel in Birmingham, Alabama. Inside, American Values Party leader Robert Martinez and his entourage have been greeting the attendees of his gala fundraiser dinner for the past hour, and is at this very moment preparing to enter the ballroom to what will surely be enthusiastic applause. But the real story tonight is taking place out here, in front of the hotel, where the largest anti-AVP demonstration to date is taking place.

"Police have estimated that over five thousand supporters of *Brigada de Proteccion Hispana*—the Hispanic Protection Brigade—have now amassed on two sides of the hotel, and the mood is definitely more hostile than it has been in previous demonstrations this week. Twice in the past fifteen minutes, Birmingham Police have pushed the crowd back behind the barriers that were erected to mark the fifty yard perimeter around the hotel entrance that the protestors are not allowed to cross. The last time, just a few minutes ago, some of the protestors were pushing back, although they did finally retreat behind the barrier.

"So far, no arrests have been made, but a source within the Birmingham Police Department told me that one more move by the protestors beyond the area covered by their permit will generate a more aggressive police response, which I took to mean arrests. In the past five minutes, three buses belonging to the police department, normally used to transport prisoners, have arrived and are parked on Richard Arrington Boulevard, right behind me. Whether they will be called into use to take unruly protestors to jail remains to be seen.

"Meanwhile, the chants of the demonstrators have gotten louder and more adversarial. Early this evening they were shouting, "We love America too." Now they are chanting, "Down with Martinez!

"This is Kristen Connelly, PNN, reporting live from Birmingham."

PETER RACED INTO the lobby bar area and turned right, heading for the entrance to the ballroom. He could hear the band play the opening strains of *The Yellow Rose of Texas* as a crew-cut man sporting a black suit and a headset ran past him into the employee washroom, likely to let Stephenson know it was time for the grand entry. Peter saw Martinez and Sally McDaniel standing just outside the now-closed doors of the middle ballroom entrance, him wearing a look of annoyance and her an expression of downright anger. Two somber-looking security guards flanked them, one prepared to open the left door and the other prepared to open the right.

Damn! Peter had to speak with Miriam, but there was no way he'd be able to get into the ballroom until Martinez had worked his way to the dais, and he'd probably be stopping to chat and glad-hand as he crossed the room, milking the moment as much as he could. Just as Peter was considering an attempt to barge through one of the other entrances, he heard a voice behind him. "Peter!"

He turned to see Miriam rushing toward him, coming from the direction of the Camellia Room. He hurried to her and put his hands on her arms. "I did it," he said, panting. "Now I need to get outside and talk to a reporter. Get inside the ballroom as soon as you can. Go to our table and stay close to Mark and Abby. You should be safe as long as you're around a lot of other people."

She looked scared out of her wits, but she nodded. "You'll come back in right away, won't you?"

"Yes," he said, nodding vigorously. "I'll get done outside as quickly as I can. I shouldn't have any trouble getting a reporter's attention. All the action is in here. Just wait for me, okay? Don't leave that room. I need to know how to get to you as quickly as possible. We'll probably be leaving here in a few minutes."

"Peter, please be careful," she said, her voice quivering.

"I'll be surrounded by people, like you'll be. I don't think there's anything he'll be able to do. But the sooner we disappear, the better."

He started to turn away, but she grabbed him. "Tell me what he said. Did he threaten us? Did you learn anything more about him?"

"Not now," he insisted. "I'll fill you in once we're in the car. Now go! And stay at our table until I come get you."

With that, he turned and hurried away toward the hotel lobby. As he passed the lobby bar he glanced to his left and saw the door to the employee washroom open. Stephenson stepped out, followed by the security guard who had gone in to get him. Stephenson saw Peter and locked eyes with him for a moment. For a moment, Peter was afraid the man would follow him outside, but instead he turned and walked briskly in the direction of the ballroom, where the sound of the band was almost eclipsed by the raucous applause and cheering for Martinez.

Relieved, but concerned about Stephenson's next move, Peter turned and rushed through the lobby toward the main hotel entrance. Just before he reached the doors he saw Lieutenant Greene looking anxiously outside as he talked on his cell phone. Not bothering to stop, Peter grabbed the detective's arm and started pulling him along. "Lieutenant, please come with me. It's urgent!"

Greene tried to pull his arm free and said, "Mr. Hoffman, you don't want to go out there. It may get nasty."

"I have to," Peter said, nearly shouting. "And if you want those answers you've been talking about, you'll come with me."

ARTHUR STEPHENSON—ANWAR—raced ahead of the Arrowhead guard and stepped through the now-open middle doors to the ballroom. The noise in the room was deafening, and he could see Martinez moving past the front row of tables as he made his final approach to the dais. It was exactly the kind of spectacle they had wanted, but it held no interest for Stephenson now. He glanced first to his left and then to his right, where he saw Ben Wycliff pressed against the wall, eyes still focused on the podium. Stephenson stepped close to the man and spoke directly into his ear. "Now."

Wycliff turned to him, a bewildered expression on his face. "What?"

Stephenson shouted this time, his voice carrying over the noise of the band and the cheering crowd. "I said, *now!*"

Chapter 33

PETER RAN OUT the doors of the hotel, stopping next to the valet parking stand, where the uniformed attendant was staring nervously in the direction of the park across the street. Lieutenant Greene caught up to him. Dropping his cell phone into his coat pocket, he said, "I told you it may get nasty out here. You should go back inside."

Ignoring him, Peter looked across the street. The shouting mass of protestors in the park was on the verge of pushing through the barrier of yellow tape and blue uniforms that separated them from Richard Arrington Boulevard and the entrance to the hotel. He glanced in the other direction and noted the proximity of the surging crowd at the end of the semi-circle that ran between the Weston and the Uptown restaurants. Both crowds seemed to pulse with anger, and Peter could tell that it wouldn't take much to ignite this tinderbox and turn the previously peaceful demonstration into a full-fledged riot. But that was not his concern. He and Miriam could reach the parking garage from inside the hotel and make their escape before getting trapped in the melee. What he needed to do right now was find a reporter who wasn't in the middle of a broadcast about the volatile situation that had developed.

He scanned the area and saw a camera light go off, right outside the windows looking into the lobby bar area and entrance to the ballroom. He saw a female reporter lower her microphone from her mouth and recognized her as Kristen Connelly from PNN. He'd watched several of her reports in recent weeks and knew that she was familiar with the AVP leadership. She would certainly know who Arthur Stephenson was—had probably met with him a few times—so she'd immediately recognize the implications of what he had to say. With Lieutenant Greene continuing his pleas for Peter to go back inside the hotel, he headed toward Kristen.

"Come with me," he said to Greene as he picked up his pace. "You need to hear this."

Peter pushed his way through the crowd of reporters and pulled a sheet of paper from his coat pocket as he reached Kristen Connelly. A man holding a shoulder-mounted camera tried to block Peter's access, but he pushed the man aside. "Ms. Connelly, I need to speak with you."

She glanced back and forth between her cameraman and the obviously excited young man in the tuxedo, looking as if she were unsure what to do. "I have a story for you," Peter shouted. "The story of your career!"

She held up her hand to hold her cameraman at bay. "Hold on, Mitch," she said. "Let me see what he has to say."

With Greene right on his heels. Peter stepped close to her, waving the sheet of paper in his hand. "You know Arthur Stephenson, right?"

"Of course," she said.

"Well, there's something about him that you don't know. And it has the potential to turn the AVP movement upside down."

ANWAR WALKED OUT of the hotel and scanned the crowd of reporters and police. He could tell from the sound of the protestors that they'd been whipped into a frenzy, probably to the dismay of Carlos Guerra and the rest of the Brigade leadership. Well, that's what they deserved for trying to create such a massive demonstration. There were men moving among them who they didn't know—men who had their own assignments. And a peaceful protest wasn't on the list.

He glanced to his right and saw Peter Hoffman waving a sheet of paper and talking in an animated fashion to Kristen Connelly. Anwar wasn't surprised, nor was he alarmed. This was going to work out even better than he'd thought just a few minutes earlier. Not only would the Hispanic Protection Brigade be completely discredited once it appeared they had started a riot, but those two meddlesome women who'd seen his true face in Dallas would be dealt with as well. And now the man who had somehow uncovered his biggest secret was standing right outside the windows of the lobby bar. His position was perfect. The Brazil account might be salvaged after all.

He stared at the other rider and sneered. A man could live for a thousand years and nothing he ever experienced would be quite as sweet as the exquisite taste of revenge.

MIRIAM KEPT HER EYES focused on the entrance to the ballroom, praying that Peter would appear. But several minutes passed and there was still no sign of him. Abby was trying to engage her in conversation, and she knew her disinterest was apparent to both her and Mark, but she didn't care. After tonight, she'd never see them again anyway. All she cared about at this moment was seeing her husband walking toward their table.

Suddenly there was a halt in the din of conversation and laughter in the ballroom, and she heard Abby say, "Mark, what's going on?"

Miriam looked at Abby, and then followed her gaze to the dais, where Martinez sat between Mayor Simpson and Senator Carson. But a man in a black suit and with a curled wire protruding from his left ear was bent over the political maverick, simultaneously whispering to him and lifting him from his chair. Martinez looked left and right, saying something to the mayor and the senator before pushing his chair back from the table. The man in the black suit then grabbed Martinez's arm and ushered him off the stage and through a door behind the curtain.

The astonished crowd began to murmur again, people looking around the large room for some sign of trouble. The woman seated next to Mark said, "Someone told me that it looks like there's going to be a riot outside. Maybe they're taking Martinez back upstairs until they get things under control."

"A riot?" a man at the next table said. He then whispered urgently to his wife and the two of them hurried toward the exits. Others, apparently concerned that no announcement had been made about Martinez's sudden departure, did the same.

Mark leaned in front of Abby and tapped Miriam on the arm. "I don't like this. Let's get out of here until someone explains what's going on."

Miriam shook her head. "You two go ahead. I have to wait for Peter. I told him I'd be right here. He should be back any moment."

Looking worriedly around the room as more and more people began to leave, Mark said, "We'll wait with you then. I don't want to leave you here alone."

"No, go ahead," Miriam said. "I'll be fine. Why don't you go to the Camellia Room? Steph and Courtney should be in there. Maybe they've heard something. Peter and I will meet you there."

"Are you sure?" Mark asked.

"Yes, I'm sure," Miriam said. But she wasn't. She couldn't help but believe that whatever was going on had been precipitated by Peter's encounter with Stephenson. And that meant that whatever was going on wasn't good.

As Mark and Abby hurried away, she again focused her attention on the doors to the reception area. *Where the hell are you, Peter?*

PETER KNEW HE HAD Connelly's attention now, as well as Lieutenant Greene's. He opened the folded piece of paper he was holding and thrust it toward the reporter. "This is proof that Arthur Stephenson is not who he appears to be. Or, at the very least, that he has a lot to hide."

Connelly accepted and glanced quickly at the piece of paper and then at Peter. "What are you talking…?" She stopped in mid-sentence as she looked over Peter's shoulder and her eyes went wide. "There's Stephenson right now. What's he doing out here?"

Peter turned quickly and saw Stephenson standing about thirty feet away. The man was staring right at him as he smiled and retrieved a cell phone from his coat pocket. It was the most sinister smile Peter had ever seen.

Suddenly there was the sound of glass shattering as a brick or large rock crashed into the window behind them. Peter's head turned back toward the crowd to his left just in time to see another brick flying through the air and landing on the hood of a parked limousine with a loud metallic *thunk*. The protestors had moved past the barricade and were rolling toward the hotel entrance like a screaming human tsunami.

Peter quickly glanced back in the direction of Stephenson, who stood smiling amidst the growing chaos as if unfazed. But it was the scene behind Stephenson that chilled Peter's blood. The crowd in the park was moving across Richard Arrington Boulevard like a charging medieval army, as a flaming projectile flew from their midst and landed right behind the parked limo, which was suddenly engulfed in flames. Someone had thrown a Molotov cocktail! This was not the result of a crowd becoming agitated after hours of protest. This riot had been planned.

Peter looked back at Stephenson, who gave him a nod before turning and walking quickly toward the advancing mob in the semicircle. "We have to stop him!" Peter shouted to Greene and took off in pursuit.

Greene grabbed his arm and shouted, "Are you crazy? Get back inside the hotel, now!"

Peter twisted his arm free and continued to follow Stephenson. If the man was concerned about his tuxedo identifying him to the crowd as one of the enemy, he didn't show it. Still grinning insanely, he glanced back at Peter and then either ran into or was tackled by a protestor wearing an orange tee shirt. The two went down in a tangle of arms and legs, and Peter hurried toward them. A few demonstrators stopped to help the men back up, but most simply veered around them as they continued their assault on the hotel entrance.

Peter reached the spot where Stephenson had gone down, and saw him lying on the pavement, apparently unconscious. Relieved that he had him, he grabbed the man's arms, prepared to restrain him if necessary. That was when he noticed Stephenson's eyes. They were open and unfocused. Peter felt the man's neck for a pulse, but there wasn't one. He was dead.

Oh no! Peter looked up and his worst fears were realized. A dark-skinned man in an orange tee shirt was continuing to push his way against the tide of humanity storming toward the hotel. He was carrying a cell phone. He locked eyes with Peter and smiled.

Peter continued his pursuit. There were police everywhere, but none paid attention to his shouted pleas for help. They were fighting a losing battle, trying to hold back the advancing crowd. Peter caught a glimpse of orange and pushed his way toward it. Suddenly there appeared to be a scuffle about ten feet in front of him, and a couple of seconds later the sound of a woman's scream. Peter shoved people aside as he made his way to the spot, and looked down in dismay at the body of a young man in an orange tee shirt lying on the ground. He didn't have to check for a pulse this time. He knew the man was dead.

He glanced around frantically, looking for the sight of anyone focusing on him. He hadn't seen the collision, so he didn't know what to look for. Anwar could be anyone out there. He could still be moving against the tide, or with it. He was completely *incognito* now, a faceless demon in a faceless horde of humanity.

Despite the pointlessness of it, Peter continued to push forward. More slowly now, watching for any sign of someone who looked as if he were trying to get away. But there was nothing but a sea of faces—some looking angry, some looking scared, but none looking at him with any trace of recognition. It was useless to continue. Peter knew he'd lost him. The only thing to do now was try to get back into the hotel and find Miriam so they could get away from here, from Birmingham, as soon as possible.

As he turned to reverse his direction, he caught a glimpse of a solitary figure standing on the steps leading to the back entrance of one of the restaurants. He stood out because he was higher up than everyone at street level. It was a Hispanic priest, wearing the traditional black shirt and white clerical collar, but with jeans. The priest was scanning the crowd, as if he too was looking for someone in particular. And then he looked straight at Peter and smiled.

The priest was holding a cell phone. Now he held it up in one hand, as if showing it to Peter. And slowly, dramatically, he extended the forefinger of his other hand and moved it toward the phone screen. For a fraction of a second, Peter wondered why Anwar would stop amidst all this madness to make a phone call. And then, before he could even complete the thought, a massive wave of heat hit him in the back, throwing him forward. Although he never really heard anything, his ears were ringing as he found himself lying on the pavement with glass raining down on him like a summer shower.

Chapter 34

THE ROOM WAS filled with smoke. It was difficult to see where he was going, even to see his own feet, but Peter kept moving. He wanted to close his eyes, to shut out the swirling haze that was burning them, causing them to water so much he couldn't make out any details of his surroundings. What he wanted even more was to be able to close his ears—to shut out the moans and the pleas for help. And the screams.

He realized this was exactly like his dream. Except this time, he wouldn't be waking up. This time it was real, and he hoped against hope he wouldn't face the same outcome he'd had when the nightmare had caused him to wake up shrieking in terror.

When he had picked himself up from the street outside he'd been dazed for a minute or so. He had brushed off the coat of ground glass that covered his tuxedo, as if he were shaking off a layer of snow. In the process he suffered multiple tiny cuts on his hands, which stung and helped shock him back into reality. The pavement around him had been covered with wounded people, most screaming and holding their hands over bloody faces as they thrashed around blindly. Peter realized that if he'd not been facing the opposite direction, watching Anwar, he would have suffered a similar fate. No one this far from the hotel appeared to have life-threatening injuries, but many had likely been blinded by the unexpected torrent of tiny glass shards.

He looked at what had been the source of the flying glass, the windows that had separated the lobby bar area of the hotel from the valet area outside. All he could see were huge holes where the wall had been, with black smoke pouring out and occasional burning embers lighting an otherwise darkened section of the building. The spot where he'd been standing with Kristen Connelly and Lieutenant Greene just two minutes earlier was now a blackened patch of cobblestone strewn with bodies that were mostly still.

To the right, the hotel lobby appeared to still be lit, but the scene was one of chaos, with masses of people scrambling and fighting to get outside before there were more explosions. There was no way he'd get through those doors. So he'd taken the direct route, climbing over bodies and charred rubble, entering the building through the blown-out windows. He had moved across the reception area as quickly as he could in the blinding smoke, and now stood in what remained of the center doorway to the ballroom.

The smoke was so thick he couldn't see the far wall where the dais had been, but remembered that the table where he, Miriam and the Sheffields would have been seated was near the stage, slightly to the left of where he now stood. He was breathing heavily, which exacerbated the effects of the smoke, causing him to double over coughing. When he did, he saw that there was a space of a foot or two above the floor where the air was clearer and visibility was better. Again remembering his dream, he crouched low and began to alternate between crawling and duck-walking as he moved in the direction of their table.

As he traversed the room, he inspected every woman's body he found, many of them with clothes so shredded and burned he couldn't tell what they'd been wearing. As a result, he found himself saying a prayer with each one that it wouldn't be Miriam. The effects of the explosion were devastating. Many of the bodies were missing arms or legs; one was headless. It was a nightmare, a scene of carnage that would bring horrendous grief to dozens of households.

And for what purpose? Why would Stephenson have detonated a bomb that would kill loyal AVP supporters, and possibly even the founder himself? Stephenson had said in the washroom that he and Martinez were equal partners, and that they would one day *share* the power of the presidency. There would be nothing to share if Martinez didn't live to lead his party to power. And besides, Arthur Stephenson himself no longer existed, a direct result of Peter's encounter with him. That had probably not been part of his sinister plan, so now his intentions would never be known. How could they be? Peter could never tell anyone that Stephenson had been responsible. Witnesses would remember seeing Stephenson lying dead on the pavement moments before the explosion…an explosion detonated by a young Hispanic priest.

He continued his slow, horrifying trek across the ballroom. He was surrounded by screams of agony and moans of semi-conscious suffering, but he didn't stop to help anyone. He couldn't. He had to find Miriam; had to see if she had, by some miracle, survived the vicious blast. For a moment, he harbored hope that she had been one of those who had fled the ballroom when the riot had started outside. But he remembered—he would always remember—that he had told her to wait at the table for him. And he knew deep in his heart that she had obeyed.

He continued his journey, moving as quickly but as deliberately as he could. When he bumped into a hard surface and saw that it was covered in tattered felt, he knew he had reached the dais. He started edging to his left, certain that his and Miriam's table—or whatever was left of it—would be in that direction. He kept calling Miriam's name, but the only responses were cries of pain and confusion. Feeling his way with both hands as he crab-walked between bodies, he suddenly felt a hand grab his right pants leg. His heart brimming with hope, he grabbed the hand and followed the arm until he could see a face through the smoke.

It wasn't Miriam. It was an older woman, probably in her seventies, although it was hard to tell, and she was babbling incoherently. He saw that one leg was twisted at an awkward angle and the other looked as if it were barely attached below the knee. The poor thing was obviously in shock. He could now see the back and forth movement of beams of light, and realized that first responders were now arriving. He loosened the woman's grip on his pant leg and said, "Hold on. Help is coming."

He then shouted, "Over here!" and saw a light beam swing in his direction. Knowing the woman would momentarily have someone there to take care of her, he prepared to resume moving further to his left. The old woman continued to jabber as he crawled another foot, frantically searching for Miriam. And then he found her. She was sprawled across the floor on her stomach, her right hand extended toward him, as if pleading for him to come to her. Beneath her body was a pool of blood almost as black as her dress. Her head was turned so that her left cheek rested on the glass-littered floor, but he could tell that side of her head had been severely damaged. Her eyes were open...dull and lifeless.

It took a moment to register. She was gone. Miriam, his love, his life for over six and a half centuries, was gone. Her near immortality was not enough to save her. She had succumbed to the power of the devastating blast just like most of the others that had been in the room. Being a rider had kept her soul alive for centuries, but it had made no difference tonight.

He picked up the extended right hand. It was still warm. He caressed, kissed it, held it to his face, and then crumbled. It was his nightmare all over again. Almost identically. But he wouldn't wake up to Miriam hovering over him, quieting his screams. So he continued screaming. Again and again.

He didn't even notice the activity behind him as two paramedics attended to the old woman, who still cried and shouted incoherently. One of the men put a hand on his shoulder and said, "Sir, I need you to move. This is a rescue scene. If you can walk, we need you out of here. Please."

Peter tried to protest, tried to explain that he'd found his wife and that he couldn't just leave her lying there. But the room was beginning to fill with forms moving through the swirling smoke, shining flashlights all around and shouting out when a live victim was found. The paramedic now grabbed Peter's elbow and started to lift him to his feet. "Stay low, and move toward those lights over there," he said. "Please, sir, you have to give us room to work."

Peter nodded and put his hands on the floor to try and push himself to a standing position. The old woman began to thrash violently, causing the other worker to shout, "She's going into shock! Where's the diazepam?"

She then grabbed Peter's coat sleeve, tugging urgently as she continued her unintelligible murmuring. Peter tried, gently at first and then more forcibly, to pry her fingers away but she held on tightly. Finally he was able to pull his arm free but she immediately gripped his open jacket, pulling him down toward her face as her lips twitched and tremored as if she could no longer control them. One of the medics pressed an injection cartridge to her thigh and was just about to activate it when she gave Peter's jacket one more surprisingly strong tug, pulling his head down so that his ear was by her mouth. She was still trying to speak, but he couldn't understand her. And then he heard it, as clearly as anything he'd ever heard in his extraordinarily long life.

"Stay strong, *kochanka*."

Epilogue

"THIS IS KELLEY MICHELLE, reporting from the Birmingham Westin Hotel, the site of last night's horrific bombing at a fundraiser for the American Values Party. Miraculously, AVP founder Robert Martinez was ushered out of the packed ballroom just a minute or two before the explosion and was reportedly in a service elevator on the way up to his penthouse suite at the exact moment of detonation. Many of the attendees were not so fortunate. Although quite a few had sensed danger and were on their way out of the ballroom area, many more remained in the path of the devastating blast. At last count, twenty-six dead and over seventy critically injured, with several on life support.

"One of the deceased has been identified as Arthur Stephenson, wealthy Texas industrialist and Martinez's closest advisor and the chief of operations for the new party. Stephenson's body was found just outside of the hotel, in the short street that forms the Westin entrance and then loops around between several popular uptown restaurants before reconnecting with Richard Arrington Boulevard, where I'm standing now. His cause of death remains unconfirmed, but campaign sources have said that other than some superficial cuts on one side of his face, Mr. Stephenson did not appear to have any serious injuries. It is speculated that he died from a heart attack brought on by the stress of what is being termed by Martinez as a 'heinous and cowardly terrorist attack.'

"Although Birmingham Chief of Police Emmet Frazier stated in an early morning press conference, shown here on PNN, that neither his department nor the FBI are prepared to assign responsibility for the bombing at this time—just fourteen hours after the blast—I have been told by multiple sources that nearly all of their attention is being focused in one direction. *Brigada de Proteccion Hispana*—The Hispanic Protection Brigade—was holding a massive protest rally here last night, which was taking an uncharacteristically violent turn just as the bomb detonated. In fact, over a dozen Brigade protestors who were advancing toward the hotel entrance, despite having been warned by the police to stay at least fifty feet away, were injured by flying glass. Two required hospitalization.

The blast appears to have emanated from the stage area at the far end of the ballroom, possibly even the speaker podium. Brigade founder Carlos Guerra remains in police custody and has been unavailable for comment, but one of his spokesmen stated emphatically that no one from their organization had been inside the hotel at any time, and there was therefore no way that they could have been involved. This, of course, begs the question as to who else would have gone to such drastic measures to kill Robert Martinez, presumed to be the primary target, risking hundreds of civilian casualties in the process.

"Regardless of who is ultimately determined to be responsible for this deadly attack, one thing is certain…the political process in this country will be changed forever. And protestors, whatever their side or agenda, will be subjected to more scrutiny than ever before. The American ideal of a peaceful and orderly selection of our leadership has been marred by violence before, but never on this scale. Lives were lost here last night. Innocent lives, guilty of nothing more than exercising their right to support a movement that proposes an alternative to the Democratic and Republican parties which, particularly after the last election, have left so many voters feeling disenfranchised.

"On a personal note, this news network was one of several who lost members of our broadcast family last night. PNN reporter

Kristin Connelly had just completed a live broadcast from outside the hotel, ten or twelve yards from where I'm now standing, when her life was taken by the horrendous blast. Kristen was a rising star, a young, immensely popular political journalist. She died doing what she loved to do. She will be missed.

"This is Kelley Michelle, PNN, reporting live from Birmingham, Alabama."

PETER TURNED FROM the wall-mounted television and walked back to the chair he'd occupied for the past twelve hours. He hadn't learned anything from the PNN report that he didn't already know, other than the exact number of casualties. In fact, he could tell the news people a thing or two. Like the fact that Arthur Stephenson's body may have been found outside the hotel, but the devious soul who had occupied it had escaped, first into the body of a protestor, then into that of a Catholic priest. And it was him, not the Hispanic Protection Brigade, that had detonated the bomb. .

Peter was in the ICU Visitors Lounge at UAB Hospital, waiting for an update on the status of the elderly woman he'd found next to Miriam's body in the shattered ballroom of the Westin Hotel. The woman who, despite appearing to be nearly delirious from the pain of a severed leg, had struggled to pull him close enough to whisper in his ear. "Stay strong, *kochanka*," she had said. At least, that's what Peter had thought he'd heard. But now, hours removed from the shock of seeing Miriam's ravaged corpse, he was terrified by doubt. What if he had imagined it? What if his immeasurable grief had tricked his mind into hearing words that had not really been spoken? Words that only his beloved Miriam would say?

He prayed for the hundredth time that he'd really heard those words, proving that Miriam had managed to jump into the body of the old woman—who he now knew was, or had been, a prominent Birmingham society matron named Margaret Van Fleet—shortly before she herself succumbed to her devastating wounds. Despite being more exhausted than he could ever remember, as well as being covered in soot and blood, and wearing a tuxedo that was scorched in several places and reeked of smoke, he would not leave until he had his proof.

Mrs. Van Fleet's son, Stephen, had arrived from Nashville around four that morning. Peter had been pointed out by the nurses as the Good Samaritan who had found the old woman in the smoke-filled remains of the ballroom, had summoned paramedics to her side, and had followed the ambulance to the hospital.

"Do you know my mother?" Stephen had asked.

"No. She'd just been seated at the table next to mine, so when I went back in searching for survivors, she was the only one I found in that part of the room."

Stephen had extended his right hand while wiping tears away with his left. "Thank you. You've done more for a stranger than anyone could ask. You look beat. Why don't you go on home? I'll go back and see Mom when they give me the okay, and then I'll drive back to Nashville and make arrangements to move her in with us while she recuperates. The doctor told me that unless she develops some complications after the amputation, she should be ready for discharge in five or six days."

Peter shook his head and managed a weak smile. "I've waited this long. Might as well hang out here with you until she's out of surgery."

They didn't have to wait long. A nurse dressed in surgical scrubs came out a few minutes later and said, "Mr. Van Fleet, your mother did fine in surgery. It was really just a matter of cleaning everything up and restructuring the wound so it'll heal in a way to accommodate a prosthesis. She's in cubicle 4 if you want to peek in on her. She's awake, but still very groggy."

When Stephen followed the nurse, Peter took the elevator down to the first level and bought two items in the gift shop. Carrying the small bag, he arrived back in the ICU waiting room just a couple of minutes before Stephen walked back in. He was wearing a tired smile as he approached Peter.

"She's still out of it, but her color is good and the doctor said her vital signs are strong. I'm heading out now, but wanted to thank you again for your tremendous support. My mother and I will think of you often."

Don't be so sure about that, Peter thought. He shook the man's hand and said, "I was honored to help in whatever way I could. I'm glad she appears to be doing well."

Stephen wiped a stray tear from his eye. "Well, thanks again, Peter. It has been a pleasure meeting you."

As he started to walk away, he turned back and said, "I'm embarrassed that I didn't ask this earlier, but I suppose I've pretty much been in a state of shock. Did you lose anybody in the blast?"

Peter looked down and shook his head. "Don't know for sure yet."

Stephen gave him a sad look and said, "Let's hope not."

With that, he pushed the button for the elevator. The doors slid open immediately and he stepped inside, turning around to stare back at Peter as they closed.

Peter waited until the lights above the elevator indicated that the car had reached the ground floor. He then walked briskly through the double doors into the ICU, and began searching for cubicle 4. It was just a few feet down the corridor on his right. He made sure no nurses seemed to be paying attention, and then pulled back the curtain and stepped inside.

The old woman on the bed looked frail and ghostly white, but the monitor beside her indicated a steady pulse and normal breathing rate. There was a needle inserted in one arm, delivering a bag of fluids, and an oxygen tube strapped to her nostrils. But what Peter noticed most was the flat sheet below the right knee.

He moved to the side of the bed and reached into the gift shop bag, pulling out a small glass globe holding a single Gerbera daisy, Miriam's favorite flower. He placed it on the bedside table and then grasped a small, crepe-skinned hand. He squeezed it and whispered, "Miriam, it's Peter."

Her eyelids seemed to flutter for a moment, but remained closed. He squeezed her hand again and continued to whisper her name, but got no response. He had hoped to be able to look into her eyes, to search them for a sign of Miriam, but realized she was still too sedated to respond. He supposed that was a good thing. Whether she really was Miriam or not, he didn't want her to be in pain.

He glanced around, making sure no one was close enough to observe what he was doing, and then knelt beside the bed. He reached for the second item in the bag, leaned his head close to hers, and held the hand mirror above them in a shaky right hand. He barely had a chance to glimpse the reflection before his eyes brimmed with tears and the image blurred. He lifted the edge of the bed sheet and wiped his eyes until he could see clearly again. His heard pounded and his eyes flooded again as he stared at the two faces.

A freckle-faced young man with green eyes and long red curls, and a beautiful teen-aged girl with long brown tresses. A reflection he'd first seen in a clear, shimmering pond outside of Strasbourg… six hundred and seventy years earlier.

Acknowledgements

W riting is a solitary endeavor; perfecting a manuscript is any-thing but. Sometimes, what makes perfect sense in the writer's mind comes across as illogical or misplaced when it is transferred to print. I am blessed to have a team of dedicated and competent first readers whose input made this final draft significantly more readable than the first.

My darling wife, Mary Lynn, has an eagle-eye for any grammatical and punctuation mistakes. On many occasions I have handed her a chapter that I had proof-read a dozen times, only to have her find anything from a misplaced comma to an incorrect pronoun. Anything that she considers explicitly sexual also catches her attention. Sometimes I listen; sometimes I don't.

Kelley Brown and Courtney Wright have helped me do a better job of character development. Their questions about why a character would do or say certain things always make me think, and in most cases leads to needed revisions.

Dianne Querbes is my "big picture" reader. She always starts her critique with the premise that anything I have written is great (in the interest of full disclosure, she's my sister), but then manages to work in a few suggestions that make the story more believable, compelling and complete.

Friend and fellow community servant Arnold Singer read the very first draft and asked some pertinent questions that made me rethink, and subsequently re-write, certain sections. A fresh, unbiased perspective almost always opens new paths to explore.

I also wish to thank good friend and fellow thriller writer Rod Riley for his help. In addition to being a great story teller, and a good judge of stories, Rod is my go-to source for anything related to guns. If this book contains anything inaccurate about a firearm, the blame is entirely mine. He told me the right thing. Sometimes technical facts can get lost in translation, or perhaps literary exuberance. At least, that's my excuse.

A special note of appreciation to former crime scene investigator and good friend John Greene for providing insight into homicide investigative procedures and for allowing me to use his name for one of my characters. Thanks John. To demonstrate the depths of my gratitude, I'll buy your breakfast at a future Kiwanis meeting.

Finally, I want to express my sincere gratitude to my readers for investing their money and time to read my books. There is no greater reward for my efforts than to have one of you tell me that a story entertained you, a character moved you, or a theme made you think. You are the reason I spend my time doing this, and I am grateful for your encouragement and support. Please visit my web site, **www.rkbbooks.com**, for synopses, sample chapters, and ordering information for all of my books, and please take the time to use the email link to tell me what you like and what you don't. Reader comments through the years have covered the critical spectrum—the good, the bad, and the ugly—but are always welcomed.

One more thing. If you are interested in knowing what comes next for Miriam and Peter, please turn the page and read an excerpt from the next installment of their epic story, *Storm Riders*.

Take a look at the following excerpt from the continuing saga of Miriam and Peter, *Storm Riders,* coming in May, 2019.

Chapter 1

THE LONGER HE STUDIED her, the more convinced he became that she was the one. This was the second time he'd observed her in this pub on Birmingham's Southside, an area teeming with restaurants and bars frequented by young medical students and other health professionals associated with the nearby UAB medical complex. He specifically wanted a nurse this time, preferably a student, but a practicing nurse would be okay too, as long as she was young and attractive. He didn't like to think of himself as being shallow, but looks really did matter. He stared at her as she stood next to the bar, laughing and chatting with two other young women, and tried to picture her naked. Her hospital greens were baggy and loose fitting—clearly not designed to be flattering—but she filled them out in the right places well enough to give him a pretty good idea of what lay underneath.

Oh yeah, he thought. *You'll do. You'll do just fine.*

She was a little taller than average, maybe five foot six or seven, and slender. Despite appearing to be a regular in this particular bar—he'd seen her here twice within three nights and the bartenders seemed to know her—she didn't seem to be a heavy drinker. The most he'd seen her drink in one night was two glasses of red wine. She had the lean, healthy look of an athlete, perhaps a runner or a tennis player; something that required both agility and endurance. Obviously, a healthy specimen. On top of everything else, the way she interacted with others indicated a good personality, although that was not important. If things worked out the way he hoped, she wouldn't need her personality after tomorrow.

He was anxious to speak with her, but knew he might get only one chance. So he was patient—as calm and unrushed as a sniper on a rooftop, waiting for that perfect shot. Finally, after nearly an hour of standing by the crowded bar, one of his target's friends glanced at her watch and then pulled her wallet from her shoulder bag. The other friend looked at her watch too. They were getting ready to leave. Whether his girl left with them would be decided within the next two minutes. It was time to make his move.

He left his perch on a high stool in the corner and strolled over to the bar. He managed to shoulder his way through the crowd and squeeze in between her and a bearded young man he'd noticed glancing frequently in her direction over the past hour. He signaled one of the bartenders and ordered another Guinness. Leaning one elbow on the bar and turning in her direction, he waited as the two friends argued over who would pick up the tab. The debate was settled when one of them handed a credit card to a bartender just as a foaming pint of beer was placed on the bar. Picking it up and appearing to be jostled was all it took to start a conversation.

"Oh, my God, I'm so sorry! I just spilled half of my beer down your back."

She turned suddenly to see who had launched the brew attack, but any semblance of aggravation seemed to disappear when she saw the handsome young face poised just a few inches from her own. She smiled as she brushed a strand of chestnut hair from her equally brown eyes. "No problem. I was just leaving. It'll dry when I get outside."

"Well, please let me pay to have this cleaned."

She laughed. "They're cotton scrubs. They go into the washing machine."

He smiled back at her. "I suppose I could offer to wash them for you, but that might seem a little creepy."

She nodded, still laughing. "Yeah, seeing as how we've never met, I think it would."

He wiped his beer-soaked hand on his shirt before extending it to her. "I'm Peter."

She glanced down at his hand before taking it. Her grip was firm. "Jennifer."

"So, Jennifer, now that we've been introduced, do you want me to wash your scrubs?"

"I appreciate the offer, but I think I can handle it."

"Well, could I at least buy you another drink? You're wearing most of my beer, so I have to order another one. Will you join me?"

She glanced back at her two friends who, as their knowing grins indicated, were enjoying the show. "My friends and I were just about to head out for dinner."

"But you don't have to go right now, do you? Just one drink? It's the least I can do."

She started to shake her head as she turned back to her friends, so he said the only thing he could think of that might compel her to stay. "Let me buy your friends a drink too. You can put dinner on hold for another twenty minutes. It'll give your clothes time to dry a bit."

She again looked back at her friends, and the one who had paid the bill glanced at her watch. Feeling the tide was shifting against him, Peter interjected, "You could call the restaurant and move your reservation back a half hour, couldn't you?"

They all three laughed as Jennifer said, "Mellow Mushroom doesn't take reservations."

Peter smiled and waved for the bartender. "Then it's settled. What will you ladies have?"

A few minutes later when they had all been served, Peter clinked glasses with each woman in succession. "Down the hatch."

"Which is better than down my back," Jennifer said with a coy smile.

Three barstools had opened up, so the women sat and Peter stood next to Jennifer, which gave him the opportunity for a semi-private chat with her. He knew his time was limited, so he tried to use it effectively to learn as much as he could about her, in preparation for asking the all-important question that was the true purpose for their "accidental" meeting.

"Are you a nurse or a student?" he asked, starting the interview.

"Both, actually. I graduated in June with my nursing degree, and next week I'm starting a graduate program in infusion therapy."

"Infusion therapy? Like in chemo?"

"Yes. My mother died of ovarian cancer my first year in nursing school. I spent a lot of time in the infusion lab with her and just fell in love with the nurses who cared for her. They're a very special breed, a rare mixture of technical competence and genuine compassion. I decided that's what I want to give patients."

Peter studied her face. "What about your dad? Does he live here in Birmingham?"

She looked down and then took a sip of her wine. "No. He and my mom divorced when I was in the third grade. I don't have much contact with him."

Peter sipped his own drink before saying, "Well, he doesn't know what he's missing. He should be very proud. Is he at least helping with your education costs?"

"Nope," she said quickly, a trace of bitterness in her tone. "I'm on my own. That's why I'm wearing these beautiful scrubs. I'm working three day weekend shifts at the hospital, and I'll have classes Monday through Thursday."

"Never a day off?"

She smiled. "Classes don't start until a week from tomorrow, so I'm off for the next four days. After that, I'll just be off on holidays, unless they fall on a weekend, and then I'll be working."

He paused a moment before entering the most critical line of questioning. "Well, since you have a few days off, would you be interested in making a little extra money?"

Her smile disappeared immediately, replaced by a look that led him to believe she was either puzzled, insulted, or both. "What do you mean?" she asked icily.

He held up a hand and spoke quickly, thinking she might be on the verge of storming out. "No, please, hear me out. This is completely on the up-and-up. There's an elderly woman, a friend of mine, who just got out of ICU. She was severely injured in that bombing at the Westin Thursday night."

Jennifer's eyes widened and her mouth fell open in an expression of shock. "Oh, my God! She was at the AVP dinner? I got called in to help at the hospital that night. Every nurse in the city did. It was horrible!"

"Yes," he muttered. "It was."

She stared at him, seeming to notice for the first time several small cuts and peeling skin from a burn on the left side of his face. "You were there too?"

"Yes. But I wasn't in the ballroom when the bomb went off. I managed to get back in there before the first responders arrived and I found my friend. Her name is Margaret…Margaret Van Fleet. She was in pretty bad shape. Lost a leg and a lot of blood. I didn't worry as much when she was in ICU, but now that she's in a regular room I'm just afraid she won't get the attention she needs. I've spent as much time with her over the past three days as they'd allow, but I have some things I need to take care of and can't spend as much time there as I'd like. I just want someone to be there with her a few hours each day while I'm gone. In case she needs something."

She smiled sadly as she shook her head. "That's very caring of you, Peter, but the hospital can help you find a volunteer to sit with her. You won't have to pay a thing."

"I don't mind paying," Peter said. "I just want the right person. Someone knowledgeable, but also someone who is kind and understanding. Someone like you."

She was still shaking her head. "I don't know. I only have a few days off before I start…"

"I'll pay a hundred dollars an hour. Cash."

Her eyes went wide again. "A hundred dollars an hour? How many hours a day are we talking about?"

"No more than four. And it will only be through Wednesday or Thursday. Her doctor told me that if she continues to improve, she'll be released before the end of the week. She has a son in Nashville who will come get her and take her to his home for a while. Until she can get by on her own."

"She doesn't have a husband?"

"Killed in the blast," Peter said.

"Oh, that poor woman."

Peter nodded. "She has a lot of recovering to do. Both physically and emotionally. I just don't want her spending so much time alone before she's back with family. She has a lot to process. Not the least of which is losing a leg."

"What time would you need me there?"

He smiled inwardly. He had her! "Noon to four tomorrow would be great. Maybe you could help her with lunch. I'd make sure I'm back by four, and then we could agree on the schedule for Tuesday and Wednesday. And Thursday, if that becomes necessary, but I doubt it will. Margaret is a very strong woman. I'm sure she'll be ready for discharge by then."

"Well," Jennifer said, gazing down as she chewed on her lower lip, obviously considering the impact of twelve hundred tax-free dollars on her expenses. She looked up at him and thrust out her hand. "Okay, I'll do it. Noon tomorrow. Where do I need to be?"

He shook her hand, again noting the firm grip and that the skin was a bit dry…probably the result of numerous hand scrubbings each day. "Room 610, North Pavilion. I'll be there waiting for you. I'm sure she's going to like you."

"I hope so," Jennifer said. "She sounds like a very special lady. In fact, she must be, having a guy like you be so concerned about her."

He smiled. "You can't imagine."

Five minutes later he paid the tab and bade all three ladies good-night before heading for the door. He was convinced that Jennifer was a perfect choice. He knew it was possible she might change her mind and not show up, but he didn't believe that would happen. He felt certain that she would walk into Room 610 tomorrow at noon… but Jennifer would not walk back out.

About the Author

Suspense writer **R. K. Brown** is a native of Mobile, Alabama. He has lived in New Jersey, Georgia, and North Carolina, and currently resides in Birmingham, Alabama. He is the author of the mystery/suspense novel *Sonnets*, which won an Honorable Mention at the 2008 London Book Festival, as well as *The Neighborhood, A Stone of Hope,* and *Blind Luck. Riders* is his first foray into the supernatural realm, and is the initial installment of a series. He and his wife, Mary Lynn, divide their time between Birmingham and Lake Martin.

Visit his web site at **www.rkbbooks.com**

CPSIA information can be obtained
at www.ICGtesting.com
Printed in the USA
FFHW02n1606031018
48668109-52667FF